GENTS

STEAMY STORIES from the AGE OF STEAM

edited by
MATTHEW BRIGHT

UNZIPPED BOOKS
AN IMPRINT OF LETHE PRESS
AMHERST, MA

Published by Unzipped Books
AN IMPRINT OF LETHE PRESS
lethepressbooks.com

'Mombasa Vengeance' copyright © 2017 Mike McClelland
(a version of this story first published in *Gay Zoo Day*,
Beautiful Dreamer Press, 2017).

All other stories copyright © 2018 to their authors and
original to this collection.

Extracts from *Sins of the Cities of the Plain, Teleny* and
My Secret Life are public domain texts.

ISBN: 9781590214350

Cover and interior design
by Inkspiral Design

EDITOR'S NOTE: THE IRRESISTIBLE ALLURE OF TABLE LEGS

THERE'S A COMMON story recited about the Victorians that they were so afraid of sex that table-legs had to be covered, lest their phallic nature cause arousal. As absurd an idea as this is, it's passed into the realms of accepted fact. It's a succinct summary of how history has painted the Victorian era: buttoned up, repressed, completely at odds with human sexuality.

There's elements of that which are true. But there's also elements of that which are wildly wrong.

The Victorian view on sex was less one of repression, and more one of 'that which we shall not speak'. The act was far less taboo than we might imagine, but to speak of it publically by far the greater crime, socially speaking. And so naturally, in such an environment, pornography in the written form flourished. For a brief period, there was a boom in the printing industry producing written erotica (to the point where one enterprising printing press in Cornwall employed only blind or visually impaired employees in order to protect against the threat of blackmail). The demand was huge; a particularly infamous novel that involved the prolific deflowering of nuns was smuggled into the country hidden inside sarcophagi shipping in from Egypt. (This kind of historical artefact was two for a penny at the time, and no-one was bothering to pay them much attention.) It might have been the polite thing to do to not talk about sex, but behind closed doors, everyone was at it, and the people of the time were no less fascinated by it than we were.

Photography was also coming into its own throughout the Victorian era, and naturally, being the filthy creatures that we are, we immediately started getting our kit of in front of them. Accustomed as we are to seeing the controlled, sombre photographs of the era, pornographic photographs of the time are often disarmingly carefree. This book features a number of photographs from the time, but one of the notable entries is from a set generally known as the 'flowers in his hair', which features two youths in a variety of increasingly inventive sexual poses, garbed in semi-female attire, and with a posy of flowers ringed on each of their heads. The photographs are uninhibited, gender-blurring, and flagrantly arousing—and from the distance of a century or more, quite beautiful.

Which brings us to the queer experience during the Victorian era. I hesitate to use the word gay—that itself is a more modern concept, and in the late 1900s you were more likely to see the terminology of the 'invert' or something with similarly medical overtones. 'Gay' wasn't yet an identity one claimed as distinct from heterosexual, but that wasn't to say there wasn't plenty of same-sex relations going on. Whilst buggery was still highly illegal, in some respects it wasn't significantly more covert than a host of other couplings deemed taboo by polite society (there were more arrests on record in Britain through the 1960s for homosexuality or similar crimes than there were during any of the Victorian era, for example.) The Cleveland Street scandal cast a very public light on a previously hidden part of this—the messenger boys who were also for rent, and the various high society figures who had enjoyed them. On of the figures in this scandal was immortalised in the probably-fiction-but-maybe-a-little-true story of Jack Saul which opens our collection, but there are a host of other stories that have reached us from the time: unofficial 'drag queen' marriages; the anything goes decadence of the Hundred Guineas Club; and of course, the most high-profile tale of them all, that of Oscar Wilde. But even in the predominantly heterosexual erotica of the time, there is plenty of casual same-sex interactions which are usually perceived as the natural end point of sexual experimentation and not given overmuch significance (such as in *My Secret Life*, which is excerpted later in this book.)

When I set out to put together this set of stories my aim was to curate a collection that was both arousing but also grounded in the real history of a time that holds a deep fascination for me. This book has it all—from the absurd to the moving, from the fantastical to the sensual—and it's my hope that you'll find plenty in here to excite you. It certainly seems like there was plenty happening to excite the men of the day, despite what we imagine now. After all, that story about the table-legs? That originated from a satirical cartoon at the time that mocked the staid gatekeepers of the day for their conservative mores; just because stories weren't often told doesn't mean they weren't happening.

The men who lay with each under the covers might have had to keep their affairs secret, but between these covers they're all laid out for your reading pleasure. I welcome you to a fog-shrouded world of assignations secret, encounters thrilling and kisses stolen. I doff my hat to you, lovers of every type.

Matthew Bright
May 2018

EXTRACT:
SINS OF
THE CITIES OF
THE PLAIN

Jack Saul

OF ALL OF the (surprisingly voluminous) annals of Victorian erotica, Jack Saul stands out as one of the most notorious. It remains one of the handful of the exclusively homosexual from that era, and is one of the earliest ever published in English. It purports to be the story of Jack Saul, a 'mary-ann'—a rent boy, hustler. In the first chapter Jack is encouraged by a paying customer to recount his story, and the book that follows is that very account.

Jack Saul himself was real—a prostitute of Irish birth referred to 'Dublin Jack', who became embroiled in the infamous Cleveland Street scandal. Some believe this story to be his true account, related to the writer of the book. Others believe it simply be inspired by what was known of him at the time, and be pure fiction. It's likely we'll never know, but either way, *Sins of the Cities of the Plain* remains an iconic piece of pornography of the era.

Sins of the Cities of the Plain was my first window into the true sexuality of the Victorian era, and if, like mine, your preconceptions of the Victorian age were that of prudery and bashfulness, Jack Saul blasts those out of the water. With a contemporary reading it is both a startling picture of a rarely spoken history and, on the purely arousing level it was originally intended, astonishingly erotic.

INTRODUCTION

THE WRITER OF these notes was walking through Leicester Square one sunny afternoon last November, when his attention was particularly taken by an effeminate, but very good-looking young fellow, who was walking in front of him, looking in shop-windows from time to time, and now and then looking round as if to attract my attention.

Dressed in tight-fitting clothes, which set off his Adonis-like figure to the best advantage, especially about what snobs call the fork of his trousers, where evidently he was favoured by nature by a very extraordinary development of the male appendages; he had small and elegant feet, set off by pretty patent leather boots, a fresh looking beardless face, with almost feminine features, auburn hair, and sparkling blue eyes, which spoke as plainly as possible to my senses, and told me that the handsome youth must indeed be one of the "Mary-Ann's" of London, who I had heard were often to be seen sauntering in the neighbourhood of Regent Street, or the Haymarket, on fine afternoons or evenings.

Presently the object of my curiosity almost halted and stood facing the writer as he took off his hat, and wiped his face with a beautiful white silk handkerchief.

That lump in his trousers had quite a fascinating effect upon me. Was it natural or made up by some artificial means? If real, what a size when excited; how I should like to handle such a manly jewel, etc. All this ran through my mind, and determined me to make his acquaintance, in order to unravel the real and naked truth; also, if possible, to glean what I could of his antecedents and mode of life, which I felt sure must be extraordinarily interesting.

When he moved on again I noticed that he turned down a little side street, and was looking in a picture shop. I followed him, and first making some observations about the scanty drapery on some of the actresses and other beauties whose photographs were exposed for sale, I asked him if he would take a glass of wine.

He appeared to comprehend that there was business in my proposal, but seemed very diffident about drinking in any public place.

"Well," I said, "would you mind if we take a cab to my chambers—I live in the Cornwall Mansions, close to Baker Street Station—have a cigar and a chat with me, as I see you are evidently a fast young chap, and can put me up to a thing or two?"

"All right. Put your thing up, I suppose you mean. Why do you seem so afraid to say what you want?" he replied with a most meaning look.

"I'm not at all delicate; but wish to keep myself out of trouble. Who can tell who hears you out in the streets?" I said, hailing a cab. "I don't like to be seen speaking to a young fellow in the street. We shall be all right in my own rooms."

It was just about my dinner hour when we reached my place, so I rang the bell, and ordered my old housekeeper to lay the table for two, and both of us did ample justice to a good rumpsteak and oyster sauce, topped up with a couple of bottles of champagne of an extra sec brand.

As soon as the cloth was removed, we settled ourselves comfortably over the fire with brandy and cigars, for it was a sharp, frosty day out.

"My boy, I hope you enjoyed your dinner?" I said, mixing a couple of good warm glasses of brandy hot, "but you have not favoured me with your name. Mine you could have seen by the little plate on my door, is Mr. Cambon."

"Saul, Jack Saul, sir, of Lisle Street, Leicester Square, and ready for a lark with a free gentleman at any time. What was it made you take a fancy to me? Did you observe any particularly interesting points about your humble servant?" as he slyly looked down towards the prominent part I have previously mentioned.

"You seem a fine figure, and so evidently well hung that I had quite a fancy to satisfy my curiosity about it. Is it real or made up for show?" I asked.

"As real as my face, sir, and a great deal prettier. Did you ever see a finer tosser in your life?" he replied, opening his trousers and exposing a tremendous prick, which was already in a half-standing state. "It's my only fortune, sir; but it really provides for all I want, and often introduces me to the best of society, ladies as well as gentlemen. There isn't a girl about Leicester Square but what would like to have me for her man, but I find it more to my interest not to waste my strength on women; the pederastic game pays so well, and is quite as enjoyable. I wouldn't have a woman unless well paid for it."

He was gently frigging himself as he spoke, and had a glorious stand by the time he had finished, so throwing the end of my cigar into the fire, I knelt down by his side to examine that fine plaything of his.

Opening his trousers more, I brought everything into full view—a priapus nearly ten inches long, very thick, and underhung by a most glorious pair of balls, which were surrounded and set off by quite a profusion of light auburn curls.

How I handled those appendages, the sack of which was drawn up so deliciously tight, which is a sure sign of strength, and that they have not been enervated by too excessive fucking or frigging. I hate to see balls hang loosely down, or even a fine prick with very small or scarcely any stones to it—these half-and-half tools are an abomination.

Gently frigging him, I tongued the ruby head for a minute or two, till he called out, "Hold, hold, sir, or you will get it in your mouth!"

This was not my game; I wanted to see him spend, so removing my lips, I pointed that splendid tool outwards over the hearthrug and frigged him quickly. Almost in a moment it came; first a single thick clot was ejected, like a stone from a volcano, then quite a jet of sperm went almost a yard high, and right into the fire, where it fizzled on the red-hot coals.

"By Jove, what a spend!" I exclaimed, "we will strip now, and have some better fun, Jack. I want to see you completely naked, my boy, as there is nothing so delightful as to see a fine young fellow when well formed and furnished in every respect. Will you suck me? That is what I like first; frigging you has only given me half a cockstand at present."

"You must be generous if I do, or you will not get me to come and see you here again," he answered with a smile, which had almost a girlish sweetness of expression.

We were soon stripped to the buff, and having locked the door, I sat down with my beautiful youth on my knee, we kissed each other, and he thrust his tongue most wantonly into my mouth, as my hands fairly travelled all over his body; but that glorious prick of his claimed most attention, and I soon had it again in a fine state of erection.

"Now kneel down and gamahuche me," I said, "whilst I can frig your lovely prick with my foot."

Seemingly to enter thoroughly into the spirit of the thing, he was on his knees in a moment, between my legs, and began to fondle my still rather limp pego most deliciously, taking the head fully into his voluptuously warm mouth, and rolling his tongue round the prepuce in the most lascivious manner it is possible to imagine.

I stiffened up at once under such exciting tittillations, which seemed to have a like effect upon his prick, which I could feel with my toes to be as hard as a rolling-pin, as my foot gently frigged and rolled it on his bended thigh, and he soon spent over my sole as it gently continued the exciting friction.

I now gave myself more and more to his gamahuching, now and then seizing his head with both hands, and raising his face to mine, we indulged in luscious love kisses, which prolonged my pleasure almost indefinitely. At last I allowed him to bring me to a crisis, and he swallowed every drop of my spendings with evident relish.

After resting awhile, and taking a little more stimulant, I asked him how he had come to acquire such a decided taste for gamahuching, to do it so deliciously as he did.

"That would be too long a tale to go into now," he replied. "Some other day, if you like to make it worth my while, I will give you the whole history."

"Could you write it out, or give me an outline so that I might put it into the shape of a tale?"

"Certainly; but it would take me so much time that you would have to make me a present of at least twenty pounds. It would take during three or four weeks several hours a day."

"I don't mind a fiver a week if you give me a fair lot, say thirty or forty pages of note-paper a week, tolerably well written," I replied.

And the arrangement was made for him to compile me "The Recollections of a Mary-Ann," which I suggested ought to be the title, although he seemed not at all to like the name as applied to himself, saying that that was what the low girls of his neighbourhood called him if they wished to insult him, however, he said at last, "the four fivers will make up for that."

"Now," he added, "I suppose you would like me to put it up for you, or rather into myself. But can you lend me such a thing as a birch? You are not so young as I am, and want something to stimulate you; besides, I want you to do it well, as I fancy that moderate sized cock of yours immensely. Do you know that I am sure I like a nice man to fuck me as much as ever a woman could?"

The birch was produced, and he insisted upon tying me down over the easy chair, so that I could not flinch or get away from the application of the rod.

He began very steadily, and with light stinging cuts which soon made me aware that I had a rather accomplished young schoolmaster to deal with my posteriors, which began to tingle most pleasantly after a few strokes. The sting of each cut was sharp, but the warm, burning rush of blood to the parts had such an exciting effect that, although I fairly writhed and wriggled under each stroke, I was rapidly getting into a most delicious state of excitement.

The light tips of the birch seemed to search out each tender spot, twining round my buttocks and thighs, touching up both shaft and balls, as well as wealing my ham, till I was most rampantly erect, and cried out for him to let me have him at once.

"Not yet; not yet, you bugger. You want to get into my arse, do you? I'll teach you to fuck arseholes, my boy!" he exclaimed, chuckling over my mingled pain and excitement.

"How do you like that—and that—and that—and that?" The last stroke was so painful that it almost took my breath away, and I knew he had fairly drawn blood.

I was furious, my prick felt red-hot, almost ready to burst, when he unloosed my hands and ancles.

I seized him in a perfect fury of lust. His prick was also standing like a bar of iron; he had got so excited by my flagellation. He was turned round, and made to kneel upon the chair at once, presenting his bottom to my attack. No one to look at it would have thought the pink and wrinkled little hole had ever been much used, except for the necessary offices of nature. The sight was perfectly maddening; it looked so delicious.

As I stopped for a moment to lubricate the head of my prick with saliva, he put his fingers in his mouth, and then wetted the little hole himself, to make it as easy as possible for me.

Coming to the charge, I found him delightfully tight, but I got in slowly as he helped me as much as possible by directing the head of my cock with his hand, whilst I had him round the waist and handled that beautiful tool of his, which added immensely to my pleasure. At last I felt fairly in, but did not want to spend too soon, so only moved very slowly, enjoying the sense of possession and the delicious pressures which he evidently so well knew how to apply.

My frigging soon brought him to a spend, and catching it all in my hands, I rubbed the creamy essence of life up and down his prick and over his balls, and even on my own cock as it drew in and out of his bottom.

My delight was perfectly indescribable. I drew it out so long, always stopping for a little when the spending crisis seemed imminent, but at last his writhings and pressures had such an irresistible effect that I could no longer restrain the flood of sperm I had tried so long to keep back, and feeling it shoot from me in a red-hot stream, the agonizing delight made both of us give vent to perfect howls of extasy.

We both nearly fainted, but my instrument was so hard and inflamed that it was a long time before it in the least began to abate its stiffness.

It was still in his bottom, revelling in the well-lubricated hole, and he would fain have worked me up to the very crisis again, but I was afraid of exhausting myself too much at one time, so gradually allowed Mr. Pego to assume his normal size, and slip out of that delicious orifice which had given me such pleasure.

A week after this first introduction Jack came again, and brought the first instalment of his rough notes, from which this MS. is compiled.

Of course at each visit we had a delicious turn at bottom-fucking, but as the recital of the same kind of thing over and over again is likely to pall upon my readers, I shall omit a repetition of our numerous orgies of lust, all very similar to the foregoing, and content myself by a simple recital of his adventures.

If you'd like to read more, *Sins of the Cities of the Plain* is an opensource text free to read in a number of places online. It can also be found in paperback, edited and with an introduction by Wolfram Setz, from Valancourt Books.

HIRAETH

Rhidian Brenig Jones

"OI, MORGAN! STANDIN' there in a dream. Them peas won't weed theirselves."

Staring at Gomer, the head gardener, Will imagined what a fine thing it would be to drive his hoe into the old ratbag's neck, lever his head off and watch it thud into the cabbages—shut him up for ever—but instead he forced a smile and filled his lungs with sweet morning air.

For sure, he faced another twelvemonth of toil under Gomer's jaundiced eye, but a year would soon pass and until that blessed day arrived...well, the sun was shining, the soil was light and friable and the fair would be arriving in Llangain that evening. But best of all, best of all...the memory squirmed in his guts. The scent of hair oil. The touch of warm fingers. Long, dark eyes and the quiet, *Am I hurting you?* He slid his hand into his pocket and fingered the handkerchief, the linen stiff where wetness had dried, and squeezed the head of his cock.

Taking his own sweet time about it, Will unshouldered the hoe. As much to annoy the head gardener as to have a reason to discuss the man who filled his thoughts he said, "I got talkin' to Miss Jenkins's sweetheart last night."

"Lord Henry? What business have the likes of you got talkin' to him?"

"He come into the rose garden. He was after a few blooms for her."

Walnut features scowled into fissures. "You didn't touch none of my Madame Hardys, did you? They be needed for the weddin'."

"I did not. I cut him some Cramoisis and some pinks alongside."

"Don't take that tone with me. Wouldn't put it past you."

"Well, I didn't." After a moment, Will slanted a glance from the corner of his eye. "Don't seem right, though."

"What don't?"

"Lord Henry and Miss Jenkins. Old maid like her. Got a waist like a Clydesdale mare."

Will shot out his arm and grabbed the flying fist before it could land. He wrenched it back, twisting. Many a time he had felt that hand bang on his ear, or slam between his shoulder blades. But he was not a boy any more. He was of full age, vital and strong, and no man's punching bag. Softly, menacingly, he said, "Drop your hand, Gomer Rees. You don't rise it to me." He flung the fist away in disgust. "If I wants to say she's a old maid—*and she is*—an arse-licker like you ent goin' to stop me. She's dried up as last week's bread, that's the truth of it. The whole county knows the master bought him for her." He bent to the peas, ignoring Gomer's glare. "She's pleasant enough in her ways I grant you, I'm not sayin' no different." His hand slid back into his pocket "But pleasant don't do much for a man between the sheets, do it?"

THE LAWNS HAD been mown the previous day and grass cuttings stuck to the men's shoes. The shorter of the two frowned and rubbed an irritated toe against his calf. "Damnable stuff." Ralph Vernon glanced around. The ladies had walked on, taking their butterfly nets down to the lake. He indicated a fallen elm. "Shall we sit here for a moment?" He gave a little cough and adjusted the knees of his trousers. "Look here, Harry, old man, I've been meaning to talk to you. One wouldn't normally, ah, mention, but..."

"But?"

"The marriage. You're determined to go through with it?"

Lord Henry Follain, only son and deeply disappointing heir of the Earl of Brandfordham, nodded.

"I see. Of course, one has to marry, one accepts that but..." Ralph faltered again. Damned awkward situation, this, damned awkward. But they had been at school together, dash it all. One had to speak up; one owed a chap that.

Henry produced two cigars from his pocket and offered one to his friend. "Spit it out, Ralph. Or shall I say it for you? Jenkins made his money from trade so I shall be marrying far below my station. Violet is plain and she's been hawked around for years with no takers. But don't you see? She has one marvellously redeeming feature.."

"Oh?"

"She is very, very rich."

"I say, Harry—"

"My father put it rather well, I thought—here, let me light that for you. Did I tell you? He asked me directly, one day in the library at Brandford. A storm was threatening and the men were fixing 'paulins over the windows to keep the rain out. *Are you a sodomite?* he asked. *I'm not entirely sure*, I replied, *although I very much enjoy the feel of a cock in my arse.*"

A gout of smoke ballooned from Ralph's open mouth. "Christ, you did not!"

Henry smiled and tugged at a tuft of unmown grass between his feet. "No, I didn't. I said nothing, which he took for assent. *In that case*, he said, *it won't matter much who you marry, will it?* And it's true. My wife could be a costermonger's whelp or the Queen of Sheba but she'd still have a cunt, not a cock. You know how things stand, Ralph. The family's been living on capital for years. Somewhat injudicious, wouldn't you say? No, he and Jenkins have struck a sound bargain. I get the money, Violet, God help her, gets me."

"She gets an ancient name. She'll have your title."

"Which is what her father is paying for." Henry studied the tip of his cigar. "And do you know, I intend to make a decent husband. If one decides to play the game, it behoves one to play with a straight bat."

Ralph bit at a hangnail. "But, I mean, will you be able to...?"

"Fuck her? I think so. I'll lay her belly down and take her from behind. One hole feels much like another, or so I'm led to believe."

"Pretend she's me."

Henry looked at him, but it was not Ralph's face he saw.

It was insufferably hot in the house and having dressed early for dinner, Henry slipped out to walk in the relative cool of the grounds. He encountered Will in the rose garden, desultorily raking gravel.

"Lovely evening."

"It is, my lord, and set fair for tomorrow." Will looked at the high cloud in the west banded with salmon, and Henry looked at him. The loose corduroy trousers of a working man hid the intimate contours of his body, but his shoulders were powerful and his chest broad above a supple waist. The triangle of skin between his neckerchief and shirt was oily with sweat.

Because Henry wanted to keep looking at the handsome young gardener, and was enjoying picturing the length of cock that might hang between his thighs, he said the first thing that came into his head. "I wonder, might I have a rose or two for Miss Jenkins?" He indicated a bush of crimson roses, blowsy as peonies, at the back of the bed. "Those are nice."

Will weaved between the bushes and quickly cut five half-opened buds with his pocket knife, then bent to the under-planting of pinks. His arse and braced legs seemed so ridiculously inviting to Henry that he had to smother a bark of disbelieving laughter.

With a curse, Will jerked upright and raised his hand to his mouth.

"What is it? What's the matter?"

Will sucked hard and spat. "Scratched myself."

"Let me see. Here, man, let me see...Good God." A fine spray pulsed from Will's inner wrist. Henry drew back, shook out a handkerchief and pressed it against Will's skin. Instantly, the linen coloured. "I think you might have nicked a blood vessel. This should be stitched."

"Like sickles, some of them thorns. Near as big, too. No need for stitchin', though." Not at the price the local medical man charged.

Although there was no hint of breeze, Will's scent came to Henry, a mingling of sweat, good earth and the freshness of green, growing things. He raised his head to find Will watching him, his blue gaze intent. Nothing was said to break the silence, no gesture made, but recognition grew between them and the son of an earl and the son of a labourer understood each other.

But, no matter how tempting, a gentleman did not fuck his host's servants.

For a few seconds more their eyes remained locked, then Henry loosened his grip on the handkerchief. "Am I hurting you?"

"No, my lord. Thank you."

"What's your name?"

"Morgan."

"Very good. Press hard and it should stop."

Will gingerly lifted the handkerchief to peer underneath, then pressed it back. Henry fished in his pocket. "Here."

Will grimaced as he saw the proffered coin, shaking his head, but Henry tucked it firmly into Will's waistcoat. "Can't have you cutting yourself to pieces on my account. Take your girl to the fair with it."

"No girl for me, sir."

For one moment of madness, Henry believed that he would kiss the young gardener, press his mouth to those beautiful lips and feel the prickle of that glinting, golden stubble against his own meticulously barbered jaw. But instead, he picked up the spilled flowers and, saying nothing more, strode away across the gravel.

Returning to himself with a sigh, Henry ground his cigar under his foot. He rose and brushed the seat of his trousers. "Once I'm married, Ralph, there can be no more...no more...connection between us. I can't love her or even care much for her but I know what people are saying and so does she. I can promise her very little by way of affection but I can spare her the particular humiliation of being tied to a cad."

"She wouldn't know. I very much doubt she has any idea that men like we exist."

"Nevertheless, I intend to be faithful."

"Do you now? In that case, I shall come to you tonight. Make hay while the sun shines, eh?"

They strolled across the lawn to the small stone bridge that spanned a neck of the lake. The other weekend guests were some distance away, taking tea in the shade of a cedar of Lebanon. Violet waved enthusiastically as they approached. Implacable corseting constrained her figure, but thick fingers and large feet suggested heavy bones. Not for the first time, Henry thought sinkingly that she resembled nothing so much as an amiable Guernsey heifer. He ducked under the brim of her hat to peck her cheek and wondered how in the name of Christ he would ever manage to get hard enough to fuck her.

She touched the rosebud in his lapel with a coquettish gesture. "Mama has told the servants that they may go to the fair tonight, Harry dear. Lavinia and I would like to go, too."

"Would you, my dear? Then we certainly shall."

"There's to be a bioscope and a menagerie with an elephant and a Ghost House. And because the servants have the evening off, Mama says we'll have a cold collation for dinner." She frowned. "I believe she still means to dress, though—oh!"

"Violet?" Henry caught her as she swayed, colour draining, lips ashen. "Violet? Sit down, here on the step."

Ralph swept off his hat and thrust it at her cousin. "Fan her, Lavinia!" He ran to the lake and soaked his handkerchief in one of the little cascades and raced back to the bridge. "On her wrists, wet her wrists!"

By the time the others, alarmed and calling out, had hurried from the tea table, a little of Violet's colour had returned. She licked her lips. "Silly me," she said faintly, "dashing about in the sun."

Ralph caught Henry's eye. *Women. Better get used to it.*

They rose as Helen Jenkins came into the drawing room. "I'm afraid Violet is indisposed."

"Oh, I'm so sorry. Is she very unwell?"

"Dear Harry! Not at all. A little too much sun." But dissembling did not come naturally to Helen, and her fingers shook as she touched the brooch at her throat.

Henry felt a sudden pang of pity for the woman. Her anxiety that something would happen to prevent the marriage was almost palpable. How she must have cursed the fate that had given Violet her father's bull-necked looks rather than her own porcelain prettiness. "Of course," he said. "The sun has been very strong." He added a small kindness. "Violet has such fair and delicate skin."

Helen touched a Sèvres bon-bon dish on a side table. "One hesitates to ask... but Violet is fretting. This fair at the village...Lavinia is so looking forward to it." She smiled tremulously. "Do you think...would it be a dreadful imposition to ask you to take her?"

Henry possessed the exquisite manners that only a Scottish nanny and five years at an English public school can instil. "Not at all. We should enjoy it immensely. In fact," he said jovially, "I shall do my utmost to win a coconut for you and a goldfish for Violet."

Like Jacob's angels, Will thought, watching the crowd ascending and descending the steps to the bioscope. *Roll up, roll up!* Paraders stalked the stage in front of the gaudily painted backdrop, chests puffed, dazzling in their spangled finery. A troupe of youths in harlequin costumes pranced and tumbled to the throbbing roar of the showman's engine. One threw himself into a series of back-flips and it passed through Will's mind how much he would enjoy having that supple young body in his bed.

One of the Jenkins stable hands slapped his shoulder. "You comin' in, then?"

Though Will would have liked to see the show, he had no money to waste. "No, I see you later on." He pushed off the newel post and made his way through the crowd. Poppy-cheeked children squealed, darting about or stood, round-eyed, watching Mr Punch belabour the Baby. Smells drifting from the food stalls made his stomach growl: toffee apples and hokey-pokey ice cream, hot doughnuts, crisp with sugar, fish and chips... His mouth filled with saliva. He could just do with a salty cone of chips, drenched with vinegar. Wouldn't cost hardly nothin'.

As he dug in his pocket for a penny, a trill of laughter drew his attention. A few yards away, Lord Henry and his friend were standing at the coconut shy. The young lady with them bounced on the balls of her feet and clasped her hands to her mouth, tittering as both missed again. Lord Henry rolled his shoulders. "Dashed things must be nailed on."

Perhaps, Will thought, it would be worth foregoing the chips. He approached the shy and paid for the three wooden balls, knowing he'd only need one. He drew his arm back and whipped it forward. The largest nut leaped out of its cup with a *thunk*. Will took it from the stallholder and approached the watching trio.

"I've got no use for it, my lord," he said, and held it out to Henry.

For a second, Will thought that Henry would show him his back; certainly, his brows had knit in vexation, but the gent seemed to think better of it.

He nodded stiffly and took the bloody thing with as much grace as he could muster. "Thank you, Morgan. You have a good eye." He added to the others, "Morgan here is a gardener at the house."

Lavinia stared through Will with vacant blue eyes. "Harry," she said, plucking his sleeve, "I want to see the Ghost House. Too thrilling!"

"Too terrifying for me, darling. Ralph will go with you. I'll wait here."

Swallowing his irritation, Ralph offered Lavinia his arm. "I warn you, my dear, you'll have to hold my hand."

Burningly aware of the man beside him, Will strolled with Henry toward the entrance to the Freak Show, where they paused to consider the attractions on the poster.

"A lovely night for a fair," Henry remarked, breaking the singing silence.

"Night like this you don't hardly want to be indoors, bein' so warm and the stars so fine."

"Quite."

"Nights like this, I likes to sleep out. Couple of nice, clean sacks from the shed, set 'em out in the orchard. See the stars shinin' through the plum trees."

"Do you?" said Henry, dry-mouthed.

"Reckon I will tonight." Will looked him directly in the eye. "Yes, reckon I will. I'll say good night, then, my lord."

Will shouldered his way through the crush of people, pausing at a sweet stall to buy a bag of doughnuts. As he sank his teeth into the first, he looked back to where Henry stood, staring blankly at the picture of The Mighty Atom and his unusual wife. He grinned and swept his tongue over sugary lips.

"Grayson, I find the heat oppressive. I'll take a stroll in the grounds before bed. Might I have a key to one of the side doors?"

"I shall wait up for you, of course, my lord."

"That won't be necessary. Just a key, please."

"Very good. I'll have one brought immediately. Will that be all?"

"Yes. No. Bring me a glass of brandy, will you?"

"Yes, my lord. At once."

Hanging huge, so near he felt he could almost touch it, the full moon cast its light on the garden, edging the borders with silver. Moths danced in his wake, drunk on the potent scent of stocks, sweet rocket and tumbling honeysuckle. Avoiding the paths, Henry cut across the lawns, where his footsteps would make no sound. A good hundred yards behind him, the house lay dark and silent, but he was plagued by the conviction that someone had drawn back a curtain and was following his progress with curious eyes; he should have kept his coat on to hide the glowing whiteness of his shirt and waistcoat.

Just there: the gate in the wall. He slipped through it and turned sharply left, trailing his fingers along bricks still warm from the heat of the day. His heart began to knock in his throat when, out of the gloom the bulk of the potting shed appeared, the faint glimmer of candlelight at the window. A sudden rustling in the undergrowth beyond the fence—a fox or a snuffling badger—startled him and he hurried on, hand outstretched, groping for the door latch.

A musty smell of loam and the acrid sharpness of kerosene. Rough-hewn planks under his trailing hand, threatening splinters. He bumped against a tower of clay saucers, sent them crashing, and Will laughed as he stepped from the shadows.

He was naked. He seemed to accept Henry's breath of appreciation as no more than his due, with a jut of his chin and a turn at the waist to display the sinuous line of rib and flank. The muscles of his abdomen tightened as he raised his arms and held his hands clasped above his head. He looked down at his erect cock, then took it in his fist and stroked a finger around the deep split of its head.

Henry took a step and laid his hands on Will's chest. Nipples sprouted like tough little seeds from the warm and hairless planes of his breast, stiff against Henry's palms.

Will tilted his hips. "Take a hold of it, won't you?"

"Open your legs."

The skin moved easily, up over the crown, down to fold at the root. Up again. Down. Will shifted his feet on the gritty floor, spreading his thighs to allow Henry to caress his balls. Through the haze of lust that fogged his mind, Henry realised that Will was dry in his hand, as some men are; his own prick was seeping, soaking his drawers.

Will's mouth pressed against Henry's ear. "I'll fetch all over you, you keep on doin' that."

"I'd like you to."

"Lie with me and I shall."

"Help me. Hurry, for God's sake."

The pearl studs in his stiff shirt front were fiddly to unscrew, even with steady hands. Henry clinked them one by one into a saucer, along with his watch and cuff links.

"You ent wearing nothin' under," Will said wonderingly. Henry was, indeed, bare under his shirt.

"Drawers only. Too hot for comms."

"Hairy chest like that, don't need nothin' else to keep you warm."

"Oh, God. Touch me."

Will rubbed the heel of his hand against Harry's fly buttons, and nosed like a starving wolf cub against his face. Aroused almost beyond endurance, Henry pushed him off and kicked his way out of drawers and trousers, all in one. He stood naked, as confident of his own looks as Will was of his, slender but well-muscled, with the tell-tale length of bone from ankle to knee that is the hallmark of good breeding. They stared at each other, shuddering with lust until, with a gasp, Will fell against Henry, colliding with him so violently that he was almost knocked off his feet...

...and then they were kissing, kissing as only two men can kiss. Nothing restrained. Nothing withheld.

With a whooping breath, Will broke away. "Outside."

"Do you think we should? Would it not be safer—"

"*Jesus, come on!*"

Will grabbed Henry's hand and led him out of the door. They tumbled down on to the cold ground, the shock of it making them gasp until they found mouths again, and the grass under them grew warm. Belly to hard belly they lay, Henry's leg over Will's thigh. Henry grasped his own cock and nosed it to Will's, wetting the crown and making him moan. At Henry's whispered urging, Will buried his face in Henry's neck and searched between his legs. His fingertips traced a path from Henry's balls, across the bridge of his perineum, and further to the crisp hairs of his arsehole. Hugging each other, they began to thrust, hips bucking wildly, grunting with loss when one cock slipped off the other. Too soon, too soon—Henry cried out and the spurt of his ejaculation, the scent of the slippery wash, brought Will's semen fountaining onto Henry's prick.

Trembling, they held each other as the aftershocks faded, and even when world righted itself they continued to embrace, nuzzling eyelids and temples and noses, gently, gently, under the winking stars.

"How do you bear it? Or do you have a particular friend?"

"I sees a fellow lives over Monmouth way now and then."

Henry thought of certain clubs tucked away around St James's, discreet gatherings at friends' country houses. He thought of the parties at which thick-pricked guardsmen were anyone's for the taking, for the beating, for the fucking. "It must be difficult for you. Lonely."

Will shrugged and finished tying his boot lace. "Won't be lonely where I'm goin'."

"Oh? Where are you going?"

He pronounced it in the reverential tone that the rector might have used for *The Kingdom of Heaven*. "Australia."

"Australia?"

"Soon as I saves enough for the passage and some extra to keep me till I gets work."

"What will you do there?"

"Make my fortune."

Henry felt a sudden, despondent envy. "But your people, your friends? Don't you have a family who will miss you?"

"Ent no-one I cares about enough to stay. Had a brother—Ronald. Died a year last March. Typhoid. Ent no-one else."

"I see." Henry fastened the last of the studs and ran his hands through his hair, feeling for leaves. He found a twig and pulled it out. How strange that very little money, pocket change in the great scheme of things, would set Will free, yet the riches of Croesus would bind Henry in golden shackles. He shrugged his arms into his waistcoat. "How much do you have saved?"

Will got up from the overturned bucket he'd been sitting on. "What you want to know that for?"

"I was wondering how much more you needed."

Will's tone became glacial. "Why? You offerin' to pay for what we done?"

"Well, I—"

"Think I'm some kind of fuckin' Mary Ann, sellin my arse for money?"

"No, of course not—"

"*Because I ent!*"

"I didn't mean to suggest, to imply...oh, for God's sake, man!"

The icy glare faded. "All right, then." Will breathed out heavily through his nostrils and tucked the tails of his shirt into his trousers. "Better get goin'."

Henry caught his arm as he made to pass. "I could lend you the money, you know. If it would help."

"Lend me? Why?"

Because, Henry thought, *I lack the courage to jilt Violet and hook it to India or Malaya. I could not bear exile, scorned by decent society as the worse kind of remittance man. Not that there would be any money to send, and I am supremely unqualified to earn a living.*

But perhaps Will could stand proxy for him. Will, at least, could be freed, freed for him and for all men who loved men.

"A loan to be paid back when you've made your fortune. Come, how much are you short?"

He said slowly, "Three pound, near enough."

Three pounds; Henry had lost ten times that on the turn of a card. "Will you be at work tomorrow?"

"Should be."

"I shall walk in the garden after breakfast. The roses are so lovely at this time of year."

"MR REES, WILL ent here this mornin'."

"No, he ent, nor will be. He've slung his hook. He come by for his wages then buggered off. No loss."

The little apprentice's mouth shook. He looked from the head gardener to John, the lumbering simpleton who carried out the heavy laboring in the grounds. There would be nobody now to stand between him and Mr Rees, to protect him from the worst of the thumps and slaps. "Ent he ever comin' back to work, then?" he asked drearily.

Gomer slid cold eyes over the boy. "What's it to you?"

"Nothin."

"Better be nothin', too. Left Mrs Powell owin' two weeks' rent, evil young bastard. He've gone and good riddance." This was a lie: Will had cleared all his debts before he left and had given his landlady a shilling in addition to his rent, because she had always been kind to him.

OCTOBER 1913. LONDON.

A GENTLEMAN, THERE was no doubt about it. A colonial, of course, but none the worse for that. Edgar glanced at the tall figure, his back turned, running the brim of his hat through his hands. Lovely bit of suiting, and if he wasn't mistaken, the shoes were Lobb's. Edgar scraped a testing fingernail over the gent's card and pursed satisfied lips at the engraving. Passing through the drawing room toward the library, he took care not to disturb the post-luncheon somnolence. He narrowed his eyes as he approached the portly figure of Mr Trengrouse, up from Cornwall, snoring off his sole and beef; the poor old boy had neglected to fasten his flies again. Edgar reddened in vexation and gestured furiously to a junior club servant idling in a corner. Slapdash, slapdash! Young whippersnappers, no eye for proper service. Words would need to be had, music faced. At the far end of the room he spotted Henry, Earl of Brandfordham, at his favourite desk near the window, his elegant gray head bent over a letter.

"My lord."

"Yes, Edgar."

"A visitor, my lord, a gentleman to see you."

"Oh?" He picked up the card and examined it. "'*Morgan*'. Do I know a Morgan?"

"I couldn't say, my lord."

"Very well." He licked the envelope and laid it on the pile. "See that these catch the post, will you?.."

Henry strode into the hallway, straightening his tie. Morgan...Morgan... His stomach turned over and he stopped as if he'd walked into a wall. Oh, Christ...Not him. It couldn't be him. He'd been fool enough once to give the creature money. Was he now back, on the leech for more? Where had he been all these years? Prison? But wait... Edgar had spoken of a gentleman and that colossal snob was never mistaken. Somewhat reassured, more curious then than alarmed, Henry smoothed down the hair above his ears and pushed open the door.

It seemed that he had strayed into Mr Carroll's world of wonders—although a white rabbit checking a pocket watch would have been less astonishing than the man now looking at him, a tentative half-smile on his sunburned face.

"Brandfordham. How do you do."

Numbly, Henry took the outstretched hand. "How do you do."

Will indicated the portrait of the King and Queen above the fireplace, glittering in their coronation robes. "Magnificent Mary. A lady who knows how to wear a jewel."

With an effort, Henry pulled himself together. The man was his guest. No matter the circumstances, nothing excused a lack of civility. "I do beg your pardon. Will you sit down?"

Laying his hat and gloves on a small side table, Will remarked, "I see you're surprised."

"I must confess, I am, rather," replied Henry. Dreadfully bad form to notice a fellow's clothes, his bearing, *his manner of speech,* but the transformation was so astounding that the training of years fell away. "How do you come to be...I mean to say, what, what has happened?" He recalled what had been said to him almost twenty years before and the vehemence with which he had been told it. "You've been in Australia?"

"There and other places. But that's a long story." Will reached into his pocket and brought out a narrow velvet case. "I have come to repay a debt long owed." Henry watched as the case was opened, a fine chain unfastened from its bed and held up. Catching the light, the stone twirled lazily, flashing peacock colours, the fluid whorls of its platinum setting almost lacklustre in comparison.

"I hope the Countess isn't superstitious. The legend that opals are unlucky stems only from the fact that they're delicate and can crack if carelessly treated. The best blacks are found near a place called Lightning Ridge. This stone is one of the finest I've seen."

"This is too much. I couldn't possibly accept—"

"Please. I've waited many years for the pleasure of being able to repay you."

"It's utterly beautiful. And is this how you...?"

"Made my fortune? At first. I seem to have a nose for opals and a head for business. Put the two together in a rapidly growing country and...shall we put it back?"

"Thank you," Gently, not wanting to discomfit the man, Henry said, "You couldn't have known, of course, but my wife died some years ago."

"Died? I see. I...I'm sorry, Brandfordham. My condolences."

The correct use of his title intrigued Henry. "Yet you knew that my father had died?"

"Yes. It was reported in the Sydney Herald. We see it occasionally, although it's months out of date. The obituary mentioned that you have three sons?"

"Tom, Frank and Giles. Dreadful scamps. Away at school, of course. And you? Have you...?"

"No, I haven't been that fortunate." Will looked around for his hat. "Well, I must be on my way."

Henry stood with him. "Thank you again for the opal. I shall keep it for Tom's wife, for when he marries. I, er...how long will you be in town?"

"I sail for New York on Thursday. I need to see my man of business before then. He's looking for a house for me." He hesitated, as if unsure whether the confidence would be welcome. "I'm coming home."

"Are you, by Jove? In that case you must regale me with your Australian adventures before they're over. I wonder, if you're not engaged, would you care to dine with me this evening?"

"I'm not engaged."

"Excellent. Shall we say half past eight? My house is in Chelsea, at the end of Egerton Crescent. The cabbie will know it. There won't be ladies present so... shall we waive the formalities?"

His guest nodded and picked up his gloves and hat. "Black tie it is. Good afternoon, Brandfordham."

"Harry, please. Good afternoon...Will."

Henry stood at the window, looking out. Passers-by battled the wind, hands on hats, as leaves whirled around them, chasing their tails. A trio of shop girls came tripping along, arm in arm, laughing and turning their faces from the squalls that lifted their skirts and tangled their hair. As he ran his fingers over the velvet case in his pocket, Henry thought of the years that had passed. Half a lifetime...Yet as he watched Will cross the square and disappear around the corner, he felt grass under his back. The weight of a lithe body covering him. A rigid cock thrusting against his own—

"Can I bring you anything, my lord?"

"Cyril, you startled me!"

"I'm very sorry, my lord. I was wondering whether I could bring you anything."

"No, I— wait, yes." Henry unscrewed his pen and scrawled few words on a sheet of writing paper, folded it and addressed the envelope to his butler. "Have this taken to my house, will you." Coombs and Mrs Wells would be put out at the short notice but it couldn't be helped. "I shall dine at home tonight," he added, turning back to the window.

HEAVY DRAPES SHUT out the night. The lamps' yellow light glinted on crystal and lent a soft golden luster to silver. A portrait of Lady Arabella Follain, handsome in silks and powdered wig, gazed with disdain at the table, able to seat twenty but laid for only two.

Henry cracked another nut and returned to the fray. "But it would be such a damnable bother, Will. The whole house turned upside down and for what? I like gaslight. Electric light is so harsh, one almost has to shade one's eyes."

"Nonsense. It's clean and pure. A clear, white light."

"Nothing wrong with gas light," Henry insisted, chewing.

"It hisses abominably and there's always that slight odour. No, Harry, it's electricity for me. I shall have it in my new house, come what may."

Henry considered his port. "Where exactly do you plan to settle?"

"On the Welsh border. Are you familiar with the word *hiraeth*?"

"No."

"It's difficult to translate exactly. It means the longing or yearning for Wales that the exile feels. I like Australia, it made me what I am, but...at times, and increasingly so of late, I feel I should like to be home. Do you know Tintern

Abbey? I fancy settling near there. In the Wye Valley, certainly."

A coal collapsed in the grate, sending a brief flare into the chimney. The taller of the footmen bent to the fireplace but Henry called out, "Leave it. We can manage. Off you go to bed. You might tell Berry that I'll ring for him in the morning. No need to wake me too early. Have Mr. Morgan's things been sent round from Claridge's?"

"Yes, my lord. A person delivered them an hour ago."

"Good. Goodnight."

Once the servants had left, Henry leaned back in his chair and pushed the fragments of nut shell into a little heap on his plate. "Tell me now, if you don't mind my asking—your transformation. How did it come about? It really is remarkable."

"It's easy enough if one has a good teacher and the means to pay him. So much is a matter of voice, of accent, don't you think? It's not what one looks like but what one *sounds* like that matters. I had made my fortune but manners maketh man, and I realised that if I were to move with ease and confidence in certain circles, I would need a good deal of polishing."

Henry studied Will over the rim of his glass. They had agreed that, in the absence of ladies, they might remove their jackets. Will's chest was broader than Henry remembered, with just the suggestion of a hard curve of belly under his waistcoat. His fair hair had been bleached to silver by age and a merciless southern sun. Deep lines cut into his forehead and bracketed the corners of his mouth. Gorgeous mouth. Henry's cock tightened on his thigh at the memory of kisses, the tongue that had moved so greedily in his mouth.. "Go on," he said, recovering his train of thought with some difficulty.

"I met Charles in Sydney. I was there to buy land. He'd been a captain in the Blues, left under a cloud, some almighty stink about a lady and some letters. The lady was his commanding officer's wife."

Henry grimaced.

"Disowned by his family and so on, so short of money. Charlie needed funds, I needed refining. It was harder than I'd expected, but we got there in the end." Will gave a rueful laugh. "He taught me, drilled me, even made me study Speakers until he was satisfied that I would pass. I think he thought it a fine joke."

A note in Will's tone gave Henry the opportunity to turn the conversation, as he had been longing to do for some time. His heart began to gallop and he cleared his throat. Tentatively, he ventured, "You and he...were you...?"

"Lovers? After a fashion. But Charlie has catholic tastes. Men, women, black, white. He'd fuck a kangaroo if he could pin one down for long enough."

Henry laughed. "Would he now?" But the smile faded from his face when he met Will's steady gaze. The air in the room stilled, singing with sudden tension. "And you? How do your tastes run these days?"

Will picked up his glass and finished his port. "To men," he said. "Only to men."

Will's forearms were tanned as nut brown as his face, but the covered parts of his body were as pale as milk. Henry found it strange that the texture of his skin didn't alter at these margins, rough becoming satiny smooth, discernible to his tongue. Eyes closed, he licked the inner bend of Will's elbow and the bronzed vee below his collarbones, but he found no change. He propped his head on his hand and ran his hand over Will's broad abdomen. Young himself, he'd lain with a young man; neither was young now. But maturity had its compensations: skin might have lost its bloom, slackened somewhat, but it covered the powerful musculature of a mature man. He bent to kiss a nipple, and the warm belly under his palm clenched into cobblestones. No youthful Adonis, but a magnificent Zeus. And magnificent his prick, the tracery of veins engorged with blood and slippery with Henry's spittle. As Henry stared at it, a glimmer of moisture formed at the deep slit, and his own prick jolted, spilling out a more generous drizzle of clear seed.

He murmured, "Bring your legs up."

Will shifted on the bed and hooked his hands behind his knees. His scrotum bulged at the root of his shaft, drawn up to reveal his anus, tight-closed in a ruff of hair. Henry settled between his legs and hunched over him, and stroked the tip of his cock against the little slot. Misunderstanding, Will gave a shaky little laugh. "Take care, will you? It's been some time for me."

"I will. But not yet."

The fluid from his own body would not be anywhere near enough to ease penetration, but it excited Henry to stimulate Will in this way. He caressed in circles, around and around and slid a fingertip in, just an inch, and worked the rim of the ring as if marking the hours of a clock, stretching and loosening, and making Will moan with pleasure.

"You like this, don't you? Having a man's finger in your arse?"

"Yes. And other things."

"Other things?"

"Pricks. Tongues."

"I wonder...I have something else that you might enjoy." Henry reached across Will to a small table and fumbled in a drawer. He brought out a small jar and another object.

The old Javanese had been a master of his craft. The serpent's head was smooth but the ivory of its broadening body had been carved into deep scales, rippling bumps that would bring an unsurpassed intensity of pleasure as they slid through a man's opening. Henry held it up for Will to see.

"Would you like this? Would you like to feel this inside you? Before I fuck you?"

Will dropped his head back to the pillow and covered his eyes with his arm. "Yes."

Henry took fingerfuls of creamy ointment and eased them into Will's anus. The fragrance of amber mingled with the scent of his body was redolent of the love between men, and Henry's cock cramped violently as he breathed it in. Plenty on the snake, a generous coating. Gently, so gently, Henry slid the head into Will's body.

"Oh, God, oh, God—"

Deeper in, the anus expanding around its girth. In and out, in and slithering out, the sensitive flesh swelling and contracting at the passing of each scale. In to its full length. Henry brought his hand away. Yes, maturity had its compensations, not least of which was mastery of one's body. Although he let out hoarse cries and his head tossed on the pillow, Will was able to control his release. But as Henry stared, he felt the iron erection in his fist soften. Time, now, for completion. He drew out the ivory and tossed it aside. No need for more ointment; Will gaped, his hole oily and spasming.

"Oh, Christ..." Henry dropped down and as the strong legs wrapped around his hips, he slid deep, deep into Will's guts.

Since the day of his marriage, Henry had remained faithful to Violet. He had grown fond of her over the years and had mourned her sincerely when a failing heart took her to an early grave. And even afterward, he had denied himself the joy of men's bodies, conscious of the catastrophe that would ensue for his sons if he were exposed as a sodomite. Only once had he slaked his thirst, marvellously, far away in Java, where the lissom, sloe-eyed youths had smelled of the jasmine and honey that flavored their semen. Years of abstinence come to an end in the feast of this body.

Hard, then, and fast. No danger of hurt from a cock of flesh. Henry thrust, and found Will's mouth and Will held him and rocked upward and twisted to bite into his neck. Hard and fast, balls slapping, bone thudding against pelvic bone. Hard and fast, a delirium of fucking.

Henry felt the breaking gush from Will's prick. He thrust again and again, sliding on sweat and semen. One last convulsive push and he stilled. His body seized. He emptied high, high into Will's rectum and the world around him turned white.

HENRY DREW LAZY patterns in the wet on Will's belly. Licking his fingers, he thought that next time he'd suck, hold Will's semen in his mouth for a long time before he swallowed. He settled his head more comfortably on Will's shoulder, but his eyes snapped open: was there to be a next time?

"I told you that I sail for America on Thursday."

"Yes."

"When I return in the New Year, I should like to see something of you."

Henry's heart leapt. "I'd like that very much."

"Good."

"You don't think you've seen all there is to see?"

"Not everything. And besides, some things bear repeated viewing."

"So they do."

Will kissed the top of his head. "I shall have electric lamps installed in my new house, so we'll be able to see very clearly indeed, you and I."

Henry smiled.

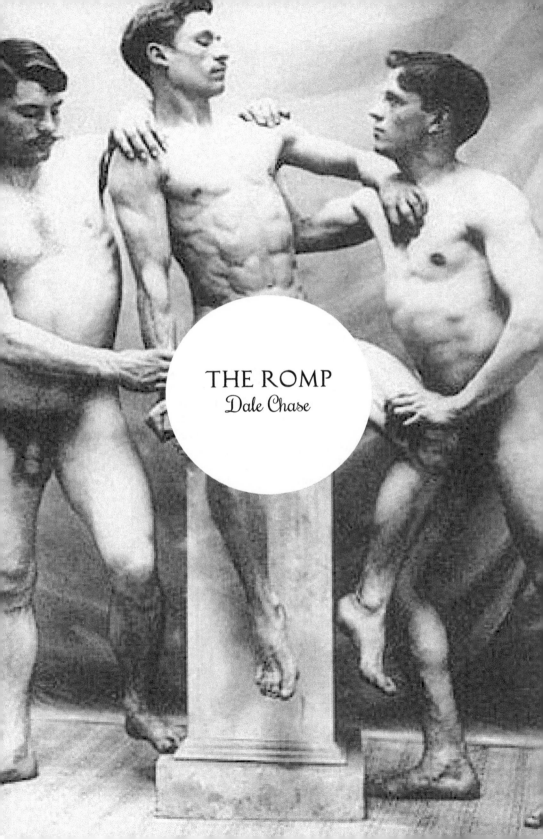

THE ROMP

Dale Chase

"If it's so select," I asked Freddy, "how did *you* manage an invitation?"

My friend smiled and squeezed my arm. "Because, dear boy, I *am* select."

"The hell you are. What did you do to get invited? Or should I say whom?"

"Please, Tom, I must remain discreet."

"You've never been discreet in your life," I noted. "Ah, that must be it. Lord Whitfield wants young men to spice up the party."

"Trust me, the party needs no assistance from anyone. Now, do you wish to join me?"

"How can I refuse?"

Freddy and I had been friends since school where we discovered a predilection for pulling each other's cocks. Now that we'd grown up and gone into business—he clerking for a solicitor, me at my father's bookstore—we kept up the friendship, giving it the old school pull, so to speak, and sometimes far more. Freddy had boyfriends while I fell to more restraint, though I did on the odd weekend venture to the low part of London to gain release.

I kept some distance from the lofty circles that Freddy moved in, and so I scarcely knew of Lord Whitfield. With little interest in the aristocracy, I approached the party with a mix of disdain and curiosity. Esterbrook, Lord Whitfield's realm, was an imposing estate, the manor house equal in size to several downtown buildings strung together. "How many rooms?" I asked Freddy as the house came into view on a lovely summer morning.

"Enough," he replied as I gazed out at the imposing building and its vast grounds.

As our carriage reached the house, I saw a large tent just beyond a terrace. "Is it a garden party?" I asked.

"Of sorts, yes," said Freddy, affecting a cat-eaten-the-canary look. I wondered what it was he knew. No doubt something good, possibly something wicked. Perhaps some notable would be present, some man of such beauty and vigor that we'd near spend in our trousers.

Servants descended before the carriage had even stopped. We were ushered to the door, our luggage seen to, leaving me unencumbered and free to take in the grandeur of the place. Lush green vines wrapped around tall columns fronting the entrance, and fancywork was plentiful on the stone facade. Freddy had to urge me on, lest I remain fixed on none but the porch.

Inside I found us dwarfed by a grand hall with twin staircases curving up at the back. A butler stood waiting; I left it to Freddy to issue commands since he'd frequented places like this far more often than I had. "Mr. Frederic Minter and

Mr. Tom Drury," he announced.

"Very good, sir," replied the servant. "I am Royce, at your service. May I show you to your room?"

"By all means."

I was still gawking at my opulent surroundings. "Can you believe this?" I asked Freddy as we climbed the stairs.

"Shush," he said, nodding towards Royce. A subtle scolding from him—and of course he was right. One mustn't reveal one's less than stellar class to servants.

We were ushered into a bedroom larger than my entire lodgings in the city. "Are we to room together?" Freddy asked Royce, sounding somewhat put out.

"Yes, sir. It is at Lord Whitfield's direction."

"Very well."

"Instead of a formal luncheon," Royce advised, "food will be provided at the performance which begins at one."

Soon as Royce retreated, Freddy threw off his jacket and flopped onto the bed. "Apparently the Lord of the manor likes boys to share a bed."

"What's going on?" I asked. "Royce said a performance. You know something, don't you?"

"Not a thing, dear boy. Party, performance, whatever. It's at one o'clock."

"Possibly some entertainment," I decided. "I do hope it's not some boring string quartet."

"Somehow I doubt that."

I strode to a large window to view the grounds. Low hedges surrounded flower beds bursting with color while lawns stretched into the distance, stopped only by a row of trees. "Nice change from London," I offered. "Shall we go for a walk before the festivities begin?"

"Good idea."

We washed up and set out, only to be met by Royce at the bottom of the stairs. "Gentlemen, where are you off to?"

"A stroll around the grounds."

"I'm sorry, but Lord Whitfield discourages such activity before the performance. He means for his guests to rest in their rooms. Please return there. You may come down at quarter of one."

"This is becoming rather strange," I noted as Freddy and I climbed back up the stairs. No other guests were to be seen and I wondered if all had been similarly admonished to their rooms. "What gives?" I asked Freddy who again flopped on the bed.

"Who cares. Something is going to happen in that tent at one."

I took off my jacket and lay on the bed, gazing at a fine white ceiling while recalling the dingy gray at my flat. Confinement to such a room was not a hardship.

"Want to get up to something?" Freddy asked. I looked over to see his pants undone, his prick in hand.

"No," I said. "I'd rather not get sweaty before the performance."

"Then suck me." He wagged his thing. I chuckled and took him into my mouth. Freddy was a scamp, the most relentless fellow I'd ever known, and I thoroughly enjoyed his antics. Soon I had a mouthful of his issue and he was asleep. I crept to the basin, rinsed my mouth, and checked my watch. Half an hour more before we could descend to who-knew-what.

I wished I could sack out like Freddy, but I was too wound up over what might lay ahead. Doubling us up in the room lent credence to the idea that something wicked might be afoot, but I called up the idea of a boring recital so as not to be disappointed. I checked my watch repeatedly as I moved from chair to window to chair until the appointed time finally arrived. "Up," I told Freddy as I shook him. "Time to find out what's in store."

He popped up grinning, and hurried to the basin. Emerging fresh and clothed into the hallway, you can imagine our surprise to find two other doors opening, pairs of handsome young men stepping out. Nods were exchanged, but nothing was said and we descended the stairs as a group. Royce guided our party to a terrace, directing us to follow steps into the garden and thence into the tent.

"Finally," I said to Freddy, nudging him as we went along.

The big white tent was unimpressive on the outside and spectacular within. Rows of fine chairs were set before a large curtained stage while at the back were tables offering a veritable feast served on fine china and silver. We filled plates and set about gorging on roast meats, puddings, and pies. Wine was plentiful and we indulged fully. Some fellows ate while seated, others stood in groups. I began to relax in such company, noting all present were around my age—twenty-two— and all were most appealing. Little was said and I saw how none had any more idea of what lay ahead than I did.

Half an hour passed in eating and drinking before Royce stepped in front of the curtain. "Gentlemen, please be seated," he announced. "The performance is about to begin."

We took our seats, Freddy insisting on first row. Anticipation filled the room like some pungent scent, and then a stunningly handsome fellow, dark haired with flashing eyes, stepped from between the curtains. He looked upon us at length, then said "A fine audience, truly fine." This brought murmurs and some low laughter, after which he continued.

"On behalf of Lord Whitfield, I wish to welcome you to his new production, *The Romp*. For those of you new to Esterbrook Theater, the play was written by Lord Whitfield and he is a featured player. Also for your entertainment are Adrian Harding and yours truly, Lance Ramsgate. And now, gentlemen, on to *The Romp*."

The fellow disappeared behind the curtain and we had but a few seconds before it parted to reveal a drawing room with settee at the center, overstuffed chairs on either side, a painting or two on surprisingly real looking walls, and a couple small tables. I was surprised a tent theater could offer staging similar to that seen in London. The Lord of the manor obviously took great care with his productions and I became eager to see what was to unfold.

Suddenly there came a high-pitched squeal. A woman in a voluminous dress rushed onstage with none other than Lance Ramsgate in tow. She had blond hair piled high with curls, jewels at her neck, and a dress with plunging neckline, tight waist, and yards of skirt. A vision of pink and lavender satin, it contained a sizeable bosom which the lady proceeded to thrust toward Lance. "Oh, Pamela," he exclaimed, slipping his arms around her.

Pamela in turn fairly engulfed him, pulling him into a mighty embrace as she fixed her mouth to his. They were thus entwined when a door slammed offstage. "What's that?" cried Lance, looking back over his shoulder.

"Oh, damn," said Pamela. "It must be my husband. He was down at the stables and I thought he'd be occupied for a good while."

Lance attempted to break free of Pamela but she held him fast, even as footsteps were heard. "Pamela, I must flee!" Lance cried.

"No time," she countered, and she lifted her petticoats and bade him crawl under. He did so and once the dress was smoothed into place, the lady of the house appeared most calm.

"Dearest Reg," she said as a graying fellow entered.

"Is that Lord Whitfield?" I asked Freddy in a whisper.

"Shush," he countered.

"I thought you had business at the stables," Pamela said.

"I did," replied Reg, "but I made short work of it. It's too fine a day to spend with the horses."

Pamela began to wriggle as her husband moved to a table where he turned his back and took up a cigar. As he spent time lighting it, Pamela's skirts began to rustle and she in turn began to squirm. She issued a muffled squeal, drawing herself up, and I had to laugh, as did the entire audience, for it was certain the fellow under her dress was tending her privates.

"What's that, dear?" asked Reg as he turned her way, puffing on his cigar.

"Oh, nothing. A moth fluttered by. I was startled."

He nodded, gathered a newspaper, and settled onto the settee to read. Pamela's mouth, meanwhile, had fallen open, her tongue lolling about as she further squirmed. Her hand came to her neck as her breast began to heave and for a few seconds she was in motion, face red, head thrashing this way and that while biting her lip. Then she burst forth a great breath and set to fanning herself with one hand. Once quieted, she moved delicately to one side where Lance managed to slip from under her and hide behind a chair. She then excused herself. "I'll see about luncheon," she announced as she fled.

Reg had looked up to watch her leave, and once she was gone he set down his paper, got up, and strode about the room. We could see poor Lance as he peeked out from behind the chair to follow Reg's progress. At last Reg slipped behind the settee where he leaned to one side to view the hiding lover. He cleared his throat, then spoke. "Mr. Ramsgate isn't it?" he said, at which Lance cautiously rose.

"Sir," said Lance.

"You are acquainted with my wife?"

"Uh, yes, somewhat, yes. We, uh, we met, we met at, at, we met at the Granger's party last week."

"Ah, yes, the Grangers. And now you've come to call?"

Lance began to wring his hands. "In a manner of speaking, yes."

"Then come out from behind that chair. Let me have a look at you."

Lance turned to gaze at the audience, as if he might gain strength from us. This sent a ripple of laughter around the tent. He ventured to center stage, looking from us to Reg, as we waited with him to see what torment the wronged husband might inflict. How curious we were when Reg, still behind the settee, began fumbling with something out of sight. He then drew a long breath and strode into full sight to reveal a hard cock escaping his trousers. My gasp was audible, as were several others, while still others laughed.

"You've accosted my wife which is, as you well know, unacceptable. What is acceptable, dear boy, is your coming over here and dropping your trousers."

Lance broke into a smile and turned to offer us shrug before doing as told. Moving to the settee, he shed his trousers, at which Reg bent him and moved in. This, unfortunately, blocked the coupling from view. What we got was Reg's backside as he pulled down Lance's undergarments and mounted Lance with what appeared a most vigorous intercourse.

"Are they really fucking?" I asked Freddy, whose eyes were wide, as was his mouth. His hand was in his lap.

"I'll never tell," he replied.

"Meaning?"

"Meaning the audience is meant to draw their own conclusions."

"But he's gone so far as to present his hard prick. What else is he to do?"

"What he presented, Tom, is an India rubber cock."

We passed this exchanged without ever taking eyes off the scene. Reg was now thrusting madly and Lance was moaning something awful. "But the false cock is *in* Lance, right?"

"It would appear so, but I really can't say. It's a play, so nothing may be as it seems."

Reg put an end to our speculation by crying out he was coming and he gave several hard thrusts along with a lengthy moan. He then withdrew, put his member back into his pants and pulled up Lance's linen. Only after these movements, did Reg step aside so we could see Lance in his undergarments.

There came Pamela's call from offstage. "Reg, darling, luncheon is served."

"Begone you rascal," Reg commanded, and Lance pulled up his pants and fled. Reg, drawing himself up to full height, adjusted his privates and strode offstage, at which the curtain closed to thunderous applause. Then Royce stepped out.

"Gentlemen, there will be a brief pause while the set is changed for Act Two," he announced before disappearing behind the curtain. Freddy chuckled while I sat in dismay. Murmurs swept through the audience, no doubt others pondering the situation. One had to wonder what could possibly be next.

After sounds of moving furniture, Royce came back out. "Gentlemen, we present for your entertainment Act Two of *The Romp*."

The curtain opened to a bedroom scene, large bed at the center with dresser, tables and chairs scattered about. It became obvious that the bed was occupied, but the occupants were well under the covers, so much so that they could not be identified. After a few whispers, the audience quieted, while the scene before us did the opposite. The covered bodies began to move, at first seeming to gently comingle, then one clearly mounted the other. I was impressed at how much coupling could be conveyed out of direct sight. Thrusting became most obvious, accompanied by the occasional squeal or moan as we watched the invisible act. I was hoping they would bare themselves when there came from offstage the voice of Pamela, lady of the house.

"Reginald, love, your Pamela is near. Are you ready for me, darling?"

Now the covers were thrown back, revealing Lance and Reg, both naked. "Hide," commanded Reg and Lance slid to the floor and crawled under the bed. Reg, meanwhile, drew the covers over himself just as Pamela swept in. She wore a pink ruffled satin dressing gown, open to reveal a lavender chemise. It could hardly contain her large bosom while cinching her waist to impossible size. I marveled she could breathe. "Darling," she cooed, "I can wait no longer."

"Pet," replied her husband, "I fear you must. My rod is quite asleep."

"Then allow me to wake it," she cried. "I am eager to sit upon your magnificence."

Here she crawled onto the bed, throwing back the blanket. "There it is! My salvation, my reward. Let me bring it forth, husband, so I may ride my stallion."

Reg eluded her by hopping from bed, taking up his dressing gown, and wrapping it tightly about himself. "Dearest, at the moment I am honestly not equipped to meet your demands. Please forgive me, but even a stallion must occasionally rest."

"Nonsense," she said and she leaped from bed, charging at her husband, at which he ran around to the bed's other side. There ensued a chase of sorts, Pamela squealing with delight at such play while Reg, fearful of same, attempted flight. At one point Lance emerged for a look, catching sight of Reg who kicked at him. Lance withdrew back into hiding just as Pamela came by again. "Pet," Reg said as he stopped his flight, breath now short, "might I attend you later on?"

"But my need is now," she replied, fanning herself with her hand. When he didn't immediately reply, she gave him a long look and said, "Why should you be in such condition that you cannot pleasure your own wife? You haven't been abusing your thing again?"

"No, dearest, of course not."

"A maid then? Or a gardener? Stable boy? Horse?"

Reg rolled his head in such an exaggerated manner that we all laughed.

"None but you, my love," he assured his wife. "Still, you must understand I am a man of years. Sometimes my thing, as you call it, may not rise to the occasion and I fear this may be such a time."

"But don't you see, my darling," persisted Pamela. "I am the one appointed to bring you to full splendor. Let me at you, please." Here she kneeled and attempted to pull open the dressing gown. Reg, however, grabbed her hands and pulled her to her feet. "I have a better idea," he said and before she could object he kissed her.

Once weakened from such attention, Pamela allowed herself be freed from her dressing gown, revealing more of her fine figure. She was then laid on the bed, head on a pillow, at which Reg climbed on. Of course his dressing gown didn't allow us full sight of what was happening, but we were given indication when, after he obviously fumbled with the chemise, Pamela's legs were raised high and wide. "Ah, there it is, my pet," Reg growled before diving down and proceeding to feed in a noisy manner.

As this went on, Lance slipped from under the bed, gathered his clothes, and was about to make an exit when he caught sight of the couple's activity. He stood watching—he had a much better view than we did—and he soon took his cock in hand and began to stroke, leaning toward the couple to gain a still better view. There passed a long interval of attention to Pamela, during which Reg surfaced once to wipe a hand across his mouth, draw a loud breath, and dive back in. After further effort there came at last Pamela's cry of release, after which all fell silent. Pamela's legs came down and Reg emerged, obviously much fatigued from his effort. When he saw Lance he became renewed, tongue emerging. With a snore now emanating from Pamela, Reg crept to the side of the bed where he began to suck Lance's cock and pull his own. As the two so engaged, there came a knock at the door. This was ignored as both men were well into the throes of ecstasy. Another knock and Royce entered. Laughter erupted from the audience; the butler sported a large red India rubber cock from his open pants. He moved about in perfect servant form, nose high, air elegant. "Sir?" he inquired. "You gave instructions to be up at ten. I see you are just that."

Reg gave no reply as he was obviously swallowing Lance's spend. Lance, arched forward, was thrusting madly, head thrown back. Once he quieted, Reg pulled off and turned to see his faithful servant at the ready. He pushed Lance away, and, still holding his prick, nodded to Royce. As Lance gathered his clothes and fled, Royce moved in. Reg got off the bed and stood facing the dresser, bottom thrust back. Royce, ever loyal, strode over, parted the buttocks, and shoved in the dildo at which Reg cried out, "Faithful servant!"

The butler, thrusting slowly, looked back over his shoulder, smiled, and shrugged. This brought a close of the curtains and thunderous applause. "Well that was certainly real," I told Freddy. "They were naked and that sucking was unmistakable. And I've no doubt that red cock is still up the master."

"You may be right," said Freddy, issuing a great sigh, hand down between his legs. "I may need some relief."

"You and everyone else."

"Gentlemen," came the call and we turned to the stage once again. There stood Royce, absent the red cock and thus returned to formality. "Lord Whitfield thanks you for indulging him in his play. Supper will be served in the dining room at eight. We do not dress for dinner so please remain in your daywear. You are now free to enjoy the house and grounds."

"Enjoy we shall," declared Freddy, all but sprinting to the wine at the back table. Everyone took a glass or two, attempting to quell the heat brought on by the performance. Oddly, there remained little mingling among the group. We were all paired and once the wine bottles were empty, everyone hurriedly departed the tent. "Well, we know what they're up to," said Freddy, watching them go. He raised an eyebrow at me. "How about we go upstairs?"

"I prefer out of doors," I replied, emboldened by the wine.

"You naughty boy! Of course. What a grand idea."

We finished our wine and went out onto garden paths. "Look," said Freddy as we saw two couples running toward the trees. "Let's watch. I'm sure we'll see a bare bottom or two."

We walked slowly along a path and, just as predicted, bare flesh was observed among the trees. We kept on in that direction, enjoying the view while getting further worked up. It felt like a log in my trousers, such was my arousal. Finally Freddy pulled me to one side. "Forget the trees. This is better."

A tall flowering shrub was circled by a chest high hedge. Freddy peered over. "In there," he said, pushing through. When I hesitated, out came an arm to pull me in, at which I saw the appeal. A straw mulch covered the ground and as I sank onto it, Freddy removed pants and linen, ending up on his knees, stiff cock in hand. "The real thing," he said. "I'm ready to blow."

When I was slow to disrobe amid Lord Whitfield's garden, Freddy reminded me of the play's content. "Surely a man who writes such things cannot be prudish. He's bound to know it's fucking madness out here and I wouldn't be surprised if he isn't standing at some window, spyglass in one hand, cock in the other."

My prick throbbed in agreement. I stripped my lower half, and Freddy fell to sucking me. I came almost instantly, primed as I was. When I drew back, Freddy said, "All fours. I need a fuck." I was then mounted, though only briefly before Freddy gasped and issued into me. When he finished and withdrew, we fell onto our backs and gazed up at the clear blue sky.

"What a party," I managed.

"What a fuck," he replied, squeezing my hand.

"My pleasure."

"Indeed."

We drowsed, the sun slipping past, awaking some indeterminate time later.

I told Freddy I thought the onstage sex was real. "It's a play, Tom," he replied. "All acting."

"Hellish good, but I do believe Lance was penetrated in the first act."

"No. It was grand simulation, the dildo up between the buttocks. He'd have required lubrication to go in and I saw none."

"Ah, I hadn't considered that."

I rolled toward my friend and propped my head up. "I want to thank you for inviting me along," I said. "It's a most remarkable day. And I must confess, dear boy, that I'd never seen a dildo before."

Freddy laughed. "I had no idea you were so sheltered. They are much in use."

"I can't imagine having one up me."

"You do know they've been in use for ages?"

"No, I don't believe it," I said.

"Good God, Tom, you are indeed sheltered. Shakespeare even wrote about them in one of his plays, *The Winter's Tale* I believe. They've been made of wood or even stone, so these India rubber things represent great progress. When we get back to London I'll get one and we can play around with it."

"Where on earth would you get such a thing?"

"The Strand, of course. It's not only French postcards sold in those shops."

I gave Freddy's prick a friendly tug. "The things you get me up to," I said.

We passed a quiet interval, then Freddy spoke. "What I especially liked," he said, "was old Royce getting in on it. Did you note how that red prick was shiny wet? Now that was reality. He did fuck Reg, not a doubt. One has to wonder how a servant feels when made to engage in such acts.'

"Perhaps, based on what Lord Whitfield writes, things on the estate run toward permissive."

"More like debauched," countered Freddy. "Imagine what Royce has seen."

"And done."

Freddy and I played around a bit more before dressing and easing back through the hedge. We emerged to find the other couple we had observed earlier also making their sheepish return from the undergrowth. Freddy drew a long breath. "Spunk is in the air," he said. "Glorious perfume."

We retreated to our room for a wash and a rest and at eight descended to the dining room. Others were already seated at a long table sporting silver candelabras, heaps of flowers, and stunning silver service. Royce supervised the staff, all of whom were male except for a rather flighty girl in skimpy black and white dress uniform. "French," said Freddy as she poured wine for each man. She danced along, sweet thing that she was, and I noted slim legs, tiny waist, and big bosom. As she poured, she managed to rub against each and every shoulder, giggling like some innocent, though she was clearly no such thing.

There was little talk among the group at large. Pairs conversed with each other, but this stopped when the first course was served. Back came the French girl who managed to make rather a production of getting the fish onto the plates. The same theatricalities occurred with each course, though the male servants remained subdued and watchful. It was only as we devoured a wonderful pudding that Freddy nodded at the French girl and said, "You do know who that is?"

"Who?"

"Lord Whitfield. He loves to dress up."

"I don't believe it," I said. The girl seemed most feminine.

"Oh, Tom, enlighten yourself. He was Pamela in the play."

"Well, I certainly don't believe that," I protested. "He was the husband."

"No, that was Adrian Harding."

I took more wine as I attempted to digest these revelations.

"It's why Lord Whitfield hasn't joined us," Freddy continued. "He prefers to appear in costume."

"As a woman."

"Yes."

"Good Lord."

Supper went until ten, after which we were free to amuse ourselves. "Upstairs," Freddy said and I didn't argue. I was quite loosened from the wine and the revelations.

The moment our chamber door closed, Freddy stripped naked and demanded I do the same. "I'm not up for anything," I told him, reeling from too much wine.

"Not to worry," he replied.

Curious, I thought, but this faded quickly. I crawled beneath the covers and was immediately claimed by sleep.

When I woke later there appeared to be a horse in the room.

Bleary eyed, I managed to see Freddy awake and sitting up. "What steed have we here?" he asked the horse, which on further inspection I now perceived to be a man in high boots, long black cape, and sporting a gold colored papier machier horse head.

"Your stallion calls," announced the horse. It approached the bed. I sat up and shook my head to make certain I was fully in possession of my faculties. "What in hell?" I said, but Freddy shushed me.

As the horse drew near he parted his cape where emerged a prick of great proportion. A true horse cock, if you will. I sat stunned at the sight, but Freddy sprang from bed and bent to offer his bottom to the steed.

The horse issued a neigh that was quite convincing, then proceeded to mount my friend. It was the only time I'd heard Freddy cry out in pain, what with having an accommodating bottom hole, at least to man-sized pricks.

The horse was most vigorous; Freddy broke into a sweat and grimaced throughout. I remained wide eyed, fully awake now and taken with this new play. Then the horse withdrew from Freddy who gasped and crawled onto the bed. "Now you," he managed and when I looked at the horse, the big golden head nodded.

I had less experience than Freddy, but caution gave way to the promise of such a member which, dripping as it was, confirmed it quite real. No more India rubber cocks. I slid off the bed, took the position, and felt the prick tear into me.

I cried out in pain as I was ravaged, but within this was arousal such as I'd never known. My prick sprang to life and I began to stroke it as the horse cock went where no other had. When I issued my spend seconds later I announced it. "Horse, you are driving the spunk from me!" The horse neighed approval.

His thrusting began to gain speed. Tears sprang to my eyes, but I did not protest. Then he drove in mightily and I got his spend, thinking it might well be a real horse fucking me. When he finally withdrew, I turned around. wanting to see the magnificent rod and there it was, dirtied now, a string of spunk hanging from the tip. A hand crept from the cape and took hold, stroking as if to calm the thing.

"Thank you, Sir Stallion," Freddy said. "You are a wonder."

The horse snorted, turned, and swept from the room.

His issue slid from me. "If my passage wasn't so ravaged," I said, "I'd declare disbelief."

"We may not sit for a day," Freddy replied.

"Or two."

LATER, AS WE lay in bed, I asked Freddy if that was Lord Whitfield.

"Undoubtedly," he said.

"Did you know about all this beforehand?" I asked.

"All I knew was he likes to dress up."

"And?"

Freddy laughed. "And do things. The horse, however, was a complete surprise."

I took this in, chuckling, then said, "I do wish I could see the real Lord Whitfield."

"My dear friend, you just did."

THE BLACKSMITH'S SON

Katie Lewis

I AM RUNNING out of paper, light, and lead as the final bar in my pencil wears down. I draw until the spring inside the silver case fully extends and the pencil's metal tip scrapes the page.

With the last of my lamp oil burning out, I step back and study my design.

The blueprint is sound. Gears and weights all in their proper place would make an automaton that would wind with an elegant handle and play a set of chimes.

Unfortunately, nothing will come of it. I have barely enough money to buy lead for my pencil, and I will either have to sell more scrap to purchase lamp oil or learn to sleep when it gets dark.

This design, like all my others, is nothing more than a fantasy. I rub my eyes.

Perhaps it's time to join the steam engine trade. Much as I loathe the idea, there is simply no demand for the things I'd like to build. I cannot keep starving myself and chasing dreams while avoiding sleep.

A loud knock pulls my focus. The front door opens wide, and I squint.

It seems I've worked through the night again. Blast. Opening the windows would have saved oil.

I stand to greet the man in my doorway. He's dressed in fine clothes: top hat, woolen coat, silk ascot, and shoes unmarred by the muck of the streets. A nobleman, perhaps.

"Good morning, sir," I say. "How may I help you?"

His voice is high. "Do I have the pleasure of addressing Mister Rory Sullivan, clockmaker?"

I've never sounded so important. "I am Rory," I answer.

"I have a letter for you, sir. Moreover, a business opportunity." The man hands me a folded piece of parchment sealed with wax. I break the seal and unfold the paper. Script so elegant is a struggle to read. Perhaps the page is upside down.

"Shall I save you the trouble, sir?" asks my guest.

"If you can, please."

The man removes his hat. "Your skills have been noted with appreciation by my employer. Let us call this individual, 'Vee.' Vee wishes to offer you a job in London and hopes that you will come presently."

With a scan of the letter, I pick out enough words to surmise that what he says is true to the note.

"But my things are here," I say, though I've not much attachment to them. My master was a bitter man and only left the shop and tools to me because he had no one else. "What would I need to do in London?"

"Vee wishes that you work with two accomplished metalsmiths in their forge to help design a new kind of armor."

Manners dictate some response, but I struggle to comprehend. Perhaps sleep would have helped.

"You will be handsomely paid," says the man.

I sit on the wooden stool beside my lathe.

"I'm not concerned about payment," I say. "I don't understand how I would help build armor. Surely there are better candidates than a twenty-year-old clockmaker from Kent."

"Ah," says the man. He folds his hands behind his back. "My employer is aware of your skills and circumstances. The combination of your youth, imaginative designs, and lack of family makes you a most excellent choice for this project."

His frankness is startling. My aloneness has not gone unnoticed. That is oddly comforting.

He bows his head and says, "Apologies. There is, as you may have surmised by the fact I haven't given you my name, a rather clandestine nature to this project. A family man may not wish to be involved."

I tilt my head.

He adds, "There is nothing unlawful in the business, to be sure, but secrecy is essential."

Curiosity brings me nearer to my guest. "How long would I be in London?"

"Until the project's completion," he answers. "Three months, perhaps, if you and the Wyndham's perform as well as my employer expects. However, you would be welcome to stay as long as you wished. There will likely be continued demand for your skills."

I glance around the room, see the tools of my trade and my most recent designs. There are a few clocks here and there that need repair, but I've created nothing new in months. I miss building.

"What would happen to my shop?" I ask.

"That much is up to you. Presumably, it would be here when you returned. If you wanted to return."

I look down. A box of spare gears and winding keys lays untouched and forlorn in the shadow of my guest. The pieces will rust and decay without use. No one here needs them.

"What is the purpose of this armor?"

The man answers eagerly, as if he's been awaiting my question. "It is a suit for a single man. One that will be lightweight and durable. One that will aid his senses and strength to make him more than human."

I laugh, skeptical. "Metal can protect, certainly. But no element on earth can do what you have described. My clockwork won't help."

The man backs into the beam of sunlight, smiles, and opens his coat.

A brilliant copper breastplate unlike any I've seen before shines like fire. Gears in the center connect to black metallic rods that follow the shape of muscle down to his waist and disappear beneath his trousers. He backs up another step and bends at the knee. My eyes widen as he jumps in the air so high that I no longer see him through the doorway. He lands crouched like an animal in a cloud of white steam.

He says, "With respect, sir, you are mistaken."

My eager eyes absorb every visible detail of his armor. I suspect I understand bits of it already, enough to know that the make is ingenious. Truly innovative.

I could improve it.

"Give us a few hours," I say. "I'll be ready."

It's impossible to tell day from night in the Wyndham's shop. Darkness, however dreary, is a necessary element to smithing. Windows remain closed to help gauge the fire's temperature from orange to yellow to white and all stages in-between.

Judging by how dry and tired my eyes feel, it must be morning.

The glass lenses I wear allow me to see delicate bolts and tiny fasteners. My world is simultaneously narrowed and expanded to dainty copper gears and fine, iron tools. I have nearly finished.

My lamp burns out and leaves the workstation too dark.

I shove away from the desk. "Blast it all!" My tools clatter to the ground where I throw them.

A warm laugh startles me. I rip the lenses from my face and turn to see Asher Wyndham by the forge in the center of the room.

"Good morning, Rory," he says, his elbow propped on the bellows. "Have you slept, yet?"

I smooth my hair. "Morning, Asher," I reply. "I did mean to, but—"

"Time got away from you," he says and reaches for his leather apron.

It hangs from the wall his father beat him against yesterday. My stomach clenches as I banish several violent images from my mind.

"And I will keep insisting that you call me Ash until you do," he says with a grin. "Even if it takes another two months."

I look down at the earthen floor. "Sorry. Ash."

"Do you need rest?" he asks.

"No," I reply.

"Perhaps a break from your clockwork, then," he offers. "Will you strike for me a while? My father's still asleep, and you are getting rather good at it."

My face warms. I pretend it's from the rising heat of the fire that Asher tends with the bellows, discard my work, and reach for a hammer. Asher approaches.

"Apron," he says and hands me the one from his hands. "Safety."

I am standing too close to him. My mouth goes dry.

Weary shadows underline Asher's hazel eyes. A bruise surrounds one. Mr. Wyndham beat him hard yesterday, and Asher sleeps outside on the cobblestones, even though there's enough room in the shop for another mattress apart from mine.

I slip the neck of the apron over my head and ask, "Does it hurt much? Your eye?"

Asher laughs and answers, "Oh, it feels jolly. I love a good half-mourning."

I say, "Better than a whole-mourning."

"That is true," Asher replies. "One good eye is better than none."

He returns the twenty-pound hammer to me one-handed, yawns and stretches. His fingers touch the blackened beams that run along the ceiling. His untucked shirt raises, and I glimpse a thin line of dark hair in the center of his abdominal muscles.

I shift my gaze to the fire. Asher's arms fall to his sides.

"Come on, then," he says with a step toward the forge.

Since moving to London and working here, my body has grown accustomed to heavy exertion. Muscles swell in my arms and chest where previously there was no definition. Asher holds a piece of red-hot metal in a pair of tongs and taps to indicate where I should strike. I raise the hammer over my head.

We toil for hours without the need of words. Firelight and soot color Asher and I the same, but beneath the grime and glow, his skin is tan while mine is pale. His dark hair reflects the color of the flames, but my white-blonde locks absorb it. We are the same age, the same gender, and working on the same project; there's not much that links us, otherwise. Yet, there is an unspoken, indefinable connection. I'm tortured by its existence. I doubt Asher even feels it.

He appraises our work, and I find myself staring once again at the base of his throat. Sweat drips down in streaks of salt and pools in that enticing hollow. Each artful strike from his hammer molds red-hot steel and flexes the pillar of muscle in his neck. It's very distracting. The thought of it keeps me awake nights.

"Agh, Christ!" he shouts with sudden vehemence as he flings his tongs aside and abandons hot iron on the anvil. He turns and buries his head in the cooling tank beside the forge. His knees hit the earthen floor. I would like to put a hand on his shoulder, but will take care of the iron, instead—-what looks like a component of the lower leg piece—-and return it to the coals.

Asher flings his head back to take a breath. Wet hair sends water droplets flying. They steam as they land on any surface hot enough. A few touch and cool my face.

"Are you all right?" I ask.

He sits back on his heels, chin low. "I'm fine." His arm rests on the edge of the tub.

"Is it your eye?"

His fingers flex and bend. "It bloody hurts," he replies with his jaw clenched. "This heat makes it damned near intolerable."

The swelling has grown considerably since this morning.

He grunts. "I've half a mind to bleed the bruise."

The thought is sickening. "You'll scar yourself if you do."

Asher wipes water from his face with his open palm. "It matters not to me."

"It will matter to someone someday." I turn my back under the guise of adjusting the iron. "A woman, I mean."

Asher scoffs. The sound is sad. "If she cannot stand a little scar on my face, she'll not enjoy the rest of me." His gaze fixes on the bricks of the forge.

My words fly off without permission.

"Why do you let him hurt you?"

The look he gives makes me want to hide. Then it softens, and I melt at his openness.

"My father is a boxer," he explains, "though he doesn't compete much anymore. He taught me to fight, but mostly he wants me to know how to take a hit."

I fold my arms over my chest. "Why, though?"

Asher smiles. The expression is not entirely bitter, but neither is it happy.

"It's like how metal is forged," he says. "The hotter the heat, the more pressure applied, the stronger the finished product."

My fingers clench. "But you're not a piece of metal."

He laughs bitterly.

I decide not to say anything else and extend my hand. He lets me help him to his feet.

His slight height advantage makes my stomach flutter. My gaze drifts to his mouth, his full lips, and the air seems to thicken.

Asher's eyes meet mine.

The door opens, and I step back. Asher's father enters the shop.

Cole Wyndham is a tall man with forearms like wooden beams. He can toss a hammer as if it were paper and hold his hand above a flame without suffering blisters from the heat. When it comes to disciplining his son, he seems not to withhold one ounce of his considerable strength, but he has never said a harsh word or raised his hand to me.

It's still difficult to like the man.

He makes the day's first prowl around the room and stops at my table.

"This looks excellent, Mr. Sullivan," he says while holding the mechanism in his large, calloused hands. "And this goes along the right forearm?"

"Yes, sir. It will allow the wearer to switch the inside lines from water to fuel depending on his needs: steam or fire."

"I have approved the blueprints, lad," he says. "I do know what it does." He studies the copper gears up close, then sets the whole piece down on the table. "Though I will not pretend to know how it functions."

He turns to Asher. All of us tense.

"Let's see your progress, then," he says.

Asher backs up and waits. Mr. Wyndham inspects the newest additions to the armor at the worktable. It seems he's satisfied; then something catches his eye—the piece I placed in the fire. It's losing its shape. Was it not iron? Asher looks to me. Panic.

Mr. Wyndham grabs the loose cravat around his son's neck. I step forward. Asher chokes as Mr. Wyndham yanks him off his feet.

"Are you trying to undo our work, now?"

Asher gasps for breath.

My spine is straight as a fire poker.

"I'm sorry," I say. "That was me. I put it in the coals. I thought it was pure iron."

"You're a good lad," says Mr. Wyndham without looking at me, "but your kindness won't teach my son responsibility. He should keep a sharper eye on things."

Mr. Wyndham releases Asher with a shove and takes his place at the anvil. His next words are echoes of various speeches made over the past month.

"We must all remember that one day very soon, a man's life will be depending on this armor."

Asher retrieves the metal from the fire and passes the tongs to his father without meeting his eyes.

"We cannot for one moment forget the importance of our work," Mr. Wyndham continues as Asher hands him the leather apron from around his front. "The three of us are entrusted with his safety."

Whoever 'he' is. Whatever purpose the armor will serve. I've been given no answers and asked no questions. I'm building something exciting, machinery the world has never seen before, and am doing so in mostly good company.

Asher reaches for the sledgehammer and his apron. I pass both to him and make sure our fingers don't touch.

"Now let's get back to work," says Mr. Wyndham.

IT'S NIGHT. My shoulders are sore. Hands are blistered and dry. I'm outside in the cold, wet, London air, and Asher is with me. His hands reach out as I back against a brick wall. His body follows. The rough touch of his leathered hands on my skin as he reaches under my shirt makes me quake, but then he leans forward and brings his mouth to mine.

I wake with a start, in bed for once, though with scraps of paper, my mechanical pencil, and a lamp still burning on the table beside me. Outside, it's raining. Between my legs, my member is erect and dripping. I lay on my back, breathless. My hands are fists at my sides. I want nothing more than for the blasted, throbbing nuisance to disappear, or to touch it, myself; but I can't.

It's improper and unmanly to self-pleasure. I've heard the warnings a thousand times. If Asher weren't so damned ingrained in my thoughts, I would stop having these dreams. But he is. My God, he is.

I roll onto my belly, thinking to flatten the damned thing, but the feeling is intensely pleasurable. My hips arch back and roll forward into the mattress. A groan leaves my chest. This friction is hot. This rutting is mindless. Asher's face looms before my closed eyes. Pieces of him—ropy forearm muscles, the wide base of his neck, the curve of his square jaw, and his warm, hazel eyes—they torture me with their exquisite, forbidden beauty. My hips thrust faster, harder.

I want to explode. My consciousness sinks deep into the black pit of my mind as my body claims what it wants. I prop myself up on my elbows and toss my head back, panting in the humid air while my hips molest the mattress.

I should not do this. Should not do this. It's so shameful.

Air pulls into my lungs in gasps and leaves in quiet moans.

It feels so good. Oh, this exquisite sin will kill me. I free my member from my undergarments. It jumps into my hand, and I give it what it wants.

Let me go to hell. Let me be unmanly and uncontrolled. I'm broken anyway. When I think of women, my blood runs cold, but when I think of him...

Asher's name leaves my lips as my seed spills in my hand. I grit my teeth, eyes closed, and catch my breath. I'm dizzy. It feels like I could sleep for a day—like I've lost ten stone of weight in one moment. I clean my hand on a scrap of paper.

"Rory?"

Blood freezes in my veins. I turn to marble with terror and pray that I'm dreaming still. With a determined breath, I glance over my shoulder and see Asher propped against the wall with his legs splayed before him. His eyes are wide and fixed on me. My face floods with heat.

"Did...?" I clear my throat. "Did you see?"

"I'm sorry." His voice is strained.

I stagger to my feet.

His words are rushed. "It was raining, so I moved inside."

If vomiting wouldn't slow me down, I'd be very tempted to do so in the chamber pot. My hands tremble as I hurry into my trousers and gather the rest of my clothes and belongings into my arms.

"Rory," Asher repeats, more forceful. "Why did you say my name?"

I race past him out the door into the cold night and run. My body is hot from my depravity and the fire I worked beside all day. Perhaps I should have thrown myself into the forge and been burnt to a crisp. If Asher turns me in for my unnatural proclivity, surely I will be punished. My father told me not to pleasure myself, but the concept of me being attracted to men was so far from his mind, he never spoke of it. I've never discussed it with anyone. I've barely let myself believe that's what I want, but now it is impossible to deny. The blacksmith's son is in my thoughts. I'm ruined for life.

I do not know where I'll go from here, but I must flee to escape the shame. The thought of leaving a project undone kills me, but the armor is almost finished. They have my blueprints. I'm no longer needed. They could replace me with someone whole.

"Rory!" Asher shouts. Moonlight and the rain create a white frame around his body as he rushes my direction. Heart pounding, I hurry into a narrow passage and struggle to put my vest on over my shirt. Both items are drenched and sticky. I smack my elbow against a stone wall, and the pain snaps whatever tether to composure I'd managed to hold onto. I lean with my shoulders against the damp bricks, lift my face to the rain and let it hide my tears.

Asher appears at the mouth of the alley, panting. His dampened shirt sticks to his muscles, defining each crest and valley. Lascivious thoughts poison my brain and roil my body.

He approaches slowly. His chest swells with heavy breaths. If he wants to do me harm, I will welcome the punishment. Perhaps pain can heal my sickness.

"Why did you run from me?" he asks. His voice is deeper than usual.

I choke out, "You saw what I did." My hand hides my face, but nothing can shield my embarrassment. My voice breaks. "I'm so ashamed."

He stands before me, the wall of the other brick building at his back.

"Rory," he says with as much weight as a hammer. "Don't be. Contrary to what people may do in the country, not all Londoners are so strict as to condemn a person's nighttime activities." He leans forward and quiets his voice. "I've done the same before."

Breath enters my lungs, a cold, short one that gives me hope.

"But," he continues, and my blood runs cold. "You said my name."

I freeze. Wish I was part of the stone.

"Why did you say my name?" he asks.

I turn my head aside. My jaw clenches, followed by my hands. Pain twinges in my elbow.

"I... I don't know if I can explain." My throat closes—makes it hard to speak or breathe. "Your presence, or rather, you in general. Or rather you, specifically."

He focuses on me with so much attention, my thoughts jumble.

"That is, it makes me..." I bite my lip, lower my chin, and whisper. "You make me..." The pain of hiding my desperate longing to touch him becomes too vast to hold back. I cry and whimper, "Asher."

He steps close. "Ash. Please."

His eyes are kind. I'm so raw from exposure there is nothing left but honesty. I feel naked and hollow and embrace his inevitable judgement as if welcoming death.

"Ash," I say. "I want you."

He takes a breath. "I want you, too."

My gasp is stifled when his mouth meets mine. His body presses me against the bricks. Fingers slide across the skin of my stomach, and I shudder with shocked pleasure.

I dreamed this. But it's real.

"Rory," he says, eyes bright in the darkness, hair dripping wet and plastered to the sharp curves of his face. "I have been waiting my whole life to find someone else like me." His barely contained smile breaks with a nervous bite of his lip. He rests his forehead against mine. "I am so glad it's you."

I'm stunned. I haven't moved. My arms are stiff by my sides.

"What do you mean, 'like you'?" He's so far above me.

He smiles, white teeth glinting. He reaches for my hand and brings it to the front of his trousers. I marvel at what I touch.

"You do this to me," he says in a husk.

My eyes close to better feel him with my hand. This forbidden contact makes me shake. He reaches out and presses his palm flat against the swell between my legs.

He says, "I do this to you."

The heat from his hand is maddening. I groan. He rubs up and down, and my knees go weak.

He whispers in my ear. "It's special." Breath tickles my neck and causes chills.

I press into his insistent touch, even as I battle inside.

"Isn't it sinful?" I ask.

Asher flattens a hand against the wall beside my head. "If it is," he replies with an exhale. "Then forgive me."

Our eyes meet. His voice is thick and coarse with the ardency of his words.

"But first, let me sin."

I HAVEN'T BEEN right since then. I cannot focus, sleep or eat. And it's the first time in my life I have been truly happy. Asher has made me a whole person. No one can know what we are to each other, but that is a small burden compared to the one that has been lifted from my shoulders by knowing that I'm not alone, and I can have him, if only in secret.

When we're together, I gaze at him openly and catch him doing the same. We spend every possible moment at each other's sides and most nights exploring.

It wasn't clear what we should do at first, physically. My education about how a man and a woman come together in bed is barely adequate to make me functional in that arena—and Asher's is the same. But we are learning.

A month has passed, and my appetite for him grows each day. The marks on my body indicate that the same applies to him. The hidden echoes of his touch make me grin throughout the day.

Mr. Wyndham looks my direction. I force the smile from my face and furrow my brow in mock concentration.

The first draft of the armor is finished, and Asher is wearing it to test how it works. We've been told that his body type is similar enough to Vee's to mold the armor to his shape, and it looks damn good on him. The suit is a mix of copper, heat-treated iron, and bronze. My design is elegant, but Asher's body makes it stunning.

He beams from inside the armor, flexing his fingers to try out the fluidity of their mechanisms. His father stands with the blueprints and triple-checks every bolt and fastening while I stand with the master key that will wind the gears when we are ready to test the suit.

"Well, gentlemen," says Mr. Wyndham as he ceremoniously returns the blueprints to the table along the wall. He turns and looks at Asher. I have never seen a more genuine smile on his face. "Look at what we have accomplished."

Orange light from the forge glints in the armor and reflects back to us.

"This is history." Mr. Wyndham circles around Asher and claps a hand on his shoulder. "We have come a long way from our first prototype," he says and looks to me, "thanks entirely to the addition of your genius, Sullivan."

I startle from the compliment, but blush deeply from the way Asher is smiling at me like he couldn't be prouder. It seems indecent, his expression. His father is right here.

"And now I think it is time that everything comes to light. No more secrets." Mr. Wyndham drops his hand from Asher's shoulder and places himself so that if he were to reach out with each hand, he would be able to strike us both.

I share a nervous look with Asher.

Mr. Wyndham crosses his arms over his chest and lowers his chin. Uneasy anticipation settles over the room like a fog. Asher sweats in his armor.

Perhaps we've been too careless with our gazes. Is there a bruise on his neck from me?

"You must be curious about the identity of Vee."

The breath I let out is long and controlled. Asher meets my eyes with a reckless relief that borders on glee.

It takes discipline to tune back into Mr. Wyndham's words.

"You must want to know why we were given the task of creating a suit that could not only protect the wearer, but enhance his strength and be a weapon itself."

Mr. Wyndham stares at Asher with so much import that Asher turns from me, his smile completely erased from his face, to gaze at his father.

"The suit is for you," he says. "Vee is the queen's guard. You are the first of Her Majesty's Clockwork Sentinels."

The fog of anticipation turns into a lightning storm of confusion. Asher gapes open-mouthed at his father and steps backward.

"What?" he asks.

Mr. Wyndham advances toward his son.

"The streets of London have grown increasingly dangerous," he says. "Her Majesty's wish is that armed guards such as yourself, unofficially affiliated with the crown, will take care of the worst sort of criminals in a way that will immediately nullify them as threats."

Asher's eyes bulge. He shouts, "The queen wants me to kill people?" Bits of armor hit the floor as he peels them loose and continues backing toward the door.

"Asher," says Mr. Wyndham in warning. "This is a great honor. You've no idea how long I have been working toward this for you."

Asher's movements become erratic. His hands shake. He's stuck in his shoulder armor, and his father is gaining ground on him.

"Wait, Mr. Wyndham," I call.

It's as if Asher hears and sees nothing. He breathes heavily. His hands work fast if not with accuracy. Mr. Wyndham stalls.

"Give him a minute," I say in what I hope sounds like a respectful tone. Asher races out the door. Mr. Wyndham steps toward it, and I place myself in the way.

"I will speak to him," I say.

After a moment, Mr. Wyndham nods and backs down. "The boy does seem to like you," he concedes. My stomach flutters. "Very well. But you understand the significance of this, do you not? The honor? The responsibility. London needs men who can keep her people safe. Asher can be that for her."

"I understand," I reply. "I will speak to him."

I DISCOVER ASHER in the alley where we first revealed our souls to each other. He's crouched against the wall on his haunches. When I step between the buildings and he looks up at me, his eyes still wide and his hands still shaking, my heart breaks.

"This does not feel real," he says.

I hurry to him and crouch down so our knees touch. He stares at his palms.

"My father cannot be serious. He made the whole thing up, surely. Another trial. Some new way to hurt me."

"I think not," I say. "Where would he have gotten the money for parts and my salary? He must have had a wealthy patron."

Asher grabs my hands and hisses, "But the queen?"

I grip his fingers and try to keep him steady.

His voice is strained. "Lucifer's muff, man. I have never even seen the blessed woman. I have never even been in a fight or witnessed a crime. I cannot kill anyone. My father is barking!"

I lean forward and kiss him. He tenses, then softens, wraps his hand around my neck, and pulls me close. When I lean in, he surrenders his head against the brick wall and allows me to tilt his jaw, as if grateful for being overpowered. I pull back.

"I have no idea what your father was thinking," I say and bring my hand to the side of his face. "But I do know that if I needed protecting, I would trust my life to you. It seems incredible, what your father says, but also... I believe him."

Asher's eyes look vibrant as they search mine.

"If the queen's guard needs London-dwelling, undercover crime-combatants in metal suits, you really are a natural choice."

He laughs. The sound and expression jolt my heart. I want to kiss him again, but instead, focus on what's most important at this moment.

"But it is your life."

Asher takes in my words and stares at my collar bone.

"If you don't want any part of what your father suggests," I say. "I will leave with you right now. We can disappear together."

He grips my arm tightly.

I press my forehead against his. "I'll teach you how to build clocks, and we will move to a place where they don't know what time is yet and become rich."

The sound of his laugh is weaker now. I add, despite my selfish desires to have him to myself, safe and happy, "But if you wish to stay..."

He meets my eyes.

"I have the utmost faith in you, in your judgment and strength. So does your father." I lower my voice. "And I know your heart. I know why you are scared."

He purses his lips, the same ones that stain my body red and black with passion. The hollow in my chest reserved for him and only him grows larger in necessity. Should he wish to stay and walk this dangerous path, he will need a partner, and I will need to be strong.

"You can protect people without taking anyone's life."

Asher stares at the ground. Several moments pass. With a deep breath, his body stops shaking. His lips press gently against mine, then part when he speaks.

"We did build a hell of a contraption."

I chuckle. "We did."

"It would be a shame to waste." Asher's eyes burn bright with mounting excitement.

"It would," I say, drop my chin, and swallow my fear. "If you break her, we will have words."

He wraps an arm around my shoulder and pulls me close. "Will we?" he asks. His tone sends a chill of excitement through my bones. "I think I would like to hear that, Mr. Sullivan."

I nip at his neck and lick the hollow that torments me so. "Try me, Ash."

His fingers thread through my hair. "With pleasure."

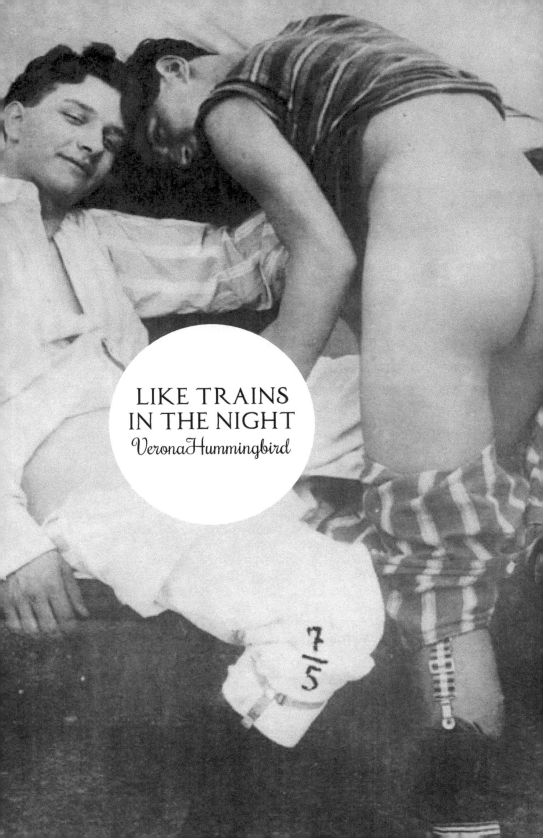

LIKE TRAINS
IN THE NIGHT

Verona Hummingbird

A SENSUAL HAZE settled over the train yard, gliding around the boxcars situated on the newly constructed tracks. Max strolled between the snake-like locomotives, admiring their angles and bolts and sheer sturdiness.

Working the graveyard shift wasn't so bad. Max often went nights at a time without seeing anyone, and when he did see someone he got to tackle them to ground and hand them over to the constabulary, which was exciting at least. Better than his last job at the icehouse.

He especially liked the scents of the yard. The smell of metal on metal, of oiled joints and friction-heated iron. Though the area was quiet while he was on shift, it still retained echoes of the day's activity. The steam engines groaned occasionally as they settled. Deep sounds, earthy, like the sighs of something primal.

Late one summer night, while Max was inspecting a loose track spike, he heard one such groan emanating from the back of the yard. This particular noise wasn't quite what he was used to, and an eerie shiver worked its way down his spine. This sounded more like an animal, more like...

Another moan echoed between the cars, this time unmistakably human. Max moved toward it, holding his lantern high and doing his best to keep his boots from grinding too heavily on the gravel. Stealth was not Max's primary virtue. But that was fine. The company didn't employ him because he was stealthy. They employed him because he was big—because he could wrap his huge, dark hands around another man's waist and haul him bodily away. Because he could throttle would-be bandits into submission. Because he could be counted on to slide his bulky frame between a gaggle of robbers and their prize.

Max kept the goods on the pallets. He was proud of that.

The groaning turned into grunting the closer he came to the sound. Someone was certainly putting their back into it—whatever *it* was.

The trains wound through the yard, forming long corridors between them. The grunts lead him to a car far afield of the office and guard house. Light eked out from beneath the train, casting shadows into Max's path, revealing at least two men.

He turned down the gas on his lamp—he'd never get the jump on whoever it was if they caught his shadow just as he'd caught theirs.

For a moment, though, he was confused. This train was empty, ready to be loaded at first light. There was nothing to steal, and yet—if the grunting and the shadows were anything to go by— the two men were doing some very heavy lifting.

The deep, hungry growls were occasionally punctuated by high, breathless keening. And now that he was close, Max could smell bitter cologne, and detect a muffled smacking of lips.

It took him a moment to ease out of the guard-dog mindset enough to fully comprehend what was happening on the other side of the tracks.

"Richard," a man gasped, his voice rough and needy. The one-word entreaty carried so much desperation, Max faltered. His heart skipped a beat, and heat filled his cheeks and coiled between his legs. His cock gave an interested twitch in his trousers as his imagination provided him with images to go with the noises. In his mind, two fully-naked young men grasped at one another, struggling for dominance, rutting blindly against each other's hips, cocks thick and leaking.

"Richard," the man whined again.

"Shh, shh. Quiet, love."

"*Don't*," the first man demanded. "Don't say such things to me—as though I'm some delicate waif who needs declarations of your devotion. Don't talk to me like I'm Claudia."

"I don't call her *love*. Could never—"

"Shut up—"

There was a breathless pause. They must have been kissing.

"I can't be your chaperone anymore," the first man said after a moment. "I can't watch you court her."

"Oscar, I'm yours at night."

"I don't care."

The grunting picked up again. Max palmed himself through his trousers, fully hard now. His pulse pounded in his ears and his cock, and he could feel sweat prickling across the back of his neck, despite the slight chill of the night.

He knew he should leave. It was the polite thing to do. Men like them, men like *Max*, had enough troubles in the world.

But, perhaps that was why he shouldn't leave. If one of the other night guards discovered the couple, things could go badly for them. They would be arrested—or worse.

Maybe I should warn them, he thought. *Tell them to take it someplace else, spare them public humiliation at the price of a private embarrassment.*

Leaving his lantern behind, he rounded the front of the train, stepping deftly over the tracks to come within line-of-sight of the two men.

They were still fully clothed, which surprised him. Gentlemen's clothes, no less; both wore double-breasted waistcoats and ascot ties. One man had the other backed up against the train car, boxing him in with his arms and his hips. They were both lithe and tall, but much smaller than Max. The lamp they had with them sat near their feet, casting strange shadows over their handsome faces.

They didn't notice Max, and he let them be for a while longer, entranced by the way they touched one another. Richard, he learned, was the one crowding Oscar against the car. His hair was longer, tied back at the base of his neck with a ribbon. He rutted into Oscar's belly while he kissed up and down his neck.

Oscar didn't know what to do with his hands—they alternated from clutching at Richard's hips to clawing at the car behind him. It was as if he didn't feel he had the right to touch Richard, like he was holding back. Whether it was because Richard was courting the absent Claudia or because Oscar had not yet come to terms with his desire for another man, it was hard to say.

As Richard kissed the edge of his jaw, Oscar gasped, drawing Max's attention to his mouth. It was such a pretty mouth, with a plum bottom lip that bowed just right and begged to be bitten—begged to have a cock sliding over it.

Max widened his stance, shifting uncomfortably as his erection throbbed. He imagined Oscar on his knees, taking Richard's cock between his lips. Or, maybe, taking Max's...

I should stop them, Max thought pragmatically. *Should let them keep a bit of dignity.*

But then Richard's hand slid down Oscar's chest, creeping lower and lower, until he cupped the bulge in his trousers. "You want me," he said against Oscar's lips, eyes hooded.

"Always," Oscar admitted breathlessly. "But we should stop. We have to stop."

"If you wanted to stop, why did you come out with me this evening?"

Oscar's eyebrows sloped upwards in an expression of injury. Richard already knew the answer to his inquiry, and was asking simply to be cruel.

With the way the two of them played off one another, it was easy for Max to imagine they'd known each other intimately for some time. Since childhood, perhaps. The heartbreaking devotion on Oscar's face told a story; he'd never been able to deny Richard anything, least of all himself.

Richard dove forward, claiming Oscar's mouth, desperately kissing the pain away—pain he'd caused. Their grinding grew more frantic, more needy.

With a feral growl, Richard yanked Oscar's shirt free of his trousers and worked at the buttons trapping his cock. They continued to kiss, but Oscar's expression became more and more panicked. "Wait. Wait, please."

"I don't want to," Richard said. "We've always been denied—always been told to wait, not to touch. I need to touch you."

Oscar pushed Richard away. "We have to stop."

"Why?"

"Claudia."

"Forget about her." He took hold of Oscar's jaw, gaze fixed on his mouth. He kissed him again, pushing his tongue between his lips.

After taking it for a moment, getting lost in feel of Richard's tongue sliding against his, Oscar grudgingly turned his head, breaking away. "She's my sister, I can't."

"You'd rather I marry someone else? Some other woman from some family we don't know? Have no cause to see you so often? No reasonable excuse to stay at your home, in your rooms?"

Oscar rolled away, out of the box of Richard's arms. "Maybe that would be best."

With more force than was necessary, Richard grabbed hold of Oscar and pinned him to the car. "I don't want that," he said darkly. He moved his hips forward, crowding Oscar, trapping him. He ducked his chin into the crook of Oscar's neck, mouthing at the tendons at the top of his shoulder though the fabric of his shirt.

Closing his eyes, Oscar gulped. He was warring with himself, wanting to get lost in Richard's heat, in his skin, but knowing it would only make things more difficult. "Stop. I don't want to go on if I can't have you."

"You'll always have me."

"Don't pretend to misunderstand. You know what I mean."

Richard refused to back away, holding onto Oscar's biceps with a white-knuckled grip. He pressed his groin against Oscar's, and they both gasped. "I need you..." Richard insisted. "I need to be inside you..."

Oscar sucked in a sharp breath. "*Richard,*" he warned, pushing at his friend's chest. "Don't do this to me."

Over the last few minutes, Max had become inexplicably protective of Oscar. Perhaps it was because he reminded Max of a boy he knew in his youth—Edward. So trusting, so loving, and things had gone so wrong for him.

Now, as he watched Oscar struggle, halfheartedly fighting, Max's instincts took over. He didn't want to see Richard *take* what already belonged to him. He didn't want Oscar to have to suffer through a betrayal like that. Richard wouldn't *force* him, no, it wouldn't be like that, but it would hurt Oscar none the less. It would break his heart.

Max stepped forward, out of the dark, insides reeling at the indecency—knowing he had no right to approach such fine gentlemen unintroduced. "He already told you to stop."

Both men startled, breaking away from one another, putting a gaping distance between themselves. Richard twisted, as if to bolt off into the night, but to his credit he stayed. He wouldn't abandon Oscar.

Now that they were both looking at him, Max could fully appreciate the pair's attractiveness. Richard was clean shaven, with big brown eyes and a commanding stance. Oscar sported a bit of scruff, and—with his shirttails dangling free, wide pupils crowding out his green irises, and pouty lip flushed from kissing—was much more disheveled.

"It's alright," Max said soothingly, holding out his hands. "I'm not going to report you. I'm—I'm like you." He kicked himself as soon as he said it. Just because they shared an attraction didn't mean they'd share anything else. It didn't mean they wouldn't report *him.*

Max eased his way toward Oscar, who was still plastered to the train car. "Are *you* alright?" he asked pointedly.

"Yes, thank you," he said sadly, trying to maintain his dignity. Realizing he was in an indecent state of undress in front of a man he didn't know, Oscar tried to tuck his shirt back in.

"Leave us be," Richard demanded. "I don't know what you think you heard, but there was no impropriety—"

"Oh yes," Max said scathingly, "I'm quite sure the two of you got lost on your way to some fine dinner party. But it *is* my job to keep the tracks clear at night."

Richard crossed his arms, but said nothing else.

Oscar shuffled uncomfortably, looking around for his jacket. Max spotted it tucked against the tracks and picked it up for him, dusting off the fine velvet before bringing it over. He held it tentatively for Oscar to take. "I'm sorry," Max said, keeping his voice low. These words weren't for Richard. "About the two of you, I mean. It happened to me, too—losing someone to another. I know how it feels."

Oscar's gaze narrowed as though he was unraveling the confession, deciding what to do with it. Their fingers brushed as Oscar took his coat. Max expected him to take the jacket, pull himself together, and run off. Instead, Oscar's hand lingered. He let his fingers slip beneath Max's thumb, tracing the underside with his knuckles.

Max recognized it for the invitation it was. Mild, subtle, but so sexual his flagging erection immediately swelled. Max also recognized the *intent*. Here was a man so in love with someone he couldn't have, he was willing to do something radical in an attempt to keep him—to claim him permanently.

If Richard didn't understand why seeing him with Claudia hurt Oscar so much, Oscar would make him see. He would show him what it was like to watch your lover with another.

Do I want to be that for him? A tool? Max asked himself. His heart went out to Oscar, but did that mean he was alright with being used?

Oscar licked his lips, biting the bottom one for good measure. Those lips— which looked so soft, so plush. Those lips that *begged* for something against them, something between them. Those lips that Max had wanted to taste from the moment he'd noticed them.

In addition to his teasing mouth, Oscar's eyes pleaded for Max's consent: *take me, kiss me, have me. Show him what it's like.*

A tremble ran through Max, caused by a heady mix of anticipation and fear. A lot of time had passed since Edward.

Would I have done this the night Edward left, if the opportunity had presented itself? Would I have tried this? Would it have made a difference?

His heart fluttered at the thought. In truth, he'd tried everything at his disposal to convince Edward to stay. He'd exhausted all options available to him, and would have exhausted a hundred more if fate had sent them his way.

So, yes. He would have.

With a gruff grunt, Max nodded, and Oscar visibly relaxed—glad his plan had been well received—before tensing again as Max tossed the jacket aside and advanced.

Clearly, Oscar *wanted* Max to take control, even if letting a stranger make such decisions prickled his nerves. He waited pliantly for Max to make a move—

to do more than invade his personal space—perhaps expecting him to encircle his wrists with his big hands, to maneuver him. *Manhandle* him. Max could, easily. He could pin Oscar's arms above his head, shove his face into the side of the car, and yank down his trousers. He could have a finger inside Oscar, stretching him, before Richard understood what was happening. But he wouldn't dare be so bold.

He wanted *Oscar* to govern the encounter, to make all of the decisions. This was Oscar's game; Max was simply a willing pawn.

Oscar licked his lips once more, before leaning in and tilting his head up. Grabbing Max's suspenders, he guided him forward. "Kiss me."

Richard's crossed arms fell limply to his side as he tried to comprehend what Oscar was doing. He took a breath, opening his mouth to speak, but before he could formulate any words, Max was already obeying.

He took Oscar's face in his hands, treating this as the gift it was. The other man's stubble was coarse against his palms and would be coarse against his face, but he didn't care. Gently, he moved his mouth over Oscar's in a tentative, open mouth kiss. But Oscar didn't want gentle. He shoved his tongue into Max's mouth, demanding roughness and desperation. The man tasted like high-society; lemon scones and fine tea and a touch of cigar smoke. Max knew he tasted like the tracks; metallic, dusty, perhaps with a bit of woodiness. The two flavors complimented one another, inflaming Max's arousal.

His cock throbbed deliciously.

Richard shook himself out of his initial stupor and rushed at them, pulling Oscar away. "*Stop.* What are you doing? You deny me, but will have a stranger?"

"You deny me, but will have my sister?" Oscar shot back.

"It's not the same."

"Isn't it?" He pulled himself out of Richard's grasp and returned to Max. "What do you want?" he asked Max, glancing side-long at his friend. "I'll give you anything."

"You're insane," Richard barked. For a moment, Max thought he would leave and the game would be over. Oscar wouldn't continue if he didn't have Richard as an audience, he was sure. But something made Richard stay. Curiosity, denial—didn't matter.

Both men waited for Max's answer.

What do I want?

Max reached up to touch Oscar's face again, pressing the pad of his thumb against that sinful bottom lip. "I want you on your knees," he said, slipping his thumb forward, watching it disappear into Oscar's mouth.

Oscar hummed his approval, closing his eyes for a moment to savor Max's digit. He sucked hard, hollowing his cheeks.

"Don't you dare," Richard said.

Oscar's eyes flew open, and his expression turned stony. In an instant he slipped to the gravel and began working Max's trousers open.

Max caught his hands. "Are you sure?"

Oscar stood again. This time, it was *his* gaze that lingered on Max's mouth. His eyes that took in the broadness of the man before him. His fingers that trailed down Max's torso, admiring the strength beneath the cotton. "I want you," he said, his voice dark. Winding his hand around the back of Max's neck, he pulled him in for another rough kiss. "I want to taste you," he said, rocking his hips forward, letting Max feel how hard he was. "Do you want me to taste you? Slick you with my spit? Make it easier for you to—"

"Yes," Max growled.

Oscar sank to his knees again as Richard rushed forward.

"Get up," Richard demanded, attempting to haul Oscar to his feet, but Oscar shoved him away. He pushed Max's trousers aside, letting his cock free.

It was thick, and long, with a wide, flared head. Oscar's open mouth watered at the sight. He leaned in and took a deep breath, appreciating Max's muskiness. He dragged his stubbled cheek back and forth across the shaft, making Max shiver.

"Jealousy has always been your weakness," Richard gritted out, still trying to keep his voice low. He clenched and unclenched his fists ineffectually at his sides. "We're *gentlemen*, Oscar. We can't afford to be jealous. We don't get to keep boys on our arms. You and I can't exchange vows. There are expectations—"

"Then leave me be," Oscar said, still admiring Max's hard length. He let his mouth trail across the velvety skin as he spoke. "I came here to fuck. If *you're* not jealous, then it shouldn't matter that I'm on the ground for another."

"Fine," Richard snapped, throwing his hands in the air, rushing at Oscar. "Fine." Instead of trying to yank Oscar away once more, Richard crowded into Max. For a moment, Max feared a slap to the face.

A new wave of lust mixed with surprise slammed into him when Richard grabbed him by the hair and forced him to bend his neck. "If you're going to have him, then I will too," he growled at Oscar, his heated gaze grazing over every inch of Max.

Oscar didn't protest. Instead, he made an indignant whimper before sliding his lips over Max's cock, enveloping it in wet, smooth heat.

In retaliation, Richard devoured Max's mouth.

Max returned the kiss eagerly, trying to keep his hips still, wanting so badly to grab the back of Oscar's head and slam forward. It was all so good. Oscar had a talented mouth—clearly he'd had his lips wrapped around Richard many times. And Richard's tongue knew just how to tease. It added that extra tingle of pleasure—enough that he had to concentrate, to reign himself in.

He didn't want this to end too soon.

In fact, he had an idea. Smiling to himself, Max tangled his fingers in Richard's hair, pulling it free of its ribbon. The strands were silky, and framed his face just so. "You—" Max began, punctuating each word with a kiss, "Should—join—him—in—the—dirt."

At first, Richard appeared confused. Max gave him a helpful press on his shoulders, illustrating that he should get on his knees. Remarkably, he complied.

Now Max could watch Oscar worship his cock. The man looked pleased, so happy to have his mouth stretched wide. But his eyebrows went up in shock as Richard settled in beside him. He pulled off with an obscene slurp, a long string of saliva still connecting Max's cock to those spit-shined lips.

Both Richard and Oscar paused, evaluating how they'd gotten here. Their eyes met, and they had a silent conversation in seconds. Apologies were made, glances of devotion exchanged. Diving forward, they collided in a violent, open-mouthed kiss, their tongues licking at one another obscenely.

Max was sure that was the final curtain. The night's drama was over, at least for him. He should tuck himself in and go back to work. But then they simultaneously turned, including his cock in their kiss.

Two tongues swirled over his shaft, leaving cool trails on his hot skin. They licked over and under, occasionally pulling up to simply explore one another before dropping down to slather his cock with attention. They left butterfly kisses on the head, suckling away the precum that dribbled from the slit.

Max gasped and fidgeted, trying to find a handhold on the boxcar. They were so good—not just talented, but eager. Eager as he'd been the first time he'd given a blow-job to Edward. They hummed around him, sending little vibrations up his shaft and through his testicles.

Their licks were wildly explicit, lewd in their sensuality. The shine of spit, the press and pull and roll of their soft, pink tongues in the low light looked as good as it felt. He could watch them like this for hours.

After a time, Oscar once again took him down, hollowing his cheeks as he sucked. Richard ducked to mouth at Max's sack, hot breath tickling his perineum.

Muffled moans and slurps filled the quiet night around them.

Max had restrained himself for as long as he could—kept himself subdued and passive. This was about *them*, after all. He was only a conduit, an extra thread of connection they needed this strange evening. But he wanted to touch them, to praise them and pet them. His hands found their hair, stroking and grabbing to encourage them. "That's good, boys," he growled. "Yes, like that. Your tongue, Oscar—my god, *just like that*. Mmm, Richard, *harder*. Mmm, yes, good boy."

Everything between Max's legs throbbed divinely. He could feel his sac tightening as pleasure swelled in his abdomen. They were winding him tighter and tighter, soon he'd snap. The pressure built with every slide in and out of Oscar's mouth.

"Al-almost—" he groaned. "So close, boys."

That spurred them on, each working that much more frantically, both that much more eager to push him to the edge.

Richard's hands went to Max's hips, steadying him, while Oscar palmed at the base of Max's shaft, pushing himself down until he'd taken Max as deep as he was able. With a few calculated swallows, Oscar triggered the landslide.

Pleasure washed over Max, spiraling from his groin through his limbs, making his brain go fuzzy. He barely had the presence of mind to try and turn to the side—to come on the gravel instead of down Oscar's throat.

But Richard wouldn't let him get away. Oscar pulled back and Richard moved in beside him. They pressed their cheeks together, taking hold of Max's pulsing shaft to make sure he painted their lips.

Max attempted to deny them—it was too intimate, felt intrusive. But they wanted it, and his pleasure was too thorough for him to argue. He allowed them to milk him while the waves of his orgasm sloshed through his body and brain. Globs of sticky-white hit their lips and dribbled down their chins.

They were obscenely pretty like that—mouths messy, eyes wide and dark.

When the last few pulses of pleasure subsided, Max slumped against the car, panting. His cock still bobbed semi-hard in front of the two men, and they proceeded to clean him and each other, lapping at the errant drops of come on his cock head before turning to one another. Half-kissing, half-licking each other, they smiled.

After a few moments, Max regained his wits and tucked his over-sensitive cock into his trousers. The way Richard and Oscar were staring at one another was his cue to leave. He knew they wanted to be alone, that they would pick up where he'd first found them.

"I'll keep a lookout," he told them gruffly, rolling his shoulders, standing straight, trying to shake away the fact that he'd just gotten off while on the job.

"Thank you," Oscar said, favoring him with a sly smile.

"My pleasure," he said, though not facetiously. With one last nod to the couple, he slowly moved away from their lantern light.

Max wasn't sure if anything had changed for them—would Richard still court Claudia? Would he run away with Oscar? Was this their last night together?—but one thing was for certain: they would always be in love. That's what he'd been to them: proof of devotion.

He allowed himself to glance back, knowing they wouldn't mind if he took a peek or two. They were so beautiful together, it would have taken a much stronger man to ignore their lithe bodies thrusting against one another.

This time, Oscar had Richard pinned to the train car. They spoke softly, sweet desperation in their eyes. Richard nodded and turned. He braced himself against the metal while Oscar thrust his hips against Richard's still-clothed backside in a promise of what was to come.

When Oscar yanked Richard's trousers down, exposing the round globes of his ass, Max turned away. Soon the grunting that had drawn him in the first place picked up again, punctuated by the slapping of skin-on-skin.

Max stood stiffly and scanned the perimeter, watching over the train yard and its precious contents, as usual. He let himself think about Edward—wonder what had become of him, if he was happy.

Max hoped so. That was what love was all about, after all.

MOMBASA
VENGEANCE

Mike McClelland

THE FIRST THING I thought upon arrival in Mombasa was: how was I ever to achieve my end when I could not even walk ten feet without sweat burning my eyes?

The second was to note with surprise that the city was not at all as I had envisioned during my crossing from England. As we drove from the port into Mombasa, I was surprised by the city's eclectic but predominantly European appearance. The city had been founded hundreds of years before and for that reason I had assumed it would be African through and through, which in my mind meant constructed of wood, mud, brightly colored fabrics and rough animal hides.

Instead, Mombasa looked like the result of an allied effort between Portugal, England, and Arabia. Most of the newer buildings were white stucco, wood, or brick and featured gables and Baroque windows, nearly in the Queen Anne style except with lower roofs. The older buildings resembled Portuguese forts, lower to the ground with a pinkish-orange hue and blocky construction. Finally, there were an abundance of mosques and other stone buildings with large overhangs and patterns carved or painted into their exteriors.

The residents of Mombasa varied wildly. There were fewer Africans than I'd expected, but we still passed a few, of both sexes, in light, one-shouldered robes. There were plenty of Arabians in white clothing and extravagant headwear, the men in bright red fezzes and the ladies in *jalibib*. Most abundant, however, were Englishmen. There were a few ladies, but mostly the streets were filled with ambling men in black suits in a style a bit more current than my own, with baggier trousers, no waistcoats, and looser-fitting coats. Several wore smocks, which was probably a smarter alternative with regards to the heat but made those wearing them look like coalminers. And a very small amount, likely tourists on hunting holidays, wore white leisure suits, looking like big, lace-swathed infants.

We arrived in front of our destination at half past four in the afternoon. The Bender's Arms was a lovely three-story building made out of deep brown wood. The building had three gables were each ornamented with finely lattice reeds of what looked to be bamboo, making it look like a sort of African gingerbread house. I grabbed my son's hand and pulled him inside with me, and we both sighed in relief in the inn's blessed coolness. The room was two storeys tall, long and wide and filled with tables and chairs. A large bar took up nearly the entire wall opposite Charlie and I. There were staircases to our left and right, leading up to a balcony that ran around three sides of the room's interior. Rooms were visible along the balcony at the top, six rooms visible and presumably more out of sight on the third floor and out back.

Half of the twenty-some barstools were filled with men of various background, shapes, and sizes, and the diversity was a striking contrast to most of the public houses I frequented in London.

I felt the comforting weight of the pistol tucked in my waistband and scanned the room. I saw no sign of the man I had come here for. I'd met him quite a few times, knew what I was looking for: a tall, rail thin man with bright, straw-colored hair and a thin, scraggly beard. He had the spare, chessboard teeth of a man who'd survived a hungry childhood and as a result his cheeks were sunken, making his wide cheekbones look even larger. But he was nowhere to be seen.

I was both relieved and disappointed at his absence. Nevertheless, there would be time. I guided Charlie forward, sitting him down at one of the tables.

"You stay here, my boy, while I get us some drinks. If anyone speaks to you just yell for me." I removed his leather jacket and put it on the back of his chair and gave Charlie's shoulders a squeeze.

The barman was a hideously ugly man, his face ruddy and pockmarked on one side and almost entirely destroyed by a lumpy pink scar on the other. The scar ran from his ear in to his left eye, which it had rendered milky white, and down through the left side of his lips. It pulled top lip up and bottom lip down, revealing teeth that looked soft and yellow as honey cake.

He eyed me with what appeared to be vigorous dislike, although it was hard to tell on account of his grotesque visage. Behind him, a striking black African in a white collared shirt and tight black trousers was pushing wooden barrels up into the bar area from a large doorway, presumably the basement. I leaned against the bar and the African came up and joined the barman at the bar.

"Could you have your boy bring a pint of ale and a half pint of *Apfelwein* to our table?" I said to the barman, motioning towards the black African.

The African's head shot up and his eyes narrowed.

I wondered if he spoke English, and why he staring at me so angrily. My hand again returned to my back, where I felt the comforting heft of the pistol.

"I own this establishment, and I'm no one's *boy*," he said, and I didn't know if I was more surprised by his proclamation, or by the fact that he said it in a Scottish accent.

I was momentarily at a loss for words. Instead, I just stared at the man and his ugly bartender, waiting for inspiration to strike.

"I know you Limeys have trouble with black people doing anything other than serving," he said tersely. "So if this is a problem for you, you know where the door is."

"I don't have any problem with that," I said after a moment, and I meant it, although it was a new concept to me. I couldn't even recall seeing any black faces back at home.

"Good," he said firmly. "I'm Musa, and this is James. My employee."

Embarrassed, I decided to get straight to the point.

"This establishment is listed as the address of a man named Ezekial Greyhorn," I said, watching both men for their reactions. Musa's face remained blank, while James' registered recognition.

"Do you know him?" I asked James.

"Zeke! Poor Zeke, he's…"

A loud thump had come from somewhere behind the bar and James was now hopping on one foot.

Musa said, "Why do you ask?"

I wondered how I should spin it. Then, remembering that I was an angel of vengeance—a hero, not a coward—I said, "I intend to kill him."

THE TALE OF my journey to Mombasa requires little prelude. I intended to kill the coward Ezekial Greyhorn, and I would do whatever it took to ensure my goal. Unfortunately for Greyhorn, I was a very rich man. I could, and would, track him to the ends of the Earth.

The details by which I tracked my mark to this godforsaken public house are complex, but I shall furnish you with the scantest of details. By the time I learned of the craven act for which Greyhorn had earned my hatred, Greyhorn was long gone, his home in Clapham sold. But, being a merchant, Greyhorn relied on business relationships, and it didn't take me long to find that he'd left a forwarding address with Burroughs Wellcome & Co, a pharmaceutical supplier in Wandsworth. According to their impressionable young secretary, a hefty young man with a strong chin and a full, inviting mouth, Greyhorn had seen the light of the Lord and left to establish and outpost for the import of medical supplies to aid missionaries in British East Africa. I was certain this had less to do with Greyhorn's yearning for God's grace and more to do with the deep pockets of the Imperial British East Africa Company, which was throwing money in every direction in order to justify their expensive and deadly railway, which linked the port city of Mombasa to Nairobi in the northwest and then westward still into Uganda.

The Mombasa address that Greyhorn had left with Burroughs Wellcome was that of an inn called The Bender's Arms.

At first I intended to send my son Charlie off to boarding school while I travelled to Africa. The logical part of my brain told me this was the right decision, but as my chequered personal history would no doubt attest to even the most casual of observers, the logical part of my brain was rarely in control. Sentimentality convinced me to bring Charlie along, to begin his teenage years with the adventure that my own had lacked. Further, I came to the conclusion that I would not be returning to England. If all went according to plan, Charlie would return to London with a large inheritance, sun-kissed skin, and memories of his brave father.

Which was how Charlie and I found ourselves boarding the S.S. Berwick Castle on the famous Union-Castle Line, headed south to Mombasa directly from Southampton on a cool day in April of 1910. Charlie scurried along by my side, trying to simultaneously take in the sights while keeping up with me. I'd dressed him in his own little sailor suit; a white canvas set with blue tapes sewn on to mimic a naval uniform. At ten, he was almost too old for it, but Charlie had a keen sense of whimsy and I wanted him to feel as light-hearted as possible, if only to offset my bloody intent.

A loud horn sounded through the air as we strolled towards our room. It sounded like some kind of mythic goose, wild and free. I couldn't yet feel the boat move but I could see the landscape slowly begin to shift.

"We're going to Africa!" Charlie hollered, jumping up and down beside me.

I looked at Charlie but my mind's eye was on Ezekial Greyhorn, on his blood coating my fingers as the life bled out of him.

"Yes we are," I said, smiling.

"I INTEND TO kill him."

James' mouth dropped open. Musa looked at me like I'd just belched in his face. All around us at the bar, men gasped.

James sputtered, "What do you mean, kill him? Where do you think you are? Texas?"

Musa joined in. "This isn't some lawless American outpost where you can just shoot people! This is Africa! We have *rules!*"

"Nevertheless, I am here to kill him, and I have reasons that neither God nor man would blame me for."

I fought to control my voice but there must have been something in the quiver of my words that persuaded my audience that I was not merely a lawless interloper. Musa's eyes softened slightly. "Well, that as may be," he said. "Either way, I'm sorry to say that the Lord has done your work for you."

Musa appeared genuinely sad, but I didn't get his point.

"What do you mean?" I asked.

"Ezekial Greyhorn in dead. An accident while working on the train. Was doing some labor to supplement, I think. Damned thing's killed more than it's transported, I believe."

I just stared at him, not understanding.

"But… *I'm* supposed to do it…" I said hollowly.

"Why don't I help you and your son getting settled in a room?" Musa said.

I said nothing. I just looked back to Charlie, who had downed his *Apfelwein* and started on my ale.

Musa rounded the bar and gently grabbed me by the elbow. "Follow me," he said grimly, and pointed towards the door.

I GOT AN already-sleeping Charlie settled in the smaller of the suite's two adjoining bedrooms and met Musa in the lounge. He'd brought a bottle of whiskey and two glasses along and set them on a small yellow table in the middle of the dim room. Calling it a suite was a stretch, but it was much cooler than the main building had been and was clean.

Musa stretched himself out in a chair, his long, lean body looking distractingly inviting. The top two buttons of his shirt were unbuttoned, which seemed entirely inappropriate, but the look did suit him. I removed my frock coat and sat across from him. I'd worn one of my bright blue waistcoats to accentuate my eyes and I found myself wishing I'd applied more cologne before exiting the boat. I comforted myself by remembering that when I'd planned my outfit I'd been intending to murder a merchant, not seduce an innkeeper.

Musa poured us each two fingers.

"So, how is it that you have a Scottish accent?" I asked him, wanting to discuss anything other than my failed mission.

"This isn't Scottish, it's African! A Kikuyu accent, I swear!"

I narrowed my eyes and he laughed. It was good to be distracted.

"Here's the short version," he said. "Years back, the Church of Scotland sent a bunch of missionaries down in their own attempt to 'civilize Africa.' They stole babies from their villages, raised them in English-speaking schools, sent them to church on Sundays, and told them all that their families died in battle or of disease. I was one of those babies. However, when I was fifteen, an awful flu spread through the settlement that had been built up around the school in Rabai. It killed most of the white people, leaving us to fend for ourselves. Eventually we made our way to the closest Kikuyu village, where I spent the next couple of years learning my native language and culture. So now I live in both worlds, though the Europeans are still doing everything they can to wipe out African culture."

"I'm sorry," was all I could think to say.

He gave me a hard stare and then shrugged. "Seems like you've got your own problems," he said, and took a drink. "Now," he continued, his eyes kind, "tell me your story. What drove you to want to kill Ezekiel?"

I knocked back my whole glass. "It's a sordid tale," I said.

Musa poured me another and smiled. "I like sordid," he said.

I swallowed the second glass, felt it burn bitter on my tongue and down my throat, as if the flesh of my mouth was briefly aflame. "Ezekiel killed my wife," I said, staring off into the darkness above Musa's head.

I saw Musa's face fall into a one of sympathy, but I'd had quite enough of that these few months, and so before it could continue, I began my story.

"My wife and I met at one of a series of horrible dances the upper crust arranges in order for their children to find spouses of a similar social class. We were both eighteen. I had maneuvered Jonathan Howard, the sixth son of the Marquess of Pembroke, into the coatroom. I had just managed to get hand down the back of Johnny's trousers and was showing him some of the more mysterious parts of his anatomy when my future wife, Cornelia, fell through the door, wrapped in carnal embrace with Eugenie Cavendish, the ninth child of the Duke of Devonshire."

I looked up to see if Musa was horrified by my revelations, but he was eying me a cautious amusement.

"Johnny and Genie both nearly died of shame and fled the coatroom. I was scared as well, terrified that my secret would get out. But Cornelia looked me in the eye, threw her head back, and laughed. In that second I knew that she was the woman I would marry."

"We were the first of our siblings on either side to be married and all of our brothers and sisters were nearly mad with jealousy and fear that our union could result in us stealing their promised titles. Neither Cornelia nor I had any desire for such things, but we did both like children and we delighted at torturing our families, so as soon as we were married we decided that we needed a baby.

"However, as you know, it's only healthy for a child to be conceived out of love. And so, Cornelia and I set out to fall in love, if only for one night. We thought about dressing me up in ladies' clothing but it didn't work for either of us. So, Cornelia cut her hair short, which wasn't a problem as she'd inherited dozens of lavish hairpieces from her late mother, and then she spent a few months exercising vigorously to grow some muscles. I hated for her to do it, but she claimed to enjoy it. After a few months, on a dreary Wednesday evening, she let me see her naked and I must say that her effort was rather splendid. She insisted on having me call her Johnny, who I did always view as a missed opportunity, and bent over on all fours. Nine months later we had Charlie!"

At this, Musa looked a surprised at last.

"That can't be true," he said.

"It is! I swear it! After Charlie was born, I can honestly say that we were in love. Unconventionally, of course. The only problem was that we'd both always wanted adventure, to travel and see the world, but we were frightened. London was dangerous enough for people like us; the rest of the world was even worse."

Musa nodded in vigorous agreement.

"Given our shared love—and lack—of adventure, I wasn't surprised when Cornelia fell head over heels for Abigail, the wife of a seafaring merchant we frequented at Borough Market. She was just Cornelia's type: gorgeous face, loose brown curls, bright blue eyes, a bawdy sense of humor..."

"You could be describing yourself," Musa said, his voice deep.

"You didn't let me finish!" I laughed, my cheeks reddening. "I was about to say, 'with tits that could float her to Australia!'"

Musa snorted his whiskey and then wheezed. I shushed him, not wanting to wake Charlie, though I knew the boy would be sleeping for quite some time, given the combination of heat and alcohol.

"Abigail and Cornelia began a rather torrid romance, either coming to our house or frolicking around at Abigail's when her husband was out of town. Then, one day, the police came to my door. The said that Cornelia and Abigail had both been found dead at Abigail's home, a bottle of arsenic clutched in Cornelia's hand. The police said it was a suicide."

My voice lost its volume and I realized that I'd never once told the whole story to another soul. Musa put his hand on my leg.

"I am ashamed to admit that I believed the police. I was so angry. I couldn't imagine how Cornelia could leave Charlie. And me!"

I took another sip of whiskey and continued.

"I would have stayed ignorant if the merchant—who was, as I suppose you've guessed by now, Ezekial Greyhorn—hadn't fired his butler, O'Brien. O'Brien, upset with Greyhorn for leaving him jobless and destitute, wrote me to say that Greyhorn had witnessed our wives offending our masculinity through sinful acts and that Greyhorn had countered his humiliation by offing them."

I was shaking and Musa kept his hand on my leg.

"So I decided to kill Greyhorn. To avenge her."

"In that case," Musa said quietly after a few moments. "I'm sorry that he's dead. For you. I knew him to be a good man. But good men do evil things."

I couldn't think of the way forward. Murdering Greyhorn had been my only goal. I was left adrift.

Perhaps sensing my desolation, Musa rose quickly, grabbing me by the shoulder and pulling me along.

"Come with me, I have something to show you," he said, and led me out the door.

I'D BEEN HESITANT to leave Charlie alone in the suite, but Musa assured me that the area was quite safe and that we'd be close enough to hear Charlie call if he woke. Musa led me down a small dirt path that lurched out from the road behind the Bender's Arms into a thicket. I feared the brush served as a resting place for venomous African wildlife, but Musa boldly ventured forward, pushing branches aside as he led me further inside. It did cross my mind that I barely knew this man, that he could be leading me anywhere, but he had an inherent sturdiness that led me to believe in his good intentions. That, and I liked the view of his strong shoulders straining to push heavy branches apart.

Eventually we reached a small clearing. The late afternoon light was nearly extinguished here, but after a moment my eyes adjusted. Directly in front of us sat a row of a dozen or so uneven headstones. Squinting, Musa moved in, looking closely at each stone before calling me to him.

"Here," he said, gesturing to the low, crooked stone in front of him. "Here's what remains of Ezekial Greyhorn."

Leaning towards the stone, I noticed that something had once sat atop it, perhaps a cross or an orb of some sort, but it had been knocked off, stolen perhaps, making the stone resemble a headless bust.

The words had faded. They didn't look old, but the stone was cheap. Barely legible in in the dark, I traced them with my fingers as I tried to work them out.

"To the fine men who perished in the construction the Empire's Greatest Railway— our trains glide atop your shoulders."

And below, in smaller print: "The Imperial British East Africa Company."

"He didn't even get his own stone?" I asked.

"Who would have paid for that? If your story is true, he killed his only family."

I felt something crack within me, allowing some thick emotion to trickle out into my chest. Not sympathy, but deep sadness, a sadness for how lonely the world was, and what a damned fool Greyhorn had been for making himself even lonelier. Now here he was, the only memory of him certain to sink into the dark red mud.

DESPITE THE SOFTENING of my heart towards Greyhorn, I was in a stormy mood when we returned to the suite.

Musa interrupted my misery. "May I ask you one question?"

"What?"

"Why did you bring your son?" he asked.

I didn't even need to think.

"I brought Charlie along to see me do it, so that, even if he couldn't look up to his father as a man, he'd know he did the manly thing, just once."

"And murder is the manly thing?" Musa asked quietly.

I felt horribly bleak and didn't know how to express my thoughts clearly. Instead, I looked at his lips, which were thin and dark, almost blue. Like ice. I fell forward, pushing my lips against his.

He froze at first and I wondered if I'd guessed wrong. The signs all seemed to be there. Then he pushed his tongue into my mouth and grabbed my face, pushing deeper.

I put my hand between his legs and when I felt what he had there, I made a noise of surprise. To my disappointment, Musa slapped my hand away and pushed me back, putting distance between us.

"I won't fulfill your fantasy of having some African savage brutalize you, if that's what you're after," he said, his voice dark and his eyes pained.

Of course not, I wanted to say. But then I wondered if that would be a lie. So, instead of speaking I stood up, grabbing his hands and pulling him up, too. Then I turned him around and pressed myself against his backside, biting him on the neck, holding his hands behind him.

He whirled around forcefully. "Oh, is it that you want, to debase the unwilling slave? I won't do that for you either."

God, he was difficult. But he was also right; I was fetishizing him. He was so foreign to me and I didn't know what to do with him.

"I don't know how to do this," I said miserably.

"Stop thinking," he said. "Let's enjoy each other."

WITHIN MOMENTS WE were both naked in the suite's master bedroom, the door locked behind us. The room was illuminated by two small gas lanterns on tables on either side of the bed. Musa had undressed faster, whipping off shirt, his trousers and flannel drawers, and was sitting on the bed, his yard sticking out of a tidy bit of curly black hair like a fencepost. I had more straps and clasps to deal with, and I'd worn a wool combination underneath. I assumed Musa would avert his eyes while I disrobed but instead he watched me hungrily. I blushed but continued boldly, turning my round rear to him as I peeled the undergarment down, bending slightly forward as I dragged it over me, exposing myself to him. I knew it was a pleasing view and, though my face burned, my cock was granite hard as I pulled the woolen garment down and let it fall to the floor.

Finally naked, I turned, leading with my cock, and I saw him eye it with satisfaction. It was perfectly proportionate to my body: lean, long, and firm, and emerged from an attractive tuft of light brown hair, my light pink bollocks hanging heavily beneath. My equipment may have suffered in comparison to Musa's but I felt no shame. I knew my own beauty. I was so sensitive that a mere look was enough to turn make me flush. Everything, from my lips to my nipples to my balls to my entrance was a sexual pink, the color of erotic strain.

Everything that was light and flushed on me was dark and deep on Musa. He was entirely beautiful, every muscle and curve glimmering in the dim light. Where I was light and lean, he was dark and full. He wasn't pure stone—his chest was broad and soft, his nipples the same purple as his lips. His thighs were broad, while his legs below were long and almost delicate, like those of a ballet dancer.

While his body had me panting with desire, his face was what sent me over the edge. He stared at me with complete desire. I wanted him inside me; I wanted to be inside him. I wanted him to take me apart, to use me. I wanted to bend him over and see him spread, to make him moan as I fucked him vigorously.

He motioned for me to come to him, his eyes bright in the flickering light. He was alternately cool and hot, his movements assured and brisk but his body radiating heat. As I approached the edge of the bed, I was unsure of how to engage. I was used to fleeting encounters in dark corners: the pulling down of breeches, desperate thrusts in the dark.

"I want you on my lap," Musa said.

I turned and backed towards him.

"No, face me," he said.

I hadn't done it this way before. Tentatively, I bent my left knee and placed it outside his right leg on the edge of the bed. Then I placed my right knee outside his left leg. I arched my back and sat on his lap, his root settling in between my ass cheeks. I felt gloriously exposed, and I was breathlessly aware of his cock sliding over my hole.

I was both in control and submitting to Musa, which gave me pause. His face was aligned with my chest and he smiled before closing his mouth around a nipple, staring up at me while he sucked gently on it, his tongue rolling over the sensitive nub. I reached back and gripped the base of his cock, then went lower, fondling his big bollocks.

Musa moaned against my chest, vibrating my nipple. My dick hardened further and ground against the hard muscles of his abdomen.

I brought my hand back up, spit on it, and then went back to the base of his yard, working it slowly. Musa broke his face free of my nipple and gave me a shameless smile.

"God, you're beautiful," I said. In response, he flexed his cock, which was gliding between my ass and my hand.

His own hands, which had been rubbing my thighs, moved to my ass, each one cupping a cheek. He squeezed, pushing my ass into his dick, and I let out a low, quiet moan. I arched my back, my chest running against his face, and he sucked on my other nipple.

He worked up my backside until both hands were close to my entrance. He spread my ass wide, pushing the head of his cock against my hole. I moaned again, hungry for it.

He grabbed my forearms and moved my hands to my own backside, replacing his with mine. I held myself open while he raised the middle finger of his left hand to my mouth. I understood his intentions and sucked it in hungrily. He then moved the finger to my hole and pressed it gently inside. The pain was sharp, but it subsided quickly as he hooked his finger and hit the spot with expert precision.

Musa reached his free hand up and grabbed my chin, bringing my mouth to his. He kissed me deeply. I kept my eyes open and so did he and we stared openly at each other. All the while, his long middle finger pushed in and out of my ass.

He pulled back from the kiss. "You're so hot inside," he said. "You're so ready to be fucked," he whispered. His words made me even harder and I ground my cock against his stomach.

"Yes. Fuck me," I said. He added another finger, stretching me slightly.

Musa reached over to his pants, which were lying on the corner of the bed. He extracted a small jar of oil.

I laughed. "You came prepared."

He smiled and removed his fingers from me, smeared them with oil, and pushed them back into my ass. He began to work them faster, hitting the spot over and over again, making my mind blank with ecstasy. I watched his face while he fingered me. His eyes were dark and he breathed heavily, his lust playing out across his face.

I reached back again to tug his cock. I rolled my hand up its length and was rewarded with a bead of moisture at the tip. He was definitely aroused.

"Okay," I said. "If you don't fuck me now I'm going to finish too quickly."

Musa removed his fingers and poured some oil into my hand.

"Get me ready and then climb on. You're in charge."

This was a first. Usually, in my frantic encounters with men, one of us bent the other over and went at it. Musa was putting me in charge. Though he was doing the fucking, I was in control.

I oiled up his cock, slightly scared of its size. But, when it came to cock, I was nothing if not ambitious. I met his eyes and arched my back, pushing up on my knees. I lined up the head of his cock with my hole. Then I sat back, taking it in a half-inch at a time, slowly lowering myself onto him.

Musa appeared to be in such a state of ecstasy that I feared his eyes would roll back in his head. I enjoyed the power that came with controlling how much of him was in me. I made it about halfway down his cock, already feeling full, and then, noting Musa's increasing arousal, took the second half into me with one swift thrust downward.

There was pain, the also the immense pleasure of being so incredibly full. I moved my hand to my own root and worked it to distract myself from the pain, watching Musa's face all the while. His mouth was open in a wide 'O," which was followed by a smile of sheer appreciation.

Musa returned his hands to my ass, kneading my cheeks as I pushed my knees up and then fell back on his cock, feeling his heavy bollocks against me as I took him in fully. I relished the control, the mix of being taken and being in charge.

Musa brought his mouth back to my chest as I rode him, sucking my nipples alternately. My hair fell forwards over my eyes as I rocked myself up and down on him and I wiped it away.

Soon, too soon, I could feel myself approaching release. I removed my hand from my cock but it was too far-gone and still rubbing against Musa's chiseled stomach.

"I'm close," I said raggedly.

Musa smiled mischievously and said, "Let me finish you off, then."

"You can do whatever you want to me," I said, and he bit my nipple in response.

Then he pulled back and said, "Kiss me."

I bent forward and kissed him and, as I did, he gripped my ass and began thrusting upward into me.

His cock hit that amazing spot inside me again and again and I held my mouth over his as he thrust with increasing power up into my ass. It was relentless and the slap of his bollocks on my ass made it all the more visceral.

Musa pushed his tongue into my mouth as he pounded me and I relished having him in me on both ends. I thought that he had to be fucking me as hard as he possibly could, but he took it to another level still. The feeling spread from deep inside me, from that spot where his root relentlessly slammed into my center, and radiated outward, taking over my entire body. It spread outward, into my cock, which erupted violently, covering Musa's dark stomach in streams of sticky white.

He looked down in wonder as volley after volley shot out of me and then came himself, shooting deep inside me.

Trembling, I pulled out of our kiss and lowered my head to his shoulder. He stayed inside me, his cock still hard. I was empty and full at the same time, exhausted and energized.

After a few minutes, Musa gently slipped out and rolled over. I fell forward, face down on the bed. I turned my head to look at him and found him looking too aroused for someone who should be spent.

I stared at him, content, and it was only then that the tragedy of my situation returned to me, but though the old horror of my situation remained, I found it muted by a creeping sense of relief, relief tempered with a small amount of hope. Maybe kindled by Musa, maybe kindled by being so far away from London.

Musa having cleaned himself up a bit, rolled back onto the bed. I put my arms around him, my face meeting the back of his neck, which I kissed slowly and gently. He murmured and arched into me contently. I kissed down Musa's neck and along his shoulder. Already, Mombasa had shown me things I'd never seen before. I didn't' believe in that old Herbert phrase, "living well is the best revenge." But now that seemed to be my only way to honor Cornelia. To do right by Charlie and to give him the life that she would have wanted for him: a life of freedom, of adventure, of discovery. Here, deep in Africa, seemed to be the perfect place to do just that.

I hugged Musa closer to me, thinking to myself as I tasted the salt sweat of his neck with my tongue that good things could still occur in the world that tragedy left behind. If it had simply been a fuck then life would continue on, but perhaps there was a chance, fragile but undeniable, that this was more than that, and as I hardened against him, I let myself forget the sadness of the world, if only for a little while.

EXTRACT:
MY
SECRET LIFE
Anonymous

If size matters, *My Secret Life* beats off all comers, pun fully intended. The book, released in eleven volumes, comprises over a million words. In any circumstance this would be an impressive achievement, but even more so when one knows that *My Secret Life* is wall-to-wall filth—there's a truly astonishing range of encounters details throughout the book, in repetitive, obsessive detail. Published between 1888 and 1894 at a cost of £60 (a cost almost more obscene than its contents, being equal to approximately £4000 in current money), it was banned immediately and remained so for nearly a century.

The book is ascribed to an author known only as 'Walter', although there is very little conclusive evidence for who this might be, (though the most likely candidate is a man by the name of Henry Spencer Ashbee who went by the pseudonym "Pisanus Fraxi", a lewd pun derived from praxinus=ash and apis=bee). Whether the book is fact or fiction is up for debate, though some argue that the inclusion of mundane details and the general lack of exaggerated, unbelievable situations makes it likely it as least partly true. Though if this is the case, the number of assignations that 'Walter' engages in is jaw-droppingly high.

My Secret Life is almost exclusively heterosexual, though there is a noted ambivalence towards encounters outside of this realm. Many of the women 'Walter' encounters discuss lesbian affairs, and as the volumes wear on the diversity of sexual encounters begins to widen. And though we shall make no comment that before anything even mildly homosexual occurs, 'Walter' has already explored voyeurism, watersports, and some very dubious cases of consent, placing a same-sex coupling quite some way down the line of 'extremity', there is a notable section in which 'Walter'—consumed by curiosity of a homosexual encounter and arranging a bisexual threesome as a method of initiating said meeting—discovers himself suddenly sexually obsessed with the male of the trio and proceeds to explore this further.

His first encounter is relayed here, and his later explorations continued later in this collection.

The evening came. I felt so nervous and even shocked at myself that I wished I had never under-taken the affair. — It was in vain that I argued with myself, and spite of my conviction that there was no harm in my doing it, when I came to her door I nearly turned back. I had been trying to strengthen my intention by thinking over my former wishes and curiosities, of the various amusements I should have with him, and how much I should learn of the ways of a man, to add to the lot I knew about women. All was useless, I almost trembled at my intention. I entered, saw Sarah. "He is in the bed room — such a nice young man, and quite good looking, I never saw him till I went to buy the things." I said I felt nervous. "That is stupid, but you are not more nervous than he is, he's just said you were evidently not coming and he was glad of it, and would go." Again she assured me that he was all the charwoman had told, a young man out of work, wanting bread, and not a sodomite.

I followed her into the bedroom. Saying, "This is the gentleman," she shut the door and left me with him. He stood up respectfully and looked at me timidly.

He was a fine young man about five feet seven inches high, rather thin looking as if for want of nourishment, with a nice head of curly brown hair, slight short whiskers, no moustache, bright eyes, and good teeth. He was not much like a working man and looked exceedingly clean. "You are the young man?" "Yes sir." "Sit down." Down he sat and I did the same.

Then I could not utter a word more, but felt inclined to say, "There is a sovereign, good night," and to leave him. All the desires, all the intentions, all expectations of amusement with his prick, all the curiosity I had hoped to satisfy for months left me. My only wish was to escape without seeming a fool.

With the exception of the sodomite whom Betsy Johnson had got me, it was the first time I had been by myself in the room with a male for the clear intention of doing everything with his tool that I had a mind to. My brain now had been long excited by anticipation, and wrought up to the highest when this opportunity came, and every occurrence of that evening is as clear in it now as if it were printed there. Altho the exact order of the various tricks I played may not be kept, yet everything I did on this first night, all that took place, I narrate in succession, without filling in anything from fancy or imagination. I could even re-call the whole of our conversation, but it would fill quires (and I did fill two or three). — I only now give half of it, and that abbreviated.

I sat looking at him for some minutes — I can frig him, thought I — but I don't want to now. — What an ass he will think me. — Why does he not unbutton? I wonder if he is a bugger — or a thief. — What's he thinking about. Is he clean? — How shall I begin — I wish I had not come — I hope he won't know me if he meets me in the street. — Is his prick large? — These thoughts one after another chased rapidly thro my brain, whilst I sat silent, yet at the same time wishing to escape, and he sat looking at the floor.

Then an idea came. "Would you like something to drink?" "If you like, sir." "What?" "Whatever you like, sir." — It was an immense relief to me when I called in Sarah, and told her to get whiskey, hot water, and sugar. — Whilst it was being fetched I went into the sitting room, glad of getting away.

Sarah, in the sitting room, asked, "How do you find him?" — I told her I did not know and was frightened to go on. — "Oh! I would now, as you have had him got for you, then you'll be satisfied." — Again she assured me he was not on the town, and I need not be afraid. The whiskey was got, and behold me again alone with him. I made whiskey and water for myself and him and took some into Sarah. I began to ask him about himself. He was a house decorator in fine work, such work was at its worst just then, being a young hand he had not full employment, had been out of work nearly two months, he had pawned everything excepting what he had on. This all seemed consistent. He told me where he lodged, where he was apprenticed, the master he worked for last, the houses he worked at. "If you are a decorator your hands will be hard, and if you kneel your knees will." "Yes but I have had scarcely anything to do for two months, and but one day's work last week. Look at my nails." — They were stained with something he had used. Then he had had one day's chopping wood which had blistered both his hands, for it was not work he was accustomed to. Blisters I saw. There was evident truth in what he said.

This relieved me, together with the influence of whiskey and water. I got more courage and he seemed more comfortable, but not a word had transpired about our business, and an hour had gone. Then my mind reverted to my object, and I said, "You know what you came for." "Yes sir." He changed white, then red, and began to bite his nails.

My voice quivered as I said, "Unbutton your trowsers then." He hesitated. "Let me see your cock." One of his hands went down slowly, he unbuttoned his trowsers, which gaping, shewed a white shirt. Then never looking at me, he began biting his nails again.

The clean shirt, coupled with his timidity, gave me courage. "Take off your coat and waistcoat." He slowly did so. — I did the same, gulped down a glass of whiskey and water, sat him down by me, and lifting his shirt laid hold of his prick. A thrill of pleasure passed thro me, I slipped my hands under his balls, back again to his prick, pulled the foreskin backwards and forwards, my breath shortening with excitement. He sat still. Suddenly I withdrew my hand with a sense of fear and shame again on me.

"May I make water, sir, I want so badly," said he in a humble way, just like a schoolboy. "Certainly, take off your trowsers first." He looked hard at me, slowly took them and his drawers off, and stood with his shirt on. I took up the pot and put it on the chair (my baudy brain began now to work). "Do it here, and I'll look at your cock."

He came slowly there and stood. "I can't water now — I think it is your standing by me." "You will directly, don't mind me." The whiskey and excitement having made me leaky, I pulled out my tool and pissed in the pot before him.

He laughed uneasily, it was the first sign of amusement he had given. Directly I had finished, I laid hold of his prick and began playing with it, I pulled back the skin and blew on the tip, a sudden whim that made him laugh, and his shyness going off, I holding his prick, he pissed the pot half full — I was delighted and wished he could have kept on pissing for a quarter of an hour.

The ice was now broken, I took off my trowsers, and then both with but shirts and socks on, I sat him at the side of the bed and began my investigation of his copulating apparatus.

"I want to frig you," said I. "Yes sir." "Has any man ever frigged you." — No living man touched his prick since he was a boy, he declared. — Then I began to handle his cock with the ordinary first fucking motion.

I had scarcely frigged a minute before I wanted to feel his balls. Then I turned him with his rump to me, to see how his balls and prick looked hanging down from the back. — Then on to his side, to see how the prick dangled along his thigh. Then I took him to the wash stand and washed his prick, which before that was as clean as a new shilling, but the idea of washing it pleased me. Then laying him down on his back, I recommended the fascinating amusement of pulling the foreskin backwards and forwards, looking in his face to see how he liked it. — He was as quiet as a lamb, but looked sheepish and uncomfortable. His prick at first was small, but under my manipulation grew larger, tho never stiff. Several times it got rather so for an instant, and then with the desire to see the spunk come, I began frigging harder; when instead of getting stiffer it got smaller. I tried this with him laying down, sitting up, and standing, but always with the same result — I spoke about it. — He said he could not make it out.

His prick was slightly longer than mine, was beautifully white, and with a pointed tip. I made it the stiffest by gently squeezing it — I had had no desire in my own doodle, but as I made his stiff once when he was lying down, my own prick came to a stand, and following a sudden inspiration I laid myself on to his belly, as if he had been a woman, and our two pricks were between our stomachs close together. I poked mine under his balls, and forced his under my stones, then changing, I turned his bum towards me, and thrusting my cock between his thighs and under his balls to the front, bent his prick down to touch the tip of mine, which was just showing thro his thighs. But his prick got limper and limper, and as I remarked that, it shrivelled up. We had been an hour at this game, and there seemed no chance of his spending. No sign of permanent stiffness or randiness or pleasure. He seemed in fact miserably uncomfortable.

Then he wanted to piss again from nervousness — I held his prick, squeezing it, sometimes stopping the stream, then letting it go on, and satisfying my curiosity. That done, I made a final effort to get a spend out of him, by squeezing, frigging slow, frigging fast. Then I rubbed my hand with soap, and making with spittle an imitation of cunt mucous on it, titillated the tip. "I think I can do it now," said he — but all was useless. "It's no good, I'm very sorry, sir, but I can't, that is a fact. — I don't know how it is."

The last hour had been one of much novelty and de-light to me, tho he couldn't spend; but the announcement disappointed me. It came back to my mind that he might be, after all that Sarah had said, an over-frigged bugger, who could no longer come. For I had heard that men who let themselves out for that work at last got so used up that it was difficult for them to do anything with their own pricks, and that all they could do was to permit men to feel their cocks, whilst they plugged their arse-holes. So I repeated my questions, and he again swore by all that was holy that no man had ever felt him but me; and he added that he was sorry he had come, but the money was a temptation.

I laid him then again on the bed and felt his prick. We finished the whiskey, and I sent for more; and in a whisper told Sarah that there was no spunk in him. She brought in the whiskey herself, and laughed at seeing us two nearly naked on the bed together.

Then I asked him when he had a woman last, if he liked them, how he got them, and so forth. He told me that he liked women very much — sometimes he got them for nothing, and they were servant girls mostly. When at houses if servants were left in them, or even if the family were only for a short time out — young fellows like him often got a put in; or else made love to them, and got them to come out at nights. He warmed up as he told me this, and his prick began to rise, but on my recommencing to masturbate him, it fell down again. He declared that the woman he last had was ten days previously, when he gave her a shilling out of the trifle he had gained, and that he had never spent since. Then he began biting his nails, adding that he hoped I should give him the money, for he could not help not spending, and was desperately badly off — "I have had some bread and cheese, and beer, but I have not tasted meat for six days."

Three hours with him passed, the frigging seemed useless, but talking about women had brought my steam well up, so I began to think of letting him go, and plugging Sarah to finish. "Sarah is a fine woman isn't she? Did you ever have her, or see her naked," I said suddenly, thinking to catch him. — She was fine, but he had never seen her in his life, until the day but one previously. — "Would you like to see her naked." Oh! would he not. I knew Sarah would do anything almost, so called her in, told her his cock would not stand, and that we wanted to see her naked. "All right," said she, and began to undress.

He kept his eyes ardently fixed on her as she took off her things — I remarked to him on her charms as she disclosed them. He said "Yes — yes" — in an excited way. Then he ceased answering, but stared at her intently. When her limbs and breasts shewed from her chemise, a voluptuous sigh escaped him, and he put his hand to his prick outside his shirt. Feeling him, I found his prick swelling. "Don't pull off yet Sarah." She ceased taking off her chemise. "Pull off your shirt." Helping him he stood naked with his prick rising. — "Now show us your cunt." Down Sarah lay (after stripping off her chemise) on her back, one arm raised and shewing her dark haired arm pit, her legs apart, and one raised with the heel just under her bum, the black hair of her cunt curling down till shut in, by her arse cheeks, the red lined cunt lips slightly gaping. — It was a sight which would have made a dead man's prick stiffen, and mine was stiff at the sight altho I had seen it scores of times. I forgot him then, till turning my head I saw his splendid cockstand. — His eyes were fixed full of desire on her, and he was a model of manly, randy beauty. — "Is not she fine?" said I. "Oh! lovely, beautiful, let me do it," addressing her. "No," said I, "another time perhaps," and I seized his tool with lewed joy.

For an instant he resisted. Sarah said, "Let my friend do it, you came for that." I frigged away, he felt its effects and sighed — I frigged on and felt the big, firm, wrinkled ball bag. A voluptuous shiver ran thro him soon. "Oh! let me feel her — do." "Feel her then." Over he stooped. "Kneel on the bed." Quickly he got there and plunged his finger into her carmine split. Again I grasped his tool and frigged. He cried out, "Oh! I'm coming. — I'm spend — ing" — and a shower of sperm shot out, covering her belly from cunt to navel. I frigged on until every drop had fallen. Then letting go his prick, he sat down on his heels, his eyes shut, his body still palpitating with pleasure and now fingering his still swollen doodle.

The effect on me was violent. Sarah's attitude on her back at all times gave me a cockstand — it had stood whilst frigging him. — There she lay now, a large drop of his spunk on her motte seemed ready to drop down on to her clitoris, higher up on her belly little pools lay. Tearing off my shirt, scarcely knowing what I did, crying out, "Move up higher on the bed" — which he did, I flung myself on her and put my prick up her cunt. — My prick rubbed the spunk drop on her thatch, my belly squeezed the opal pools between us, the idea delighted me — I fucked away, stretched out my hand, grasped his wet prick, for he was now conveniently near me, and fucked quickly to an ecstatic termination.

The greater the preliminary excitement, the more delicious seems the repose after a fuck — the more it is needed, and I had had excitement enough that night. At length I roused myself. My cock did not seem inclined to come out of its lodging. I felt that I could butter her again without uncunting. So keeping it in, I raised myself and looked at him sitting at the head of the bed, naked and still feeling his prick, which was again as stiff as a ramrod.

"He can spend after all," said I, my prick still up Sarah. — "I told you he was a nice man." "Should you like to fuck her?" "Just give me the chance." The tale of the soldiers putting into each other's leavings came into my head. "Do it at once." "Lord," said Sarah, "you don't mean that." But I did. "Do it now." — I rose on my knees. — As I took my belly off of Sarah's, they were sticking together with his spunk. It made a loud smacking noise as out bellies separated. — My prick drew out sperm which dropped between her thighs. — As I got off, he got on, and as quickly put up her. The next minute their backsides were in rapid motion.

The second fuck is longer than the first, and I had time to watch their movements. — A man and woman both naked and close to me, were copulating — I could see and feel every movement of their bodies — hear their murmurs and sighs — see their faces. — There stood I with my prick now stiff again watching them. — My hands roved all over them — I slipped my hand between their bellies — I felt his balls. — Then slipping it under her rump it felt the wet spunk I had left in her cunt, now working out on to the stem of his prick as it went in and out — I got on the bed and rubbed my prick against his buttocks. I shouted out — "Fuck her, — spend in her — spend in my spunk," — and other obscenities I know not what. — I encouraged his pleasure by baudy suggestions. A sigh, a murmuring, told me he was coming. My fingers were on his balls, and I let them go to see his face. He thrust his tongue into Sarah's mouth. — "You are spending, Sarah." — No reply. — Her mouth was open to his tongue, her eyes were closed, her buttocks moving with energy, and the next second but for a few twitchings of his arse, and their heavy breathings, they were like lumps of lifeless flesh. Both had spent. The fancy to do her after him came over me — my spunk — his spunk — her spunk —

all in her cunt together. I will spend in her again. — The idea of my prick being drowned in these mixed exudations overwhelmed me libidinously. — "I'll do it to you again. — Get off of her." — "Let me wash," said Sarah. — "No." — "I will." — "You shan't. — He was getting off, she attempting to rise, when I pushed her down. — "It's wiser" — I didn't know what she said scarcely. — "No — no — no — I want to put into his spunk." — Her thighs were apart, her cunt hole was blinded, hidden by spunk which lay all over it and filled its orifice. I threw myself on her, my prick slipped up with a squashing noise — I know no other way of describing it. I think I hear it now.

I felt a sense of heavenly satisfaction. Her cunt was so filled that it seemed quite loose, the sperm squeezed out of her and up, until the hair of both our genitals were saturated — I pushed my hand down, and making her lift up one leg, found the sperm lay thick down to her arse hole — I called out, "Your spunk's all over my ballocks," and told all the baudy images which came across my mind. I told him to lay down by the side of us, and made Sarah feel his prick at the same time I did — I felt my pleasure would even now be too short and stopped myself. Sarah with a sigh cried, "Oh — my God — go on," her cunt tightened, she got his prick and clasped my buttocks to her — I held his prick, and tried to lengthen my pleasure but could not, her cunt so clipped me. Abandoning myself to her the next instant almost with a scream of pleasure, I was quiet in her arms and fell asleep — and so did she, and so did he — all three on the bed close to-gether.

Awakening, I had rolled off close to Sarah on to my side, my prick laying against her thigh. — She lay on her back asleep, he nearly on his back. All three were nearly naked, myself excepted who had on an under shirt next my skin. — She had silk stockings and black merino boots on. My foreskin had risen up and covered the tip of my prick. In the saucer at the top was spunk which had issued from me after I uncunted. — The lamp was alight. Two candles (they had been short pieces) had burnt out, and the fire had all but expired. The room had been hot all the evening, for there were three of us in it, three lights burning, and the fire. Now it had got cold, and a sensation of chilliness was over me.

I got up and looked at the pair. — She a splendid woman, firm and smooth skinned, and of a creamy pink tint — with the dark hair of her cunt in splendid contrast. He a fine young man with white flesh, and with much dark brown hair clustering and curling round his white prick, and throwing his balls into shadow. His prick still large was hanging over his thigh, the slightly red tip half covered by the foreskin pointing towards Sarah, and as if looking at it. Then sexual instinct made me pay attention to her. — She lay there with two libations from me, and one from him in her cunt. I desired to see how it looked and felt it, but was so distracted by my various erotic impulses that I cannot recollect everything accurately. — All I know is that I laid hold of her leg nearest to me, and watching, pulled it slowly so as to leave her legs slightly open. I put my finger down from the beginning of the cleft. It felt thick and sticky, yet but little spunk was to be seen — looking down towards the bum cheeks, I saw the bed patched in half a dozen places with what had run out from her — I thrust my finger up her cunt and she awakened.

She sat up, looked round, rubbed her eyes, said, "it's cold." Then she looked at him. "Why — he's asleep too, have you been asleep?" — Then she put her fingers to her cunt too, got off the bed, and on to the pot — looking at me smiling. — "You are a baudy devil and no mistake — I don't recollect such a spree since I have been out." "Your cunt's in a jolly state of bat-ter." "It will be all right when it's washed" — and she proceeded to wash, but I stopped her.

He was snoring and had turned on to his back — his prick which seemed large lolled over his thigh. "He's a fine young man and his prick's bigger than yours, and what a bag," said she gently lifting up his prick and shewing his balls. I saw it was very large, as it had seemed to me when I squeezed and felt it before, but then I had been far too excited to notice anything carefully. Now I began to frig him as he lay. "I thought you had done me, for two hours I could not make his cock stand." "Ah! it was nervousness. — He has never been felt by a man before, some would give ten pounds for such a chance and you are to give him a sovereign." "Do you think he can spend again?" "Yes, see what a lot he spent over me; if he was well fed, that young chap would be good for half a dozen pokes, he's been half starved for two months."

I gently laid hold of his prick, and pulled the skin down. One feel more and it rose to fullish size, and lay half way up his belly. "I thought it would directly you touched it from its look," said she. Said I, "I will frig him," and commenced in the slowest and gentlest manner, scarcely touching it. The stiffening began and the foreskin retired, the tip got rubicund and tumid, an uneasy movement of his thigh and belly began, and muttering in his sleep his hand went to his prick. — I removed mine. Soon his hand dropped by his side again, and he snored and muttered something.

Sarah, who had put on her chemise, then laid hold of his prick and frigged it. — "He can't spend, he's done too much already," said I. "I think he will tho." Then I, jealous of her handling, and lewedly fascinated, resumed the work. — Had he not drunk and eaten heartily, and been very fatigued, he must have awakened, but he didn't. Not spending, I spat on my finger and thumb, and making a moist ring with them, rubbed his prick tip through them. That did it. He muttered, his belly heaved, and out rolled his sperm, as he awakened, saying, "I've had a beastly spending dream, and thought I was fucking you." Seeing us laughing he seemed astonished, and was angry when told of our game. We all washed, we men put on shirts, and he got good humoured again.

I had scarcely eaten that day, felt empty and said so

Sarah said she was hungry, he that he could eat a donkey, for he'd not had food since the morning — I had never eaten in Sarah's lodgings, for the style didn't suit me, but felt that I must eat now. "Shall I fetch something at once? It's near midnight, and all the shops will be closed." — We had been five hours at our voluptuous gambols, but it did not seem half that time.

I gave Sarah money. She fetched cut beef and ham, bread, cheese, and bottled stout, and also whiskey. — Whilst she was away, he recovered his temper and felt his cock. He said he hated "beastly cheating dreams." "Are you fond of feeling men?" "It's much nicer to fuck a woman," I replied and told him that for many years I had never put finger on a prick but my own.

Spite of dirty knives and a dingy table cloth, we all fell to at the food. — He ate ravenously and told me that the last time he had meat, a mate gave him some of his dinner. I gave him a cigar, we had more whiskey and water, the room was hot again, we sat round the fire with our shirts only on — Sarah was dressed. — He told me again about himself, and soon the conversation drifted into the fucking line. He had lost his modesty and with it much of his respect for me. Instead of only answering and saying "sir" he began to ask me questions. Just as a woman's manner alters towards a man, directly he has once fucked her, so did his alter now that I had frigged him.

I asked if he liked being frigged. — No he did not like — "spending in the air" — did I? "No" — but I did such things at times. Then Sarah alluded to his big balls, we both felt them, and such a large bag I have never seen before. He said the boys at school joked him about it. Boys know the sizes of each other's pricks.

I wanted to go on. The novelty was so great that I could not see and feel him enough; circumstances which I did not expect had brought Sarah into the fun, which increased the amusement. I am in the prime of life, and altho never attempting such wonders as some men brag of, can easily do my four fucks in an evening with a fresh woman, and sometimes more, altho then used up a little next day. I had now only spent twice and my prick seemed on fire. Wine, beer, and a full stomach soon heat a young man who has not spent for ten days. I pulled his prick about as we sat round the fire, and it readily swelled. He prayed me to desist, he'd had enough that night, but I had not. So I made Sarah take off her clothes to her chemise, and sit opposite. I sat next him smoking and looking at his prick, and feeling it at intervals.

Often in my youth, my prick has stood before my dinner was finished. A dozen times have I got up and fucked in the middle and finished dinner afterwards. — This meal began to tell on all. Sarah raised her chemise to let the warmth of the fire reach her legs, and showed her silk stockings and red garters. — "What a fine pair you have," said he — and down went his hand to his shirt. I saw a projection, and pulling up his shirt, there was his prick as stiff as ever.

"I'll frig you, and you look at Sarah's legs." He objected, had had enough of that, he would sooner fuck Sarah. — I had not brought him to fuck my woman — my letch was for frigging him. — Whilst this talk was going on I held his prick. Sarah showed us one of her thighs and told him to let me do what I liked — I had a stiff one and was dying to let out my sperm. I would frig him, and he should fuck her afterwards. A young man with a standing prick always thinks that there is enough sperm in it for any amount of fucking. — How often I have thought whilst my cock was standing and burning to be in a cunt what wonders I would do, and directly after one coition did nothing more.

I put Sarah on the bed, myself by her, him by the side of us on his back, and upside down; his belly so placed that his prick was near my shoulders, and I could conveniently feel it. His prick was throbbing with lust — I laid on Sarah with prick outside her and began frigging him. He sighed and cried out, "Oh! let me do it to her — do — oho — do." I meant to play with him long, but Sarah was lewed, placed her hand between our bellies and put my prick up her. — Then all went its own way. — If a woman means you to go on fucking when up her you can't help yourself. Without moving their bums, they can grip with their cunt muscles and grind a man's tool so that he must ram and rub. I was soon stroking as hard as I could, but holding my head on my right hand resting from the el-bow, so as to see his prick which I went on frigging. It was a longer job than before, with all our lewedness and good will, for both of us. At length out came his sperm. At the sight of it out shot mine into Sarah, who responded with her moisture, and all was quiet.

We reposed long, then I got off. "Now you may have her." — Sarah washed. He laid on the bed, and after wiping up his now thin spunk from his belly, began frigging himself up. Sarah laid down by his side an(let him feel her clean cunt, but it was useless; an(after some violent fisting of his tool, he rose saying "I'm done up" — and again we all sat down before the fire, smoking and drinking, and talking about fucking the causes and the consequences thereof.

This talk went on for an hour or so. Sarah said jeeringly to him, "Why don't you have me." — Every ter minutes he frigged his cock uselessly. Then he ate more food. — Sarah went to the watercloset, which was in a yard, and dressed partly to go there, for it was cold. — His prick looked beautiful but lifeless. — My baudiness was getting over and I was tired, but thought then came into my head — a reminiscence of my frolics with French women. But tho I had done everything but one with Sarah, I did not suggest what was in my mind before her — I had a stupid lingering modesty in me. — We were both fuddled and reckless, and Sarah now down stairs. I locked the door, saying, "If you'll promise not to tell her, I will make you stiff enough to have her." He promised. — I laid him on the bed and putting his prick in my mouth began to suck it, first with the skin on, and then gently with the skin off. The smoothness delighted me. I no longer wondered at a French woman, who told me a prick was the nicest thing she ever had in her mouth. I did exactly as it had been done to me as nearly as I recollected; spit out after the first taste, and then went on mouthing, licking, and sucking. It took effect directly. — "Oh! it's as good as a cunt," said he. It was stiffened by the time Sarah came back. I went to the door and unlocked it, he had resumed his seat, then Sarah washed her backside and went back to her seat by the fire. He'd never had his cock sucked before.

We finished the whiskey — it was getting towards one o'clock — Sarah said, "It's time we got to bed — why don't you both stop all night? — it will be cold, !or I have no more coals." The lamp was going out, and she went to the next room to fetch candles. When she came back, "If he is going to fuck you, he should begin," said I. "Yes, and I am going to bed whether he does or not." She stripped to her chemise and got into bed. "If you don't have her now, she is not to let you when I am gone, get outside the bed." — Sarah did. — With cock stiff he got on to her in a minute. I saw by a cross twist of his buttocks and a sigh that he was up her — Sarah gave that smooth, easy, wriggling jerk and upwards motion with her buttocks and thighs, which a woman does to complete the engulfment of a doodle — I put my hand under his balls. His prick up to the roots was up her cunt.

Then not a word was spoken. A long stroke ensued, and gradually after hard quick ramming, their last pleasure shewed itself. My randiness increased by watching him, I made him leave her cunt before he had well finished spending and again plunged my prick into her reeking, slippery, slimy vagina. I gloried in feeling their sperm upon me. I was not in the habit of giving Sarah wet kisses, but as I thought, I longed to meet her mouth with mine, and with our tongues joined, and hard thrusts, a pain in my pego, and slight pain in my arse hole, I spent, and Sarah spent. "My God I'm fucked out," said she.

It was three o'clock a.m. — eight or nine hours had I been in one round of excitement — I had frigged him three times and he'd fucked thrice — I had fucked six times —I had fucked in his spunk, and had sucked his prick — Sarah had been fucked quite eight times. How many times I had spent I did not then know, being bewildered with excitement and drink. — As Sarah got up she seemed dazed, sat in a chair, and said, "Damned if ever I had such a night, I'm clean fucked out." Then paying them I left. It was at our next meeting that Sarah said I had fucked her six times. In my abbreviation of the manuscript, I have omitted some of our lascivious exercises, which were in fact but a repitition of what I had done before.

I was thoroughly done up the next day, not only with spending but with excitement. My delight in handling his white prick in repose, half stiff and in complete rigidity, was almost maddening. The delight of watching his prick glide in and out of her cunt was intense. The desire and curiosity of twenty years was being satisfied. My knowledge of copulation and of the penis getting perfected. — Yet I went home in an uncomfortable frame of mind about what I had done with him. There was no one in my home just then to wonder at my being so late, to notice my excitement, or to question me, which was fortunate.

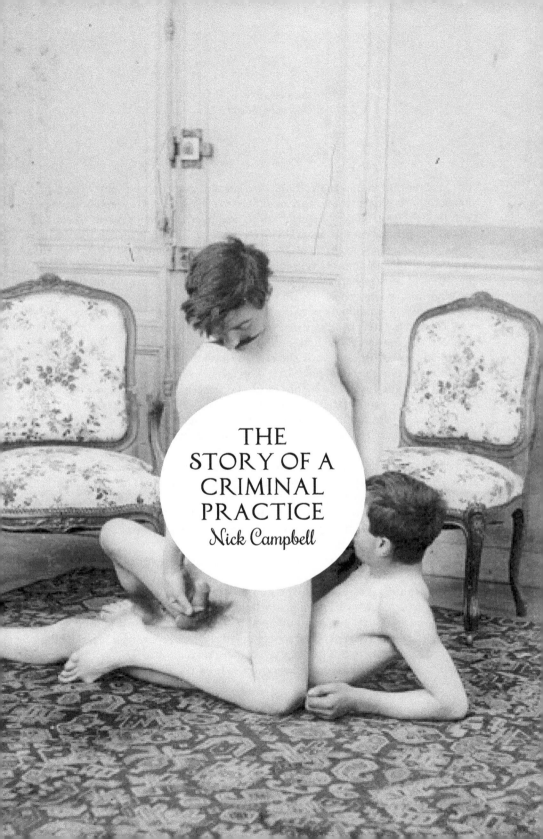

THE
STORY OF A
CRIMINAL
PRACTICE

Nick Campbell

*With apologies to E. W. Hornung
and George Cecil Ives*

"BUT MR EDWARDS," comes the refrain, whether at dinner party, literary salon or club outing, "is it true that you are on first name terms with the great Mr George Cecil Raffish?" At the very mention of his name, any women present affect to swoon, and gentlemen turn from their conversations, bending an ear, their eyes alight with schoolboy excitement. Mr Raffish of the Vauxhall Titans is a name to conjure with: it summons the very image of youthful virility, normality and clean character, of tousled hair falling over green eyes that glitter with intelligence, and of gleaming white sports kit smeared with good, clean English mud.

"Indeed," I unfailingly answer, "though I cannot claim intimacy with the man. The fact is, I struck Mr Raffish very hard before either of us were introduced, and he struck me—and what a humiliating story that is to tell!"

Nonetheless, while that is the story of how I first encountered with Mr Raffish, there is a great deal more to it than I shall ever unfurl in such company. I should be exiled from such soirees at the very least were I to go further, besmirching the name of the Church of England, not to mention the true spiritual institutions of the land: for the truth is that England's most accomplished sporting thoroughbred is a darker horse than readers of the Times would ever countenance.

I am, myself, no stranger to sport. At Magdalen College, I was drilled in a green, timeless atmosphere, playing ball games of many kinds, not infrequently coming out top. Nevertheless, coming as a grown man to the metropolis, and making my name here as a professional writer of sorts, I never thought to continue playing or even following such games, maintaining my physical acumen in the more solitary art of figure skating.

I also took long walks alone, which piqued my taste for games of quite a different hue.

One winter's afternoon, at the end of the last century, I was combining several of my interests with a visit to the floating Glaciarium, moored on the river off Charing Cross, an enterprise I understand nowadays to be losing some of its buoyancy, financially speaking, since London discovered some new fad. Nothing is assured its solidity in this great city, any more than my late father, addressing the faithful at Canterbury Cathedral, ever assured them of their immovability from this mortal sphere.

I was not looking at the crowd, as I swept across Ives' patented artificial ice. One is so constantly surrounded by the faces of strangers that, for much of the time, they blur into patterns. I was meditating on a telegram, received that morning in my rooms in Mayfair, when one saturnine face in particular became abruptly recognisable and close at hand. A second later, we were both fighting for purchase, clinging together for stability. The fact that I had been awakened out of a reverie in so violent a manner, without quite falling, should, perhaps, have been an indication of how the whole strange story was to play out for me, but alas I was not in the mood just then for reading omens, and was merely grateful to have clung to a little dignity. One does not necessarily object to being watched by a face in the crowd, but by the whole crowd—never.

They revolved around us, trying not to notice what had happened and to whom: skates sighing over the ice, ladies' skirts swishing by like columns of dark cloud, their partners in tweed knickerbockers and caps. My own cap was knocked awry, and I felt quite disarranged as if shocked suddenly out of a dream: I could not help but notice that my partner was perfectly composed, in fact hardly out of breath. This surprised me not at all. Even one like me, who did not follow sporting affairs in any detail, knew the star of the English rugby union team when he was toe-to-toe with him, not to say moustache-to-moustache. Already, I had marked the strength of his grip on my forearm through the heavy blue serge of my overcoat (without giving, I felt, any outward sign of interest in his physical prowess).

"My hat!" Mr G. C. Raffish exclaimed, for it was he. "No wonder you kept your poise so beautifully, sir. Surely I am not mistaken: you are Mr Benson Edwards, and your skill on the ice is entirely a matter of professional pride."

"You flatter me," I replied, cordially. "It has indeed been my great pleasure to fly the flag in that capacity. I must freely admit, however, that my true talents lie elsewhere. I am no Gilbert Fuchs."

"There is only reply worth making to such a statement," said the young man, with a devilish look in his eye, "and I fear I don't dare utter it here for fear of a lifetime's ban."

"Then I can surely be in no doubt of your identity," I answered, blushing. "In my experience, only a rugby player would even contemplate such a remark, and only the most untouchable amongst them would actually voice it to so new an acquaintance, Mr G. C. Raffish."

"You have me," he said with a pout. "I must apologise for such ribaldry: I am too used to the rowdy company of rugger players and quite forgot myself. Would that this were the place to sink to my knees!"

"No apology is required," I replied, with a tight smile. "I remember such youthful irresponsibility with affection. It is an honour to make your acquaintance."

I had the feeling Raffish sought to impress, for some reason: I was put in mind of undergraduates competing to win a favourite schoolmaster's esteem through feigned maturity, not able to quite disguise the disdain for authority burning in their eyes. Amusing though such displays of contradiction are, they are one of the reasons I left playing fields behind me at Magdalen, the changing room atmosphere becoming more tiring than the sport itself.

"Too kind, old boy," said Raffish, sounding almost insolently like a student addressing his tutor. "Would you forgive my irresponsibility enough to join me for supper this evening? I believe Fate has thrown us a thread, and I always grab hold of such things—if I like the colour of the wool."

"Alas, it is impossible this evening," I said, betraying myself with an involuntary smile. "I am already invited elsewhere."

"Of course," said he. "No doubt you are the recipient of constant invitations, given your rising literary profile. I have myself read your most recent volume of ghost stories, and by jove, but it made me quake."

I could not resist grinning at such praise. "How gratifying to hear that. I must say, I would never expect a fellow as solid as yourself to be moved by my queer little fantasies."

"Never say that, old boy," Raffish responded, patting me on the shoulder. "You are positive you cannot even join me for drinks this evening—perhaps you might bring your companion? The more the merrier, they say!"

"I'm afraid it would be out of the question," I said, blushing again; this time, at the enthusiasm of his pursuit. "I am meeting on business relating to my work as a writer—quite a delicate matter, you understand."

"I hope you don't refuse for fear of being seen with a bear like me," he went on, glancing about at the circulating crowd. "I fully understand the risks a man runs. I had the misfortune to dine the other night with Algernon Halfleigh—you know the name, of course."

"One of my rivals in the dark world of supernatural fiction," I said. "We see one another now and again in the British Museum reading room."

"And in exactly that capacity, I asked the fellow to my residence in Russell Square—" at this, the rugby ace casually passed me his card "—and you won't credit it, but the bounder turned out to be the most dreadful occultist. Desperate beyond belief to enlist me in some magical brethren he's assembling in South London."

"How awkward," I remarked.

"So you see," he said, "I do understand your scruples in choosing how to spend your time and with whom. You are a careful man, are you not?"

"My dear Mr Raffish," I said hotly, "Please rest assured I do not bracket you with occultists, communists or any other objectionable creed. I hope that in very short order, I will have the pleasure of your company at my own modest apartment in Mayfair."

He smiled. "I shall hold you to that promise, Mr Edwards. Tightly!" And with that, he skated away, and a short time later, it seemed, he vanished from the rink entirely.

I was somewhat relieved at this, having always found small talk irksome. Conversation in fictional narrative is always to some purpose, whereas in real life it frequently serves no more purpose than a dozen other perfunctory acts of social etiquette. It was flattering, of course, to be so intently pursued, and by a handsome celebrity as well, albeit one whose conversation would undoubtedly in the event prove impossibly restricted. In addition to this, discussing my appointment with such a thoroughly decent type as Raffish gave me an odd feeling of excitement. It was like the moment in a story where a man says, what a very comfortable and well-appointed room, I shall sleep well tonight, and both author and reader know that something perfectly thrilling is waiting outside the window.

A delicate matter, relating to my work as a writer? Well, that was true. And if I played my part well, perhaps there would be business, of a kind unknown or at least unmentionable to the likes of Mr Raffish.

How long had it been since Joe's first letter—typewritten and tentative—had arrived in my hand? Only a month? Or was that supposed to be a short time? The days spent in anticipation were as difficult to estimate as the depth of a valley viewed from the brink; yawning troughs of meaningless waiting.

> Dear Mr Edwards,
>   Every night I read your *The Face at the Window* in bed. Before I begin I extinguish my bedroom lamp and read by candlelight even though I know it is bad for my eyes and even somewhat dangerous. You see I am determined to create the correct atmosphere. Every night when the story is finished and the candle is out I lie trembling beneath the counterpane with an exquisite sense of terror. Ever since having seen your photograph in the newspaper I have felt a strong kinship in you, for surely you must also have experienced this sensation at the climax of your own extraordinary stories or you could not reproduce it so completely in a healthy young man like me who has been in the navy and never yet before had any thoughts in my head that resemble what you set down.
>   There are only six stories in *The Face at the Window*, plus one other—*The Cold Hands*—that I found in a copy of *Pearson's Magazine* I got at a Charing Cross Road bookstall. I read some stories over and over. I felt you should know of my feelings for your work, but I hope you do not misinterpret.

The frequency of our letters had risen. When the afternoon post was still not arrived, I found it hard to settle to my work: my stories took on unpredictable imagery. On one occasion, the half-completed manuscript had to be burned. Yet the reading of each letter was never quite the cresting pleasure that I hoped for. From the first, the meaning of each of Joe's letters looked forward to the next one, the next, however I induced him in my own handwritten replies—giving the personal touch, that I longed to have from him—never delivering the personal dimension I felt he owed me.

Dear Benson

I still cannot quite believe that you enjoin me to call you that, and me no more than a clerk while you are such a very great man: not only as a writer, of course, but as someone who I think feels as so many men who do not feel, and expresses it so subtly in your tales that only such as I who have felt the same way can know precisely what you are writing for us about.

Since you ask, yes, I do indeed read your letters in bed as I always have done your stories. Even the matter which does not relate to the supernatural I find is matter enough to bring me out in gooseflesh, and so I think the setting is highly important. It is so exciting to think that a man might speak so directly to another, and hear his voice in his head as if he were intimate with one.

I of course sent him copies of other stories, including the manuscript for one that *Pearson's* had rejected on the basis of being too close in imagery to an earlier story. In these early letters I was solely motivated to stoke inside him the strange sensation of which he spoke, the kinship that I understood—despite his naïve phrasing—only too well. Hadn't I felt that particular pleasure aroused in me again when the masculine, normal and proper George Raffish talked about 'quaking' about my scary stories? Hadn't I imagined men such as Raffish and my reader, turning the pages in a suspension of disbelief as my stories unravelled, following my misdirection, laughing at my jokes, becoming relaxed and susceptible at just the moment I told them to be: then recoiling, from the very roots of their soul, as something nasty transpired on the very next line, and uttered an incoherent moan that was calculated precisely to lower the blood to just below freezing temperature.

My Dear Benson,

Your most recent letter gave me great pleasure, though I cannot believe everything you set forth in it. I have hidden it as you suggested—I could not bear to destroy such intriguing works of fancy. I will need to read them again, I know, to extract full satisfaction from their meaning, which I suspect to be a code I am halfway to breaking.

Your explanation of the inspiration for *The Cold Hands* excited me. I have attempted to understand precisely what you meant by it. I think I am very unworldly despite my experiences and there are some things for which I do not yet have the words.

Since you ask, I will describe myself to you: I am twenty-four, a little over six foot, and my hair is fair...

The prose was not particularly scintillating, but the sentiment was irresistible and the frank manner in which he described his feelings could not help but lead me on. In an effort to explain some of what I understood him to be feeling, and perhaps even lead him to some degree of indiscretion (for surely a man who has lived at sea among sailors could not be really so innocent as this young man claimed to be) I gave him more detail about the manner in which I had enjoyed myself at Magdalen, and some of the adventures I had become involved with since renting my flat in Mayfair, which affords such easy proximity to those great Royal Parks, popular with Her Majesty's servicemen. In retrospect, perhaps I enjoyed our correspondence at the fullest when I was writing my replies, and utilising the same narrative devices as in my supernatural fiction (which, as had already been made quite clear, he was quite the aficionado of).

I engaged his sympathy and then piqued his curiosity, evoked a scene and established the parameters, holding back just enough to ensure it was his own imagination with which he was truly engaged. I pictured the counterpane gathered up around him, the pillows on which he lay, the look on his face as he read.

At last, I proposed a meeting.

> My Dear Benson,
>
> In the light of your expressed desire to meet with me and do all that you suggest we do, I have reread all your messages since received and begin to harbour suspicions as to your character and purpose. Remember that I am only a clerk, whose body and character was formed healthy and true in the strict confines of Her Majesty's naval services and in the strict obedience of Lord God Almighty.
>
> I have only been concerned all these months for your fictional writing about the condition of our immortal soul, and the dangers of such unholy presences as we are told lie in waiting to threaten, tempt and otherwise endanger our selves as we were created by the Almighty. In the light of all you have related since we met, I cannot help but imagine that you are more in the likeness of those unholy things than concerned with all that is good, as I know your late father to have been.
>
> I do beg your forgiveness if I have mistaken your character.
>
> Your dear friend,
>
> Joe

This reply had finally delivered the electric shock for which I had been labouring, desperately, it now seemed. A terrible shame rent me, and I thought several times to destroy all he had already sent me; several times, too, I composed replies to my dear reader: mollifying explanations of how he had misread me; desperate, tragic confessions of all I had meant; livid, coruscating letters accusing him of everything he had fingered me for. I wrote, reread and rewrote again and again the paper trail that led from my Mayfair flat to his rooms in the south west of the city.

And after all of that strife: a telegram from Wimbledon.

> Benson—
>   If you still wish to meet, I am in town tomorrow and will be in the Criterion at six if it pleases you. Be sure to destroy this telegram.
>   Your reader

There was next to no time to consider the proposal, besides which, I did not attempt to deceive myself: I had already decided I would go, before even I had finished reading his message. I did not think my heart could stand to live with the great burden of regret if I missed this opportunity. Then there was Joe the clerk himself, who had put his heart on paper for me so many times, even when (so it very much seemed) he had no sense of what that meant in the long run, or what it might mean if one were bold. The abhorrence in his last letter: might that not be something he directed at himself? Could I in good conscience, the son of a churchman, leave a benighted man to dine alone? And let some other hungry quean, for the Criterion was populous with them, move in and make a claim, after all that we had discussed together?

His instruction to destroy the telegram, and his choice of the Criterion bar, were both instructive. This man, I told myself repeatedly, knows to be careful.

Nonetheless, a great mystery hung over the whole affair.

The noise of the Long Bar always takes me by surprise when I enter: the effect, I suppose, of spending so much of my day in the solitude of pen and paper. The street itself is hardly less quiet, particularly in that busy district of London, where it seems men of every walk of life coincide. The place reminds me of the raucousness of the public baths when visited at the wrong time of day: a few screens and palms doing nothing to subdue the acoustic effect of so much tilework, gleaming white on the floor and fiery gold on the domed ceiling. It is always jostlingly full of every sort of man with money in his pocket, from the businessman to the brigadier: the greater number of whom, one is forced to assume, are perfectly normal men, who wouldn't bother to imagine one of them without his hat, never mind anything else.

I was drawn to my reader as though psychically he had called my name: a well-built, fair-headed man with a glass of gin before him. He was sitting alone at a table, his gaze raking the crowd. The very openness of such a look protected him; his endearing earnestness, one would have thought, pinned him as the very opposite of the 'Earnest' regulars of the Criterion.

I introduced myself, and was startled to find he was exactly as I had imagined him: heavy-lidded eyes suggestive of late night reading, a masculine purse of the mouth suitable to a man who had been some years at sea. A second later, the face had altered, as the sea changes under a shaft of sunlight, with the outbreak of a boyish smile. "I am pleased you could come, Mr Edwards," he said, in a low voice. "You look every inch your photograph."

"There's good reason for that," I said, tipping my bowler. "I was grateful of the opportunity to repair my character with you, Joe, after such a— misunderstanding." I offered him a cigarette; he accepted, and I sat down opposite him.

"What brings you into the city?"

"Nothing exciting, I'm sad to say," he replied, shyly. "I had to meet with a fellow at my bank. Money is a slippery thing, just now. I'm trying to ensure it doesn't slip away from me altogether."

"You are still engaged as a clerk?"

"That's right," he said, "in Wimbledon. It's steady. I laid a bit of money by when I was a sailor. My Dad's advice, god rest his soul."

"My own father gave me reams of good advice," I replied, politely. "I may still take some of it up, one of these days."

"It must be hard to follow in the example of a man good enough to be Archbishop," he said, with a shy smile down at his drink. "Not that you are not a good man. You show admirable charity in meeting me at all, after the message I sent you."

"Not at all. It was I who came to ask your forgiveness, if what I wrote was—misjudged," I said. "You wrote me a great many more friendly letters proportionate to the one unfriendly, remember."

"I remember," he said, and knocked back the last of his gin all of a sudden.

I waited for him to say more, and for a minute—or longer, it felt—we sat unspeaking, not quite looking at one another, as the Criterion crowd thundered on with its indistinguishable cataracts of dialogue. I observed, in quick glances, the short fair curls on his head, the clean-shaven contours of his tightly clenched jaw, the strong hands, the nervous tic of his thumb smudging beads of condensation from his glass.

"I heard men at work talking about this place," he said at last. "I never saw anything so lavish in my life. It's like a fairy palace. Have you ever been here before?"

"A number of times," I said, "when I feel in need of company. What did your colleagues say about it?"

"I only got the sense it was the sort of place a gentleman like yourself would feel most comfortable in meeting me," he said.

"Would you care to dine here?" I asked him. "Perhaps it could be my way of making amends."

"It really isn't necessary, sir," he said, looking me in the eye. "I was wrong to write you such a strongly worded letter in the first place. It was simply embarrassment at the thought that a great man like yourself should show an interest in a man like Joe Smith."

"You must disabuse yourself of such notions," I said, my heart suddenly soft as a stick of butter. "You can't tell how I looked forward to hearing from you, Joe. I felt, from the start, precisely the kinship you spoke of in your very first contact letter."

"You really enjoyed reading me?" he said, cringing a little, like the puppy he was.

"Didn't I just say it, Joe?"

"And am I not a disappointment, now that you see me off the page?"

"You look very fine," I said. My heart was beating at this point. I realised suddenly that I had not even tasted my whiskey and soda, and reached for it now.

Joe was watching me. "Very fine? Even in a room like this, full of other men?"

"You have every advantage over them, in my view. Shall we leave it at that?"

"Must we?" he said.

"Well," I said, glancing about, "exactly how much further do you see me taking it?"

"I've no idea, sir," he said. "As I believe I made clear, I've no experience in this area."

"Would you like another cigarette?" I asked him, having smoked mine down to the end. His was still alight. "Perhaps you would rather we went somewhere we could talk more freely."

"Certainly, if you are sure, sir," he said, picking up his cap. "I am staying the Victoria in Northumberland Street. It's ten minutes' walk away from here."

I wish the reader to be under no preconception. I had been in the Criterion, as I told Joe, a number of times—a great number of times might be more accurate— and there were other places, too, where I had had conversations of this kind before: a number of conversations, a great number of men. For the most part, they were guardsmen, but as often they were clerks, poets and peers. I had felt my heart race, soften, speak for me, before, and precisely as it did here. It did not mean I was accustomed to the feeling. I am a writer of supernatural fiction with a wide readership, and it does not surprise me that men, even well-educated and socially secure men as myself, should repeatedly put themselves in the positon of being frightened, three, four or five times a month if he can.

But this occasion was to prove different.

For one thing, we were not going to my rooms in Mayfair. Naturally, I would not usually advance the expense of room hire when my own bed did perfectly well, and was centrally located too. The idea that Joe, whose true character I felt I was beginning to delineate, had rented his own room for our use was touching and exciting. It also felt unprecedentedly safe.

The Hotel Victoria had something of the look of a fortress from medieval times, with over six floors of increasingly small, close-set windows. I almost imagined to glimpse a bowman crouching at one of these, but didn't think Joe would understand my reference. It was plain that Joe had given the place a false name, and as the doorman closed the grille on our elevator and took it to the first floor, I had the most serene feeling of stepping completely outside of my own life, into a zone of discreet, unencumbered freedom.

"I'm not sure if it's quite what you're used to," said Joe nervously, letting us into his room. "It was the cheapest they had, and I naturally can't judge such things."

"Neither can I, I'm sure," I reassured him, and he gave me a brief, hunted look.

We crossed to the window. The world went on, like a stage-set before the curtain has raised, unaware that it was observed: taxis trotting from Trafalgar Square to Charing Cross, men and women striding along like dolls moved by invisible hands, lost souls loitering sadly for warmth under the great gas lamps.

Joe drew the curtains and switched on the electric light, which buzzed. He locked the door, threw his cap down on the bed and began to unbutton his coat. "I feel I should ask you to tell me a story," he said, nervously.

"I suddenly can't think of any," I said, laying my hat down on the hotel dressing table.

"Can't you just make them up, like that?" he asked me, throwing the coat down and bending to untie his laces. He moved as if he was going against the clock.

I went and crouched beside him, put my cold hands on his, and kissed his angry-looking mouth. He resisted for a second, then closed his eyes and softly parted his lips, as if to speak, admitting my tongue. I gently stroked his brow, the nape of his neck, as if comforting a panicked animal. He suddenly lost his balance and fell over with a laugh.

"My," he said, "but you are well-practised, aren't you, sir?"

"Let's go carefully," I said. "I want you to enjoy yourself to the utmost."

Joe's reply was interrupted by a sudden shocking report, and a smashing sound.

We both leapt to our feet. Joe went straight to the window and pulled the curtains back almost angrily. Someone had fired from the street, directly through our hotel window.

"Do you see anything?" I said, and then thinking more clearly, "For God's sake, man, get away from the window."

"I knew it," the young man said, puzzlingly. "You wait here. I'll be back in a second."

Before I had drawn these strange events into one unified narrative, I was alone in the hotel room. I was quaking, through fully-dressed. What awful events were transpiring? Who was it outside the window, and where had my reader— my lover—gone in pursuit of him? I did not doubt that Joe would chase down his man. He was tall, athletic, and his dander was well and truly up. He had not even had time to untie his shoelaces before the peculiar attack.

Did I dare wait for Joe? Could I bear to leave him, after what we had shared?

I crept once more to the window and peered out into the starless night. As I stirred the curtains, something dropped almost absurdly from the curtains. I picked it up and examined it. It was a champagne cork.

There was a knock at the door. I turned, but could not summon breath to speak. This little mattered, for the door handle turned and swung open, admitting the unexpected figure of England's sporting champion and my interlocutor of that morning: Mr G. C. Raffish. He was carrying a jeroboam of champagne.

I balled my fists and assumed a boxing stance, vaguely recalled from my sporting days at Cambridge. Raffish looked at me with an air of bewildered good humour.

"And a very good evening to you too, old boy," he said, setting down the bottle next to my hat on the dressing table. "I've experienced warmer welcomes." Fishing in his coat pockets, he produced two fluted glasses, and began shining them on his muffler. He looked cool as the wine itself.

"Tell me what you've done with Mr Smith," I demanded.

"Mr who?" He was seemingly more occupied in pouring two glasses of fizz than in acknowledging my insinuations of violence. "You mean your coquettish young companion for this evening?"

"You know perfectly well to whom I am referring. Where is he?"

Raffish paused to consider. "I should say by now he would be approaching Pall Mall," he replied, his brow knit. "I observed him run for a train in Clapham Junction this morning, and he certainly has a lot of power, not to say stamina. If Tiger's been able to lead him correctly—and we had a terrific rehearsal this afternoon at the Oval cricket ground, you know, really invigorating—he should be able to lead him all the way into Green Park."

"I shall go and fetch the hotel manager this instant," I told him.

"Must you? Your Duval-Leroy will be quite flat by the time you get him up here," said Raffish, proffering a flute. "Besides which, in your present condition, I think he might raise his own suspicions and evict the pair of us."

"What condition is that?"

"On the very brink of sex," said the rugby stay, looking me up and down. "I'll admit, I look at you myself with the perspective of a self-confessed criminal, but then, he will certainly have a filthy mind of his own." He succeeded in giving me the glass of sparkling wine, and clinked his own glass against it. "Good man."

"A self confessed criminal?" I said, perching on the edge of the bed. "Will you please explain what dark deed brings you into my life this evening?" I tried crossing my legs to disguise what remained of my erection, but it was too uncomfortable and I abandoned the idea. Raffish sat beside me. I could smell a mingling of cologne and perspiration, and the sweet scent of Macassar on his neatly coiffed hair.

"Villainy of the blackest stripe," he said, sipping his champagne. "To whit, blackmail."

A chill went through my spine. "You fiend," I breathed. "I know, of course, that such things are done. A part of the modern world, even: the price of growing liberty, and a warning to the foolish. But such deeds are the refuge of the self-loathing, the wretched nihilist and the pauper."

"Certainly, I can't but agree," said Raffish.

"How, then, can you defend your actions?"

His eyes burned into mine. "The very idea of ascribing some moral reason for one's individual actions belongs rather more to the present century than the coming one, don't you think, Mr Edwards?" he said, in a low purr. "A Frenchman would understand me in a second, though I do wonder whether some of your own fiction doesn't show the influence of Joris-Karl Huysmans. No? I could lend you a copy, if your French is up to it. I wouldn't go as far as our mutual acquaintance, Mr Halfleigh, by invoking Satan in a parlour in Lower Norwood—but a few years ago, I involved myself in a criminal practice that has come to liberate me, body and soul, from the moral rectitude, western materialism and the utterly Victorian prudery that, together, have typified the evils of our age."

He put a hand on my thigh, and slowly moved it upwards till it found—without, I'll admit, any confusion—the raging hard-on in my underwear.

"You speak like a madman," I said, longing to kiss him.

"I'm an amateur cracksman," he replied. "A housebreaker. A trespasser. And a practicing sodomite to boot."

"And now," I said, "you've inveigled your way in here to blackmail myself and Mr Joe Smith? Are those the plain facts?"

Raffish unbuttoned my trousers and reached inside. "Quite the reverse. I'm here to steal your letters away from Mr Jonathan Smythe, who has already blackmailed eight of our brethren in the last six months."

I drew back. "Surely you are not serious, Mr Raffish?"

"It is a very serious matter, Mr Edwards," he said, leaning in and pressing me against the bed. "That being said, at this very moment I'm just having a good time."

"But how did you know I was meeting him here?" I asked, succumbing to his strong, sure touch and the weight of his muscular frame, accentuated by his rich fragrance.

"Ah, I've been too close, haven't I? You see, I've been watching him for some time," he said, undoing my waistcoat with a housebreaker's ease. "One of his victims involved me. We noticed him make your acquaintance at the Criterion in autumn last year."

"I don't recall that," I said, arching my back in pleasure as he undid my shirt and kissed my body through my woollen vest. "He looked familiar to me this evening, but I thought—"

"His technique is well developed," said Raffish, descending kiss by kiss down my abdomen and into my open trousers. "A colleague of mine has been monitoring his telegrams. I've been moving as carefully against him as he against you, Mr Edwards."

"Call me Benson," I said, watching him take my member in his mouth.

"Benson," he said, licking me with extreme joie de vivre, "you taste like a man who's enjoyed months of titillation. I don't know you can have borne it."

"What was all that business at the ice rink today?" I asked, returning the attention at last by unbuttoning his expensive linen shirt with trembling fingers, while he caressed me with a strong but delicate grasp.

"I contrived to run into you there," he explained, as he went in less than a minute from a uniquely well-dressed man to one who was not dressed in the slightest. His athletic musculature rippled in the breeze from the broken window. "I was trying, in a manner of great subtlety, to warn you. But you were drunk on lust, weren't you?"

Once more, we grappled together on the hotel bed, his neat coiffure now a lacquered mess, the taste of his person, oozing like butter on hot bread, delicious in my mouth. What a heroic creature, I thought, when I did think, and alternately, what a true scoundrel.

Now he withdrew, smiling like the devil himself. "I'm glad you met him, though. I like a man who runs to catch the ball, even when circumstances are against him. Besides, it's good that you see this."

"See what?"

"My proof," he said. "Perhaps it'll teach you a lesson, you soft-hearted marjorie." He dropped to the floor and pulled a leather briefcase out from under the bed. "As soon as he left this morning, I inveigled my way into his house in Clapham. It was easy: like his house wanted me inside it. But there wasn't a sign of the papers—which means, he must carry them with him." He clicked open the case. "See."

I leant in, and I saw—clothes. A shirt. A change of trousers. Underwear.

Raffish rifled angrily through Joe's things. "Not here," he said tersely. "Of course—the hotel safe!"

At that very second, we heard raised voices in the hall. One of them was unmistakably Joe's. Heart pounding—when had it stopped that evening?—I ran to the window and threw up the sash. Outside was a narrow parapet. "Out here," I said, urgently. "Now!"

Raffish was pulling on clothes and stuffing them simultaneously back into the case. His hair was tousled, but he moved with practiced cool, even when a fist pounded heavily on the door and a voice demanded, "Open up! I am an officer of the law!"

The amateur cracksman was out of the window, the sash lowered, the curtains drawn, at exactly the instant the door swung open and the aforesaid officer stormed in, accompanied by so-called Joe Smith and a fit looking young man wearing a rugby jersey and a hangdog expression.

"Right! Let's get to the bottom of this, shall we?" The officer flung the door shut, straightened his tunic and stood to attention as though expecting the arrival of a superior officer, at which point he seemed to register my state of undress, not to mention the pink, hard prick sticking out of my trousers. "Well," he said. "This affair seems to grow stickier by the minute, don't it, gents!"

Joe was looking at me penetratingly; I also noticed him, noticing the suitcase.

The other man was intently inspecting his hands.

"Tiger!" I exclaimed, making the stranger raise his reddened face. "How have you been caught up in all this? Officer, accept my word as a gentleman, this lad is innocent as the day is long."

The police officer narrowed his eyes. "Is that so, Mr...?"

"Benson," I answered. "Mr Edward Benson, of Mayfair."

"Oh," he said. "Yes, I thought I knew the face. Well, sir, the fact is that the length of a day is what you'd call a variable quantity. At this time of year, it can be rather dark and suspicious looking even by early afternoon. And this fellow was being pursued through Green Park in a decidedly murky twilight."

"Indeed, officer," I said, thinking he was laying things on a bit thick.

"I don't wish to make trouble, officer," Joe said in a thin voice.

"Whatever you wish ain't necessarily on the cards, my dear fellow," said the solid fellow in blue. "You are apprehended, pursuing a man through one of the most notorious sodomitical pleasure grounds north of Vauxhall; you claim he has some vendetta against you, but can give no detail; your hotel room, I discover, contains one rather excited-looking writer of the fantastic and sometime champion figure skater. If that's not trouble, I don't wot but what it is, sir." He beckoned to me. "I'm going to go outside and take statements from these two men, sir, and I'll be coming back for you—potentially with reinforcements. Do you comprehend me, sir?"

Joe was watching me now. The face that had earlier been flushed was now white; the innocent smile he had earlier shone me, he now looked incapable of. I wondered whether, had Raffish not intervened, this might not be the point in the evening when, satisfied and sticky, he made his first demands of me, and began the slow destruction of my life.

Instead, I followed the other pair into the hall, shut the door of the hotel room and never saw hide nor hair of the bounder again.

Raffish was waiting for us, wearing (I saw at once) the suit of clothes we had found in Joe's suitcase. Joe's cap was on his head, his coat was on his shoulders. He carried a small packet of papers. "Good heavens, Benson," he said, with a concerned look. "I've just been reading your letters. You're absolutely filthy, aren't you?"

"Jolly good," said the police officer, placing his hand on my arse. "Do I get to read them? I think I deserve some sort of payment after that little performance in there. You should pop in and see his face, Raffish."

"Performance?" said Tiger. "You want to get chased through the capital by a six foot bugger who thinks he's just been shot at! You had the easy job, Maurice."

"In any case," said Raffish, "you really ought to straighten yourself up, Benson. You make me feel like I'm in a bordello. And we ought to leave before the manager gets too good a look at me and notices that I'm nearly a foot shorter than I was this morning."

"But can it really be," I said, when, having regained my composure and refastened my collar stud, we arrived at Raffish's rooms, "that the three of you are accustomed to working as a team in such affairs?"

"The three of us? God bless you," said our host, leading us to his bedroom, from which arose the murmurings of conversation. "Don't you know how many players are in a rugby squad? Come, let me introduce you to the team, and we can finish what was so rudely interrupted."

Our two companions went in ahead of us, and a cry of welcome went up from a great quantity of interesting-sounding men. I hesitated before entering, determined to thank Raffish for his daring rescue: for preventing my moral and financial ruin, and my humiliation.

"My dear fellow, you've no need to thank me," he said. "I've not had such a successful day in ages. Not only did I burgle that villain's instruments of darkness, and his hat; I also stole a delicious looking figure-skater from underneath his nose, and he'll know that by now, the poor bugger." He kissed me with sudden excitement on the mouth. "This calls for more Duval-Leroy, I think. To toast the splendour of a life of crime!"

And I don't think I could agree more.

PROGRESS
BE DAMNED

Rob Rosen

TRUTH WAS, I simply missed my father. Poor soul was laid to rest barely sixth months ago, taken from us under mysterious circumstances. Mother was still beside herself with grief, which is why, when I saw the sign tacked to the wall of the pub, I decided to act upon it.

Spectacles were all the rage up in London these days, drawing enormous crowds of onlookers, all eager to witness the mediums who communicated with the dead, who conjured ghosts. I'd heard it was quite exciting to behold, though I remained a skeptic just the same.

And so, for mother's sake, if not my own, I made plans to attend the event the following week's end. London was only an hour away by train, which I generally only used to visit Brighton, to act the tourist, London being too large for the likes of me, too modern.

And, yet, to London I soon found myself travelling.

The train cars were packed, people bustling this way and that in all their finery, making the most of this new luxury now afforded them. The men were dressed formally, clad largely in dark tailcoats and trousers, in matching dark waistcoats, bow ties, shirts with winged collars. They were, by and large, clean-shaven, which had again become the style. As for me, I still wore my beard long, figuring the custom would eventually return, thereby saving me the chore of shaving.

The women, I noticed, were fancier than the men, most wearing the boning that made their waists as small as possible. I wondered, as I stared at them, how they breathed, especially with the high collars that seemed to threaten to throttle them at any moment. Then again, women held little fascination for me, and so my wonder was fleeting at best.

In any case, quickly bored with staring at the latest fashions, I gazed out at the countryside instead. I'd not been to London in quite some time, and was amazed at the shrinking cattle land, at the disappearance of farms, all of it giving way to more and more towns, as if London was expanding ever outward. I mused at what the future held. Mused, that is, and feared it just the same.

Father worried about such things as well. Is this what lead to his untimely death? Would the medium be able to shine some light on that? All this I thought about as the city grew nearer and nearer with each passing second.

We rounded a bend. London came into view. The women around me squealed in delight. Even I was caught up in the excitement, especially once we pulled into the mammoth station a short while later, the train screeching to a deafening halt.

Minutes after that, I was standing in London proper. Massive brick and stone and glass structures rose high above. Gone were the wood and mortar buildings, the dirt roads giving way to cobblestone. The streets were teaming with life, children running between the horse-driven carriages that seemed to outnumber people these days. In the distance, I saw smoke belching up from factories. The London from my youth has almost completely vanished. And I? Well, I felt like a bee in a hive, Queen Victoria leading the entirety of the bustling apian colony.

I was not alone in my desire to see the great mystic perform; evidence to this were the several hundred people who had already amassed by the time I'd arrived, all of them paying their entrance fee without complaint, clamoring around the makeshift stage, eager to see the show. Even I, naysayer that I was, grew excited. After all, I was on a mission to perhaps speak once again with my late father, to perhaps ask him questions from the beyond the grave, to discover some hidden truth; I found myself pushing through the crowd, eager to see the spectacle from up close.

Then, suddenly, from behind a curtain appeared a man dressed all in silken reds. I could see that he was young, handsome, the features magnificently etched across his face. He spoke with a megaphone, his voice deep, resonating, piercing through to my very soul. The crowd hushed in an instant.

"Friends," he said, his sparkling eyes of blue taking us in, clothes billowing in the breeze. "I, the great Mephisto, have been given a gift, a gift that allows me to bridge the gap between the living and the dead. I have travelled a great distance to share this gift with you today." He moved the megaphone away from his face. He smiled so beguiling that my prick throbbed within my slacks. As if he could sense it, his eyes suddenly caught my own. "Friends, prepare to be astounded!"

A giant puff of gray smoke all at once erupted form the stage. The crowd coughed and shrieked, but otherwise stayed in place. When the cloud at last broke, Mephisto was no longer standing; he was now seated at a table that had magically appeared on stage, a heavy cloth covering it. The megaphone was again held up high. "Friends," he said again. "I require a volunteer!"

Every hand in the crowd eagerly went up, my own included. Shots of, "Pick me! Please, pick me!" rose up from every direction, echoing off the great stone structures that ringed the area we found ourselves in.

Mephisto scanned the crowd. He pointed to an older women dressed in outdated clothes, a mess of unkempt hair towering above her head. She quickly bounded onto the stage. "Whom do you wish to speak with, my dear?" he asked her.

Her eyes went wide. "Me husband," she replied, in a thick cockney accent. "Bugger hid me money before he croaked."

The audience laughed, nervously. Mephisto nodded and again lifted the megaphone. "Spirits!" he shouted. "Bring forth this dear woman's husband!"

The stage beneath us shook as another great burst of smoke poured forth from seemingly everywhere at once. My eyes burned, and I coughed as a tear streamed down my cheek.

When the smoke again cleared, Mephisto was still seated, except now his chair was floating a couple of feet higher than before. The crowd gasped as one, myself included. I tried to look beneath the table, but the heavy cloth prevented me from doing so. Said table shook as the stage had previously done, my body trembling right along with it.

I stared at Mephisto. His eyes had curled back in his head, his neck tilted in reverse. When he spoke, he no longer needed the megaphone.

"Honey, that you?" It too came out coarse and cockney.

"Charles!" shouted the woman. "It's me husband, Charles!" She was crying. There were actual tears. If she was an actress, a plant, she was surely adept at her craft. "Charles!" she shouted again. "Where's me money?"

The chair that Mephisto was seated in floated an inch higher, swaying as it did so. Again, the crowd gasped. There was a pause before the spirit replied. "I'm sorry, love," it eventually said. "I gambled all the money away."

The woman moaned. The crowd tittered. The chair floated back down to the stage. Mephisto turned to the woman. "Did that answer your question, my dear?"

The woman frowned. "I shoulda listened to me ma. She told me not to marry that louse."

The crowd exploded in laughter. Clearly they were getting their money's worth.

This went on for quite some time: Mephisto chose his volunteers, there were great theatrics, Mephisto spoke in numerous voices. It was impossible to tell what was real and what was not. The crowd dispersed when the show had ended, seemingly elated with the outcome.

Me, I wasn't so sure. Not to mention, I hadn't been chosen as a volunteer, hadn't spoken with my late father. And so, with the crowd going in one direction, I went in the other, heading behind the stage.

I found him alone, in a small wooden makeshift room. "I've been expecting you," he said, with a smile, a swarm of butterflies suddenly loose inside my belly.

Up close, I could see he had makeup on, some sort of white powder. Still, he was handsome, those eyes of his shining through like starlight. "You have?"

He shrugged. "The great Mephisto sees all, knows all." Without the megaphone and the echo of the buildings, he sounded less, shall we say, *great.* "You've come to speak with someone, yes? Someone who has passed?" I nodded, eager despite my misgivings. The smile rose on his face as my prick rose inside my slacks. "Twenty shillings, my friend."

Twenty shillings was a week's worth of pay for me. Still, I'd come prepared. I moved in, gazing into those maginificent pools of blue. "Ten, and maybe we can come to some sort of... *understanding.*" I winked. I stroked the silk of his shirt, my finger twirling around a pert nipple within.

A deal had been struck in the moan that followed. He backed an inch away. The smile remained, though now tinged with something more like lust than showmanship. The red shirt was lifted above his head. Mephisto was lean, his torso dense with tight muscle, a smattering of ebony hair splaying his chest. He'd clearly been a laborer at one time, perhaps a farmhand. His lot in life had seemed to improve as of late.

I watched intently as he kicked off his slippers, the silken slacks falling to the ground next, his cock springing free. He was slight; it was large. Here was a beguiling dichotomy to behold.

My moan echoed his as I sunk to my knees, eager to suck him down my throat. He moved in, the one-eyed beast charging my way. I blinked. It parted my lips. I blinked again. It went all the way inside, my lips now brushing the wiry hairs that sprung from his heavy balls. I breathed him in. He smelled of musk, of sweat. You could become rich and successful, but that intoxicating rutting aroma stayed with you.

I stared up, locking eyes with him, my fingers through his thick bush and up his flat belly. He fucked my face all the while. Still, ten shillings these days got you far more than merely that.

I popped his prick out of my mouth. He sighed as his meat swung free, glistening in the dim light of the kerosene lamp that illuminated the small enclosure. I smiled up at him. "Do you prefer to act the bull or the cow?"

He grinned. He sunk to his knees, joining me on the dirt floor. He brushed his lips across mine. Men tended not to kiss other men, at least not out in the country. Perhaps things were different in the city, or perhaps simply in that shack of his. Either way, I kissed him back, relishing his tongue as it snaked and coiled around my own. He then fell on his back. "*Moo*," he said, by way of an answer.

He lifted his legs up and out, rigid prick pointing to the wooden ceiling, balls draping down. I'd never considered men beautiful before; Mephisto was the exception. And yet I wondered just how exceptional he was, at whether he was a swindler or not. Either way, of course, he was still getting good and fucked.

I undressed, spit into my hand and slicked up his hair-rimmed hole before my own thick prick, which throbbed in my grip. In I slid, slowly, gently. He sucked in his breath. His hole tightened. I waited until he nodded for me to continue. Further I slid, further still, goosebumps forming up my arms as my eyelids fluttered, a moan escaping from between my lips. As I fucked him I took hold of his prick, stroked him.

I grinned. The great Mephisto at least lived up to his name in some ways, I quickly realized.

I plunged harder now, deeper, filling him up to the quick. His prick was so thick in my hand it was almost impossible to keep hold of it. He was panting now, thrashing on the dirt floor. Sweat was flinging off my brow and down onto his rapidly expanding and contracting chest. We were both close, so close.

"Together," I rasped.

Again he nodded. I rammed my prick into his depths one final time. He let out a satisfied grunt, his cock exploding in my grip a second later. I came with him, a geyser of come erupting inside him before dripping down to the dirt below. All the while, his cock was spewing, spunk flinging this way and that, pooling in white gobs on the otherwise brown floor.

I retracted my prick from his portal. "Now then," I said, very well spent. "Time for that spectacle we agreed upon."

He chuckled as he pushed himself onto his elbows. "I think I already done gave you one, mate," he said, his accent decidedly less posh than it had been before.

I knew it then: he was a scoundrel, a fraud, despite him being an excellent fuck. Still, I had come this far, and so I persevered in my mission. I helped him up, brushed him off, even allowed him a kiss, seeing as such delights came few and far between. Then, once again dressed, we proceeded to the business end of our arrangement.

Outside we went. He led me to the stage. The place was utterly deserted, the sounds and smells of London hanging at the periphery. A cold sweat appeared on my forehead. I knew that none of this could be real, but still my knees shook as I sat on the chair across from him.

"Who is it you'd like to speak with?" he asked.

I gulped. "My father."

He nodded. He closed his eyes. He placed his hands flat on the table.

"Spirits!" he shouted. "Bring forth this man's father!"

As before, the stage shook, the table rocked, and a cloud of smoke gushed forth from beneath table. My entire body trembled, both in fear and in anticipation. Mephisto's eyes went wide. His mouth gaped open before he uttered, "Jonathan, is that you?"

My back went rigid. Mephisto didn't know my name; I'd never given it to him. "Father?"

Mephisto's neck nodded, rigidly. "How'd you find me, son?"

I couldn't help but laugh. "Long story," I replied. "But listen, we don't have much time. Your body was found floating in the lake. I watched you swim countless times and you were strong and fearless; I cannot believe that you could have drowned?" I gulped yet again. "Were you... murdered?" The last word came out in a hushed whisper.

Again Mephisto's neck rigidly rose up and down, his eyes unblinking as a bead of saliva dribbled down his chin. Where once he'd been handsome, he suddenly appeared gruesome. This, I realized, was the true Mephisto. I shivered at the sight of him, then shivered even more so upon the answer. "It was the trains, son. They wanted our land for a new line. Progress they said. Almost the Twentieth Century, they said. I told the man they sent to bugger off. Guess he didn't take my reply too well."

I nearly cried. "Tell me who he is, father," I pled. "Tell me who he is so I can bring him to justice."

My father laughed. All things considered, it was a strange sound to be coming from a dead man. "The cad who killed me? The buffoon, the ruffian, the...fraud?"

"Fraud?" I repeated, staring into those unblinking eyes of blue that gazed back at me.

"Fraud!" bellowed my father. "And he sits before you now, son, fired from the railroad after cheating them. He now cheats others... but no longer." Again the laughter streamed forth. "Justice you asked for? Worry not about that, son, for justice I shall soon have."

With that, Mephisto at last blinked. It was to be the last time he'd ever do so. He coughed. He rasped. It seemed as if he was being suffocated, his life snuffed out from the inside as opposed to the out. He thrashed as he clutched his chest, and with his final dying breath, he said, "I see all, I know all."

I rose from the chair. "Perhaps," I said. "But certainly not any longer."

Out of curiosity, I looked beneath the table. Mephisto's foot had been on a contraption that could pump out smoke. The chair he sat on was lifted by some sort of mechanical device. He was indeed a fraud. In fact, he was a fraud and a murderer.

I kicked over his chair. His lifeless body fell to the floorboards. I walked off the stage, not looking back. "And don't worry, father," I said, staring up at the azure sky. "I'll never sell your land, not ever." A grin suddenly eclipsed my frown. "Progress be damned."

LUC
ORPHELIN
AND THE
HODAG OF
RHINELANDER

Charles Payseur

Luc was convinced there wasn't a single comfortable seat in the whole of Wisconsin. From his time in Madison, the city roiling under threat of labor riots and anarchist plots, there had been only a string of awkward meetings, first with Robert La Follette, the supposed governor, and then with his wife, Belle Case, and his daughter, Fola. Then the damnable trip aboard the decrepit Gilmore Skyship, a ratty contraption with cramped metal seats and not even a tea service to recommend it. The least the state government could have afforded an official representative of the Interstate Commerce Commission was a private berth on a Union Airtrain. Truly, it would have only cost an extra day.

"Are you even paying attention?" Fola asked, and Luc scowled, brought a hand up to twist up the end of his mustache. Probably there would be nowhere in town to buy wax, and Luc's own supply was beginning to dwindle. He could perhaps send a telegram to Washington, to President Roosevelt himself even. If he knew how his agent was being treated...but no, imagining the reaction of the President to such a request was...unpleasant.

"Sir, I said are you ev—"

"Mademoiselle Fola, I assure you that none of this captivating discussion is lost on me," Luc said. Really he needed his vanity case and some time alone, but ever since disembarking, as glorious as it was to feel solid ground again, he had been rushed to introductions and meetings, a series of wooden seats that smelled like they were fresh from the mills and were probably ruining his second best suit.

"I just wondered what you thought about Annie Taylor's claim that the disappearances are caused by—"

"Hodags?" Luc asked, and snorted. "I think that perhaps Madame Taylor is letting her...imagination get away from her."

Which was putting it lightly. But then, few would say it to her face. Not to the woman who had gone over Niagara in a barrel. Not to the woman who, after her manager had stolen the barrel and skipped out to Chicago, tracked him down and ended him to the song of her pistol's report. Newly released after her acquittal in Illinois, she was hot for some positive press, and apparently monster hunting was her new adventure. And she wasn't alone.

"Surely you must admit that the coroner's report matches the lore and the legend." The voice was decidedly British, raised above the grumbling of the crowd assembled in the small town hall. Weston Colt, Monster Hunter extraordinaire, whose adventures across Africa and Asia were serialized in *McClure's*. Utter poppycock, though the man did cut a good figure in the leathers of a trapper and a cleanly shaved face. And he did his best to match the prose. Obviously a criminal of some sort, though, with something to hide.

"What I must admit is that the coroner is a souse and logging accidents are hardly uncommon," the administrator of the meeting countered. Webster Brown was a serious man and a rich one, with connections to half the businesses in Rhinelander and three other towns besides. As the local Representative to Congress he was one of the most influential local personages. That he was strongly against the investigation and both the Governor's and the President's interest was not lost on Luc. And that mustache! It looked like a moth had taken up residence on his upper lip.

"There is something dark in the woods, Sir," said Deacon Bradley, owner of Bradley's Lumber, the largest outfit in a hundred miles. "It's those damned Ojibwa. They've conjured these beasts out of our nightmares to punish us. Madison has turned a blind eye to the clear evidence that there are tribes still hiding from relocation and this is where their bleeding hearts have led us all."

"Whatever the case, Sirs," Madame Taylor said. She stood for the first time during the meeting, and pulled up the gun belt she wore conspicuously over the waist of her dress. "I will be leading an expedition into the forests in pursuit of these creatures. If they are new hoaxes, as the esteemed Congressman believes, then we will find them out. And if they are real, then I will upholster my barrel with hodag hides."

Luc rolled his eyes. Her barrel. Her eyesore. It stood proudly on the deck of Monsieur Colt's private airship. Somewhere along the way she had it bronzed and engraved with her name and the date of her trip over the Falls. Ridiculous.

With a curt nod she turned and left, Colt trailing in her wake. The silence of her departure lasted only a moment before evaporating into a thunder of voices.

"And I, Sir, will not allow my workers to be terrorized," Bradley said. "I will take whatever means necessary to protect what is mine." And with that he left as well.

Luc maintained his seat, as uncomfortable as it was. He waited. He watched.

"I don't mean to question your investigative techniques, Sir, b—"

"A fact I much appreciate," Luc said. "For while I realize that your mother was quite keen on your taking part in discovering the truth behind these disappearances and murders, she was also quite clear that while accompanying me you were to respect my methods."

Fola crossed her arms and sighed loudly. "Not that I've seen much in the way of methods," she said, then started as if just catching his words. "Wait, murders?"

"Of course," he said. "I, too, have seen the coroner's report, and noted where and when the disappearances and attacks occurred. Axes may slip, yes, but they do not crack trees in half or leave grooves in the earth as deep as three feet. Unless the ax belongs to Paul Bunyan, but you do not look one to believe in such, how do you say, tall tales?"

Fola regarded him a long moment, wariness etched in her features, before nodding.

"But if you think these men were murdered, then are you saying you believe the reports that a hodag was responsible for the incidents?" she asked.

Luc shook his head. "No," he said. "No I do not." But he said no more. He could read Fola's eyes, and knew she, too, had more than her share of secrets, and he wasn't about to give her more.

With the departures of Madame Taylor and Monsieur Bradley, the rest of the crowd slowly trickled away, and finally Luc stood and made his way to the front of the room. When he arrived he could see the obvious disdain with which Congressman Brown regarded him. Well, at least it ran both ways.

"If I wanted a Frog I would have visited a nearby pond." He spoke not to Luc but around him, to Fola. "You can tell your father that there is no call for the federal government to get involved. As a politician and businessman I can assure you I will let it be known that such an intrusion is not only uncalled for but sets a dangerous precedent."

"As a politician *and* businessman, sir," Luc said, "you might forget that government does not exist solely to ease your turning of profits. There are people dying, *Congressman*, and I have been tasked with discovering why and how, as you yourself seem incapable of."

"Don't think that y—"

"And for your elucidation," Luc went on, cutting off whatever Brown had been about to say, "I am not French, but French Canadian. Good day." With a smile Luc tipped his hat and turned sharply.

Fola fell in beside him, stifling giggles, and they exited the hall to the bright summer day. And, of course, waiting for them on the street just outside was a small group, Annie Taylor and Deacon Bradley at their head.

"Mister Orphelin," Bradley said, sweeping off his hat in a small bow. "I wonder if we might have a word."

LUC GRIPPED THE railing of the airship, Weston Colt's *Ravager*, and tried to imagine himself in a cafe in Quebec. Happy. Before that business with Teddy Roosevelt in New York with the anarchists and the "ghosts." Before he was conscripted. Before he had ever heard of Rhinelander, Wisconsin.

A presence beside him made him turn, and there was Weston Colt himself, tall and chiseled and—the ship lurched a bit and Luc cursed and held on even tighter.

"Should you not be piloting, Monsieur Colt?" Luc asked.

Weston laughed instead of answering right away, and stepped closer still, wrapped his arm around Luc's back, pressed his body against Luc's side. For his part, Luc did not shrink away, enjoyed the warmth of their closeness even as he didn't allow himself to waver in his focus.

"Call me Wes," he said. "And try not to worry about the ship. Your Miss Fola was eager to learn how to pilot him, and I saw no reason to stop her. Knows her way around tech, does your Miss Fola."

Luc swallowed and nodded. "Indeed she does," he said. "But tell me, you said 'him.' Is it not bad luck to call your ship after a man?"

"Some say that it's unnatural for ships to fly, too," he said, and pushed just a little against Luc's side, "but I think people have a rather skewed view of what's unnatural and not, unlucky and not. Ships fly. And captains name them for their desires, regardless of how distasteful some find it."

Without entirely meaning to Luc found himself bucking slowly against the pressure, hips pushing as if imagining...but he stopped himself. It may have been a long time since anyone looked at his admittedly soft and round physique and had thoughts of a carnal nature, but Luc would not let it distract him. Yet.

"How do you find working for Madam Taylor?" Luc asked, and Wes shifted back a half-step, though his hand remained wrapped around Luc's back, an anchor as the ship trembled in the wind.

"She's strong," Wes said, and Luc waited for some qualification that never came. Luc smiled.

"It doesn't bother you that she was accused of murder?" he asked.

"That's all behind her," Wes said. "She beat the conviction, after all."

"Yes, by convincing the jury that she didn't know her weapon was loaded," Luc said. A ploy that the Chicago jury had swallowed whole, eager to see a woman clueless and clumsy, distraught at having accidentally slain her former business partner.

"If she had told them that she had killed him in an honest duel they would have hanged her," Wes said, and Luc knew that as well. A woman who was an idiot the jury had no problem with. A damsel in need of protecting. A woman who could shoot better than a man, though? That was another thing entirely. She was far more clever than the jury had given her credit for.

"You're not afraid, though, for when she finds out that you're not Weston Colt?" Luc could feel Wes tense, realized perhaps a bit late that it would be an easy thing for the man to push him over the rail and claim the meddlesome foreigner had tripped. The justice system left so much to be desired.

"I don't know what you're talking about," Wes said.

"Gentlemen," came a voice from behind them, cutting off their conversation. Wes quickly moved away, and both men turned to face the newcomer. Deacon Bradley approached with a frown on his face.

"You're sure it's appropriate to let a woman pilot your craft?" Bradley asked. Wes rolled his eyes.

"I thank you for allowing us to begin our investigation at your logging camp, Monsieur," Luc said. "You said that you are afraid that it will be the next attacked?"

"Damned right," he said. "Three camps have been hit so far, all in a direct line to my biggest operation."

"These camps that were hit, they were other large camps?" Luc asked.

Bradley shrugged. "Not really," he said. "Two of them were brand new, upstarts funded by Chicago money. The most recent was an outfit looking to expand from Appleton."

"An outfit in which Congressman Brown has a controlling interest, if I am not mistaken?" Luc asked.

"You really were paying attention. Yes, Webster was behind the move. Though I think now he'll think twice about trying it again."

"Funny that he'd be so against the investigation if he had personally taken a hit in an attack, though," Wes said.

Luc twisted his mustache between two fingers. "Not especially," he said, flashing a small smile but saying nothing more. Yet.

Wes and Bradley both frowned at him, but before they could ask a question there was the sound of the ship's foghorn sounding. They all flinched at the noise.

"Trouble," came the cry the second the horn ceased, and they saw Fola leaning against the railing outside the helm, pointing out in the woods where tendrils of smoke were beginning to snake their way into the sky.

"My camp," Bradley cried, and Wes rushed back across the deck to the helm. Luc kept his eyes on the smoke and gripped the railing firmly.

"I suggest you hold on, Monsieur," he said to Bradley. Wes was hardly going to be gentle in getting them to their destination, and for once Luc couldn't object. Too much. The *Ravager* shuddered as it picked up speed, steam billowing out of its many chimneys. Luc would really have to insist on getting a place on a proper ship for his return to Washington. Or even a train. It would be nice, after all, to not have to worry about falling out of the sky.

The camp was much as Bradley described, which is to say nothing fancy. A few barracks-style buildings housed the workers and everything else was saws and machinery to get the lumber ready to move. Luc's eyes followed the lines of smoke back to the ground. One of the buildings was on fire and it looked like one of the walls had been smashed in. And there, through the smoke and trees—what was that?

Luc's eyes widened. There did indeed look to be a creature, as big as four horses put together, moving through the trees, cloaked in smoke but just visible enough to see the features. A great tail that swished from side to side, felling trees where it struck them. Squat arms and legs, and a face of gleaming malice. It turned toward the ship, pausing a moment as Wes aimed the *Ravager* at the creature, and then plunged further into the woods, was lost to the thick press of trees as they approached.

"A hodag," Bradley was saying, voice somewhere between excited and awed. "I told you. A real hodag."

Luc pursed his lips. "So it would appear."

A search of the camp yielded little but five dead loggers and a mostly-destroyed dormitory. There were the same broken trees and grooves where the hodag had moved, but no other hard evidence.

"A good thing we scared it off when we did," Bradley said as he surveyed the damage. "We're only out a few days at most."

"And the lives of five people," Fola said. Luc nodded. Five more murders. He had seen enough.

"If you will, I think it is time to reconvene in Rhinelander," he said.

"You can't mean immediately," Bradley said. "It's nearly dark now. We'll have to wait out the night here."

'Wait in a camp that has just been attacked?" Luc asked.

"Surely the danger is gone now that we're here?" Madame Taylor said, patting the pistols at her side.

"No," Luc said. Suddenly he forgave the haste that had been required in getting him here. There could be no delay now. "No, we must return at once. Please to gather everyone on the ship, and I will meet you there in ten minutes."

"Now look, I don't know what kind of game you're playing at, Mister Orphelin, but—" Bradley began, but Madame Taylor coughed and pulled at her gun belt.

"He has a point," she said. "And as much as I'm hot to track the hodag, my bones aren't as young as they used to be. I'd much prefer the beds at the hotel over whatever passes for a mattress out here."

Luc smiled, his esteem for her rising, and nodded in appreciation. "Just so," he said. "It is not in the modus operandi of the creature to return to the same site twice, either, so any delay will just confirm what we already know."

"Then why do you need to stay an extra ten minutes?" Fola asked. At least she was paying attention.

Luc gave a tight smile. "As I said," he said, "I want to confirm one thing I already know."

The others grumbled, but gave in.

LUC BARELY CONTAINED a growl as he regarded himself in the mirror. His clothes were nearly ruined. It had drizzled on the way back to Rhinelander. Drizzled. He lit a small candle, slid it into place to melt the wax he required. Carefully he stripped, leaving his second best suit for the staff to clean. If it didn't go according to plan, at least he had left his best suit back in Washington. He dressed in fresh clothes and quickly brushed himself. When the wax was ready he sculpted his mustache and trimmed the stray hairs. Finally he looked nearly human again, and with the addition of a dry hat he was ready.

They were waiting in town hall, and from the look of them they had not taken the opportunity to freshen up. Luc walked in, paused as everyone stood and faced him.

"You'd better have a good reason for making us wait," Congressman Brown said, his ridiculous mustache making it hard to determine if he was frowning or not.

"I assure you there is good reason for everything I do," Luc said.

"Well you could have fooled me," Brown said, sneering.

"Not a difficult task, Monsieur," Luc said, "for you have been fooled by every person here."

"Now see here," he said, taking a step closer.

Luc did not back down. No, his immaculate mustache was like a shield from scorn. He would not be bullied by a waif of a man. "No, you see," he said. "See what is right in front of you. Just because you are obviously engaged in illegal smuggling does not mean that you can turn a blind eye on murder and corruption."

"I beg your pardon, sir—"

"You should," Luc said, advancing still, and now Brown took a step back. "You should beg that I do not report to President Roosevelt of your *business practices*. Why else would you discourage an investigation when it was one of your operations attacked? Perhaps because you knew an investigation would reveal no legitimate logging enterprise but one engaged in smuggling across from Michigan and Canada, using the lumber trail to trade in drugs and embargoed alcohol."

Brown retreated further still, face pale, eyes darting about as if searching for an escape. "But—but I didn't have anything to do with the attacks. Why would I, when they revealed..." He clamped a hand over his mouth. No matter. He had admitted enough.

"Of course you didn't," Luc said.

"But if not him, who?" Madame Taylor asked, hand still hovering near her pistol.

"Well among those here, Madame, you at least I can eliminate," Luc said. "You may have killed Frank Russell, but you were in Illinois still when first attack occurred, and I doubt very much you could have orchestrated this from there. Though..." He turned to look at Wes, who smiled sheepishly. Luc almost hated having to do this next part.

"Though I think Monsieur Colt has no such alibi. And as the true Weston Colt is currently on a hunt in the heart of India, there are some questions as to his true identity." The room tensed, everyone turning on Wes, whose smile never slipped.

"And there of course, there is the Mademoiselle Fola, who is such a hand with mechanics. Airships, certainly. But technologies more delicate as well, I think."

"What does that have to do with the attacks?" Fola demanded.

"Everything, Mademoiselle. Because as I'm sure you realized, the 'hodag' that everyone is so concerned with is most assuredly mechanical in nature." The room gasped, except for Fola and Luc. "Which is why your mother sent you north, to confirm what she must have suspected."

"You keep saying her mother, but wasn't it the Governor who petitioned the President, and sent you both north?" Congressman Brown asked, apparently having gotten some of his wits about him again.

Luc gave a small smile, saw the fear in Fola's eyes. Another confirmation. Well, not all secrets had to be revealed. "All of which is immaterial now. Because it was not the La Follette's who orchestrated this little farce."

"Good god, man, just out with it," Wes said. "If you get any more mysterious I'm sure I won't be able to keep my hands off of you."

Despite himself, Luc blushed. But perhaps it *was* time.

"Very well," he said. "Yes, the hodag is mechanical. And driven by a human intelligence. An intelligence of such naked ambition that it would use a mythic creature to try and kill two birds with one stone. For once the hodag had succeeded in driving out the smaller logging outfits, then this intelligence would have leave to 'take whatever means necessary' to destroy the beast. Means that would include striking at the native populations still living in the area. Means that would solidify Bradley Lumber as the undisputed king of the North Woods."

Every gaze settled on Deacon Bradley, who stood very still.

"Perhaps you forget that I am among the victims of this tragedy, *Monsieur*?" he asked.

Luc shook his head. "No," he said. "No. As you said yourself, the attack only put you back a few days. *At most.* Only a few lives. And you can buy more of those. Oh, you took steps to hide your activities. The act of the 'concerned citizen.' Housing the hodag away from your camps. But it is a machine. And machines need fuel. Those ten minutes I required before we left your camp? I was asking your site foreman if any fuel had gone missing recently. And you know what? There had been thefts on the days before each of the attacks. Days that corresponded to days you visited the site. You, Monsieur. Probably you hoped to simply write the fuel as lost during the attack. Your paper trail would have been faultless."

Bradley swallowed.

"But of course, you overreached yourself," Luc continued. "You want people to see the beast, to confirm that it is real. How convenient then that it attacks while we are on our way to your camp, and how convenient that we scare it off before it can do more damage. And wreathed in smoke, how easy to confuse the mechanical construct for flesh. But how obvious the ruse, to me."

Bradley ran. Of course he would run. Luc's voice started to rise, for there was no way he could match the man in a chase. But he didn't need to. A shot rang out, and Bradley shrieked, stumbled, and fell. Blood poured out of his leg. Annie Taylor stood, arm outstretched, pistol smoking in her hand.

"Oops," she said, lowering the weapon slowly. "My weapon seems to have fired. Silly me."

They all stared at her, and then at Bradley, for maybe a minute before anyone thought to run for help.

"You looked scared for a moment there, admit it," Wes said in between sips of whiskey. They sat in Luc's room, loose ends being wrapped up elsewhere.

"But of course," Luc said. He grinned and patted his stomach. "I do hate running."

Wes laughed. "I should be mad at you, you know?" he asked. "You cost me a job."

"You don't need it," Luc said. "You are not a poor man."

"What gave me away?"

"Your accent," Luc said. "One spends enough time around you British, one can tell who is lowborn and who is, how do you say, slumming?"

"I've been accused of worse," Wes said. That he was not more upset was perhaps surprising, but given his inclinations he was likely eager to escape from high British society. "Lord Wesley Cockburn, at your service."

It was Luc's turn to laugh. "That explains the alias, I suppose."

"Shut up," Wes said. "It's not like you're who you pretend to be, either. You might act like a proper gentleman, but I know enough to know that you are certainly *not* from money. Or breeding. And unless I miss my guess entirely, Orphelin is not just a surname."

"No indeed," Luc said. He was indeed an orphan, grew up the poorest of the poor.

"Then why not take a different name, if you don't mind me asking?" Wes asked.

"It is not something I wish to hide from," Luc said, "even if I am much happier now that I can take proper care of my mustache."

Wes put his glass down on the sideboard and stood. He slid free of his coat first, and threw it over the back of his chair. He unbuttoned shirt sleeves, then collar. His shirt joined the coat. Then suspenders. Undershirt. Boots. Pants. When all his clothes were neatly placed on the chair, he just stood a moment, completely naked. Luc admired him, the way his neck flared to shoulders, a muscled chest, a sleek stomach. His cock was half hard already and rising even as Luc's gaze lingered.

Quite a different sight from Luc's own paunch and softer features. But in Wes' eyes there was a reflection of the desire Luc felt rising in himself. He did not doubt that, and would not disrespect it. He put down his glass. He stood.

"Just be careful of the mustache," Luc said.

The most important tool for any detective was observation. So what was happening? Heat, first—the burning pressure of Wes' body suddenly pressed against Luc's, lips like fire when they met. Luc tried to still himself, tried to keep his hands at his sides as Wes tore open his shirt. Buttons flew. Regret and relief mingled. The shirt was ruined, yes, but at least his second best suit was safely out of the way. Fabric ripped and Luc found himself pushed back, angled toward the bed. He contemplated resisting but pushed the thought aside. He wanted to see where this would go. He was exactly where he wanted to be.

Hands slid across the exposed skin of his chest, his stomach. Luc's pulse raced. Arousal. Yes, definitely. All the classic signs. Breathing was heavy, body flushed, cock erect and straining against his pants. The back of his legs bumped against the bed and Luc almost tumbled backward but caught himself. He didn't want to make it too easy, after all. Wes hummed against Luc's lips and pulled back, gripped the waist of Luc's pants directly above the buttons. Surely he didn't intend—there was a loud rip and Luc rocked forward as Wes pulled sharply down and forward. More buttons cascaded to the floor.

"Not exactly a patient man, are you?" Luc asked, and Wes just smiled, let Luc's pants fall.

With a shove Wes sent Luc back onto the bed and swiftly removed his shoes, socks, and underpants. Now clothed only in a tattered shirt, Luc felt exposed, pulse spiking again. Fight or flight, he knew, and he resisted both, forced himself still. Wait, observe.

Wes crawled onto the bed, forcing Luc back, thighs brushing thighs, cocks just inches apart. Luc fought the urge to arch up, to force the contact between them, and before he could succumb Wes grabbed him by the shoulders and rolled him over so that he was face down. In rough motions Wes pulled Luc's shirt down off his shoulders and used the ripped fabric to tie his arms together, forearm to forearm.

There was a pause, and Luc felt an absence behind him. Had Wes spotted the conspicuous bottle on the nightstand? He didn't need to be the greatest detective in the world to figure out why it might be there. A warm hand on Luc's ass, spreading his cheeks, and a sudden cold sliding down his crack told him that Wes had figured it out. And then something was pressing against him, seeking entry, and Luc didn't need to be the greatest detective in the world to know what it was. He was, but still. Luc sucked in a breath and relaxed his body as—they both moaned as Wes slid inside, as Luc couldn't help but push his hips back, savoring the sensation.

The pace Wes set was not slow, was not gentle, but Luc didn't object. His arms bound, his face pressed into the bed, he tried to keep himself still. Wait, observe. But he couldn't help crying out in pleasure as Wes pulled his hips up and began pushing in with near bruising force. It didn't last long until Wes shuddered and faltered and Luc felt the tremors of orgasm in the shake of his thighs, in the sudden spurting inside him. The pause lasted only a moment, though, before Wes pulled out and roughly rolled Luc onto his back, his arms pinned under him, his cock half-hard and throbbing with want.

There was no hesitation as Wes lowered his mouth onto Luc, took him in and coaxed him back to full hardness. Luc watched, whimpered at every bob of Wes' head. He couldn't suppress the shudder as he felt two fingers explore his ass, sliding in easily amid the lube and Wes' semen. Luc tried to tell himself to hold out. Wait, observe. But the sight of Wes' face, eyes closed, mouth closed around Luc's cock, sent him over the edge, and Luc gasped.

"I'm...I'm..." he said, hoping it was warning enough, and Wes quickly pulled his mouth away and replaced it with his free hand, pumping Luc fast and hard. It was too much. He came, and came hard, ass clenching around Wes' fingers and cock twitching as it released its load across his stomach and thighs.

Luc was about to say something, something witty and charming no doubt, when a booming crash drew their attention away from their own lingering pleasure and to the window. Luc sighed. At least they more or less finished. Wes rushed to the curtains and drew them aside.

"I say, what the blazes was that?" he asked, and Luc watched as his eyes widened, as his breath caught.

"I'd say it was probably Bradley's hodag come to try and kill its master," Luc said. With some effort he managed to roll to the side of the bed and stand, arms still tied behind his back. He joined Wes at the window, both naked and glorious but probably not the most interesting thing to see at the moment.

Not with a giant, mechanical hodag crashing through a clothier's shop less than five hundred feet away. It was an impressive creature, Luc had to admit, even if this closer look made it obvious it wasn't alive. It moved like a natural thing, though, and its eyes glowed with a malicious intent. People ran in all direction away from it.

"Did you know it was going to return?" Wes asked, and Luc nodded.

"With Bradley still alive, it was inevitable," Luc said. "The man was hardly working completely alone, and his compatriots probably fear he'll reveal them and their hiding place. With a beast such as this at their call, how could they but send it to silence the man who could betray them?"

"But you knew, and you warned no one?" Wes' voice cracked, and Luc tried not to grin too broadly. "How are you so calm about all of this?"

"I never said I warned no one," he said. Though warning Congressman Brown would likely have been a fool's errand.

"But where are the police? Where are the—" The sound of an airship cut through the noise of the attack, and the hodag paused in its rampage. "Is that my ship?"

It wasn't the kindest thing he had ever done, but Luc had known that Wes would be...otherwise occupied. And the *Ravager* was by far the most logical choice of assault vessel.

"Who's flying him?" Wes demanded.

"I believe Mademoiselle Fola is piloting," he said. She really was a natural with anything mechanical. The air ship swept down, precariously close to the hodag, which swiped at it with an enormous, clawed arm.

Wes winced. "But she's not a proper pilot," he said.

Luc chuckled. "Trust me, if she and her mother can maintain a fully automatized mechanical man and pass him off as the Governor of Wisconsin, I don't doubt she can master something as simple as flying."

Wes' eyes bulged. "Wait, what? You're saying that the Governor is..."

"Not important just now, I think you'll admit.."

"But my ship."

"Is perfectly safe," Luc said. Outside the hodag screeched and the *Ravager* climbed, aiming to pass directly over the creature. "Mademoiselle Fola is not alone, after all. Madame Taylor accompanies her as well."

"Well that's—" Whatever else Wes had been about to say was cut off as a point of darkness dropped from the *Ravager* and plummeted. The hodag had time only to screech again before the evening echoed with the crash of metal on metal. Dust and smoke plumed around the impact.

"What the bloody hell was that?" Wes asked.

"I believe that was Madame Taylor's famous barrel." The eyesore. But a very effective projectile, once bronzed. The scene outside settled with the dust. On the

Ravager Luc could see Fola and Madame Taylor cheering, and the people on the street around them took up their joy and triumph.

"Now," Luc said, drawing Wes' attention back to the room, "you can either keep staring out the window, or you can come back to bed, and either untie me or not, depending on how you want the rest of the night to go."

It took only a second for the dazed look on Wes' face to shift to something... hungrier. Luc nodded. Putting up with the uncomfortable chairs of this forsaken state might be even more unpleasant after they were done, but at that moment Luc cared not at all.

THE
WHIPPING
MASTER

Dale Cameron
Lowry

THOUGH MY FATHER died when I was too young to remember him, we did not suffer. He left a sizable estate, and my mother gave me a good education, teaching me to read and write, assigning the classics to recite to her as she sat in the parlour.

This all changed when I was fourteen and my mother remarried. My stepfather was a hard-working, prosperous man and outwardly kind. Alas, my mother being his first wife, he naturally wanted her all to himself, and so one day I was put on a coach and taken many miles away to a well-known school for boys.

The school had a fine reputation, for its teachers were not slow to mete out discipline, and many a night I settled in bed with a bruised bum from the lashings they saw fit to impart. You see, although I was a mild-tempered boy and naturally hesitant to ask impertinent questions or speak out of turn, I had the misfortune of being born with an inclination to favour my left hand over my right. My mother had taught me to write with my right hand, but never punished me for the use of my left. My new schoolmasters, feeling strongly about the evils of left-handedness, saw fit to beat it out of me.

This should have been my shame. My classmates had long graduated past the cane and paddle as regular implements of discipline. And yet after every session, I could not help but feel a strange feeling of accomplishment, a warm internal radiance accompanying the ruddy glow of my abused bottom.

This was especially true when the administrator of my flagellations was Master Prevost, our Latin and Maths teacher, and quite the sterling example of young manhood. Having graduated from the same academy a few years prior, he had all the recommendations of youth and none of its failings. He was lean and strong, and possessed of clear skin and fair hair that shone golden in the light from our classroom windows. He grew a fine moustache, but his cheeks and jaw were butter-smooth much like a baby's—or so I imagined, for naturally I had no opportunity to run my fingers over his delicate skin.

I could not help but gaze at him at every hidden opportunity. As Master Prevost lectured us, my eyes would wander from his curled lashes to the sweet pout of his lips to the lengthy taper of his fingers as they held a piece of chalk or wrapped around the root of his impressive cane.

I refer here to his "cane" in the literal sense—the one much like a billiard cue that served as an extension of his hand, whether it be to point at the chalkboard or whip my bare behind. But his metaphorical cane was also impressive, a hypnotic tube disturbing his pleats, and so long the fork of his trousers could not contain it. It slid down along the inside of his trouser leg, a sausage bulging against its casing.

This was not the only feature to recommend him. He was a rare thing in the public school—a teacher who sought actually to teach. He seemed to take students' failures as an indictment on himself, and endeavoured to do better that they might understand. He often sat down with lesser students during study hours and explained the whole lesson with patience and consideration.

I was that poor chap on more occasions than one, and I prized these times together. Oh, what a pleasure to sit close to such a manly specimen, our knees on occasion brushing beneath the table as our eyes traced the page in unison, our bodies and minds acting in concert toward a common goal. When understanding finally dawned upon me, he would place his warm, strong hand on my back and congratulate me on a job well done, with a smile that softened his features and brought a rose tint to his lips and cheeks.

But I get ahead of myself.

Master Prevost did his best to ignore my obstinate ambidexterity the first week of my schooling. The second week, he took me aside, explaining if I continued in this way, I would have to be punished; it was the headmaster's decree. I was aware of this, having already been walloped in Greek and History. But still, Master Prevost sought to refrain, administering little other than the occasional stinging smack against my *manum sinistram* when I inadvertently employed it to pick up my pen.

The third week, he startled me by interrupting his lecture to say most sternly, "Mr. Wallace, I see you continue to insist on writing with the devil's hand. To my desk. Drop your trousers."

Fear thrilled up my spine and caused my nipples to press against my shirt in sharp little peaks. "Yes, sir."

I slid from my chair, my gaze falling on the prominent jewel against the front of his trousers. How I wished that mound of love were instead the instrument of my punishment. Oh, I would that he might compel me to kneel before him and kiss it as just humiliation for my impertinent left-handedness.

The eyes of every student followed me as I marched to Master Prevost's desk and bent upon it, lowering the back of my trousers to expose the ivory flesh of my virgin bottom. But the only eyes I cared for were those of Master Prevost, astute like an owl's, and the most mesmerizing shade of brown.

"Do you look me in the eye in your moment of shame, Mr. Wallace?"

Butterflies descended on my stomach. I looked away. "I beg your forgiveness, sir."

His voice gentled. "God is merciful, but He is also just, Mr. Wallace. So you understand I must be both things as well."

"Yes, sir."

"To ten. Please count."

The cane came down against my bum with a loud crack. It might as well have struck my lungs, for it fairly knocked the air from me. I wished to cry, but my body was in so much shock from the pain it could do nothing but gasp out, "One, sir," as Master Prevost had commanded.

The second blow fell further down my bum, where less fat covered the underlying muscle. I attempted to discern which type of blow was more painful, and failed.

"Two, sir."

The third blow shook me out of shock enough to wrench sharp, stinging tears from my eyes. I did not allow these to fall; I could not show myself to be a pigeon-livered meater before the manly Master Prevost.

And then a strange thing happened. As Master Prevost beat down upon my fragile bottom a sixth, and seventh, and eighth time, I became acutely aware of the pain as an extension of his hand, and thus its entire character transformed. It was still pain, yes, but also ... lovely. Its terrible sting was as desirable to me as his kiss. Heat spread into my cock and made it stand against the front of my drawers.

By the tenth strike, I was breathless and panting, my face flushed with the knowledge that I had, in a way, been taken by the school's most desirable master. I turned to the blackboard as I fastened my trousers, tugging my jacket down to camouflage my eager little prick. It refused to relax all through the rest of the lesson, even as my bottom fairly screamed in pain.

That evening in the dormitory, the other boys tackled me to the bed and pulled down my pants to poke at the welts, joking that my "arse must be as sore as that of a Mary-Ann who has given himself over in sodomy to all the gentlemen of London!" My erection returned with a vengeance, and when lights went out I was only too eager to frig it, pushing my sore, aching bum against the lumpy mattress, delighting in how the pressure reawakened the memory of Master Prevost's cane on my tender derrière.

I could barely sit the next day, but of course was required to. It was a delicious sort of torture, though I pretended not to delight in it. I appeared stoic, as a young man of good breeding ought to be.

It was inevitable that I should err again; so also was the application of Master Prevost's cane. I fought not to become aroused during these sessions, fearing the entire class might see the outline of my engorged pego as I stood or, worse yet, that Master Prevost himself might. I directed my concentration to the sting each blow brought to my abused flesh and the humiliation of having my bare bottom ogled by callous peers.

But still the arousal came, and often more quickly now—by the fifth strike, or the third, or at times even before the thrashing commenced.

Nonetheless, I did not seek out these whippings. I feared the cane as much as I took pleasure in the repercussive sensations it afforded me. In my night-time ministrations, I riled my private lusts not with phantasies of Master Provost's wooden implement on my skin, but of his tender lips and tongue, his long fingers, and his dancing member in my hand or entering the virgin orifice between my legs, causing me a kind of pain even more ecstatic than that of the cane.

Strangely, though, it was in Master Prevost's classroom that my ambidexterity took its longest to cure. For my other schoolmasters, I reformed in a matter of months. For dear Master Prevost, it took almost two years.

Poor, beleaguered Master Prevost, seeing that his cane failed to cure me, took to varying his implements in hopes of finding one which might reform me at last. The paddle left wide black bruises; the birch slashed stinging cuts into my fair skin; the belt bit stubborn welts into my flesh. But no matter the severity of pain each lashing induced, my buttocks inevitably became all of a glow, and my incorrigible pego held as stiff as an iron rod by the concluding blow.

As I stood straight, my eyes aimed to the floor, I often caught a glimpse of Master Prevost's trouser fronts and, fairly intoxicated from the scourge, imagined his manly cock to have taken on even more monstrous proportions than it possessed in its usual state.

I tucked this image away in my mind, bringing it out only at night in my phantasies. Often as I roused my member, I also roused my bedmate. We all who boarded slept by two abed, and naturally when one engaged in the pleasuresome art, the other was inclined to follow. I developed the habit of peeking beneath the covers to watch his hand frigging his inflamed member, making believe the small prick was Master Prevost's colossal column, my breath quickening when its spendings pulsed into the palm of his hand. A small thrill built deep within my belly as I imagined how much bigger the eruption from Master Prevost's mountain must be, and at this thought I inevitably fell under the wash of a tremendous spend.

Eventually I became accustomed to using my right hand for all things but frigging, and Master Prevost found rare need to administer the lash and cane for my betterment. It was then that memories of the beatings took on a romantic aspect. I could not recall them without infusing them with lofty emotions and the kind, gentlemanly comportment that Master Prevost displayed in our private tutoring sessions. Certainly these imagined floggings were just as painful and intense as the real ones, as the strength of his arms in wielding his weapons was a necessary part of my arousal. But afterward he would caress my bum so sweetly, rubbing soothing liniments into the cuts and bruises, and laying kisses on my despoiled flesh.

Oh, how I loved Master Prevost! So powerful, yet beneath it all so tender and caring—in both my dreams and in my daily interactions with him.

I remember particularly one afternoon my final year as we read *The Aeneid* together and came to the deaths of Nisus and Euryalus, two soldiers who loved each other above all else. As Nisus leapt from the woods to rescue his lover, Master Prevost's voice faltered; tears formed in his brown eyes as he read the words *tantum infelicem nimium dilexit amicum*—"he but loved his unlucky friend too much."

How I wanted to kiss those tears away, and give my master the sort of comfort Euryalus had given to the elder Nisus in their better days! But such thoughts were foolishness. The only touch we could engage in was through the cane.

So the next day, after more than two years of conformity, I took my pen into my left hand and proceeded to take notes. Master Prevost warned me thrice.

I refused to switch hands.

"Sit in the hall, Mr. Wallace. I shall deal with you after class."

When I re-entered the now-empty classroom, he looked more fearful than I felt: his brown eyes were as wide as tea saucers; the cane seemed to tremble in his hand.

But when I presented myself to him, the cane sliced through the air as quick as ever, and landed upon me with such force I thought the thing might break. What an agonizing sort of relief it brought me! For despite my dalliances with bedmates, Master Prevost's touch was the only one I truly treasured, and here I had it again. How I wanted him to strike me until the purpling marks ran so deep they could not fully heal. I longed for scars to remember him by in years to come!

But Master Prevost was a gentleman; he knew self-control. He stopped at ten and ordered me to pull my trousers back up. My cock was so inflamed I could barely button them. I did not try very hard to hide this from him, but if he noticed, his countenance did not show it.

"Mr. Wallace." He outstretched his hand.

I shook it, hanging on as long as he allowed. "Master Prevost."

Not minutes later, I was outside on the wooded grounds, frigging my over-inflated member with the hand which had held his, his warmth still radiating through my palm. Oh, what bliss! My spendings were copious, clinging in wide swaths to the bark of the tree against which I had leant. If only Master Prevost would spend against me in the same way, my joy would be complete!

It came time to leave for university. Abandoning Master Prevost was my own private sorrow to bear; I sought distractions to temper the loss. I learnt to be intimate with other men in the true Oxford style, our crimson members plunging through semen-slicked thighs. I kissed succulent lips, engorged cocks and shy pink orifices. And a few delicious times, I wheedled our head of house into using his paddle for our own private sessions of unofficial discipline.

How different were these spankings from the ones Master Prevost had given me! The head of house often had me fully naked before he dealt the first blow, and kissed my pretty bum between each blow, praising me heartily as my cock grew more and more inflamed. When he had whipped me all I could take, he would press his big cock between my two arse cheeks and slide it up and down the crevice as I squealed from both pain and pleasure. He was a sturdy young man, ever ready to come again and again, and after his first generous spending he would push the semen into my bunghole with his fingers and then mount my lubricated aperture. This afforded me great pleasure, and often I came near fainting from excitement as he pounded his hips against my bruised flesh.

Upon graduation I joined a bank in London. I thought to give up the lubricity of my university days; the gentlemen's clubs to which I sought membership did not look kindly upon catamites and buggerers. My gamahuching days were behind me; cigars were the only tubes to enter my mouth in those barren years.

Then, one evening shortly after my twenty-fifth birthday, I came face to face with Master Prevost at Mr. M's chambers.

Master Prevost was still remarkably handsome, though now being at least thirty years of age, his strength was no longer counterbalanced by the softness of youth. His jaw, though shaven, was not smooth; the depleted hairs shone visibly against his skin, casting a shadow. His moustache was fuller than before, and meticulously groomed, bringing out the full glory of his cherry lips.

Still, he was the same beauty I had fallen in love with years before.

"Mr. Wallace, what a pleasure to see you again!" He shook my hand vigorously. "I have never forgotten your face."

I flushed, and oh! As I glanced down in my agitation, I saw he maintained the same stout tree trunk in his trousers, as large and lovely as the towers of Westminster Abbey.

Over dinner, Master Prevost explained that he had left teaching in search of a better fortune, and was now a clerk as he prepared to sit for the bar. "Have you married?" he asked after I told him of my work at the bank.

"I think I never shall, or at least I shall put it off as long as possible. I prefer spending my evenings in the company of men, don't you?"

"Naturally. I am lucky no lady would have me in my current position."

"Then you'd best not become a solicitor, for then they will clamour for you!"

"True, true. I shall withdraw my application to the bar immediately!" All around the table laughed at the very good joke, but my reckless heart took it quite seriously. His knee brushed mine under the table, sending frissons of pleasure through my skin.

When we retired to the sitting room, Master Prevost took the seat next to me on the divan; draught after draught of brandy made the company more lively and congenial. At one point Master Prevost threw his arm around my shoulder as we laughed over something, and pulled me to his chest; he did not let go for much of the evening. How my heart beat itself into a divine fury of lust and admiration!

I wanted him so, and was just trying to devise a way to lure him into a more private venue when he coughed and called for his coat. "Would you amble with me, Mr. Wallace, before I retire? I am too stimulated from all the discussion to sleep just yet. The air will do me good."

We left the party. It was late, the street near empty. We walked arm in arm for several long minutes before Master Prevost spoke. "I have a confession to make. Walking was not my only reason for wanting a moment alone with you."

"Oh?"

"Tonight we laughed as if old friends, Mr. Wallace, and it warmed my heart. Have you forgiven me, then, for the unjust punishments I gave you? I have often regretted them." His face became frightfully earnest, and I feared he might kneel in the streets to perform his penance.

"They were not unjust. I disobeyed."

"Perhaps your disobedience was not the sin I thought it was. I have attended many scientific lectures since my relocation to London, and have learnt that your preference may simply be an inborn trait, as natural as my eyes being brown and yours being blue."

I startled. Master Prevost knew my eye colour, even though in the dark of night all eyes looked grey. Had he spent as much time memorizing my visage as I had his?

This thought, and the brandy in my belly, emboldened me. "An *erastes* does what he thinks best for his *eromenos*," I said, using the Greek for *teacher-lover* and *student-beloved*. "There is no fault in that."

The meaning of the words were not lost on Master Prevost; some unidentifiable emotion rippled through his countenance. "But not every *erastes* is wise. Some are foolish, and afraid to teach—and love—as they should."

"Or perhaps—" I swallowed heavily. *"Dilexistine nimium amicum infelicem?"* It was a play on the line from Virgil that had so stirred his compassion years earlier: *Did you love your unlucky friend too much?*

His eyes searched my face in the dark. It came suddenly upon me that he was close enough to kiss me, had we been in private. "More than a schoolmaster ought, John," he said slowly, using my Christian name for the first time. "Though had I been your *erastes*, I daresay the love I felt for you would have been just the right amount."

My heart fairly pounded out of my chest, but I managed to respond, "Master Prevost—"

"You may call me Rupert."

"Rupert—" I put my hand on his. "Nos cedamus amori." *Let us yield to love.*

His eyes glimmered in night's dim light.

THERE WAS NO need for discussion once we reached his apartment. He fell upon me, his delightful moustache tickling my bare upper lip, his plump lips interlocking with mine. His hands grasped at me hungrily—first my hair, then my arms, then tugging impatiently at the buttons of my coat. In all my years, I had never been embraced with such passion, and the heat ran through me so liberally that soon the fire in the hearth became superfluous.

Feeling his great member pressed against me, I entered a frenzy. I did his trousers as fast as I could, my hand wrapping around his tremendous priapus—or as much as it could wrap, for his girth was such that it required two hands to complete its circumnavigation.

I looked down at his crimson glory. It was ten inches long, set off by a profusion of blond curls and underhung by a pair of balls as weighty and glorious as the mast. I delicately drew back his sheath, revealing a bulbous head even redder than the rest of his appendage. He shuddered, his tip exuding an iridescent pearl of arousal, and he continued to kiss me until I could barely breathe. This was of no matter; breathing seemed as superfluous as the fire.

"Oh my dearest John, how long I have dreamt of your hand on me!"

Only then did I notice it was my left hand on his manly apparatus, not my well-trained right one. I retreated from his lips, smiling coyly. "Clearly I have not learnt my lesson. Perhaps you should whip me to refresh my memory."

"Or perhaps it is I who should be whipped, for condemning that which was only natural for you." To my great surprise, he plucked a switch of birch from the kindling pile and placed it in my hands. He fell over a chair in front of the hearth, his trousers slouching around his knees and his muscular buttocks high in the air.

My cock arose to full mast. I had never dreamt of my former teacher in this position, and yet when faced with it, I could not think of anything more desirable. Or, rather, I could think of only one thing.

"Remove your clothing, Master Prevost."

He obliged at once, and I made quick work of my own.

"Now count."

How natural it felt to wield the switch, to hear it sing as it sliced through the air! And to hear my dear Master Provost gasp at the first sting, and see his buttocks flush pink where the birch had struck! "One, sir," he cried. Both our pegos grew.

I whipped him again, and again, each stroke stronger than the last. I showed him no mercy; he took it all with manly discipline, biting his bottom lip rather than squeal or squirm. His composure inflamed my desire, and compelled me to equal his strength. But I was not without sympathy. I felt each lash as if it were my own bum being excoriated—an intoxicating brew of pain and pleasure.

When his count reached ten, I let my arm go limp. "You may stand, Master Prevost." But he did not move. I gentled my voice, my hand tracing the pink lashes on his bum. "Rupert."

He looked at me over his shoulder, not moving his hands from where they were clutched around the chair's legs. His eyes held that same patient look I remembered from our afternoon tutoring sessions. "No, John. My pain is not yet equal to yours. Draw blood, and then you may rest."

"But you never—"

"Please."

I could not refuse. He groaned and grunted as I recommenced, tears streaming down his face. "Seventeen, sir," he counted.

My arm felt weak. I switched over to my left hand and struck as hard as I could. He yelped, "Eighteen, sir!" as a bright streak of blood blossomed on his abused cheek.

Such beauty I had never seen. I fell to the floor, kissing his bum fervently, licking the carmine fluid which leaked from his skin, the tang of salt and iron causing my own life force to throb within me.

"John!" he exclaimed, and almost before I had my hand around his length he spurted a great jet of spend onto the hearth stones, where it danced and sizzled in the heat. He trembled and cried as another draught came, this one into my hand, so thick and creamy I could not resist rolling it around my fingers and rubbing it into my palm.

"Fuck me with my spend, dear John!" Rupert pulled me yet closer to him until we were chest to chest and mouth to mouth. I tasted blood again, now from where he had bit his bottom lip during the lashing.

"Your bum is not too tender?"

"Oh no, you must make it tenderer still! I have years of penance yet to perform." He spread his thighs for me, showing me his winking little pucker, all rimmed with a halo of golden downy fur.

I was compelled to kiss it, and to rub over his opening with my semen-slicked fingertips as I gamahuched his massive rod to the best of my ability—which alas was not very well, for his cock was so big and my mouth so small in comparison.

Yet he made the most delightful noises, and begged me to plunder him, and so I pushed the first finger in. Oh, what joy! His gorgeous passage clung to my finger as I slid in, and he let out a soft, trembling moan. He felt tight as a virgin, but soon he pled for a second finger, and then a third. "Split me open, Mr. Wallace!" he panted.

"But I have only a moderate cock, nothing like your own manly appendage. I'm afraid the only rod here capable of splitting is your own."

"Say what you will! I must have you." He grabbed me forcefully, aligning my cock with his pretty arsehole before I had a chance to lubricate it.

"Patience, Master Prevost." I spat on my hand and made my member good and wet with semen and spittle. He squirmed impatiently, but at length I was ready and began to push into his warm and tight sheath.

"By Jove, your cock feels anything but moderate," Rupert moaned.

I chuckled. "Your senses deceive you. Should I withdraw?"

"No, my darling. It's a most delicious sensation."

I kissed him. The bleeding from his bottom lip had slowed, but his mouth remained moist and delicious. I feasted as I began delicately to frig his cock, feeling it once again grow to its most intimidating fullness.

"Oh, yes, darling." he cried against my mouth. "Do fuck me in earnest, please."

It was such a polite request I had to comply. I pulled out until only my head remained enclosed in the heat of his orifice, then plummeted in until my hips smacked his tender bum and his arsehole nigh swallowed my balls. He hissed between his teeth.

"Too much pain?" I asked.

"Just the right amount."

I took him fully then. Rupert made the most pleased of moans, clinging to me with every part, his legs wrapped about my waist and his arms about my shoulders, and his mouth kissing and biting as if with intent to gobble me down.

I fell in thrall to such excessive emotion that soon my body was in a tremble all over, and the inevitable thrill came upon me. "Oh, Master Prevost!" I cried out as I had done before only in my phantasies, and shot a regular flood of spend into him, going dizzy with the strain.

He answered with thick spurts of his essence on my hand and his lovely stomach, and I thought we were done, but, "You mustn't stop!" he demanded, tightening his anal sphincter to lure my softening prick back into excitement. As insolent as I had been as a schoolboy, I had no inclination to be insolent now. I let him rouse me, and within a few minutes I was back at full capacity, and even better this time, with so much slippery semen to foster our lubricity. We spent again and again, like adolescent boys who have just discovered Eros' most precious gift.

"I fear you will have to wait to split me in two until another time," I said, collapsing on the rug. "I cannot move another muscle."

Rupert looked suddenly shy. "You would have me again?"

"*Difficile est longum deponere amorem.*" It was a play on a poem of Catallus, who loved both women and young men: *It is difficult to relinquish a long-cherished love.* "So I'd rather not, now that I've found you again."

"I feel the same." His watery gaze turned wicked. "Besides, you have so many whippings to impart to me before the score is even."

My cock somehow managed to stir with renewed interest. "That I do, love. That I do."

LONDON,
1888
Jeff Mann

(for Jane the Wickced and Jane the Good)

> "Einarr made them carve an eagle on
> his back with a sword, and cut the
> ribs all from the backbone, and draw
> the lungs there out, and gave him to
> Odin for the victory he had won."
> —*Orkneyinga Saga*

GLORIOUS AND HORRIBLE, the miasma below, a churning and a squirming of light and noise and reek and smoke. I walk the Golden Gallery, atop the dome of St. Paul's Cathedral, hundreds of feet above the streets of London, and snuffle the night breeze, wrinkling my nose and curling my lip.

The Thames is high with incoming tide, sloshing its odorous banks. Carriages clatter far below, windows glow, chimney pots fume, denizens shout and curse and groan. Weary of such abrasive stimuli, I gaze up into the clouds, focusing long enough to bring on a soft rain. Perhaps it will dampen the urban chaos and spare my sharp senses for a time.

Ah, yes. Here it is, a sweet summer-solstice storm. The sky-water's cool on my face. It glistens on the monumental dome beneath me, dulling the din of the streets. For a few moments, I question the wisdom of returning to London. Why do I come back again and again? I, who was born on a remote Scottish island at the end of the sixteenth century, a man who much prefers the company of wolves and birds of prey, of lonesome highlands spotted with heather? Why do I return to this unwholesome mess of a city, squalid tens of thousands of human souls packed in tight, numerous as grains in a windswept field of barley?

Appetite, of course. The same reason that drives other men—more human men—to endure hostile circumstances, take risks, compromise their morality, and make fools of themselves. Hungers for food and drink, hungers for erotic delight.... In my case, all those achings merge. I return to this maddening city to sample the beautiful men who stride its streets. And tonight I have a very specific quarry in mind. Wiping raindrops from my black beard, I tongue a fang and mutter his name before launching myself over the railing and taking flight.

THE GROUND FLOOR of the four-story townhouse is well lit, the upper windows curtained or revealing flickers of candlelight. Who knows how long this delightful establishment will last? The laws against Uranian activity in this country are strict, and sooner or later the authorities will raid it and shut it down, convicting both the poor boys who work here and the men of means who patronize the place. But tonight the male brothel on Cleveland Street is busy hosting eager guests.

Before the house, I gather my Inverness coat about me, savor the continuing rain, and contemplate how I'll snare my prey. I could simply lure him back to the mansion I've bought near Regent's Park, but no, tonight I think I'll need a little more sport than that. Before he falls in love with me, my bit of rough needs to be roughed up, to be thoroughly terrified.

I shake the wet from my hair, ascend the steps, and knock on the door. From a side window, a boy peers out. In a trice, the door's flung open. It's Charlie, who often mans the entrance.

"Lord Maclaine! Welcome back! When did you get to town?" Face flushed and happy, he bustles about, taking my coat from me and brushing the damp from it.

Always so solicitous. He's not the sort of boy who attracts me—too blond, too thin, too young, too neat and clean-shaven—but his manners are always immaculate and his attentions flattering. "Just this evening. How have you been?"

"Ah, well, I'm well. Busy! We've had a full house tonight. Would you like some champagne?"

"I would. And I'd like a chat with the proprietor, if he has a moment."

"For you, sir, I'm sure Mr. Hammond will have that moment. Have a seat in the parlor then. I'll be right back."

The parlor's dim, full of antiques, velvet curtains, oil paintings, decorative china, and a grand piano, accouterments meant to put erring aristocracy at ease. I've seen some uproarious evenings in this room, but now it's well after midnight, and everyone seems to have retired upstairs to share concupiscent pleasures. Everyone except a regal-looking man, clearly inebriated, who's slumped back on a divan while a redheaded boy fondles the front of his breeches. I give them a hard mental nudge, and within a minute they've trundled out of the parlor and up the stairs to continue their mercenary intimacies. I want my conversation with Mr. Hammond to be a private one.

Charlie slips in only long enough to hand me a glass of champagne filled nearly to the brim and to inform me that the proprietor is on his way. I'm picking out the melody to "Loch Lomond" on the piano when Hammond strides in. He's taller than I am, and heavier, with wavy hair and a sprinkling of beard. The man's will is strong. In the past, I've had to nip him a couple of times to get him to obey me. Tonight, I think, currency will spare me the need for that sort of sharp persuasion.

"Lord Maclaine, it's a great pleasure to see you again," he says, offering his hand.

"Glad to be back, Mr. Hammond." I rise from the piano bench. We share a prodigious handshake. He's always surprised at how much stronger than his my grip is. "The place is as elegant as usual."

"Thank you. Business is thriving, I'm happy to say. Several men of impressive position have been frequenting us. Which of our services do you require tonight?" He winks. "I do hope you aren't planning on leaving another of our poor boys chafed, bitten, and bruised, are you?"

"This one I don't plan to leave at all. At least not for the immediate future."
I slip my hand into my frock coat and pull out a clump of pound notes. "The last
time I was in town, you had a new employee, a dark Irish lad with a short beard.
Is he still working here?"

Hammond regards the money with frank greed. "Colin, you mean. He is
indeed. At thirty, he's far too old to interest our customers, and he's far too hairy
as well, so he's been handling odd jobs around the house since last autumn. That's
when you visited us last?"

"Yes. I've been in the United States since then."

"West Virginia, is it? How do you bear dwelling in such a wild and savage
place? Mountains and beasts and barbarians!"

My mouth twists into a crooked smile. Hammond and I have had enough
dealings together to feel comfortable teasing one another. "Because, as you know
better than most, there's something wild and savage in me that feels at home
there. And, as you recall, I'm from the mountains myself."

He shakes his head, looking bemused. "Yes. The Highlands and the Western
Isles. More howling wilderness, if you ask me. Crawling with barbarous clans. It's
a miracle that our Queen goes on holiday there. It's a miracle that a man of your
noble bearing hails from those parts."

I meet him grin for grin. "Indeed. Which is why I come to London every so
often for a taste of civilization. Speaking of which, on to business. Colin?"

"Ah, yes. Well, as I said, he's not one of our boys for hire, but I'm sure he'd be
amenable if offered the right sum." Hammond regards the money fixedly. "That's
a great deal to buy the night, you know. Our usual charge is four shillings."

"I don't want to buy the night. I want to buy the man."

His brow lumps up. "Buy the man? What do you mean?"

I riffle through the bills. "I mean, I want to take him with me. To be my
manservant."

"Ah, Lord Maclaine. Colin's a good worker. I'd hate to see him go."

I hand Hammond the bills. "Count it."

He does so. His eyes widen, and his cheeks quiver. "My God."

He looks up, face flushed. "He's yours then. Be kind to him, though, Lord
Maclaine. The lad seems sad all the time. No one knows why."

"I'll take care of him, I promise you." I give Hammond's hand another shake.
"Tell Colin to pack his possessions and meet me in the alley across the street."

"I shall. Let me show you to the door."

In the foyer, Charlie helps me on with my coat. I'm about to leave when
Hammond says, "Lord Maclaine? A question first? You're a man of fine parts.
You're handsome and wealthy and magnetic. Why do you patronize this place?
With your looks, you surely don't need to pay."

I pause. "Because...you and I, the men who come here, and many of the boys
too, we're kindred of a sort, are we not? We sodomites are a secret breed. The
same pious curs hate and persecute us all. I had a lover once, back where I was

born, on the Isle of Mull. He was murdered by a pack of such vile dogs."

Hammond's face blanches. "Lord God. I didn't know. I'm so sorry."

"Thank you, sir." I grimace and nod. "Now I do what I can to help our kind and to thwart the swine that would do us ill. Do you understand?"

"Yes." Hammond's face darkens. "It's a perilous existence indeed. Imprisonment or hard labor if we're found out. Cast out from polite society as if we were vicious, loathsome vermin."

Sighing, he pats me on the shoulder. "Well, enough of such gloomy chat. Many thanks for the money, Lord Maclaine. That will support the house for months. I'll send Colin out posthaste."

COLIN STANDS IN the glow of a streetlight, carrying a satchel. He's dressed in black boots and a tattered gray coat that, considering the way he's shivering and hugging himself, is insufficient to warm him against this chilly evening of lingering drizzle. He peers into the blackness of the alley, looking dubious, his brow wrinkling. By the Gods, he could be Mark Carden reborn.

"Lord Maclaine. Where are ye?"

I say nothing. Colin takes a step into the darkness. Then another. Then another. Then another.

I could simply explain the situation, name the amount of money I've paid for him, and escort him to the mansion. He should be relieved to hear that he can leave the brothel and become my manservant instead. I could explain...but where is the fun in that?

I move too stealthily for him to hear, too fast for him to retreat. In a matter of seconds, I've wrenched his arms behind him, clamped my hand over his mouth, and sunk my fangs into his neck. Beard stubble, man-scent, fright-flood of rich blood, futile thrashings, stifled screams...and now he's swooned. Chuckling, I hoist the lean boy over my shoulder, snatch up his satchel, and jaunt down the alley toward our new home.

BY THE TIME Colin comes to, I've arranged him just the way I want him, the way I prefer any beautiful, virile youth: stripped, silenced, and restrained. Wielding cruel power over such deeply desirable men is often more delicious than drinking their blood or semen.

Lounging in an armchair by the bed, I survey Colin's nakedness in the glow of an oil lamp and watch his slow return to consciousness. Inside their fringe of black lashes, his blue eyes flicker open and fix on me. When he tries to move, the realization of his helplessness suffuses his handsome face. Then begins the captive's struggle, the frantic futility, a show I've relished for over a century and—the Dark Lady, the Lord of Beasts, and the Lord of Storm be willing—shall savor for centuries more.

Glaring at me, he thrashes about atop the bed, but his prettily hogtied movements are minimal, thanks to my rope-work, all of which is deliberately tight enough to cause him pain. His wrists are bound behind his back, as are his biceps. His legs are bent behind him, his ankles crossed, knotted together, and tethered to his hands. His shouts for help have a hoarse beginning, but, as the panic builds, they grow shrill. No matter. I've tied three thick rags between his teeth and then a good two yards of rope. No one will hear him in this high, tightly shuttered room.

Ah, what a poem, the way his sinewy body flexes, contorted in the lamplight, muscles swelling and straining against restraint, the way his teeth gnaw the rags and rope, the way his blue eyes grow wet with fright. I sit back, smiling, sipping mead, and admire his youth and beauty and hapless terror. The boy has a fine frame: lean hips and midriff, a strong chest and sinewy arms. Glossy dark hair coats his torso, belly, and thighs. I've chosen well. He's just the sort of manly feast I cherish. And his resemblance to Mark is so uncanny it makes my heart hurt. Odd how I can feel lust, sadism, aesthetic admiration, and sorrow simultaneously.

I let him exhaust himself. I wait for the rage and the fear in his gaze to ebb down to a teary, glassy-eyed pleading. I wait for his violent writhing to subside to a pained, restrained squirming and slumping. I wait for his screams to dwindle down to pants and groans and a deliciously pathetic whimpering.

Good. Now he's so fatigued he can barely move. He lies on his side, facing me, wheezing and trembling. His fine face is streaked with sweat and hopelessness. A few tears slide down his cheeks. This is what I most relish: to see a man's spirit broken.

I rise, dip a forefinger into my drink, and bend over him. He jolts when I touch his brow. "Easy, lad," I mutter, tracing the Norse rune Gifu on his skin, marking him as both gift and sacrifice. The scent of his terror-sweat is as sweet as the mead.

Gently, I stroke his bearded cheek and gag-distorted lips. Gently, I finger up his tears and taste them. "Ah, you're weary, are you?" I say, brushing back a lock of dark hair. "Done with pointless protests?"

The youth takes a long, shuddering breath and nods. What I see in his face is the certain conviction that he's about to die. He must think that I'm a dangerous madman poised to off him. As if I would so abruptly end such a finely furry morsel without enjoying him for many months first.

Smiling, I peel off my clothes. Naked, we resemble one another, both of us muscular and furry, with shaggy black hair and black beards, though I am of brawnier build. Ah, well, I suppose I've always had a bit of Narcissus in me. Colin might be Irish and I might be Scots, but he could pass as my younger brother.

I stand over my prisoner, hands on my hips, eager sex rampant. I am not a skillful mind reader, unlike many of my kind, but even I can gauge from the look in his eyes—confusion melded with hopeful flickers of relief—that he's beginning to realize that this evening might be about erotic abduction, not murder. After so many months in the Cleveland Street house, he's surely heard of clients whose penchants are as perverse as mine, other men addicted to restraint and domination, fellow devotees of the delights described by that hapless French marquis.

"I've been wanting to hold you close for many months. Let's make you more comfortable first." Loosening knots, I remove the short tether that secures his wrists and ankles together, freeing him from the constrictive hogtie. "You must be very stiff. Stretch out now."

He unbends himself, emitting a pained moan.

"To the beautiful, I can be merciful. Better?"

He stares up at me, blinks, and nods.

"I've always doted on boys like you. Dark, lean, and furry. Hirsute Christs."

I lie down on the bed beside him. I touch the wound on his neck, cup his wet cheek, and kiss him on the forehead. My tenderness, I can sense, surprises him. What sort of mad kidnapper, he is wondering, would so lovingly caress his captive after binding him so cruelly tight?

"The Black Irish are a flavor I savor." The boy's nipples are tiny—pert pink stars in a heaven of thick black hair. I take the right one between thumb and forefinger and squeeze it till he flinches. "The first I had was Jimmy O'Farrell. He helped to murder my lover, Angus. Before I cut off his head, I raped him and drank from him. That was sweet retaliation indeed."

New fear floods Colin's eyes. Chuckling, I kiss his rag-and-rope-crammed mouth. Rolling onto my back, I wrap an arm around his shoulders and press his head to my chest. "I'm Laird Derek Maclaine. Do you know why you're here?"

Colin gives a slow shake of his head.

"Tonight is the summer solstice. To celebrate it, I must have a Sacred King to sacrifice."

My word choice deepens his alarm. Jerky shudders seize him.

"I saw you at Mr. Hammond's place last autumn. I thought you were glorious. You served me champagne, then stood by the window, brooding in your dark Celtic way and watching the rain. Do you remember?"

Colin gazes up at me. Wonderingly, he nods.

"Do you like my looks?" I run my hand over my chest and down my belly. I take my hard cock in my fist and squeeze it.

He bites down on his gag and blinks. Thick eyebrows, thick lashes: more of the elements of manly beauty I dote on.

"Answer me," I say, squeezing his shoulder.

"Ahh," he mumbles.

"That's 'Aye,' is it not?"

Dropping his gaze, the boy gives me a slow nod.

"Good. I thought I felt your interest the evening we met. It's always fortunate when attraction is mutual." I nuzzle his neck and lap at the wound I'd earlier made there. "This city stinks. But you, your scent is intoxicating, especially after such sweaty struggle."

My free hand strays down to his groin. I grip his sex in its thicket of midnight hair. "I wanted you badly the first night we met, but business required me to leave the city soon thereafter. With a Hibernian beauty like you, I knew that I would want more than a mere night. So tonight I paid Mr. Hammond a goodly sum for you. I promised to improve your position, and so I shall."

"Um?" Colin grunts. His fear must be receding, for now his member stiffens in my hand.

"I bought you, lad. You're mine. You'll live in this mansion as my manservant. You'll keep the place up in my absence. And you'll share your favors with me whenever I so choose." I roll him onto his back, climb on top of him, fondle his hardened prick, and stare into his eyes. "Do you understand?"

Blue eyes widen, black lashes blink with bewilderment and astonishment. Then fear resuscitates as I expose a fang.

"I'm no mere man. I have unusual appetites," I say, stroking his member. "Animal appetites. Let me show you. Lie back now. It's time for me to feast."

Beneath me, more ragged shuddering takes him, and his heart speeds up.

I press a hand over his gagged mouth. "You will keep quiet, will you not? You've done enough bellowing tonight."

He manages a spastic nod. His cock jerks in my grip.

"Good. A boy who does as he's told is always rewarded."

With that, I bend to his torso, sucking and nibbling his nipples till he's moaning with delight. Then the hunger takes me, and I sink my teeth deep into his hairy breast, the hard flesh over his heart.

Wincing, Colin yelps against my palm. After a few deep, spicy draughts, I slow down, wanting him conscious for what's to come. Head lolling, the boy trembles beneath me, rubbing his groin against me as I drink.

"Thanks, lad, for that rich gift," I say, retracting my fangs and licking blood from my lips. "Let me please you now. The pleasure will banish what remains of fear."

I shift my attentions to his prick, lapping the shaft, sucking the head, treating him to warm, slow suction till his thighs are quivering and he's close to spending, his slender hips bucking against my beard.

Chuckling, I free his salty cock and slip off him onto the bed. "I believe you're ready to be rogered, lad," I murmur. I squeeze his compact rump and run my fingers through his inky hair. "Aren't you now?"

"Ahh," Colin murmurs, nodding. His blue eyes are drowsy now, and entirely acquiescent. Around his gag, his pretty mouth musters a weak smile.

"Another 'Aye?' Show me how much you want me inside you." I give his innate passivity the slightest psychic prodding, and in a trice he's rolled over onto his belly and cocked his bum up in the air.

"What's more beautiful than a strong man eager to surrender?" I sigh, fondling his arse. I unbind his ankles and spread his legs before kneeling between his hairy thighs. "What loveliness the Gods lend us."

Awash with reverence, I nip each hirsute arse-cheek and rake them with my fangs. Spreading them, I lick his hairy cleft and probe his hole with my tongue, relishing the strong scent and taste. The boy whimpers in response and presses his rump back against my face. Greedily, I bury my beard between his buttocks, lapping luxuriously at his tight nether-entrance.

"Beg me for it," I say, tugging at arsehole hair with my teeth. "Beg me to fuck you."

And so he does, a long string of rag-stifled sounds unintelligible but expressive nonetheless, welling with the unmistakable tone of hungry pleading.

In another minute, I've greased us up and am pressing my prick against his bum-hole. Colin winces and moans as I push myself inside him. Another minute more, and I've wrapped an arm around his chest, dug my fingernails into a nipple, clamped my hand over his mouth, sunk my teeth into his neck, and begun the savage pounding that will lead us both into brutal bliss.

I STAND NAKED on the roof, high above the leafy darkness of Regent's Park, letting rain sluice Colin's blood, sweat, and semen from my body. Downstairs, he sleeps soundly, still bound, exhausted from blood-loss and a lengthy ravishing.

This is the shortest night of the year, and it is dwindling fast. But the solstice celebration is complete. I have drunk the mead, and with it I have anointed my captive Hercules. The God of the Dark has mastered the God of the Light, and now the sun will wane and the nights will wax.

I lift my face into the storm and taste the rain. Then I wring water from my hair and beard and descend into the house.

In the master bedroom, I dry off with a towel and watch my captive slumber. As lovely as he looks tied like that, as succulent as he felt thrashing and groaning beneath me, I may linger in London longer than I'd planned. I came for business, to oversee financial transactions, but with a hairy-arsed delicacy like this to possess, I might have to stay for pleasure.

He lies limp as I unbind him, but as soon as I've pulled him into my arms, he murmurs awake, smiles sleepily, and clings to me. For long moments, we lie together unspeaking, listening to sheets of rain spatter the windows.

"You're no longer afraid," I say, nibbling his ear. "Do you trust me now?"

"Aye, m'lord, I do. For a while there, I thought it was the end of me, but you were just playing a game, were you not? Like some of the patrons of Cleveland Street. *Sadisme*, I think one of the Frenchmen calls it."

"Exactly. Named after a marquis I knew once."

"So I'm your manservant now, you said?"

"Indeed you are. Do you approve of your new accommodations?"

Colin lifts his head long enough to observe the fine furnishings of the room. "Aye! This bed is grand! This place is kingly! So I may truly stay here? I no longer need to work for Mr. Hammond at Cleveland Street?"

"As long as you continue to please me, this is your home."

Colin grips my hand and kisses it. "I will please you. I swear it. I'm very grateful, m'lord."

"As you should be. Now it's nearing dawn, and soon I must leave you. But first..."

I kiss his brow, fondle a nipple, and gaze into his eyes. "You will submit to me in all things. True?"

Colin smiles, well into the cozy peace of thralldom. "Aye, m'lord. I will obey you. I will submit to whatever gratifies you. Do as you will."

"Oh, I shall. Make no mistake about that." Gently I nudge the boy onto his back. I climb on top of him, wrap an arm around his waist, slide two fingers up his well-greased bum, and fang-feast on his nipples, feeling much like a dark moth robbing the nectaries of a rare Burren flower.

Colin flinches and groans. With one hand, he strokes his cock. With the other, he cups my head, as if he were a mother and I a thirsty babe. He finishes before I do, grunting with rapture before passing out.

TWO WEEKS LATER, I'm having a brandy in the front parlor and reading the *Evening Star* when Colin enters with a package. He's looking quite natty in a new suit of clothes I've bought him.

"M'lord, another shipment from Cresswell Brooks arrived this afternoon."

"Excellent," I say, patting the divan. "Have a brandy with me, lad."

Colin takes a seat, pouring himself a drink after refreshing my own. I tear open the bundle and pull out my prizes: a collection of poems by Christopher Marlowe, Robert Louis Stevenson's *The Strange Case of Dr. Jekyll and Mr. Hyde* and *Kidnapped*, and Lord Tennyson's *Idylls of the King*.

"'Come live with me and be my love, / and we will all the pleasures prove,'" I mutter, flipping through Marlowe. "And so it has been with you and me."

"Many a pleasure, m'lord. I'm blessed to be living here. What's that you're reading?"

"It's poetry. Written by a man like me. A sodomite who knew that the way to a boy's heart—and up his bum—was to shower him with gifts. We'll read Marlowe together. You're fairly literate as it is, but you could stand to improve."

"True, m'lord. I was doing well in my ragged school before Ma and Da died, but I'd very much enjoy continuing my studies, if that would please you." Colin takes a sip of brandy, clears his throat, and hangs his head. "M-May I ask you a question, m'lord?"

"You may, my boy," I say, squeezing his knee.

"Why do you favor me with such generosity? There are many other men you could have chosen. Boys at Cleveland Street, or, well, anyone in London."

I wrap an arm around him and pull him closer. "You resemble someone I treasured in the past. His name was Mark Carden. He was a Southern soldier who died during the American Civil War, back in 1863. The memory of him haunts me still. When I look at you, it seems as if I lost him only yesterday. Yet, holding you, it seems as if I have him back again."

"You remind me of someone too, m'lord. What's your age?"

I'm tempted to admit that I was born in 1700 and turned *draugr* in 1730, but full revelations can come later, once he's made himself more at home. Instead, I say, "Thirty, lad. The same as you."

"You look thirty, true, but something about you seems far older, if you don't mind me saying so. That's why you remind me of my Da. He was strong, a powerful man like you. When I was a boy, he made me feel safe, as you do, and cared for. Safe until...."

"Go on, boy."

Colin lifts his head. Deep grief dilutes the blue of his eyes. He takes my hand and rests his head against my shoulder.

"You said that the memory of that soldier haunts you. I fear that I'm haunted too. There's a brain sickness in the family. Melancholia, a doctor called the malady. My grandfather said a witch's curse started it. Da suffered from it terribly. He thought the dark moods might lighten with new scenery, so he moved us from Limerick to Wales and got a good job in the ironworks, but that didn't help. Nothing did. Then Ma died of cholera, and one night Da walked out into the snow and shot himself. Now I suffer from the sickness too. It's as if he's passed the dark demon on to me. When it rains, when it's cold and damp, which would be most of the time in London...I wonder what life's for. Everything seems so grim and pointless I don't want to get out of bed. And I worry."

"Why do you worry, Colin?" I say, patting his hand. "As long as you choose to stay here, you'll have no material wants."

"I worry for my sister, Mary. She left Carmarthenshire and took to whoring in Cardiff. Then she moved to London and began to spend time with fine gentlemen. Carriage rides and even a trip to Paris. But then the dark moods seized her too, and she took to drink, as I admit I often do myself. Another family curse, I guess. Now she's...it so grieves me to say this...she's a strumpet plying her trade in Whitechapel. I came to London to bring her home, but she refused. She knows about me, about—"

"How you prefer the company of men?"

"Aye. She said what I do with men makes Our Lord's heart bleed. She refused my help, and we got into an awful row."

Colin sighs. "Now, Mary and me, we're hardly speaking. It's an irony, really. I came to London to beg her to give up the whoring, and then I ran out of money and ended up working in a brothel. At least Cleveland Street is nicer than the foul pubs where she looks for men."

"No more Cleveland Street for you, my lad. Tomorrow night, I'll give you money you can offer her. If you think she'll accept it. If you're sure she won't simply spend it on gin."

"I can't guarantee that, m'lord."

"Then we'll conduct an experiment. If she takes the money and we determine that she uses it wisely, I'll allow you to give her more. If she squanders it, then I'll waste no further funds on her."

"But m'lord, sometimes, like me, the poor girl loses control and—"

"Are you questioning me?" I say, baring a fang.

Face flushing, Colin drops his eyes. "No. No, m'lord. I would never do that."

"Good. In a while, let's order a hansom cab, and I'll reward your compliance with a good meal at the Cadogan, that new hotel in Knightsbridge. Now, however, take off your upper garments and get on your knees. I want to torment your nipples with my fingernails while you suck my cock."

Straightaway, Colin's bare-chested and kneeling before me. He grips my thighs and sucks me with passionate desperation, as if he were Lazarus and I were the first breath of air he takes after rising from the dead.

I DO AS every man doting on a boy has done, from Babylon through Athens and Rome on. I do everything I can to give Colin delight.

Along with expensive gifts—a fitting wardrobe, a gold watch—I take him on summer holiday. To Paris, where he grows less lean on the rich food and fine wine. To Brighton, to enjoy the pier and pebbly strand. To Auld Reekie's cobblestone streets and cozy pubs. To Llandudno's crescent beach and promenade. To the isolate silence of Mainland Orkney, former home of my maker, Sigurd.

Colin, in turn, more and more the subservient slave, treats me to the erotic amusements I favor. Kneeling, besotted, he tongues and sucks my sex in the deep green of Hyde Park, in a brougham as we bounce through Mayfair. Tied belly-down and spread-eagle on my bed, he fights his bonds, wiggles his arse, and moans into his gag, giving me a sweet show of well-trammeled discomfort as I sit back and stroke myself, readying my prick to serve him up another bum-pounding.

One September night, Colin's bent over our favorite tombstone in Highgate Cemetery, trousers down around his ankles, spreading his arse-cheeks and begging me to ravish him, when a constable appears in high dudgeon, waving his truncheon. I take advantage of the man's presence to intensify the perversity of the evening. Soon, to Colin's hot-faced humiliation, the mesmerized man's stroking himself while watching me brutally bum-fuck my thrall. Colin's so sore when I'm done that he's wobble-legged, and so I throw him over my shoulder. But first, I send home the randy constable with instructions: to feast on his wife's quim before rogering her in the arse.

"Gather ye rosebuds while ye may," said the Cavalier poet. And so I do, devouring Colin's rosebud, penetrating him to the music of our mutual rapture. In return for his blood and submission, I give him all the luxuries a working-class Irishman ever dreamed of.

Still, sometimes Colin broods. When I rise at sunset, he's often standing by a window, watching the light die, the despondent fit upon him. Sometimes, when the fit's more severe, I find him staggeringly drunk. Sometimes, to my displeasure, he's nowhere to be found. Later in the evening, he creeps guiltily in, having treated his trollop of a sister to a pub meal in Whitechapel. My mesmerism, my passionate attentions make his melancholy recede, but, I can sense, cannot banish it entirely. That failure is a profoundly irritating reminder: even I have limits.

A CHILLY TWILIGHT in early October, Colin's tending a coal fire in the parlor when I enter. He hurries over to the collection of crystal decanters and gives me a questioning look.

"Absinthe tonight," I say, flinging myself on the divan and scanning the *Evening News*. "Another beastly murder in Whitechapel. If I didn't know better, I'd say that a *draugr* with brain fever was the culprit."

Colin hands me a glass of the green liqueur. "The details are dreadful indeed."

"Don't dwell on such nastiness. Tonight, we see Henry Irving at the Lyceum in *Macbeth*. And next week's your birthday. We'll have to celebrate with a fine dinner out. Steak and oysters, perhaps? Would you like that? With a few bottles of claret?"

"Oh, yes, m'lord! You're so good to me."

"I am indeed. And I have a birthday treat planned."

"What's that, m'lord?"

"I'm going to have your initials etched into that gold watch I gave you. I should have done so when I first bought it. Fetch it now, and I'll speak to the jeweler tomorrow night."

Colin's face pales, making his black beard seem even blacker.

"Ah, m'lord, you're too kind. No need to do such a thing for me. Truly, I'm undeserving of your generosity."

"Nonsense, lad. Between your sweet blood and your tight rump, you've made me quite content. You know I like to coddle you. Off now, and bring me that watch."

Colin moves over to poke at the fire. "M'lord...I fear I've misplaced it."

"Misplaced it?" I arch an eyebrow, probe his mind, and find what I never thought I'd find there. "You lost it?"

His back to me, Colin stares at the fire. "I fear that I did. I looked for it this very afternoon so that I might wear it to the theatre tonight, but it was nowhere to be found. I'm so sorry, m'lord. I—"

"Colin, look at me."

Colin turns, meeting my eyes for only a second before staring at the carpet.

"You're lying to me. Did you really think I wouldn't be able to tell? So beautiful but so foolish. Where is that watch?"

Colin's hands are shaking as he replaces the fire poker in its stand. "I sold it, m'lord. Please forgive me."

"Sold it? You needed money? Isn't the salary I give you sufficient? Why do you need—"

I gulp the absinthe and rise. "Ah, I see. You didn't need it. That sister of yours did, the greedy harlot. Am I correct?"

"A-Aye, m'lord. I'm so sorry. She badly needed rent money."

"And gin money too, no doubt. You've never seen me angry before, have you, my boy?"

Colin quails. "N-No, m'lord. P-Please don't be angry. I made a terrible mistake. I s-shan't do so again. Please forgive me."

"You'll receive forgiveness, certainly. But only after you receive a proper chastisement. Are you ready for that? Are you ready to suffer for me?"

"A-Aye, m'lord," Colin stammers. "I'll endure whatever it t-takes to be forgiven."

"Good. Strip."

Head bowed, Colin complies. Trembling in the cold air, he stands naked before me, a study in white skin and black body hair, an artist's canvas in need of painting.

I fold my arms across my chest. "On your knees. Beg me to punish you. Plead for mercy."

Shuddering violently, he kneels at my feet. "P-Please, m'lord. Punish me. D-Deal out the discipline I deserve. B-But, please, m'lord, show mercy."

"Agony will earn you mercy. Eventually."

Growling, I grip my errant thrall by the back of his shaggy head and press his face down against the leather of my boot. "Lick, you wicked brat, until I tell you to stop."

COLIN'S WELL-EARNED TORTURE continues all night. I force him to piss into a rag I cram into his mouth and secure in place with rough cord. I rope him down to the bed and cover his heaving chest, belly, and quivering sex with candle wax. I feed from his neck till he's fainted, then slap him awake, hoist his legs over my shoulders, bend him double, and roger him till he screams. I drag him into the cellar, press him face first against a pillar, bind his wrists behind it, and beat his back with a leather whip. He sobs brokenly into his urine-soaked gag, struggles, thrashes, spasms, and swoons. When he regains consciousness, I beat him again.

Dawn's approaching when I finally cut him loose. Beneath the lash's affections, his pale skin has caught fire, striped with bleeding welts I greedily lap clean. I tie the insensible lad to a chair and leave him in the cellar, slumped, bruised, and bloody. All day, I know, he will fight his bonds and moan my name into his gag.

When I rise at dusk, Colin's where I left him, sagging against his bonds and whimpering piteously. After so many hours spent cruelly restrained, he's soiled himself. I untie him, wipe him clean with a rag, and carry him upstairs. I draw a bath, lower him into the steaming water, then peel off my clothes and join him. He sighs and groans as I bathe him and apply unguents and dressings to his wounds and rope-chafed limbs.

After drying us off, I carry him in to bed and fold him in my arms. He presses his face against my breast, and I stroke his thick hair.

"I'm so sorry, m'lord," he murmurs, his breath warm on my skin.

"I know you are," I say, kissing his cheek. "You'll never speak another falsehood to me, will you, lad?"

"No, m'lord. Never."

I run a hand over his bandaged back. "You took quite a beating. I'm proud of you. You Irishmen are made of stern stuff."

"We have to be, m'lord, considering the history of our island." Colin nestles closer. "Have I earned your forgiveness?"

"You have. Tomorrow night, I'll hie to the jeweler and buy you a new watch."

"Thank you, m'lord," Colin mutters drowsily. "I'll never part from it. As I'll never part from you."

With that, my exhausted and aching thrall slips into deep slumber. I kiss and fondle him till dawn, knowing myself even more smitten now that he's suffered so to please me. Rare are the humans I become attached to, but when I do encounter one of them, that attachment is swift, dangerous, and deep.

YE OLDE CHESHIRE Cheese is bustling this foggy evening. It's Samhain, the festival of the dead, a holiday sacred to the Old Religion, so I'm treating my thrall to a celebratory meal in one of his favorite pubs. He'll need his strength to endure the especially intense ritual I have in mind for later.

Ravenous as usual, Colin's put away four pints of ale, a plate of bread and cheeses, a beefsteak, and spotted dick with custard. Now he's into his third whisky. Another dark mood has taken him. I can tell by the steady way he's drinking and how his eyes stare dully at windows or floor or the depths of his drink. The boy hasn't slept soundly in weeks.

"What's poisoning your mind, lad?" I say, nudging his leg with mine. "The old melancholia's gnawing you, isn't it?"

"It is," Colin sighs. "I'm tight as a boiled owl, but I've still got the morbs. The drink isn't helping. What a shameful, contemptible thing you must think me."

"And why would I think that?"

"Because a man with any mettle would shake off this gloom. But I can't. You've given me so much. I don't mean to seem ungrateful, but.... Honestly, dread is clawing my guts, m'lord."

"Why, Colin? You've feasted heartily, and later tonight you'll suffer and bleed for me, and in return I'll hold you and cherish you and plow your body into bliss. You know that, don't you? No one can harm you while I'm around."

"Aye, m'lord, I know that you'll take care of me. But still...."

"Still?"

Colin gulps the last of his glass, rests his elbows on the table, and props his chin in his hands. "I went to see Mary today. We had another frightful row."

"Damn it, boy. You know those visits always upset you. She's vile to you. Why do you go? I told you to give her no more money. Did you? Do you want to be disciplined again?"

"I gave her no money, m'lord, I assure you. I just wanted to see her. She's my little sister. I can't help but be concerned about her, despite our differences. If you had siblings.... Do you have siblings, sir?"

"I did," I say, taking a long drink of ale. "An older sister, Morna. She was a ferocious glory, an incarnation of the sword-wielding Scathach if ever there was one. She helped me dispatch Angus's slayers. I slew her puling merchant of a husband before I sailed for America, and she inherited his riches. She lived a long life, enjoying the high society of Glasgow. I offered her the gift that Sigurd gave me, but she refused. One lifetime of dealing with the rank foolishness of humanity would be quite enough, she said. She died in 1781. Like Angus, she's buried back in the Maclaine family cemetery, on the Isle of Mull. I've never been able to bring myself to visit either grave."

"I'm sorry, m'lord. As long as you've lived and as deeply as you feel, you must have had to say a heartbreaking farewell to many of those you've loved."

I nod. How well I remember finding Angus at the base of the standing stone, stabbed to death, and Mark's body on the battlefield of Chickamauga, a Minié ball in his brain. "I have, and I'm not ready for another parting just yet. More reason for you to shake off the grim moods, stay out of the stews of Whitechapel, and leave your sister be. She'll be your ruination, boy. I've grown quite fond of you, and I want you safe. Do you understand?"

"Aye, m'lord. After what happened today, I doubt that I'll be seeing her again."

"Another whisky for the lad," I order a passing server. I want Colin thoroughly drunk for tonight's ritual. He'll take the pain better.

"Tell me what happened, Colin."

Colin pulls a long face. "Ah, Lord Maclaine.... I feel guilty living as well as I do, thanks to you, when she's living as she is, so that's why I've kept going back and offering my help. Especially lately. I so want to get her out of Whitechapel. What the Ripper did to that Eddowes woman...."

"The criminal is certainly a madman of the most extreme kind," I say. "But the constabulary is out in force, making regular rounds, as are the members of that neighborhood vigilance committee. You can't make your sister leave Whitechapel if she doesn't want to."

"She made that very clear today." Colin gives the returning server a nod, takes the glass of whisky, and gulps down half of it. "When I offered to treat her to supper but refused to give her money outright, she began shrieking at me. In return, I told her she was a.... Well, I lost my temper and called her profane names. And she, she was beastly drunk as usual—she seems to start drinking at breakfast and keep at it all day—and she threatened to dump her chamber pot over my head, and she called me a foul bugger, and a nancy, and a disgusting sodomite. She told me that I could take the funds I earned from the sin of Sodom and shove them up my prick-pummeled arse. She told me she never wanted to see me again. And I told her that I'd damn well oblige her."

"Do so. Stop seeing her, Colin. Every time you do, I can sense the sadness grow in you. When I slip into your mind and try to banish it, it's as if there's a black whirlpool there, an icy maelstrom, that sucks down all my efforts to help you."

"But, God, to part like that? My own shister?" he slurs.

"Yes, Colin. I think it's time."

"Ahhh, bloody hell, you're right." Colin quaffs the rest of the whisky. "Enough of her, the stubborn trull. Let's go, m'lord. I've fed well, and now it's your turn. Your beard is looking hoar-frosted. You haven't kissed my throat in many days now. Why is that? Has another caught your eye?"

"I fear that the regularity of my attentions is eroding your health. You've been looking wan lately, and thinner than I'd prefer. Like Keats' knight-at-arms 'palely loitering.'" I drop some coin onto the table and rise. "Come to think of it, tonight's Samhain blood-rite will be a strenuous one. Perhaps I shouldn't perform it after all."

Colin shakes his head. "You musht, m'lord. It's a sacred night. You musht mark it. I'm more than ready to shubmit to the rite. I feel stronger than I look. I shan't disappoint you."

"I'm not sure. Perhaps I should find some other boy to help sate my appetite and send you on holiday for a few weeks."

"Please don't." Colin stands, swaying with drink. He scowls. "I wouldn't want to share you. I'm all you need."

"Possessive brute." Chuckling, I drape an arm around him. "My little Noisiu. Hair black as the raven's wing, lips red as blood, and skin as white as snow."

I lead Colin out, through a crowd of other drunken patrons. As we pass the resident parrot, Polly, she puffs out her breast feathers and screeches. "Give us a kiss, darling! Meat and two veg! Carpe diem, cunny! Dab the dirty puzzle! Hang the 'orrible hedge whore!"

ARMS BOUND ABOVE him, Colin dangles from a cellar rafter, swaying on his toes. He bites down on the rope knotted between his teeth, flinching and moaning as I steadily cane his bum.

When his arse is scarlet and ridged with welts, I cease. I kiss his tearstained cheeks and draw my dirk. With its sharp blade, I etch runes into his bare chest—Wunjo for joy, in order to banish his sadness, and Kenaz, to symbolize the passionate connection we've found together. I quench my thirst in the blade's aftermath, an assiduous lapping of blood from his wounded breast, a shallow sucking of blood from his nipples and neck, a savory draining of semen from his pulsing cock.

Soon, he's passed out. I snuff the candles, thank the Dark Gods, and hail the beloved dead, Angus and Morna and Mark, all those who wait for me in the Summerlands. Then I bandage Colin, unbind him, lift him into my arms, and carry him up to bed.

My thrall wakes during the night, jolting up from a bad dream. He wraps his arms around me, buries his face in my chest hair, and sobs for a long time. I stroke his head and soothe him till he's exhausted himself. I lick tears from his face and cradle him like a child.

"You're all right, lad," I say, rocking him.

"Aye. Aye, I am. The beating, the pain you inflict...it helps, m'lord. My body's suffering puts to rout the sorrows of my mind," he whispers against my skin. "At least for a time. I thank Our Lord you found me."

Soon Colin's asleep again. I kiss the wounds on his neck. I rest my head on his bandaged breast, to feel the rise and fall of his breathing, to hear the steady beating of his heart. Damn that slatternly sister of his. He needs another jolly holiday to cheer him up, a change of scenery. Perhaps we'll go to Edinburgh come the Yuletide. I'll rent us a grand Georgian flat in New Town. I'll buy him a great Christmas turkey and a huge plum pudding, and the boy can eat till he's full to bursting. Or perhaps I'll simply pop his damned sister into a remote nunnery. Or, better still, Bedlam.

A SUFFOCATING WAVE of despair washes through me as soon as I awaken, as if I'm drowning in the oily water of the Thames. Slipping from my coffin, faintly nauseated, I race up the cellar stairs.

Colin is sitting on the divan in the parlor, clutching a copy of the *Evening News* and watching November rain crawl down the window glass. A half-empty bottle of whisky rests on the table before him.

"Colin? What is it?"

Colin doesn't look at me. He lifts the paper, then drops it on the table.

"She must have invited him in. She must have thought he was just another fuck."

I snatch up the paper and skim it fast. *East end fiend...insane love of mutilation... Mary Ann Kelly...cut, eviscerated, and disfigured as none of her unfortunate predecessors sacrificed by the 'Lust Morder' have been.*

"This woman. She—"

"Aye. My sister." Colin takes a long drink from the bottle. "I think. I should go to the police. I should...."

I drop the paper onto the floor. I pull Colin to his feet and embrace him. His arms hang at his sides; he leans limply against me. It's like hugging a poppet. I slip into his mind, trying to give him comfort, but all I find there is alarming numbness and a cold despair. It's like a boulder even I lack the strength to budge.

"Stay here, lad," I say, squeezing his hands in mine. "I'll go to Whitechapel and found out what I can."

Colin nods. He sinks down onto the divan, leans back, and closes his eyes.

COLIN'S STILL SLUMPED on the divan when I return, after hours of exploration and the exertion of much mesmeric energy. On the table, the whisky bottle stands empty. When the lad lifts his face to mine, his eyes are blank, emotionless, like discs of azure ice.

"M'lord. You're back. What did you find?"

I sit beside him and wrap an arm around him. He takes my hand, smiles, and stares at the carpet.

"It was your sister, lad. I'm so sorry."

Colin nods mechanically. "What happened to her? How did she die?"

"Her throat was cut, like the Ripper's other victims." After some rigorous mind-manipulation on my part, Dr. Bond, the police surgeon, shared all the horrific details with me, but they certainly aren't facts that Colin should hear.

Colin shudders against me. "What did he do then?" he asks flatly. "Is it true that she was mutilated like the others?"

I nod.

"How?"

"You don't need to know that, my boy. You're distraught enough."

Colin drops my hand and kneads his brow. "Do they have any idea who this man is?"

"Not yet. Several people on the street think they might have seen him. They have a description. And I think I got the smell of him."

Colin looks up, one beautiful eyebrow cocked. "What's that, m'lord?"

"My sense of smell is as sharp as my other senses. I misted into the room where the murder was committed, and I got a whiff.... Some men have very distinctive odors. You certainly do. This scent.... I think I'd recognize it if ever I encountered the man. Perhaps tomorrow night I should have some pints in Whitechapel and see what I can see. Or rather, smell what I can smell. If the authorities can't find the foul bastard, perhaps I can. And if I do...."

"Revenge her, m'lord." Colin takes my hand again. "Make him suffer as terribly as he did them. Let's get you down to your bed now. The dawn's nearly here."

The sun's only begun to decline, I can sense, when the lid of my coffin's lifted.

My eyes flicker open. Colin's standing there, studying me. Drowsily, I peer up at him and smile. Solemnly, he returns my smile.

"You're a glory, Derek Maclaine."

"As are you," I croak.

Bending, he kisses my mouth and my brow before lowering the lid.

The sun sets, and I rise.

Upstairs, sleet taps the windows. Colin's nowhere to be found, and the house is dark. "Off to fetch liquor, cheese, and meat," I mutter, starting up a fire in the grate. "For a lean lad, he certainly likes to eat."

I light a lamp in the parlor for Colin's return and pour him out a glass of red wine. "Time to quaff some ale in Whitechapel," I say, heading up the stairs to dress. "'The *Draugr* Detective.' Fine title for a penny dreadful."

I'm adjusting my frock coat in the mirror and admiring the polish Colin's left on my boots when I see the envelope on the bed, lying atop my pillow. Across it, my name is scrawled in Colin's blocky script. I tear it open, unfold the letter inside, and read.

My sweet Lord,

Forgive me. This is my farewell. By the time you read this, I will have thrown myself into the Thames.

The brain-blackness has me. It's like a dark fire inside my bones, and only death will put it out.

What happened to Mary is too much for me to bear, too much for me to live with. To think I could have helped her, to think that the last time I saw her in this life I called her a foul twat and a drunken slut.... To think that she died in a manner so terrible that you would not tell me the details....

I adore you, Derek Maclaine. You looked like Our Lord sleeping in your coffin. And like Him, you will arise and you will spread salvation.

You were my salvation for a long time. But I am too weak to continue. My mind is diseased. You are strong. You will continue. I will die knowing that you will live to avenge my sister and to give new life to other fortunate souls like me.

Do not forget me, Lord. And be in no hurry to meet me in Paradise...or in Hell, where, according to the Church, as a self-murderer I am bound. This is the place for you, I think. You love this world more ferociously than anyone I have ever known.

As I have so deeply loved you. I am so sorry to disappoint you. Being your servant and your lover...these have been the best days of my life.

Colin

In a fury, I crumble the paper. "You little fool," I snarl. In another second, I've dashed out into the icy night.

I CHECK THEM all, moving so fast that humans can only discern a blur. So many bridges. Waterloo, where numerous Londoners have ended their lives. Blackfriars, Southwark, London, and one in construction near the Tower. Westminster, Lambeth, Vauxhall, and Chelsea.

There's no sign of Colin, no scent. He's gone. I stop panting in the middle of the last bridge, Albert, lift my face into the falling sleet, and howl.

TWO DAYS LATER, Colin's body is found, smelling of river and rot. I identify him, I claim him—Colin Kelly, manservant. I touch his sunken face and arrange for his burial.

Three weeks after that, at the Ten Bells—a pub where Colin's sister was seen the night of her murder—I'm paying the stonemason the last installment on Colin's tombstone when I catch a long-awaited and familiar odor. There, at a corner table, is a patron who fits the description of the man seen with Mary Kelly soon before she died: short, with a pale complexion, thick eyebrows, and a moustache curled up at the ends. For a moment, I think the American author Poe has stepped out of his grave and into the pub.

When the stonemason departs, I order another pint of bitter, take a table near my odoriferous prey, and observe him as he converses with a friend and eyes the women, many of whom are prostitutes. The mad killer who has all of London in a panic is unremarkable, with the looks and speech of just another East End denizen.

Near midnight, one woman, an emaciated redhead, chats with him. His eyes gleam with fervor. He smiles. He cups her arse, fondles her breast, and escorts her out. I drop money on the table and follow them.

The pair have turned left down Lamb Street when I accost them. "You, madam," I say, gripping her arm. "You'd do well to head home now. I have business with this gentleman."

"Sod off!" the man splutters, glaring at me. "Our business is none of yours."

"Whas this?" she slurs. "Mutton shunter, are you? Frightfully l'elegant for a bloody bobby, an't you? We're just off to smother a parrot, we are. The Green Fairy calls."

"Madam," I say, gritting my teeth and giving her a hard mental push. "On your way, snaggletooth."

"Ah, shite. You're both tossers. Gong-farmers. I'm gone." With a wave of dismissal, she staggers back toward the thoroughfare.

"You bloody bastard," the man snarls, seizing my forearm. "I should—"

"What?" I shake off his hand and he takes a step back, abruptly aware, despite his rage, of our considerable difference in size. "Cut my throat and mutilate me like you did those women? Like Mary Kelly? Gashing her face, slashing her throat, hacking off her breasts, stealing her heart, removing her viscera?"

He chokes up a gasp. "How? How do you—?"

"Your scent, sir," I say, curling my lip. "You have a very individual stink. Syphilis, yes, but that's not uncommon in this city. Something else. Who knew that extreme insanity had an odor?" Smiling, I expose both fangs and, from beneath my Inverness, I draw my dirk.

He may be a madman, but he has the sense to run, bolting back toward Commercial Street. Snickering, I shift into winged form, take to the air, and follow him. He moves due east, then north along Brick Lane. After a couple of blocks, he darts into a row of flats.

I swoop down, peering into window after window until I locate him. As badly as I'd like to smash through the glass for dramatic effect, silence is as much of a necessary element of my task tonight as it was for his killings. I mist inside instead, materializing behind him as he leans against the door, panting hard and listening for sounds of pursuit.

"I don't care who you are or why you killed them," I say.

The man whirls and backs up against the door, hair unkempt and face frantic.

"I only know that what you did to Mary Kelly took my boy from me. And so tonight, sir, your vile life is mine." I lock eyes with him, probing his thoughts. Sometimes the insane are easier to mesmerize than the sane, and sometimes they're entirely resistant, like a rabid animal.

This one is the latter. With a snarl, he whips a long knife from his pocket and leaps at me.

My hand shoots out, knocking the blade from his grasp. "Is that the knife with which you eviscerated them?"

With both hands, I catch him by the throat, carry him kicking across the room, and force him down onto the filthy bed, where he lies thrashing and cursing with what breath he has left.

"Yes, that's right. Fight for your life. That will only make the ending of it more delicious. You thought you were the only monster in London? You're sadly mistaken." Growling, I straddle his chest and tighten my grip about his windpipe.

Again I flash my fangs. "I could drain you like a spider does a fly, but I shan't sully my tongue with your syphilitic blood. Instead, I'm going to treat you much like you treated your victims. Have you ever read Icelandic sagas, little man? Have you ever heard of the blood eagle?"

I bear down harder. His eyes bug. Wheezing, he claws at my fingers. He kicks like an upended insect.

I throttle him till he's barely conscious. Then I release him, roll him onto his belly, and tear open the back of his shirt. He lies there, quivering and gasping, as I remove my fine clothes, unwilling to besmirch them, and then slide my dirk from its sheath.

"I want you to feel every moment of this," I sigh, running the tip of the knife down his spine. "This is a work of art that will take both great strength and great patience. Luckily, I have both."

He whines like a dog, scrabbling at the bed. I clutch the back of his head, lift my blade, and begin.

I'VE PAID A goodly sum for Colin's headstone in Highgate Cemetery. It's a Celtic cross taller than I am, adorned with interlocking knotwork and carvings of shamrocks. Tonight, edged with snow as white as my beard, it glistens in the moonlight.

Every part of my erstwhile foe save one has been swallowed by the malodorous Thames. The heart I hold up and squeeze like an overripe plum. It deflates and collapses in my grip. Blood oozes out of it, dripping onto the snow-covered grave and trickling down my arm.

"Lord Odin," I whisper. "And You, Dark Crone of the Cauldron, and You, Lord of the Beasts. Accept this offering. Be kind to my lost boy in the Eternal Lands."

Something rustles in the boughs above, and then down they flap, two ravens, visitors from Valhalla. I drop the crushed heart onto the snow and step back, wiping tainted blood off my hands with a rag. The birds peck at the pulp, then tear it into gobbets and feast.

When they're done, I run my fingers over the name cut into the stone. Then I rise into the air and veer off toward the pubs of Hampstead. After weeks of rage and nausea, my appetite's returned. Tomorrow, I will book passage back to America. Tonight, I need to be cruel and kind to a new black-haired youth. Tonight, I need to banish sorrow and feed again on beauty's brevity.

STEAM IN ANTARCTICA

Matthias Klein

THEY TRACKED THE beast to the water's edge, where both the prints and the specks of blood, peculiar red-orange in hue, disappeared into the ocean. Thorne sent the others back to the ship to prepare for a hunt, lingering behind with his scientists to document the marks in the snow and ice. He never made detailed sketches and so finished first, warming his hands in the pits of his arms before having a smoke and watching Leland work. The man had pulled off his brown glass goggles and was squinting at the trail, thin fingers grasping the pencil tightly enough to hold it despite numbness from the cold.

Logan was swearing again. Thorne glanced his way, noted he had given up on his own documentation; there had been nothing but bloodlust in Logan's soul since Foster had been dragged under by the beast, blind rage of the sort that spoke of a deep bond.

"Off your ass, Leland," said Thorne, flicking the last of the ash in the man's direction. "If we don't hunt down the blaming thing Logan will swim after it himself."

Leland rose reluctantly, fumbling with his gloves, and shot Logan a look Thorne almost laughed at. Leland was all affront and arrogance until you got him alone. Stripped down he had a soft, aching artist's core. Stripped down he had a habit of asking for permission to come.

"I'll continue to recommend the use of an airship to track and monitor from above—" began Leland.

"We ain't studying it," said Logan. He had his goggles up still, eyes red-rimmed and searing as he glared. "We have Thorne's tarnal harpoon to send it to the devil."

"If we're intending to kill the bloody thing," said Leland, glancing to Thorne as though for help, "we ought to use the steam guns."

Thorne wanted another smoke. His bunch were an unusual lot; thanks to his own unorthodox nature, he could hardly have failed to select an odd assortment of professionals to accompany him to the Antarctic. While other expeditions were concerned with reaching the pole, Thorne had focused his endeavors on hunting down the beast credited with the destruction of a good half a dozen parties to date. There was little known about it, and descriptions from survivors were so poor that in the few weeks they had been here they had a different picture of the animal than the one they had when they arrived. Originally they had all agreed they wished to capture it alive, but wishes could change, and now Thorne's own group was splintering.

"Goggles down, Logan," said Thorne. He never got involved in their arguments. "You want to go snowblind?"

Logan grumbled all the way back to the ship, but he obeyed. Thorne had a short discussion with the crew and they were underway, leaving him to stagger down to his cabin. Alone, he had a shot of whiskey and set about cleaning his steam pistol. When the beast had streaked by he had taken several shots, damaging it enough to draw blood, but the sea salt was hard on the weapon. He should have known better than to bring anything he had not first gone over and tweaked to his standards, but he had been in a rush to get the expedition off, and his cousin could get steam weapons so damned cheap.

He did not bother looking up at the knock on the door. He already knew who it would be.

"Enter," he said, scrubbing hard at salt and rust buildup on the metal. If he had the right supplies, he could coat the metal to prevent most of the oxidation; as it was he had to clean it regularly and hope no holes were eaten in the cheap weapon.

Leland shut the door behind him and dumped his papers on the side of the table Thorne was not currently using, rubbing his hands as he sat. No doubt they were still cold, no doubt too he knew this would be the warmest place in the ship that was not full of sailors keen on harassing a lone British artist. Thorne kept a fire in his rooms every day of the year, the easier to dispose of bloody rags without raising any suspicions, helpful too in that it more fully cemented the idea of his eccentricity. Only strange men kept a fire burning daily in the summer months.

He knew what Leland wanted and he ignored the man until he took up his papers to refine the sketches he had made out in the snow. Thorne concentrated on the pistol, noticing out of the corner of his eye how Leland looked up at him every now and then. Waiting. Hoping.

God, how he enjoyed toying with Leland before fucking him. It was as if the man liked being ignored, as if the perverted kind of foreplay they engaged in only made him harder in the end.

He had been the only foreigner to answer the advert months ago, when Thorne was assembling his party for the expedition. He had strode into Thorne's New York office with his arrogant artist swagger and presented himself stiff-backed. Thorne had decided immediately that the man's moustache had to go if he wanted a place on the ship.

"Basil Leland," he had said, holding out his hand. Thorne merely eyed him from where he sat until the hand was retracted. "I'm here in response to your advertisement."

"Advertisement, huh," Thorne had said, mocking Leland's accent. The man had taken it, even looked vaguely amused. Thorne lit up, blew the smoke Leland's direction as he looked him over. "You don't look like a scientist."

"I'm an artist. I'm rather good. I was educated at—"

"And you're definitely not American."

At last Leland had scowled.

"That wasn't listed as a requirement."

"It's not." Thorne had stood, walked around the desk, circled Leland. The man seemed unable to get nervous, standing there unflinching, but Thorne saw his eyes dilate. He puffed smoke in Leland's face and watched the man grin at it.

"I'd heard Marcus Thorne was eccentric," Leland had said, "But I wasn't anticipating you'd be so...commonly American."

Thorne had grabbed the man's chin before he completely realized what he was doing; normally he did not bother testing the likes of Leland. But something about him...Leland's eyes dilated even more when Thorne turned his face to his, and he could have sworn Leland was holding his breath.

"I'm looking for scientists," Thorne had said, "or sailors, or hunters. Not squirmy little British pricks who like to scribble."

"How many of your scientists will be able to draw as accurately as I?" Leland had asked, boldly, eyeing Thorne's eyes, his lips. "Certainly you will want some accuracy with your accounts. I can use whatever style you'd prefer."

"I need people who can meet challenges. Take a pounding. It's rough out there."

Leland had seemed to pause. Thorne decided to test him. He held tight to the man's chin, kissed him full and forceful on the mouth, breath still full of smoke. When he pulled back, Leland's eyes had been closed.

"I'm your man," he had said, faint tendril of smoke seeping from between his lips. Thorne let his chin free and pulled back, taking another drag. Leland opened his eyes.

Thorne enjoyed leaving Leland wanting, just like he had that day. Watching the man become frustrated was too good; he spoke to him now without looking up.

"Pour me another whiskey."

Leland stood immediately and moved to do as bid while Thorne ignored him. His pistol clean, he began reassembling it, debating whether he had enough supplies and time to make any crude updates here. He did not particularly care to use cooking oils or anything else inappropriate to tweak the pistol, but he was well on his way to becoming desperate. As it was, the weapon was still shooting, as he had proven today, but he had no idea how long it would be before the salt rusted away too much and ruined the functioning.

"You thirsty, Baz?" he asked as he was finishing.

"Wouldn't say no."

Leland was feigning nonchalance, but he held the pen unmoving in his fingers. Thorne stood to replace his weapon and took the whiskey into his mouth. When he leaned over to Leland the man made him wrench his head over to where he could kiss him. He transferred the trickle of liquor to Leland's mouth and moved away, drinking what remained in the glass. Out the window the water rushed by, the ship on a faster clip than was safe, hot on the trail of the beast.

When the crew was finished giving the harpoon a good clean Thorne would have them move onto the steam guns. Unlike the harpoon, those had none of his little touches or modifications, and after so many months he seriously doubted they were salvageable. It should have occurred to him that the salt would interfere so much. But then, many things should have occurred to him, such as Leland nearby, breathing unevenly as he waited. The man was in love. Thorne should have anticipated that. He swore, slammed the glass down on the table.

"Anything I could help you with?" asked Leland, suddenly behind him. "Let off a little steam?"

Thorne turned, grabbed Leland's arm, and twisted it behind his back so sharply the man yelped. When Thorne slammed him facedown on his small bed the man ground back against Thorne's bulge and he responded by twisting harder. Leland moaned, a painfully lusty sound, and Thorne reached for the cravat he kept at the foot of the bed to bind his hands where he wanted them. Leland liked the feel of silk tight on his wrists. Leland liked the blindfold, too, which was ideal for Thorne. He never fucked without his partner wearing one.

"Damn," said Leland as Thorne pulled him backward, stretching his spine as far as it would go. "Please..."

Thorne ignored him, slid his other hand around and under Leland until he could feel the man's hardness. He pulled his hand back and shoved Leland forward, grinding his face into the bed. When he let him up he removed Leland's belt as the man gasped.

"Please what?" asked Thorne, pulling down Leland's trousers to reveal a pale ass. He snapped the belt in the air. Leland was blindfolded, but his ears worked well, and Thorne watched the man swallow. "Well?"

"Please don't," began Leland, choking on his words when Thorne grabbed his balls between his legs and tugged. His ass seemed to be opening to him, the hole clenching and unclenching, eager to swallow whatever Thorne would give.

"Don't what?" asked Thorne, knocking the man's legs apart farther. The time for Leland to bail out was now, but he never did. Thorne took a step back, struck Leland with his own belt. The man gasped, nearly cried out, and Thorne reached for the old piece of knotted rope. He leaned forward, pressing himself hard against Leland's ass, and gagged the man with the rough, salty length.

He stepped back and struck again, and Leland cried out into the rope. The man was blamed good at taking a beating, but Thorne was in no mood to draw it out long. Not today. His mind was only partly on the fucking. He laid the belt across the back of Leland's neck as though in warning and reached for the lubricant he was kind enough to use. Leland groaned into the rope, wriggled. The pink, raised flesh on his ass was the kind of beautiful thing that Thorne knew he would miss when it was gone. Damnation, that Leland had to go and fall in love with him.

He lubed Leland's eager, gaping hole and dropped his own trousers. With a hand he touched himself, slicking his hardened member. It was newly updated, buttersoft hide over a mechanism of his own devising, and he circled Leland's opening with his head first, teasing them both. Leland let out a little moan of begging, then a groan as Thorne entered in one sharp motion. The mechanism kept in time with Thorne's motions as he fucked Leland hard, the suction and pressure building him fast.

Leland cried out again as Thorne pounded him, head rocking back and forth under the belt.

"Not yet," said Thorne, punctuating his words with thrusts. "Go off without permission and you'll regret it." He grabbed Leland by his hair and yanked his head back, watching the man grind the rope in his mouth. The sides of his mouth were slick with salty drool, his cheeks damp. Thorne released him, set about pumping him a few more times, and rode Leland's ass through the climax.

He pulled out, cleaned up, and left Leland where he was while he waited for the mechanism to return to resting state. He poured himself another drink and shuffled through Leland's sketches, considering.

"The problem with the steam guns," he said as though Leland could respond, "is that I haven't had them cleaned since we set out. The salt rusts the cheap metal and gums up steam weaponry."

He heard Leland shift on the bed behind him.

"I'm having the crew clean the harpoon now, but it shouldn't be such a problem. I designed it myself, you know—rust-free coating. Bastard looks too big for one harpoon, you reckon?" One of Leland's drawings had a person standing next to a lump that represented the beast, and the size difference was remarkable. Thorne took another drink.

Leland let out a pleading sort of moan and began pushing himself against the bed in measured motions.

"Come before I give you permission and I'll invite all the sailors in here," said Thorne. "How do you think your ass will feel after it's been thoroughly explored by a good hard dozen cocks?"

The movement stopped, but if Thorne knew Leland at all, he was nearly there. He turned back to the bed and hauled Leland over by a shoulder so the man was on his back now, bound hands pinned beneath him, erection bobbing free. Nothing to get him off now. Thorne eased the rope gag out.

"Speak," he said. "Give me a good idea and I'll let you have what you want."

Leland licked his lips with a dry tongue.

"Capture it, like we first intended," he said.

"And do what with it? The blamed beast is larger than expected. It won't fit the ship."

"Please," said Leland. "I'll think better if you..." he trailed off, titled his ass up. "Just fuck me again. With anything. Anything. I'm desperate."

"I ought to tell you no," said Thorne, but he was hard again. "And leave you there." He moved to line himself up with Leland's ass again and pushed the man's legs back, not bothering to re-lubricate when there was still some left.

Leland's breath caught as Thorne pushed against his opening.

"Scream and I won't give you permission for days," said Thorne, watching Leland grit his teeth. Oh, this would be good. Thorne tended to come harder the second time anyway, and watching Leland's face as he struggled to be silent and enjoy himself at once would be a pleasure all its own.

Leland breathed in sharply as Thorne pushed his way in, motions causing more friction than before. Thorne grabbed his legs and dragged the man down on his cock, watching Leland toss his head. Had he bothered to remove more of his clothes Thorne knew he would find sweat beading over the man's chest, but his shirt was soaking it up, just as the blindfold was soaking up his tears. Thorne leaned hard into Leland as he climaxed a second time, grunting, but did not pull out. Instead he pushed Leland roughly and freed his hands.

"Will you let me?" asked Leland, words small in his mouth. His cock oozed precome. Thorne drew back and pushed in again, enjoying the sensation the mechanism delivered to his body, and caught the hand Leland had hovering over his cock.

"Use the other hand," he said, and watched as Leland fumbled to get himself off with his non-dominant hand. He whimpered to himself and exploded over his stomach and shirt, continuing to stroke until Thorne told him he could stop. Dutifully he waited until Thorne had permitted him to remove the blindfold before doing so. By then Thorne had his trousers back on again and was running through options in his mind.

They could open up some space in the hold and he could rework the cage to contain a larger-sized creature, to keep with the original idea. They could hunt it down and hope their weapons could kill it. Thorne had enough scientists and one professionally trained artist; they would be able to well document the beast, inside and out, upon its demise. But all of these options carried greater risk than before, when they had believed the creature to be smaller, less deadly. When his party had all agreed on what their task was.

"What course will you take?" asked Leland as he buckled his belt. He winced slightly as he sat, but made no complaint about it.

"I'll have to—" began Thorne, but a yell from outside the cabin interrupted him. He rushed out, hand on his steam pistol, Leland behind him. Any crew not currently running the engines was at larboard, leaning over. Someone, Logan perhaps, must have broken the lock to the weapons storage, as Thorne could see most men armed with steam rifles or pistols.

"Shit," said Leland. He looked like he wanted to hold Thorne back from approaching the side of the ship, but thought the better of it. "They want to kill it."

Most of the men were aiming as Thorne drew closer. He grabbed a man by the shoulder and hauled him away, peering over the rail at the beast in the water, so far beneath the surface it was only a dark blob. No one had fired yet, but every trigger finger itched for the beast to swim just a little closer. Thorne kept his hand over the pistol at his side, trying to block some of the salt spray from reaching it. He saw no blood trail in the water; whatever damage he had done earlier, it had not been much. He swore.

"We'll give him Jesse, sir," said the man aiming a steam rifle next to him. Thorne could hear how it whirred and wheezed, not an appropriate noise for such a weapon. Perhaps the weapons storage had not been as well sealed as he had assumed; perhaps salt had been rusting away at the rifles and pistols for months now. Everything would have to be individually inspected and cleaned, perhaps even torn apart and picked through to reassemble weapons with the parts from several others.

Thorne stepped back.

"Hold your fire," he said. He paced down the deck and gave the order again. Most of the men obeyed; some shut power to their weapons and were examining them, which only irritated Thorne more. They knew their rifles and pistols sounded wrong and had been about to use them regardless.

"It's surfacing," shouted Logan, and those who had not lowered their weapons trained them on the water now.

"Hold fire," he repeated, but the anger in his voice was not enough. At least half a dozen men fired; one or two shots went where intended, but the rest of the weapons malfunctioned, spraying superheated steam. Curses and yells of pain cut the air, and a round of further shots as Logan and another man continued to fire.

Thorne was pushing his way over to Logan when the ship shuddered and he stumbled, nearly falling to the deck.

"Harpoon," yelled Logan, and Thorne shouted to countermand that, staggering over to the man, who had raised his steam rifle and was aiming shakily into the churning water as the ship lurched. Thorne grabbed Logan's arm, tried to wrest the weapon from him. The ship shuddered again and both Thorne and Logan fell to the deck.

"The beast is more agile in the water," said Leland, somehow at Thorne's side to offer him a hand up. Thorne refused it, instead using the rail to yank himself to his feet.

"And it's trying to punch a damned hole in the ship," said Thorne. Another tremor ran through the deck. "Shit." He raised his voice. "All crew stand down!"

What they needed to do was back off. What they needed to do was leave the beast alone. But no one heeded orders in the chaos. Thorne kicked the back of Logan's leg, sending him toppling to the deck, and made a direct line to the harpoon. With the size of the beast, if the harpoon struck, the entire ship could potentially be dragged beneath the icy waters. For certain, that would end the expedition, not to mention all of their insignificant lives.

Thorne understood he would not make it to the harpoon in time, recognized also that the particular man working it was Mueller, one of Foster's friends, and unlikely to leave the harpoon if he had not already. Thorne paused, planted his feet against the sway of the rocking ship, and pulled his steam pistol.

"Mueller," he shouted. "Stand down." The man ignored him, adjusting the angle on the harpoon.

Thorne shot him. No one seemed to notice as he dashed over, pushed Mueller's body away, and worked at powering down the steam harpoon. The ship, however, seemed to be headed toward land, away from the beast, though the occasional thud against the hull that lurched them about indicated it was not intent on leaving them be. Thorne glanced to the helm and saw Leland there with a sailor, no doubt instructing him to drop at shore.

The ship continued to shudder as they set down, crew running to the side in time to see something large streak up out of the ocean and across the land. Thorne squinted at it, a greyish lump against the stark white of the snow, leaving behind a trail of blood. It was massive, the size of a small whale, although it resembled a seal to some extent, albeit with claws. He thought he confirmed the head was elongated and toothed like an alligator, but it was too swiftly into the distance to be certain.

"Thorne," said Leland, at his side again. They both watched a number of the crew disembark, Logan leading the way after the beast.

"I don't recall ordering you to set ashore."

"I'm sure you'll have a chance to whip me for it later."

Thorne hoped so. He desperately wanted a smoke, but for now he needed to give orders and set out after Logan. After the beast's attack, any crew not trekking across the snow and ice in pursuit more than willingly set to work on ship repairs, tending the wounded, and seeing to the state of the weapons without any complaint. He and Leland pulled on their protective goggles and set out.

The trail was easy enough to follow, the red-orange blood of the beast and how Logan's men had trampled it into the snow. Thorne had brought several vials, hoping to collect samples. He was first and foremost a researcher and inventor; he no more wanted to kill the beast than Leland seemed to, but suspected he was more open-minded to the suggestion than the artist.

They found Logan and his men clustered around a hole in the ice down which the blood trail indicated the beast had fled. It was a massive hole; Logan was pointing his steam rifle at it as though anticipating the beast would return. It looked as though the other men had brought knives rather than the poorly working steam weapons, and the second functioning rifle was nowhere to be seen.

"I doubt there's point to waiting," said Thorne, watching Logan whirl to point the rifle at him, the other men parting to give him a clear shot. Shit. "I reckon it's not coming back that way."

"Here to stop the hunt?" asked Logan. There was something very dangerous in his eyes. Thorne took a step forward. "We should've butchered the tarnal thing the moment we first found it."

Thorne nodded.

"Yes. Then Foster would still be here."

Logan curled his lip, apparently not keen on Thorne's understanding.

"I'm leading the expedition now," he said. "You brought the money, sure, but we brought the real labor, and we're the ones bleeding and dying." He motioned with his head. "Step away, Leland."

"Will you be shooting him?" asked Leland.

"That beast just took down Rogers, rifle and all. I figure fresh meat'll draw it back. I won't kill him—no point in that. Let you bleed a little first, Thorne."

"You blame me," said Thorne, silently cursing his own foolishness. Talking himself out of situations was not one of his skills.

Before he could continue, though, motion at his side caused him to turn, to watch as Leland pointed Thorne's steam pistol at him. The artist backed away toward Logan as Thorne felt his insides lurch. He had believed Leland of all people would stand by him. A familiar kind of terror gripped him, the kind he had not experienced in decades, the kind he had last felt in the midst of a conflagration he had almost lost his life to.

That time he had been reborn. He doubted he would be so lucky now. He watched Leland move to Logan's side, steam pistol trained on him.

"Looks like I ain't the only one," said Logan.

"The legs, then?" asked Leland. "He won't be able to run."

Logan grunted and aimed his rifle downward, toward Thorne's left leg. The moment he lowered the weapon Leland turned and shot him through the skull. Thorne jumped to the side, narrowly avoiding the rifle shot, and tumbled hard onto the ice.

The cold silence was hard on the ears. Thorne got to his feet, glanced around at the men. Their expressions were difficult to make out beneath their winter gear, their brown glass goggles, but none of them raised a knife.

"We will kill it," said Thorne. "But we will do it on our terms. Anyone not with me can feel free to go back to the ship and make repairs." When no one volunteered, he bent for Logan's rifle. "Fan out in groups of three and check the area. If it dove into the ice here the blamed thing could have a den nearby."

Leland went with Thorne even though he told the man to accompany a different group. Just another thing he would have to punish the artist for. Leland would be getting one hell of a ride later, after jarring Thorne like that.

"I sense you're not pleased—" began Leland.

"Go to hell," said Thorne, so sharply that Leland fell silent.

Several hundred feet away they found a waterfall of blood. Leland turned, checking for danger, while Thorne approached. This, this had to mean something. It was too cold to smell, but Thorne thought that was best, not caring to have any sensory experience of the flow beyond what he could see. He filled his vials, mind churning. He could not determine whether there was something under the ice, some colossal beast, bleeding into the snow like some wounded god of old, or if this was something else. At any rate, he was certain that they were now in the heart of the beast's territory and well out of their depth.

Where there was one, there could be more.

No one objected to returning to the ship. Preparing to meet the beast again was priority enough, even for Logan's followers, and Thorne wanted to analyze his blood samples. Back in his cabin, the warmth made the contents of the vials reek of metal.

"Hypothesis?" he asked Leland, not looking up at where the man was sulking with his papers.

"Mechanical creature," said the artist. "The 'blood' is a mixture of lubricant and rust. Explains the peculiar hue."

"Interesting. I hadn't considered man-made."

"Why would you? You believe yourself to be the cleverest man aboard."

That stung more than Thorne was expecting. He experienced a flare of rage, then the desire to make Leland justify himself, make him defend the who and the why of it all until he gave up and admitted it was a foolish suggestion. But Thorne simply stared.

"I know, you know," said Leland. When he glanced up and their eyes met, Thorne experienced a jolt in his stomach that truly disturbed him. He leaned back in his chair.

"Know what?" he asked, but he knew. Damnation, he knew what Leland was saying, but somehow he hoped that if he pressed hard enough, Leland would have made a mistake, would back down, intimidated.

"Marcus Thorne," said Leland. He was not going to be intimidated. Why should he? Intimidation aroused him. "The innovator who was only able to explore his genius when his wealthy father's home burned down and he inherited at the young age of nine."

"It's not unheard of for fathers to disagree about what their sons should do."

"But it is an oddity that a son should suddenly pursue entirely different interests, isn't it?" Leland was examining his face now, and Thorne wished he had left all of his winter gear on. "Since I've been working for you I've learned that you were different after the fire that claimed your entire family—including your twin sister."

"I did shoot a man today," said Thorne. The corner of Leland's mouth tipped up in amusement.

"As did I. For you, I'd add. I'd do it again."

"And if you don't want me to, you ought to shut your damn mouth."

"I want your trust," said Leland, and Thorne gave a sharp, short laugh. "If not your devotion. I know, and I have known. It was not difficult for me to put together, not after screwing you regularly. No variation on the blindfold. What if Alice hadn't died in the fire, but rather Marcus?"

Thorne found himself crumpling. Leland had returned his steam pistol to him, well knew he could shoot him dead, and yet he was still talking. Thorne stood.

"I'd have preferred to be called Alexander," he said. He had never admitted that to anyone. Leland nodded.

"But you had to assume your brother's identity."

"Oh, I could have run off as Alexander. I was planning to, before the fire. But the inheritance...I could do anything I wanted with that." Thorne was debating what to do now. No one had ever guessed at his past before, at who he had been forced to be before that fire. "What are you planning on, Leland?"

To his surprise, the artist got to his feet, moved around the table, and knelt before him.

"To beg," he said. "Plead. Implore."

"For what? Forgiveness, now that you think I'm a woman? Maybe I ought not to shoot you?"

"No, Thorne, you're all man. I wouldn't otherwise..." he trailed off, shook his head. "I've known for months, and I'll confess that. But I'm begging for something else."

He went silent.

"Beg, then," said Thorne, and for a moment everything was usual, Leland asking permission, Leland begging, Leland needing his authority. When he hesitated Thorne stepped on his hand, pressed down just hard enough to hurt a little. "I said beg."

"I'm going mad," said Leland. "I long to suck your cock, and you withhold. Please. Just once."

Thorne paused. It fell into place now why Leland had brought it all up, forced Thorne to consider that someone else might know. He wanted to reassure Thorne. He wanted to let Thorne know something beyond the only thing they had ever done was possible, that there was no need to hide that which was no longer a secret. Thorne could not decide whether that was a relief, or utterly terrifying.

Whichever the case, he could not stop himself from playing along, at least for now. He could decide what to do later.

"What a confession," he said, grinding Leland's hand under the sole of his boot. "You pathetic, horny little man. You really think you should be allowed a taste?"

"I'm begging you for one."

Thorne grabbed him by the chin again, yanked his head up.

"Begging. Pleading. How much will you be crying for me to stop as I'm ramming myself down your throat? I don't like men who go back on their word."

"Please," said Leland, eyes watering from the angle of his neck, the pressure on his hand. Thorne let go of his chin, pulled his foot back.

"I have work to do," said Thorne, turning away. Leland crawled on the dirty wood floor, following him to his seat, groveling.

"I'll be your assistant, your devoted assistant. Help with any experiments you want. I'll track this bloody thing to the pole and back, just promise me I can gag on you."

Thorne's mind swore. Resisting Leland was not something he was good at, and this new territory was too tempting. He felt his trousers getting tight as his cock reacted to his body's growing desire. No one had ever wrapped their lips around him, had taken him in and swallowed him whole. He could never have risked it; his cock was as perfect as he could craft, yet he knew he would be unable to fool anyone with it, not even with the blindfold. And yet here Leland was.

Time stretched peculiarly as his mind raced. There were the vials of blood on his table, waiting to be analyzed. Here was Leland, prostrating himself at Thorne's feet, hope and lust in his gaze that he carefully brought up to just under Thorne's own eyes.

He could send them after the beast and they could all die in the next few days. A smart man would gather as much information as he could and plan a return expedition. The beast itself could be man-made, as Leland suggested, or could be an undiscovered animal. The blood would reveal much.

Thorne could not think with all this blood pounding through him, hot and demanding. He decided he could trust Leland. He decided he could rely on Leland. He decided he could review and reanalyze that determination at any point. He decided he was not going to let more men die if he could help it.

He decided to set aside the vials for now.

"Very well," he said at last. "You'll still be bound and blindfolded—lustful men like you need help keeping your urges in check." He paused, gazed down at Leland. "But I will let you try out a new gag."

EXTRACT:
TELENY
Anonymous

The Librarie Parisienne was a bookstore on Coventry Street in London, run by a man named Charles Hirsch. One day, a famous writer by the name of Oscar Wilde entrusted Hirsch with a package, telling him that a friend of his would be along to collect the package, and would have with him Oscar's card by way of proof. As Hirsh describes it, "a few days later one of the young gentlemen I had seen with [Wilde] came to collect the package. He kept it for a while and then brought it back saying in turn: 'Would you kindly give this to one of our friends who will come to fetch it in the same person's name'". This occurred three more times before the book was finally returned to Wilde, but in the meantime, Hirsch's curiosity had gotten the better of him and he had dared to top unwrap the package and read it's contents.

What he found inside was *Teleny*, a 'round-robin' novel telling the story of lovers Camille de Grieux and René Teleny; it was wildly pornographic, almost exclusively homosexual, and clearly written by, as Hirsch describes it in a beautiful example of turn-of-the-century shade, "several writers of unequal merit."

Whether Oscar Wilde wrote any of the sections of Teleny remains unproven, though the book is frequently ascribed to him. Though in structure a love story, the book is startlingly explicit. The scene excerpted below is a particularly infamous (and ultimately gruesome one) that occurs three quarters of the way into the narrative.

One of the guests shewed us how to make a Priapean fountain, or the proper way of sipping liqueurs. He got a young Ganymede to pour a continuous thread of Chartreuse out of a long-beaked silver ewer down on Briancourt's chest. The liquid trickled down the stomach and through the tiny curls of the jet-black, rose-scented hair, all along the phallus, and into the mouth of the man kneeling in front of him. The three men were so handsome, the group so classic, that a photograph was taken of it by lime-light.

'It's very pretty," said the Spahi, "but I think I can shew you something better still.'

'And what is that?' asked Briancourt.

'The way they eat preserved dates stuffed with pistachioes in Algiers; and as you happen to have some on the table, we can try it.'

The old general chuckled, evidently enjoying the fun.

The Spahi then made his bed-fellow go on all fours, with his head down and his backside up; then he slipped the dates into the hole of the anus, where he nibbled them as his friend pressed them out, after which he licked carefully all the syrup that oozed out and trickled on the buttocks.

Everybody applauded and the two men evidently were excited, for their battering-rams were jerking up their heads, and nodding significantly.

'Wait, don't get up yet,' said the Spahi, 'I haven't yet quite finished; let me just put the fruit of the tree of knowledge into it.' Thereupon he got on him, and taking his instrument in his hand, he pressed it into the hole in which the dates had been; and slippery as the gap was, it disappeared entirely after a thrust or two. The officer then did not pull it out at all, but only kept rubbing himself against the other man's buttocks. Meanwhile the cock of the sodomized man was so restless that it commenced beating a tattoo against its owner's stomach.

'Now for the passive pleasures that are left for age and experience,' said the general. And he began to teaze the glans with his tongue, to suck it, and to twiddle the column with his fingers in the deftest way.

The delight expressed by the sodomized man seemed indescribable. He panted, he shivered, his eyelids drooped, his lips were languid, the nerves of his face twitched; he seemed, every moment, ready to faint with too much feeling. Still he appeared to be resisting the paroxysm with might and main, knowing that the Spahi had acquired abroad the art of remaining in action for any length of time. Every now and then his head fell as if all his strength was gone, but then he lifted it up again, and—opening his lips—'Someone—in my mouth,' said he.

The Italian Marquis, who had doffed his gown, and who had nothing on but a diamond necklace and a pair of black silk stockings, got astride on two stools over the old general, and went to satisfy him.

At the sight of this tableau vivant of hellish concupiscence, all our blood rose bubbling to our heads. Everyone seemed eager to enjoy what those four men were feeling. Every unhooded phallus was not only full of blood, but as stiff as a rod of iron, and painful in its erection. Everyone was writhing as if tormented by an inward convulsion. I myself, not inured to such sights, was groaning with pleasure, maddened by Teleny's exciting kisses, and by the doctor, who was pressing his lips on the soles of my feet.

Finally, by the lusty thrusts the Spahi was now giving, by the eager way the general was sucking and the Marquis was being sucked, we understood that the last moment had come. It was like an electric shock amongst us all.

'They enjoy, they enjoy!' was the cry, uttered from every lip.

All the couples were cleaving together, kissing each other, rubbing their naked bodies the one against the other, trying what new excess their lechery could devise.

When at last the Spahi pulled his limp organ out of his friend's posterior, the sodomized man fell senseless on the couch, all covered with perspiration, date syrup, sperm, and spittle.

'Ah!' said the Spahi, quietly lighting a cigarette, 'what pleasures can be compared with those of the Cities of the Plain? The Arabs are right. They are our masters in this art; for there, if every man is not passive in his manhood, he is always so in early youth and in old age, when he cannot be active any longer. They—unlike ourselves—know by long practice how to prolong this pleasure for an everlasting time. Their instruments are not huge, but they swell out to goodly proportions. They are skilled in enhancing their own pleasure by the satisfaction they afford to others. They do not flood you with watery sperm, they squirt on you a few thick drops that burn you like fire. How smooth and glossy their skin is! What a lava is bubbling in their veins! They are not men, they are lions; and they roar to lusty purpose.'

'You must have tried a good many, I suppose?'

'Scores of them; I enlisted for that, and I must say I did enjoy myself. Why, Viscount, your implement would only tickle me agreeably, if you could only keep it stiff long enough.'

Then pointing to a broad flask that stood on the table,—'Why, that bottle there could, I think, be easily thrust in me, and only give me pleasure.'

'Will you try?' said many voices.

'Why not?'

'No, you had better not,' quoth Dr. Charles, who had crept by my side.

'Why, what is there to be afraid of?'

'It is a crime against nature,' said the physician smiling.

'In fact, it would be worse than buggery, it would be bottlery,' quoth Briancourt.

For all answer the Spahi threw himself face upwards on the ledge of the couch, with his bum uplifted towards us. Then two men went and sat on either side, so that he might rest his legs on their shoulders, after which he took hold of his buttocks, which were as voluminous as those of a fat old harlot's, and opened them with his two hands. As he did so, we not only had a full view of the dark parting line, of the brown halo and the hair, but also of the thousand wrinkles, crests—or gill-like appendages—and swellings all around the hole, and judging by them and by the excessive dilatation of the anus, and the laxity of the sphincter, we could understand that what he had said was no boast.

'Who will have the goodness to moisten and lubricate the edges a little?'

Many seemed anxious to give themselves that pleasure, but it was allotted to one who had modestly introduced himself as a maître de langues, 'although with my proficiency'—he added—'I might well call myself professor in the noble art.' He was indeed a man who bore the weight of a great name, not only of old lineage—never sullied by any plebeian blood—but also famous in war, statemanship, in literature and in science. He went on his knees before that mass of flesh, usually called an arse, pointed his tongue like a lance-head, and darted it in the hole as far as it could go, then, flattening it out like a spatula, he began spreading the spittle all around most dexterously.

'Now,' said he, with the pride of an artist who has just finished his work, 'my task is done.'

Another person had taken the bottle, and had rubbed it over with the grease of a pâte de foie gras, then he began to press it in. At first it did not seem to be able to enter; but the Spahi, stretching the edges with his fingers, and the operator turning and manipulating the bottle, and pressing it slowly and steadily, it at last began to slide in.

'Aie, aie!' said the Spahi, biting his lips; 'it is a tight fit, but it's in at last.'

'Am I hurting you?'

'It did pain a little, but now it's all over;' and he began to groan with pleasure.

All the wrinkles and swellings had disappeared, and the flesh of the edges was now clasping the bottle tightly.

The Spahi's face expressed a mixture of acute pain and intense lechery; all the nerves of his body seemed stretched and quivering, as if under the action of a strong battery; his eyes were half closed, and the pupils had almost disappeared, his clenched teeth were gnashed, as the bottle was, every now and then, thrust a little further in. His phallus, which had been limp and lifeless when he had felt nothing but pain, was again acquiring its full proportions; then all the veins in it began to swell, the nerves to stiffen themselves to their utmost.

'Do you want to be kissed?' asked someone, seeing how the rod was shaking.

'Thanks,' said he, 'I feel enough as it is.'

'What is it like?'

'A sharp and yet an agreeable irritation from my bum up to my brain.'

In fact his whole body was convulsed, as the bottle went slowly in and out, ripping and almost quartering him. All at once the penis was mightily shaken, then it became turgidly rigid, the tiny lips opened themselves, a sparkling drop of colourless liquid appeared on their edges.

'Quicker—further in—let me feel—let me feel!'

Thereupon he began to cry, to laugh hysterically; then to neigh like a stallion at the sight of a mare. The phallus squirted out a few drops of thick, white, viscid sperm.

'Thrust it in—thrust it in!' he groaned, with a dying voice.

The hand of the manipulator was convulsed. He gave the bottle a strong shake.

We were all breathless with excitement, seeing the intense pleasure the Spahi was feeling, when all at once, amidst the perfect silence that followed each of the soldier's groans, a slight shivering sound was heard, which was at once succeeded by a loud scream of pain and terror from the prostrate man, of horror from the other. The bottle had broken; the handle and part of it came out, cutting all the edges that pressed against it, the other part remained engulfed within the anus.

HENRY/
HENDRIK

Henry Alley

It is September now and I'm in my fifty-sixth year, but all I have to do is think about the month of August, my dearest Hendrik, and I have movement in my veins again, with a recollection of the three days we spent together. You were my import from Rome, my house guest, lighting up all of Rye and England itself, but especially my home, my Lamb House, which I have newly owned for 2,000 pounds! Every room, every spreading shrub in the garden, every azalea, illuminating purple verging on violet, every yellow rose, latticed on the walls became a part of that moment when you arrived. Ever since meeting you in May and traveling back from Rome to what was a cold set of weeks for me by the sea, I started anticipating your every move as we planned on your visiting here. I would sit in the Garden Room of this red brick home, built in the eighteenth century, dictating to my secretary a story of an aging man in Paris, but I would look through that arched window and see the grass becoming a deeper green because I knew you would soon be at hand, under the changing clouds and toil of the sky. But how I anticipated, how I worried over your coming! That you would miss your train out of London, St, Paul's station, that you would sit in the back rather than forward, and spin off at Ashford, rather than coming to me in Rye, that it would not be you that would step off to meet me in your white cassock, so right for a sculptor in all the strength of your twenty-seven years. But it was you, my dear Hans, who stepped off at seven p.m.—you even got the first train of the evening! I pressed myself up against you, and because all the other passengers—including the woman in the hat with the grand ostrich feather!—had turned away, just for a moment, I could press closer and feel your hard muscles and bones all the way to the center of my chest. This was the man who carved stone on a parallel with Michelangelo in his studio. Holding you, I traveled all the way back to your workshop in the Via Margutta. I was at one with all the naked angels and naked women and naked men and cherubs in different angles of flight and embrace, reaching toward your high ceiling or in white touch, some of them, with one another. I felt your body, and decades and decades of hunger for contact were appeased in a moment. I actually became at one with you, was twenty-seven again (is it any coincidence we have nearly simultaneous birthdays in April?). Oh, the woman in the ostrich-plumed hat—she did not turn and look at us yet, and so, in the next instant, in becoming younger, I put my hand up and felt your blonde beard, touched your hair as we stood on the platform, kissed both your cheeks.

We had only a five minute walk to my Lamb House, but the streets of Rye seemed labyrinthine with you and me side by side and my gnome-like valet carrying your luggage ahead. The seagulls swooped down in one long cry. I could hardly keep my sense of direction as we moved toward my red cottage on West Street. You were a bit surprised, I think, by my imposing Georgian doorway, but I could only be thinking about climbing the stairs and situating you in your guest room—we did have a little cold supper supplied by my housekeeper—but later, I must lie awake with the candle out and hear you moving about getting ready to enter the high-canopied bed that to my eyes seemed to belong to a bridal chamber with its white frills supported by the rails and its glamorous white curtains and the rich white bedspread with its subtle rose designs. As for me, I tried sinking into sleep in my own room, but I was aware, waking or dreaming, of your life. I thought about our Roman hours together when we first met, how we talked that whole afternoon on the terrace three months prior about your grand plans of fashioning twisted, muscular gods for the great world, and how we had each lived in early years in New England, with you originally from Norway and how you were escaping your alcoholic father and tending to your dear mother and brothers and stepsister. You had had a hard life fashioning carpentry and painting ships, but you had developed a body like marble then, or hard wood. You grew into magnificent stature, and now that comforting man was only a few rooms away.

We talked of this the next afternoon in my garden under the mulberry tree, its branches ancient and splayed toward the ocean-like sky, ancient, yes, but still providing shade. That morning, I had clocked in with my dictation in my Garden Room while you were still sleeping from your journey, my secretary picking up every sentence on her typewriter, the clicking in time with the motions through my bow window, ranging, ranging across the lawn. Nearly quarter of a chapter was done before I heard you on the stairs, and I felt the life, the characters within me, who were coming out on the page, acquire a deeper, deeper physical life. Somewhere in the back of my mind two lovers, each of them married to the wrong person, came together in an Easter excursion, while cathedrals seemed built in the sky, a robin's egg blue.

Now our talk flew through the garden—where should we go, whom should we see?—there were many who wished to meet you, but I wanted you entirely to myself. It seemed to me you were coming to me again at that initial party of mutual friends in Rome, stepping toward me out of the group, out of the light from the balcony windows, with St. Peter's square in the distance, shaking my hand, and I felt, then, as though I were walking toward myself two decades ago when I was writing a novel about a handsome American sculptor, who, although a figment of words, was such a comfort, such a companion to me in my days back then. But today, and the next day, you were to be with me in the flesh, and so we planned our excursion, on the eve before you were to leave, to drive down to Winchelsea on our bicycles, and that moment of near parting was soon upon us. We mounted up and found our August-lit road, with the grass and the corn at our side, and the little creek with the floating white swan in it. There were exquisite green branches which dipped down over the road at times, but we cleared them as they reached toward us, and then there were the twisted road signs which criss-crossed and told us how far we were from our destination. You rode alongside of me. I had to stay slow to keep my fedora on. But you had your shirtsleeves rolled up, and I was aware of the veins traveling through all the long muscles that moved down toward your sensitive fingers. You were slim, so slim, but so strong! The evening light was starting to slant on us, and then suddenly there was a plummet down the hill toward Winchelsea, and with the arrival of the town, your insistence we ride another mile and a half to the beach. Oh, I felt my fifty-six years at that time, but I chased you, seeing your shoulders shift beneath your shirt, as the sun caught it up and made it an orange flame.

Leaving our bicycles, we walked toward the scalloped gray beach, and you suddenly stood still and turned toward me. I said, "My God, Hendrik, you look like you have become a god of the sea yourself! Triton or some other." A fine glow was behind the hills now, and the tide was coming in in level silver waves. You sat down on a log amidst some charcoaled pilings, and took off your shoes.

"This could be the time," you said, "to try becoming that."

I simply stood and looked, and you ran off, splashing in the tide pools. Then you pivoted and ran toward me, did an acrobatic leap and came up and kissed me on the cheek. We had the beach entirely to ourselves.

"What is the greatest gift I can give you?" you asked. "How can I repay this time which has been like a treasure, repay you for your house which has been the perfect refuge, for the privacy of your garden, and for your kindness in meeting me at the station? I know," you said, and started unbuttoning your shirt. That was off in a moment, and soon your trousers and your undergarments. You made a huge run toward the water and splashed in, your subtly muscled torso coming toward the surface. You were still reddish with exercise. Then you were up and out of the waves again and making tracks on the sand. You drew on your trousers only, and came up behind me and grasped me hard. "Feel this," you said, still naked to the waist. "Feel this."

"My dear Hans," I answered. "If you hold me too hard, I shall expire just from sheer happiness right here on the spot. Let nothing change this. Nothing change you. You don't know how much I have needed this."

But the sunset was escaping us. So was the warmth. I felt you shiver. The trousers had to go off again. Then the undergarments back on. Then the trousers once more. And your shirt. We had to be on our bicycles, and go the four miles back, not only for our supper but also so that you would not catch a chill. I was grateful for the Udimore hill, because the exertion would finally warm up your chilled body.

That night, as I lay in bed, how many times did I see you descend into the waves, and emerge, like Triton, naked and invincible? Then there were the hard facts. Perhaps in the next room you were packing already. "He is gone," I said to myself. "He is soon *gone*," and broke into a slight sob, which you must have heard, for in a moment you were in the room.

"There, there," you said, and removed your nightshirt.

You entered beneath the blankets, and tenderly removed my nightshirt as well. There was very little light from the moon coming through the window, and I did not have to see my own body, spread out in all its massiveness, but I felt yours. You held and comforted me.

"Here, here," you said, "take what you need."

And so I fed upon you. You nourished me. I partook again and again, and awoke the next morning as though I had drunk some magic elixir.

HENDRIK ANDERSEN, 1907

My dear Henry James, now you are gone again with the spring. But our Roman hours together were fine and lasting—so much more so than the last three times I came to you in Rye and Lamb House. I was hoping for something as good as that last day on our bicycles in 1899, on Winchelsea Beach and after, but then it did arrive, arrived this time in my rooms on the Piazza del Popolo, in my workshop in the Passeggiata di Ripetta, and in your quarters, finally, in the Hotel de Russie. Yes, yes, my dear Henry, we are, both of us, connoisseurs of light, you in your books, with your heroes and heroines just coming out of the veil of sunshine, and I with my gods catching every ray, blanched and white as they are, in my studio. You, my dear man, are put off, I know, by all those muscles, and arms and breasts and chests, and buttocks and privates, all tangled and reaching. But don't imagine for a moment that I don't need your approval as much as you needed mine.

I lived in anticipation of your coming this last May. I was heartbroken by the death of my brother, still, five years ago and needed comforting. You had been gravely ill. I thought that if anything would cure us both it would be us walking through Rome arm-in-arm and perhaps having more. And we did. You had arrived from Turin, and you promised to spend many days of the spring season with us. My stepsister, my sister-in-law, my mother and I had hoped you would bed down in our upstairs flat in the Piazza del Popolo, but you insisted on the hotel. You must have known. Still, you took time away from us, motoring sometimes with your married friends, making notes on the countryside. You had your adventurer friend and his wife with you, and all was being gathered for that book which you would call the *Roman Hours*. I would be named as your "sculptor friend," coming in those later pages added as almost an epilogue. You were making a farewell salute to the city that would be the foundation of your youthful dreams. All of your retinue stood breathless, waiting to call you "The Master." But I had ambitions of my own, and asked you to sit as a model in my studio. I was to make your bust. My models Guido and Roberto gathered round in that gathering Roman heat. Their bodies had formed the blueprint for the massive naked physique of The Ballplayer, who stood, naked, brash, and with clinched fists, and all in white plaster, with the three nude boys singing and holding hands toward the back of the studio, *Tre atleti cantori*. I remembered how my thumbs had formed the cavernous chest of The Ballplayer, how it satisfied a passion, the way the wide whirl of the nudes on the Sistine Chapel had satisfied Michelangelo's. The ceiling of my studio was high and cooling, the light flooded through the latticework, and you expressed appreciation for the cooler shadows as you sat and I molded the clay. In those moments, I wanted you. Wanted you! The great completeness of your life. You had finished out the last touches of the twenty four volumes of your New York Edition. All those novels, all those stories, all those essays, all those new prefaces—twenty-four volumes!—which included the crowns of your later life, *The Ambassadors, The Wings of the Dove*, and *The Golden Bowl*, books which were already emerging when I visited you in Rye for the first time. Little had I known what was coming when I heard the click of the typewriter that morning in the Garden Room downstairs.

And I? I had only a plan of a "World Centre," a dream plan for a city, filled with my colossal statues. My sister-in-law Olivia believed in me, was an heiress who could passionately patronize my projects. Still, I had only done such things as an *Angel of Life* in small scale bronze casting. I had yet to finish my *Fountain of Life*, which was to picture *Night, Day, Evening, Morning.* So far *Night* showed a naked man and woman thrown back in a rapturous white plaster embrace. That was as far as I had gotten. Was it that it was a man and woman and not a man and man that stopped me from going forward?

You looked skeptically at me, while I fashioned the bald brow in clay. It was the brow which had formulated those thousands and thousands of subtle words. I also fashioned the infinitely sensitive eyes that had guided the hand that penned out *The Portrait of a Lady*. I gave you a strong muscular jaw and neck, which was bared—senatorial and grand. It was to be my gift to you, but I knew, as a child does when he offers his kindergarten gift—a crayoned drawing perhaps—to his mother, that it fell fabulously, spectacularly short. You had created living people, who were all subtlety and nuance. My creations were all stiffness, idealism, and gesture. Oh, my dear Henry, I knew that as you sat for me in the hot studio. You had intimated as much when I had sent you a photo of my *Lincoln* and other photos of my goddesses and gods. Where is the person here? you seemed to ask. You had a right to ask it. I asked the same question of myself as my hands moved over the clay. But my idealizing touch was me.

So we later visited the foundry where some of my work was being cast, and I told you of my *Jacob and the Angel,* which was not far from being realized. We had dinner at my high terraced flat, under the loggia, where the roof top garden could give you red and yellow begonias and miniature roses—and a variety of miniature pine in pots. The view of the obelisk in the Piazza del Popolo reminded us of the sunset scenes we had seen on the beach at Winchelsea. Here the light slanted through the arch of the iron gate, and you said, "Now that project you mention, *Jacob and the Angel*, sounds promising. Can you put their story in their gesture?"

"I think so," I answered. "They are naked. The Angel has come up behind Jacob and grasped him with each hand on his beautiful lateral muscles. Jacob has grasped him in a kind of backwards full nelson, with the Angel's head on his shoulder. Jacob is bearded. The Angel clean shaven. The Angel's face is mild, because they're really not fighting."

"Such as you did for me on the beach," you answered. "You held me, rather than fought."

"Yes," I answered. "But I hadn't thought of that until now."

You helped yourself to more wine, more chicken. For a moment you reminded me of my father. You considered. "Yes, make the best of that project that you can. Keep it down to scale. And let me see the photograph. Tell Olivia to take it."

I felt as if you were once again putting me over your knee and spanking me with my pants down, reminding me not to be too grand again. My backsides felt it. But you said. "Those paintings of your brother's, which arrived the other day."

"Yes."

"I saw the one," you said, "I wasn't supposed to see."

He meant the one of myself and John Briggs Potter. I am lying in bed, on my back, one of my arms raised, and, half asleep, I am stroking a cat with my free hand, a cat, black and white, sitting on the floor. My nakedness is half disclosed, with the covers showing a huge erection. John, naked also, is sitting on the bed pulling on his socks.

"It's fine that you did see it," I answered.

"That's the kind of life I'd like to see in your sculpture," you told me. "Although it can never be in mine."

"Shall we try acting out a model for it?" I asked. "You leave tomorrow. The end of the all these wonderful days."

My other brother and my stepsister were not at the table at that moment. My mother and Olivia were bringing in more food. You knew a repast when you saw it.

"My dearest little Hans," you said. "I can't. I can't. Winchelsea and after was more than I have ever had my whole life. It would be greedy of me to ask for more."

I loved the sounds, now, of the piazza and the sight of the beautiful Tiber, as it led toward an arch, and then there were the beautiful lion fountains in the square, spitting water. The breeze from the river was cooling everything, but I was warming up. The Trastevere was in the distance.

"But I want more," I said. "I can ask for more. I'm younger. I want to take your magnificence into my being. To be together, breast to breast again. Only you can understand the tangle that is inside me."

You stopped eating. You put down your fork. How I wish I could have captured your pain, your frown in my bust. "I've had time to think. I've had time to retreat."

"But your letters," I answered. "They have all talked about wanting me, embracing me, holding me against you, drawing your hands over my shoulders."

"Yes, yes," you said. "I'm a man who has built himself on dreams, on indistinctness, on nuance, on imagined encounters. I desperately need warmth. Desperately. But I had time to think after we were together that first time. It was why I kept separate when you visited me again. Don't you understand? There's been Oscar Wilde and others. His miserable death. His torture in prison. His abandonment and revilement by his friends. Even by his own companion. They are all of them, all of them standing between you and me. And I have been so ill in between. And you—what would happen to you?"

"We are not in England," I said. "We are in Italy. There are no laws against us here. We have the New Penal Code. You are just afraid."

Yes, we were not in cold and cloudy Rye. We were here enjoying the lanterns of Italy. The obelisk was in the distance. The candles hovered around us like tiers going up to heaven.

You pushed your plate away. You wiped your eyes with the napkin. Perhaps you don't remember. That's when you said, "You may walk me back to the hotel, once I have said goodbye to your dear family."

There were kisses, eventually, and little pats from all of them. We went downstairs and walked the Via di Ripetta. For a moment I thought you would ask to see my studio again and then leave me back at my flat, but, no, we were going to your hotel. Sometimes the dark of the streets covered your face. In the distance were the screaming young cyclists, all shirtless and wild—you said they reminded you of the creations in my workshop. The dark became so dominant at one point, I swear I could see my father in you—the man I sent back to Norway to die of drink. I don't mean I saw you as a derelict, but only as the potential of what my father could have been. I had so often wanted to put my hand on his shoulder the way I was doing so now. The most I could have done until his death was to send my father money.

It was as if you aware, in some vein, of my thoughts. You said, "I was in the Protestant Cemetery the other day. I saw the graves of Shelley and Keats, and the grave of a dear woman who once loved me but who eventually jumped from a window. Her plot was covered with the most exquisite violets."

The six storeys of the Hotel de Russie were upon us. It was all lit by lamps. Almost every room had a balcony. I had not been in your quarters until now. I thought for sure we would part in the lobby. But you invited me up to your luminous room, one with marble pillars, golden cherub statues, and a set of windows festooned with bronze Austrian curtains.

You sat down on one of the sofas—for it was a luxurious room—and wiped your eyes again. You had lowered the lamps. You said, "This is the last time we will meet here in Rome. I will never be able to make this journey again. Do give me the gift that you gave me eight years ago. Be Triton for me. Be the Angel, Jacob's Angel."

I stood in the middle of the room. I took off my hat, my coat, unbuttoned my waist coat, removed my tie and collar, and then my trousers. My shirt was off and then, finally, my Union suit. I know you were never have called it that for the world. I stepped naked into the bed, which was mounted high already, stepped into it as though I were in that painting of my brother's. I was just as erect as before.

"You must come to me," I said. "If the gift is to be complete."

You lowered the lamps even lower. Then you removed what I removed. We were inside the blankets once more, but only for a moment. Then I drew myself across your ancient and wide back and slowly, slowly entered you the way my angel entered Jacob. I drew my rough chin across your skin, and then moment by moment filled you. For just instant, I understood all the tangle that was inside me. I entered, prodded and became you. Then we separated, and you said, "Thank you, my dear boy, and this shall never happen again. I feel now that I could not write another word."

Later you were to say you were the man to whom nothing ever happened. But it did. And although you were to go home and burn all my letters in the grate at Lamb House, you were to still write to me. I was to receive a letter from you just the other day. Here I am, you said, writing from my garden. With the roses and the mulberry tree just the same. You said you remembered the candle flames of our dinner on my terrace. May you also remember—acknowledge somehow!— our times together that were one sweet merger.

The author would like to acknowledge Leon Edel's biography of Henry James; *Rosella Mamoli Zorzi's Beloved Boy: Letters to Hendrik C. Andersen, 1899-1915*, Henry James; Susan E. Gunter and Steven H. Jobe's *Dearly Beloved Friends: Henry James's Letters to Younger Men*; Elena di Majo's *Museo Hendrik Christian Andersen* and Francesca Fabiani's *Hendrik Christian Andersen, la vita l'arte il sogno: la vicenda di un artista singolare*.

ON A
PASSAGE TO
THE QUEEN'S
JUBILEE

Kolo

April 1887

The *SS City of Rome* had been designed to be the fastest ship ever to cross the Atlantic. However, efficiency fought beauty and lost. And so *Rome* lumbered over the icy North Atlantic waters on her too-heavy hull of cheap iron without a care that she was such a huge disappointment to her makers. The character of her charges was similarly oblivious, the hallways peopled by lighthearted passengers dispatched from New York Harbor for the shores of England. "The Star Spangled Banner" bellowed in spectacular fashion daily, as if to herald the journey of one passenger in particular, a queen from far, far away in the bosom of the Pacific. Queen Kapiʻolani from the Hawaiian Isles would be Queen Victoria's honored guest at the latter's fiftieth jubilee celebration.

A single daub marred the perfection of this excursion: on April 23, mere days after stumbling out of Hudson Bay and onto the Atlantic, the *City of Rome* encountered strange flotsam in their path. The *SS State of Florida* had met its demise shortly before, and here was the proof: the No. 1 inflatable life raft, the sorry eyes of its passengers glittering hopeless in the search lights. Queen Kapiʻolani felt such pity for these desolate souls that she dispatched her valets to assist. They looked to Kuene, the Queen's most trusted valet, for instruction; without a word, he plunged into the fray, calling for blankets, towels and sustenance for the weary. The other valets followed suit. Kuene even requested that the musicians on hand play a light air. When the survivors had been fortified, the tears truly began to flow. The Hawaiians understood little of their words, but their woes were unmistakable. Strong liquor was administered to any who could hold it.

The night was cold and a thick fog threatened to blot out their route; all were advised to seek shelter indoors. Kuene wondered aloud where the survivors would be accommodated. "There is room in steerage for them," said a sailor. "Besides we can't have them bringing down passenger morale. We have a fortnight or more at sea ahead of us."

As the survivors were ushered away, Kuene caught sight of a solitary young man detached from the others. A sliver of a male with the sallow pale skin of these northern peoples, the young man was bundled up, trudging along with the others, shivering. Something about the man stirred the cauldron of Kuene's emotions. Their eyes met briefly and, more than anything that had preceded that moment, this sullen, defeated youth doubled over his own loss dealt the Hawaiian the harshest blow.

The festivities that night were not damped in the least by the arrival of the desolate bunch, nor were any of the future nights affected. If anything, life was all the more worth cherishing and living to its utmost, so the concerts and celebrating redoubled.

Kuene receded back into his duties. In addition to coordinating the party, he also served as interpreter for the entire entourage who refused on principle to abandon their Hawaiian tongue for the inferior English language. Among the valets, jokes abounded vis-a-vis the gibberish that the white man spoke, saying it sounded like fish sloshing in shallow mud puddles. Hawaiian, to their ears, were as birds' wings in flight: fluid and light, regal to behold, beyond reproachability. But, alas, everyone aboard-ships spoke this nonsense called English so someone among them must undertake to communicate their necessities to the commoners.

Kuene was happy enough to operate in this capacity because the white man was interesting. Hawaiian men were of sturdier, handsomer and generally more appealing nature to his eye, but these Americans and these Brits—they were made of a wholly different matter, and not just in terms of their language. In particular, Kuene was struck by the stiffness of the white man's character, his unflappability and utter lack of good humor around matters as mundane and quintessential as sex. Kuene was of a stock that treated sexuality as a means of commerce, a tool for deepening and solidifying relationships with either gender, and of course a way to celebrate life. Such celebrations Kuene partook of with several in his retinue, of most note a man named Iki, whose tenderness and affections were not reciprocated on Kuene's part. Yet they played, and frequently. But, Kuene detected, such play was not respected among the white man.

Kuene had to acknowledge as well that the white men they encountered in their travels were working their way into his heart. In San Francisco, Kuene finally culminated his desire to have sexual relations with a white man. The object of this affection was a doctor called Sullivan.

Here is how Kuene and Dr. Sullivan came to meet:

THE SAILING FROM Honolulu Harbor to San Francisco was seven days of reasonable comfort for all but one in Queen Kapiʻolani's party. Lieutenant-General John Dominis, husband of the Crown Princess Liliʻuokalani who was also in attendance, was stricken by a debilitating rheumatism that left him paralyzed with pain. Fortunately, the Palace Hotel granted the Queen's retinue access to one Dr. Adam Sullivan. It was Iki who broached the possibility of Kuene romancing the handsome doctor, saying, "This doctor has eyes like the sea. Perhaps a Hawaiian could drown in them? Or perhaps, tired of perpetually swimming, he would delight in climbing the precipices of a Hawaiian island?"

Kuene had occasion to test this when the Queen and the Crown Princess went to visit with a few Tahitian dignitaries who were also in San Francisco, leaving Kuene to assist the Doctor. So it was that the Hawaiian valet found himself out on the balcony with the beguiling American, who smoked and smiled a lot. The doctor assured Kuene that eventually the general's discomfort would pass, that there was little more they could do than wait it out, and that in the meantime they should enjoy a little whiskey. This the doctor produced from his bag of medicine, saying simply, "The drink makes pain easier to manage sometimes." They sipped from the same flask until Kuene found himself becoming giggly. The doctor's eyes were indeed pacific in nature, and the Hawaiian was reminded of the placid tide pools that he would swim in as a child.

Dr. Sullivan said, "What sort of name is Kuene?"

Kuene answered, "It's Hawaiian, and it isn't my name."

"What is 'Kuene' then? And why do they call you that?"

"It means 'servant' in Hawaiian, and it is the Queen's pet name for me."

"So you are the Queen's pet?" the doctor prodded, reaching out to touch Kuene's hand lightly. "You must be a good pet."

Kuene giggled again and the doctor took the valet's hand and put it on his crotch. "I have a pet too," the doctor said then. "It would be very happy to get to know you better."

Kuene laughed and let the doctor wrestle him to the ground beside the bed where the drugged general lay snoring softly. Kuene wondered if they would kiss in the way that Americans enjoy but that seemed so foreign to his Hawaiian sentiment. He wasn't sure if he would enjoy it or if he even wanted to do it. He decided that if the doctor wanted to, he would. But the doctor took instead to biting Kuene's neck and sucking on the tender flesh there. "I want to fuck your handsome smile," the doctor kept saying. "I want to fuck your face."

"What is this 'fuck' thing?" asked Kuene.

Dr. Sullivan was too happy to demonstrate. He stripped off his shirt and tore open his pants. Kuene saw his first American cock then: it was this pink, blotchy thing that was as swollen as Kuene's desire to touch it. Sensing this, the doctor brought his big dick to Kuene's mouth, one arm holding him in place, while the other hand guided Kuene toward his foreign member, which throbbed with importance. Kuene let himself be led to this fountain flowing now with nectar. The doctor's dick filled the Hawaiian's mouth fuller than it had ever been filled, and the doctor started thrusting his hips, shoving it deeper into Kuene's mouth then pulling it back out.

The Queen's valet deduced that this thrusting of the doctor's cock must be the "fucking" of his face that Sullivan had mentioned.

As the general roamed the corridors between the memory of pain and the dull ache of being comatose, the doctor moaned on the floor. Kuene used his hands, lips, tongue and throat as instruments in concert to make the Dr. Sullivan sing. The climax surprised neither of them: the doctor rode the waves of pleasure spreading out from his core, while the attendant kept a cadenced rhythm, tracking the oncoming crescendo. When it was done, it took mere moments for the doctor to withdraw his spent cock, clean himself up, get dressed again, pack up his effects and take his sullen leave, a look of half-surprise on his face.

THESE WERE THE thoughts flooding Kuene's mind when he locked eyes, however briefly, with that solemn youth of English decent, the valet decided. As the Atlantic voyage continued and Kuene performed his daily duties, he would from time to time think about the doctor, his cock and his own disappointment. He thought even of the Lieutenant-General, who after convalescing appeared to have registered nothing of the tryst. Though there many hours of service in the day, Kuene still had recourse to ponder on these things, especially at night when it was customary for the Queen and her royal party to retire early, leaving their valets much of the night hours to themselves. Iki and Kuene were of a single mind: mingle with the natives. But whereas Iki searched above-decks for sailors, musicians, politicians and other voyagers to flirt with, Kuene descended down to steerage.

The *City of Rome* was architected to be the fleetest ship to have ever plied the Atlantic. In this it had failed miserably. It was, however, the first liner with all-electric lighting. It was by these new electric lights that Kuene searched the ship's bowels for the steerage class.

First-class passengers on *the City of Rome* topped out at seventy-five, second-class numbering around two hundred and fifty souls. In steerage, the commoners were infinitely more numerous: a thousand of them were crowded into the too-small spaces where they were likely as not to rub shoulders with cargo and animals in transport. The survivors of the *State of Florida* would have found their sorry state sorrier still when they were led to their collective quarters on the steerage deck. For the low-class citizens of *Rome*, steerage deck was a temporary prison that they stomached with a modicum of pride, rather than venture into the light of day to be seen—and despised—by the upper class.

When his foot hit the floor, the first thing Kuene experienced was the punch-in-the-face fumes of too many human bodies in a too-confined space intermingled with what was unmistakably horse dung, human feces, burnt porridge, and slop. Without a thought, Kuene's arm flew up to cap his nose and prevent him from retching. When the nausea had passed, he opened his eyes and scanned the area.

The staircase led down to an expansive room overflowing with people and belongings: luggage, bedding, instruments, baby cribs, fishing poles, lumber and overflow cargo. The passengers huddled in the semi-darkness amongst their crammed-in possessions, the few lightbulbs barely sufficing to illuminate this dreadful existence. Some were heaped upon each other and themselves, groaning in what could only be constant discomfort, and at a glance Kuene knew that they must be suffering from an impossible mix of nausea and starvation. Further in, the bunks were afforded only a simple curtain for privacy, but the passage between them was so narrow that the movement of one person could not help but disturb their occupants.

Kuene wondered what he would do if he were forced to live in such quarters, like a commoner. His own quarters were somewhat confined and shared with others of the valets. (Iki was wisely assigned to a different cabin.) Four Hawaiians, wide of shoulder and jovial of spirit, all cramped into a single cabin seemed harsh, but Kuene acknowledged that having to bed amidst hundreds upon hundreds of others—all the sounds, smells and stuffy heat—that would simply be too much.

Panic fluttered in his chest then as he remembered the reason for coming to this forsaken place. Standing now at the threshold to what looked like hell on the high seas, Kuene thought that he should evacuate as soon as possible. It was foolish to even come here. And even if he did try to find the youth, that would be impossible in these conditions.

The opposite proved true: without good reason to plunge deeper into the steerage deck, the youth had stayed near this entryway where a breeze wandered in from time to time through the narrow staircase. There he was, standing alone, arms crossed over his stomach, eyes on the ground. The same blanket that he had received upon being rescued swaddled his shoulders.

Mere feet away from the boy, the valet wasn't sure anymore what he was doing there, or what to say to the survivor. Kuene felt exceedingly out of his element, his gut churning with the odors assailing his senses. This was a terrible idea, he decided, and he turned to leave.

"You," said a voice behind Kuene as his foot found the first rung of the ladder. The valet stopped in place and waited until the voice again said, "Hey, you."

Looking over his shoulder, Kuene found the young survivor was addressing him. "I seem to have lost my way," the valet said feebly.

"You helped us," said the youth as he stepped closer. "You helped us."

Kuene simply eyed him now. Features that he hadn't had a chance to note upon their first exchange of glances now became imprinted on his mind: the sorry-blue eyes, the crooked teeth, the thick lips and the tentative smile, the ears sticking out his head. The skeletal hands, the ankles exposed beneath the rolled-up cuffs of his pants. The Hawaiian blinked back his disbelief at having found the boy and discovering such loss behind the flat eyes. But as their eyes were locked on each other, it was as if life had returned to the dormant seas, and the Queen's valet felt the hardened walls of his heart melt and flex, allowing the organ to fill and overflow with compassion. Unable to prevent the words from escaping his lips, Kuene said, "Come with me."

"What?" asked the youth.

Without thinking, Kuene grabbed the young man by the hand and practically dragged him back up the staircase. Whether for weakness or curiosity, the boy dutifully followed. The steerage deck receded behind them as the valet led the way up several flights of stairs and down brilliantly illuminated hallways where the pair received the full surprise of passersby and continued on heedless. Kuene could think of only one place they could safely converse, away from the prying eyes of the elite, and soon they were standing in the doorway of his cabin.

The unit was dark: the other attendants were still enjoying what entertainment the night afforded them. Kuene invited the youth into the room, drawing up some water to use for a modest scrub-down; this being a second-class cabin, it boasted a private wash area with a basin and faucet that produced hot and cold water. When the valet turned around, he found the young man staring at him in mild disbelief, or perhaps distrust.

"Why am I here?" he asked.

Ignoring him, Kuene grabbed at the blanket and shucked it off of him. "Let's get you out of these rags. I have some pants and a shirt that you can change into, but you'll want to clean up a bit first."

The boy made no effort to help or impede progress: Kuene easily stripped off the youth's stinking shirt, as well as his weather-worn shoes and his breeches. The youth stood there then with only a light undershirt and underpants on, all of it dirty and blotched with overwear, the seams fraying. They stood there a moment, exchanged a glance, and then the young man averted his gaze and took the last of his garments off as well. Kuene produced a bar of soap and a rag, which were both dunked into the basin of hot-warm water. Kuene began mussing up a lathery foam. As his hands worked, his eyes took in that frail form and in his mind he thought how cruel life must be to this waif. The boy's ribs stuck out from his sides, his chest narrow with a smattering of tufts of hair; from the bounty of his pubic hair hung his flaccid penis, looking to Kuene like some burrowing creature who rarely saw the light.

Then the valet set about working. Starting at the shoulders, he scrubbed down the young man's body, using brisk, deep strokes that the Queen herself enjoyed (administered by her handmaidens, naturally). It was an adapted Hawaiian massage style called *lomilomi*: Kuene pushed down on the rag with the strength of his trained fingers, bursting the pockets of woe in the youth's tired muscles. The soapy cloth found the boy's chest next as well as his throat and the nape in the back. Down the trunk of the body it slid, propelled by one of the Hawaiian's practiced hands while the other braced the youth.

The silence between them was thick as gravy and Kuene cleared his throat awkwardly. "What's your name?"

"Jonah. Jonah Hale."

"Where are you from?"

"London."

"And you were headed to America." It came out as a statement.

"Yes." A moment later the boy volunteered: "I stole a ticket."

Kuene said nothing. He was working on the youth's hips and legs, running his hands down either side of these twiggy structures that managed to hold the boy aloft. When the moment came, he didn't shy away from washing the youth's cock: he massaged the wash cloth over the boy's sex, down over his scrotum toward his anus, then pulled back his foreskin to wash out whatever grit might have crept in.

Perhaps compelled to speech by the awkwardness of this scenario, the boy

Jonah described how he had happened across a peasant sleeping on the side of the road under a bridge not far from the harbor. Jonah scrounged through the sleeping man's effects and found the ticket to board the *State of Florida*. Thinking his luck might just be turning, Jonah stole the ticket. "But then the *Florida* sank, and now here I am." At this, he looked down at Kuene whose hands had managed to rouse Jonah's burrowing creature to semi-stiffness.

"I'd apologize," said Jonah, "but I suspect this was your intent somehow."

"Don't be silly," said Kuene, a half-embarrassed half-smirk on his face. "It's obvious you haven't been paying attention to the nuances of your body. The Queen and her regents must be of the utmost hygiene at all moments, so naturally her valets and handmaidens ensure that the royal party are always presentable."

The Hawaiian's hands abandoned the youth's sizable erection now and ran the length of his legs again. He lifted up each foot and scrubbed the soles, in between the toes, the heel. When the lather became dry or weak, Kuene would refresh it with more soap and water.

At a given moment, the young man began to cry, quietly. When the valet asked what the matter was, Jonah said, "I thought I had run away from my life... there. Steerage on the *Florida* was dreadful, worse than here on the *City of Rome*, but it was taking me away from my troubles in England." He sniffed. "I thought that soon the memory of stealing the ticket would amount to nothing and I'd forget all about it. That lad would, too, eventually, after he had damned me to hell. But now here I am: going back to Liverpool. Perhaps the police will take me away."

Kuene snickered to himself as he started wiping away the soap and suds. "They won't take you away. They won't recognize you in your new livery."

The youth Jonah continued to cry silently to himself, letting Kuene wipe down his entire body. The Hawaiian valet returned to his demonstrations on Jonah's now dry cock again, which had flagged but was growing thick again in Kuene's hands. "What are you doing?" Jonah asked sullenly.

"You're distressed," Kuene said by way of explanation.

"You won't tell the Queen's guard about my theft?" Jonah asked, blinking back tears.

Kuene guided Jonah into a seated position, saying simply, "I won't tell the Queen."

Then, when Kuene put the young man's throbbing erection in his mouth, Jonah asked again, weakly, "What are you doing?"

"You're distressed," Kuene repeated, removing the pink cock from his mouth to do so. "I'm comforting you." He stroked the boy's shaft with the same rhythm he might use to knead *poi* with his bare hands: delicately but purposefully. Jonah ceased questioning and ever so slightly pivoted his hips so Kuene could have full access to the length of him.

For reasons neither could fathom, the youth felt compelled to chatter the entire time that Kuene worked his cock and balls with his talented hands and mouth. Jonah explained that he suspected that the valet fancied him when their eyes met up on the boards. It was something about how the shadows painted his face in the dark and yet Kuene's eyes danced with an internal fire. It wasn't until later that this encounter reminded Jonah of another man who had had designs for the young Brit, whose unique features—the hook nose, the long-ish face, the ears jutting out—contributed rather than detracted from his youthful beauty. This other man, Miles, had taken a liking to Jonah from the first. Their companionship was typically platonic until Jonah went to spend a week on the coast with his newfound friend. On a pair of particularly cold winter nights when the lashing winds off the Channel beat Hastings into submission, Miles encouraged Jonah to share the bed. They spent the night trembling side by side, until Miles unceremoniously enveloped all of the waify Jonah in his large frame. The heat of their bodies awoke them in the middle of the night and that is when Jonah saw desire in another man's eyes for the first time, the same desire he would later see in Kuene's eyes aboard the City of Rome. Jonah assured Kuene that he was doing a much better job of sucking his cock, which spurred the Hawaiian on and Jonah got very close to coming before Kuene eased off. At some point, the valet began plying Jonah's asshole and the Brit winced somewhat, saying that he wasn't so sure about it. But then he recalled that Miles had tried to seduce him into fornicating with even more abandon, the older gentleman thrusting his turgid cock against Jonah's back door like a battering ram, but the youth wouldn't budge. "It hurts," he had sighed, supposing this to be the case, though his sighs belied his curiosity. As if to prove to the youth that the experience was worth any presumed discomfort, Miles slicked Jonah's cock up with spit and seated himself rather expertly on the boy's throne. Jonah moaned in Kuene's mouth as he described the exquisite pleasure of Mile's tight, slippery hole around his dick. This time when the valet tried his hand at the Brit's own hole, Jonah let himself be explored. The Hawaiian's fingers were thick and fleshy, but not wholly uncomfortable. Now the race to ecstasy began in earnest. All thoughts of that night in Hastings when Miles had ridden Jonah's erection to a heaven-harkening orgasm were flushed from the Brit's mind. There was only Kuene's hand and mouth working together on Jonah's swollen, seeping cock, the valet's fingers thrusting in and out of the boy and finding a tender spot that sent waves of radiating pleasure through the young man's body, as a guitar string sings when it is plucked. Then, in the comfort of the Hawaiian valet's embrace and at the reckoning of his masterful hands, the Brit came voluminously, his come flying everywhere: in Kuene's mouth and on his face, and on the fine down of the boy's own legs, and on his stomach, too.

The valet's quick movements dashed all traces of their sex from existence, and clothes were produced as speedily. Kuene had spoken truly: there were clothes enough and of a quality Jonah had scarcely known. The threads were delicate, the seams tight, the linens light and dainty, sheer against his now tender parts. Kuene never shed his veneer of decorum. When the young man was completely dressed again, this time in the clothing that a noble of Hawaiian heritage might wear, the valet smiled and smoothed down wrinkles at the youth's shoulder and elbow, saying, "You wear it well."

Their eyes locked then again, for an instant, before Jonah looked away. But then he touched Kuene's hand again. "You won't tell the Queen?" he asked, a plea in his voice.

"What about?" the valet replied coyly.

"The ticket... and my passage here... How I stole it—you won't tell the Queen, right?"

Kuene nodded solemnly, the cheer somewhat dashed from his face. "The Queen need not know of any of it."

Jonah nodded absentmindedly, as if to convince himself. Kuene changed his soiled shirt then, washed his face, mouth and hands with the same expedience and fastidiousness. The Brit watched with a distracted air, even going so far as to whistle something.

"I think you were right," he said finally. "I was distressed. But I feel somehow... better now. Thank you."

"We Hawaiians know a thing or two about helping others—and ourselves—relax and release tension."

Jonah frowned. "So you are from Hawaii?"

"Yes."

"But you are the attendant of the Queen and her regents?" Jonah asked then.

"I *am* an attendant for the Queen: Queen Kapi'olani of Hawai'i." Kuene's eyes lit up then with comprehension. "You thought I worked under the Queen Victoria herself?"

"Are you not an Indian?" Jonah asked, a fresh sullen expression on his face.

"I am a Hawaiian!" Kuene fairly roared. "You mistook me for an Indian!"

"I assumed, when you rushed to help us, you were Indian valets operating under the Queen's guard. Your livery was somewhat off, but I know little of the Indian ways."

Kuene scowled. "I repeat: I am a Hawaiian. I am not an Indian!"

They fell silent then for a moment. The situation unfurled itself in Kuene's mind: Jonah Hale had presumed that the "Indian" Kuene was sent to ascertain the validity of the Brit's passage to America on the grounds that foul play was afoot. When they were alone in the Hawaiian valet's quarters, Jonah decided he would let Kuene have his way. In exchange the valet would not tell the Queen's guard about how the youth had stolen the ticket.

"All the same," Jonah started then, "I was feeling pretty down on my luck. I guess what I needed was a right good fuck." He chuckled to himself then, and Kuene couldn't help but join him. After they had had a good laugh, they ventured forth to see what else the night had to offer.

MR. OKADA
AND HIS
CALOTYPE
CAMERA

Claudia Quint

No sooner did I step into the glorious box car of the Tsar's marvelous Trans Siberian Railway, when I beheld the spy.

Meticulous. Hair parted above his left eye in a rigid line, combed, oiled, groomed. A European style suit, and carrying upon his person a suspicious clutch of items, one in particular so awkward and large it could easily conceal the presence of a rifle. While sitting, he smoked luxuriantly, fingers splayed, and though I sought to keep my facade smooth and expressionless and not reveal the chase, I swore in place of his fingers extended several primary feathers, that of a bird's white wing, a crane to be exact.

The smoke curled away from his fingers, which were mere fingers after all. His gaze pierced the smoky veil to fix me as I passed down the aisle to my own car, secreting myself out of his line of vision but where I could watch his open door, mark his shadow on the opposing cushion and see the smoke of his cigarette which burned acrid tobacco, breathing in the same fume as he.

I fulminated with racing thoughts. My cargo limited to a book to pass the hours and the clothes on my back, I'd hoped to ride without incident to my destination in Moscow from a sojourn in Korea, when this damnable wrinkle formed. Did I pretend not to see him? Should I confront him?

I resolved to wait. As passengers boarded and found their places, the car crowded and filled, women sporting Paris fashions and military men, poor itinerant travelers, teeth crooked and stinking of beer from nearby taverns, they brought with them the frigid cold of the season. They found their seats. The car filled with their subdued conversation and I opened my book, a French copy of *The Count of Monte Cristo*, which I pretended to read, while I trained my vigilant eye upon the passenger ahead of me.

While the attendant arrived to check our tickets, I observed the spy rise and walk the aisle, into the next car. I used my punched ticket to mark my place and left my seat, and ducked into the spy's hold, leaving the door ajar behind me.

The interior of the spy's cabin trapped smoke. Through his windows, the Mongolian countryside raced past in great sweeps of landscape, people in the distance walking across snowy grounds. I did not steal into the spy's cab for the scenery, however; instead, I reached for his closest cargo, a valise, and snapped it open. If there were secret documents he were smuggling, I might easily abscond with them and have the Okhrana decipher their meaning. I would be well congratulated on my efforts, despite my recent—and ongoing—malaise.

Yet, when the case sprang open, the secret documents were instead photographic pieces, squares of strong smelling glossy paper still rank with their chemicals. I picked the first from the pile, holding it between thumb and forefinger to the window.

The photograph depicted two youths. They arrayed themselves in an embrace of carnal nature, crowns of laurel upon their heads in the style of ancient Greece or Rome, draped in cloths which revealed enough of their bodies to tantalize the onlooker, yet, the figures themselves did not seem to care that they were watched. One straddled the other, his head thrown back giving voice to an ecstasy that rendered him delirious; his partner, partially obscured by the fabric, sealed his mouth beneath him, angling a line from belly to sex.

I groaned, yet not in pleasure. The nature of my malaise had been many weeks in treatment now, and I had been well nigh successful in forcing those demons of self-abuse to flee my corporeal self entirely. With the help of an apparatus I acquired in Korea—the entire purpose of my journey—I had been able to stifle the unseemly and inappropriate urges. This apparatus was belted around my middle, intimate in nature, and of a series of articulated parts which allowed this metal contraption to encase my manhood, restricting my ability to touch it, preventing that temptation of which I had much abused and given into, the nature of my affliction.

Now, it seemed the apparatus worked against my interests, eliciting pain instead; yet, it fulfilled the expected duties imposed upon it. My sex thrust against the hard metal in reaction to the picture and I dropped the photograph. The picture fell from my fingers in a long spiral as I breathed out from my nostrils, attempting to dim those internal fires responsible for my lapse in propriety.

"Do you like what you see?"

I startled, stumbled, knocking over the valise. Photographs spilled onto the cab floor as I inelegantly crashed into the wall. Flailing for balance, I fell into the seat, still warm from where the spy had been sitting previously, who now stood before me in the threshold of the cab, unruffled.

"You're not a spy," I said.

He closed the door behind him, and remained standing, watching me.

"No," he said, amused.

"And that large package—"

"A calotype camera."

Blood, having previously occupied my lower half, immediately raced up to my face and embarrassed, I stared out the window without looking at anything at all.

He stepped over his spilled photos to take the seat across from me, where he offered me a cigarette. Frozen, paralyzed by shame, I could not speak and he continued withdrawing his cigarette and lighting it in the silence. I looked to the floor and perceived then, a kaleidoscope of pictures, with men arranged in various poses, some solitary, others in pairs or threes, bodies bared to the photographic lens and others plied by the mouth and tongue of their fellows.

He smiled and leaned forward, hands on his knees.

"You though—you're a spy, are you not?"

My face burned hotter.

He reached down to pluck a photograph from the many and placed it flat on the table, sliding to me.

I stared at it. A young man, reclining on a bench amid a forest scene, eyes half-lidded in an opiate haze and his body, bared, his cloth abandoned at his feet and clad only in sandals.

"Tensions between our countries have been high, have they not, *Mister Spy?*"

I nodded, placing a hand over the photograph so as not to look at it, to prevent the flush of blood from returning to my sex and reinvigorating it, only to be imprisoned by the cold metal around my waist.

"They have," I whispered.

"Naturally, it would be quite an embarrassment if a traveler such as myself, hired by none other than the Tsar's own cousin to take discreet photographs of himself and his wife, had to explain how an over-enthusiastic agent of the Okhrana ransacked my belongings on the train without provocation."

"I'm sorry—" I hastened to apologize, but he stopped the flow of my stammering words with an upheld hand, and once more, I had the impression once again of not fingers erupting from his sleeve, but feathers, before the perception revealed itself as a hallucination and nothing more.

"We should not risk upsetting the relationship between Japan and Russia," I suggested.

I nodded.

"I am traveling alone, and like to have someone to talk to," he said. "I would considerate it an act of goodwill if you would stay with me during my trip. Being a foreigner in this country, having someone to practice the language with would be a great boon."

Shamefaced, I agreed. We exchanged introductions—he called himself Mr. Okada, and I allowed him my first name, Sergei.

"Now, before we order that bitter tea from the samovar contraption your people so love, tell me—why do you look away from these pictures?"

Halting, I told him, unable to do anything else, unable to retreat to my former seat and pretend that all of this was not happening. I would have to pay for my mistakes, and I began by telling Mr. Okada that last summer, I had taken on a most embarrassing habit.

"My wife will not speak to me," I explained and Mr. Okada looked at me strangely, raising a hand up to abridge the smile on his face. "What?"

"I did not think you were the type to marry, is all."

I swallowed. "She is often away, with her friends."

"Sounds convenient for the both of you," he said, and if he were sarcastic, I could not detect it in his accent.

"I take no pleasure in her company," I said, "but rather, too much pleasure with myself. And so I've been recently seeking the help of the foremost doctors on the continent. I've been now to England, to Germany, and am now returning from Korea, where I've been seeking cures for my disgusting habit."

As I spoke, he picked up his baggage, opening up the largest which I had mistaken for a rifle, and removed the camera box which he used to capture images on the silver tone. I received a chill to watch him as he set it on the table and then turned to me.

"Tell me, do you think you might tame those fires you find so reprehensible by spending time with male friends?"

I said nothing. Before my marriage, I had frequented private parties among several of my friends who used to invite artists, dancers, and actors to their rooms. I had taken my pleasures among the men but confessed it to none, and the advantage I had was that I was unknown in their circles, unlikely to meet again and thus I might escape any stain of disapproval from the society I kept. Of course, my wife was adept, intelligent, and I enjoyed her company on an intellectual level...but on the physical plane, we did not often collide. I had hoped that marriage might be the thing to turn me away from my prior desires, and but instead, my current malaise of self-flagellation only increased, until I felt as the organ itself, a blind head seeking sustenance from any encouragement, rubbing indiscriminately upon any surface to sate itself.

Hence, the apparatus.

"I don't talk about that," I snapped.

He grinned, raising the picture box. He was taking my picture! I froze, unsure if I should cooperate or move—wouldn't it ruin the photo? But what did I care? I had become his virtual prisoner, after all, and it was only a photo, nothing scandalous. I had all my clothes on.

"No one would know, if you did," he said, and gestured to me. "Would you mind taking off your suit jacket?"

I paused, and then complied, pulling it off and folding it, setting it on the seat beside me. Naked men leered at me from the photos on the floor, satyrs frolicking. Light poured in from the window, illuminating me for Mr. Okada's picture taking.

"How do you come to take pictures of this sort?" I asked. "There's a great deal of punishment in the pornography trade."

"But a high demand. And it requires a finely tuned eye, of which I have. Do you know, a bird's eye can see a near illimitable spectrum of color?"

"I did not know it."

"Take off your shirt, if you please."

I paused. He said the question as casually as if he were discussing recent headlines in the newspaper and I felt warm around my collar, loosening the top button and then following the next, opening up my shirt to reveal the skin there, covered in a stippling of hair curling up from the chest and peeling off the shirt, setting it atop the folded suit jacket.

Mr. Okada licked his lips, planted his cigarette between them and stared, without looking me in the eyes. A flood of contradictory feelings gripped me. I wanted to run from the cab. I wanted to stay.

"May I confess, I have often been fascinated by your Mother Russia," he said. "Your stories of the firebird and Baba Yaga are my most treasured tales. I collect these folk tales from every country I travel in. Are you not fascinated by the interaction of animal and human worlds, and those figures who seem to belong to both?"

"Fairy tales," I sneered, remaining still for the sake of the camera, Mr. Okada's eye fixed firmly to the hole to see through the lens. He arranged a cloth over the camera, and moving his hands underneath, appeared to be taking out an object and replacing it, opening secret compartments in the wood calotype camera.

"We have folk tales in this manner," Mr. Okada continued. "Have you never heard of the crane, and their guises? If you would, you should stand by the door so I might picture the full length of you."

I blinked, disoriented and dizzy by Mr. Okada's pummeling of question, followed by instruction. The man had an altogether strange effect on my senses, and I rose, naked from the waist up and leaned against the door, thankful no passengers might know of the secrets unfolding beyond their gaze.

Mr. Okada set the camera. Photographs of lascivious nudes still at his feet.

"The crane, wounded, falls into the snow, where a traveler happens upon it. Do take off your trousers, if you would."

"Am I drugged?" I asked. The scenery through the window seemed to me to travel in the reverse direction. How was that possible? It slowed and sped up and filled me with dizzy sickness.

"Of course not," Mr. Okada assured me, and gestured for me to continue.

I unbuttoned my trousers, mechanical and slow. Lines of my reflection in the window filled with Mongolia, Mongolia disappearing and fleeing into new landscapes, the tracks, thunderous beneath us. I bared myself as though exposing a wound in my skin, the way we clear a gash of infection, and it stings to reveal the healthy, healing flesh.

I could no longer disguise anymore the apparatus hugging my sex, wrapped round my hips. I peeled off the trousers, and folded them, setting them on the seat. Chilly in the cab.

"What is that you wear?"

"It is to prevent me from self-abuse."

"It looks painful. It looks as though it does the exact opposite."

"It helps me," I snapped.

"The crane," Mr. Okada continued, "needed help from the traveler, to heal the wing."

To my surprise, Mr. Okada turned the camera away, toward the window. He stubbed his cigarette out in the ashtray. The light from the window, blinding. He drew close to look at me and I did not move.

"Only in that kindness, do we find the strength for transformation," Mr. Okada whispered, and placed one hand on my hip. The metal apparatus glinted in the cabin light, describing the shape of a phallus at rest, metal plates to restrain the rebellious flesh. He placed his hand on the metal. I imagined it felt cold to him, and he moved his hand over to the buckle on the side.

I closed my eyes. I thought of begging him not to remove it, and I thought of how very badly I wanted him to.

"What happened to the crane?" I asked instead.

Mr. Okada undid the buckle.

"He flew away. And the traveler returned to his wife."

The buckle opened, and the apparatus hung upon my engorged flesh, blood racing down from head to belly, filling the elastic skin there, turning it pink to red to purple through a nest of downy hair. Mr. Okada plucked the apparatus by its metal front, and pulled it away like a flower from a vase, revealing my forgotten and forlorn sex, dismissed all these weeks and now growing hard, hungry, and red with shame.

"But that was not the end," Mr. Okada said, and fantasies stormed my imagination; how I would like him on his knees before me, to take my length into his mouth and he would smile, kiss me on the mouth, look at me from upturned eyelids while he did it, the track in his hair unruffled by our tryst. Or he would take me, consume me, dominate me from behind and I give me that release I had not felt in how long? Too long.

He did neither.

Instead, he retreated to his camera, turning it about-face and bending down to set his eye through the lens and this, a greater torture yet.

"The traveler was at home one night when a knock came at the door, and a youth appeared there. A blizzard descended and he needed a place to stay for the night, so the traveler and his wife obliged, took him in and gave him shelter."

I remained still, but the rest of me did not. My length, growing, felt monstrous, and I could not help but think it would ruin the picture, but I dared not moved or speak.

"And it came to pass that the youth stayed with the traveler and his wife. Over the passage of years, and they became like family. The youth had a gift for weaving, and asked the traveler to grant him materials to build a blanket from, with a single request—that neither of them look upon his weaving, which he undertook in secret."

"They did not keep their promise?" I asked, breathless.

"Do they ever?" Mr. Okada sighed. "Touch yourself, if you would."

"But I—my purpose is not to—"

"Like the crane," Mr. Okada murmured, "those things we do in secret, we crave to witness."

I quieted, and after a moment, lifted a hand to myself. Tentative, ashamed, yet the shame too tenuous to keep a hold upon me and I found myself wrapping each finger around my freed length, taking my time with cautious, luxuriant strokes.

"What happened when they broke their promise?" I asked, my voice turning breathy with each movement of the arm, my fingers, burning faster up and down in rhythm.

"They saw, weaving behind the closed door, not a youth but a crane, using his beak to arrange the fingers and the thread into a glorious sheet. And of course, after that, nothing was the same. The youth was compelled to leave, being revealed for a crane, and they were a family no more. Transformation leads to creation and destruction by turns. Wouldn't you agree?"

My breath hitched with each motion. He lifted his camera, setting the lens upon me as my fist raced with my pumping heart. My sex craving hot warm closeness and fighting me, the pressure building, immense, and sending electric shocks up my spine, my belly sick with desire and rollicking with it, every sense raw and unhinged.

The wave approached in time with the racing landscape, I counted the beat of my heart and the rhythm of my fist to the train tracks and Mr. Okada, watching me with hungry attention and fingers, curled like feathers, at his temple, beneath the rise of his jet black hair.

The wave came, crested, arrived at its apogee and then broke apart. The excitement of the climax was poorly served by the aftermath, all the spent energy relinquished in my final, finishing moan and Mr. Okada's clinical observation, the camera taking in every aspect of my self-violence. I found I could not move, but only linger with my back against the door, eyes closed, gathering myself, warm now in a way I had not been.

After several seconds in which I came back to myself, I realized what I had done. This man had been party to it, recording it with his camera, I hunched down where the seed had spilled onto the rug, picking up the discarded apparatus. Caring not for cleanliness, I pulled it back on, the metal cold now, voicing an inarticulate gasp of dismay, of shock to encase myself in it once more.

And Mr. Okada, taking a picture of each stage of my wretched transformation—or perhaps devolution—into the unremarkable creature I had been before, desperate, strange, alienated and alone, until I found my way back to my clothes, pulling on each item to sit across from him once more.

Mr. Okada gathered the pictures from the carpet and shuffled them into a haphazard pile. He broke down his camera with expert quickness, opening up yet another of his cases to secrete it away, and soon, there was no sign anything had happened in this cabin at all. He pulled the bell above us. I stared at the window. A serving man brought us bitter tea with lemon, in the Russian style, and I fell asleep, thinking of folk tales, the ones I had grown up with and the one Mr. Okada had rendered to me.

Strange dreams assailed me. I imagined that Mr. Okada did not sit across from me as a human, but as a man with a crane head, dressed in his suit and smoking from the side of his beak. His eyes, vivacious and small, blinked and he grinned, perceiving all through the lens of his inimitable eyes.

When I awoke, the train was stopped at the station. We were to disembark and take the ferry, for the Trans Siberian Railway was not yet built across Lake Baikal, and there was no other way to traverse the body of water. Mr. Okada had awoken before me and gathered his things and I, being a light traveler, easily followed, though we did not exchange a single word during this time.

The dizziness of yesterday left me as I stepped off the train and fell into Mr. Okada's footsteps. He knew I trailed him, but it seemed that if our journey took us on the same path then I saw no reason not to keep close to him. Did I desire more from him? Was it a liking for his company, a fascination for his photography, or merely a hunger I wanted to sate?

We boarded the ferry at the edge of the lake. A boat had gone before us to break up the ice, and the ferry lurched into motion through a narrow trail of dark sea with walls of ice and snow towering at either side. I found my way across the ferry deck to be closer to Mr. Okada and though he did not look at me, he knew I was there, breathing in the same smoke he exhaled, the temperatures turning our fingers red in the half-light.

The ferry lurched to a halt. The ice had to be broken again at the helm. The passengers waited, some with heads bowed over the side evacuating what meager sustenance they'd taken in the meantime. The boat rocked precipitously and I did not like it, not at all. The temperatures proved so frigid that ice greedily reformed as quickly as they broke it apart.

Hands on deck whispered among themselves. I listened between a woman rocking a child to sleep and a soldier. Disgruntled, they felt it was too quickly approaching dark to undertake the ferry. They should wait till morning, when the sun would be on their side and aiding in the melting of the slush.

I resolved to circle back to Mr. Okada. I was unsure of what I could do in this circumstance, for with how far out we have already advanced there was no returning to shore. I had almost navigated my way back to him when the ferry took impact from a sheet of ice at port. It threw several passenger to their knees, stumbling and hefting up the ferry before crashing the vessel into the stark and frigid water once more, dousing us with lake water that froze as quickly as it hit the air.

In the confusion, I scrambled back up to my feet and saw with relief that Mr. Okada was standing on deck as serene as a man taking tea in his parlor room, though his equipment had been scattered. I saw with horror that the valise where he kept the pictures had cracked open and photos were sliding across the deck. Rather than try to recover it, he was moving away from the evidence of his trade, leaving behind too any identifying items, along with his camera. There was no time to sort through them without being caught with pornography and taken into custody.

But didn't the camera contain the pictures he had taken of me?

I could not afford the scandal, should those pictures come back to haunt me.

For now, people were still lurching back to their feet and the danger had passed. The ferry moved faster across the lake, freed from the ice, and made my way swiftly past Mr. Okada's belongings, some of which had rolled straight over the deck and into the hungry lake, and leaned down to snatch the camera box.

I looked up. Several feet ahead of me, Mr. Okada, watched me, and he nodded tight, urging me on.

I understood. If this were found, we both faced penalties. I took up the valise and heaved it overboard. In the confusion, few would care for luggage lost in the mire of the hungry lake. I let the waters eat the pictures but kept the camera tucked under my arm.

Hours stretched on; both myself and Mr. Okada pretended not to know each other. A few remarked on the preponderance of pictures floating by, but they were too far away to perceive their unwholesome nature. We both remained at our tense stations, waiting for outcries or complaint, but there were none.

I lost sight of Mr. Okada at the disembarking. I longed to say goodbye but prized the mystery of failing to, leaving us hovering, unfinished, in a liminal space neither here nor there. And though I knew I would not see him again, I harbored in my heart unwritten fantasies of chance encounters, of catching a glimpse of him on the street, of inhaling the tobacco of his discarded cigarette, still warm from his lips.

I returned to my occupation at the secret police, and returned to my wife, returned to my home, to discover it empty. A note in my wife's neat scrawl indicated she was staying at her friend's house for an extended visit when I at last entered through the front door, tired, exhausted, and heavy with all that had transpired. I set the camera aside, and promptly forgot about it, sleeping through two days and waking only to relieve myself and eat and then sleep once more. I still wore the apparatus. I still remonstrated myself for desires that I should be able to rise above, and yet failed to.

Life continued, as it has a habit of doing.

I became used to hanging up my hat above the camera box, of pulling off my coat and leaving it on the chair nearby so that it faded into the background, becoming a fixture, and noticing only when it ceased to be there.

My hand, hovering over the table where the camera box should be, describing the approximate size and shape. When had it gone? Who had taken it? Why? I whirled around the room, peeking behind chairs, under the ottoman, when I heard my wife call out to me from the parlor.

"Won't you come in, dear? I have your photos."

I stopped, erect, lips pulling back from my teeth. I could hear her in the other room, setting out tea, preparing the stage for my final humiliation. Oh, it would be just like her, so passive, so quietly needling, hinting at lives we could have had if we had not been so foolish as to lock ourselves together in matrimony, seeking our desires elsewhere, anywhere but home.

And now she would hold evidence of my secret self.

Time to face the music, I told myself, but then I paused, chose new words. Time for transformation, I thought, invoking Mr. Okada. I squared my jaw and walked into the parlor, where the samovar bubbled on its stand, where cups were set out, ready to receive their brutal tea, and where back presented to me as she adjusted the flame.

I looked down upon the parlor table.

A series of pictures fanned out. Each of them depicted the familiar box car which myself and Mr. Okada had been ensconced within. Yet, where I should have been, in various stages of nakedness and pleasuring myself, were instead scenes of cranes.

Cranes on the lake. Cranes on the countryside we had passed. Cranes in mid-flight.

I pulled a single photo out from the line with one thumb, holding it up as though on the other side of the paper, I might reveal the trickery at hand; nothing but smooth glossy surface greeted me, the crane, stately, regarding me from the picture frame where it might observe all it beheld with superior vision.

I sat down with the wind knocked from me and startled to find my wife, holding out the cup and saucer to me, depositing them in my trembling hands.

"Lovely photos, they are," she said. "Haunting, though—the crane seems so lonely to me."

"He does," I murmured. "Like we are."

She blinked, and suddenly laughed.

"Oh, Sergei," and she leaned forward to squeeze my shoulder. "Who said you had to be?"

"What do you mean?"

"I knew when I married you, that you had no interest in women. To learn what other predilections you might possess would surprise me far less than discovering you have an interest in photography. I had no idea you harbored a desire for such artistic expression."

I looked down at the photos, my brow creasing. Had I been wrong about the form my life should take? Could I perhaps change, like the crane, transform, at Mr. Okada's urging?

But that wasn't quite it, was it? Rather, it was not to change at all—but to become more truly myself.

"Yes," I said. "I quite enjoy photography."

I sipped from the cup as though all were ordinary and at rights in our world. My wife, who would visit her women friends far longer than married wives should, perhaps, and myself, thinking that I would take off the apparatus and from now on, carry Mr. Okada's camera box with me instead. Like the crane, to see those things we do in secret.

GREY
SALAMANDERS

Tom Cardamone

AMONG THE LIMEHOUSE paperboys, Wilmot Reed (everyone called him Reed) stood out, and not just because he was tall. Before his mother passed, she had taught him basic manners, and the supreme value of the pound. She had known far more than the common London whore, having received something of an education before her merchant father's financial ruin led him to suicide and her down into the oldest profession. Her bastard son had a bit more bearing about him than the usual urchin, as well as his unknown father's height. He picked up additional knowledge along the way, lessons learned in alleys, on rooftops, things not yet written in books. At least not yet.

The drunken sailors that wove the foggy Limehouse streets were easy targets for pick pockets, and if their trousers were filled with other morsels, Reed could help them there as well. Dank Limehouse public houses, close to the burgeoning docks of the Thames, attracted seamen from around the world. Gentlemen from the tonier parts of the city would occasionally partake as well, and not because the ale was cheap. Reed learned early that some men prefer the company of other men, and not just when they didn't have purse for a whore or were so drunk they'd fuck anything that crossed their path. Others liked them *young*. As such, they assessed Reed's height to mean he was long in the cock as well, and they were always pleased to see the length he produced once the amount was settled. These extra shillings kept Reed alive and indoors many a damp winter. Now, he was nearly too old to attract that very specific lot, and was about to age out as a paperboy as well.

He had spent the day hungry, looking for work on the docks without any luck, and settled at the most infamous night cellar in Limehouse, The Reversal, to drink away his last shillings. After he ordered a second glass of gin, a thin gentleman in an elegant dark tail coat at the other end of the bar caught his eye.

That tavern was a black nexus of cracksmen, macers, toolers, palmers and the mandrakes that favored such rough trade. Reed knew that the toffs, the more well-dressed, sometimes landed gentry even, prized discretion and communicated with a mere look, preferring low talk outside rather than barroom conversations overheard by blackmailers. Having met steady eyes with his own, a silent agreement was made. Both finished their drinks. He left after the gentleman, but not so quickly that anyone would make the connection. The night smelled of horse manure and the river. The river smelled of an ocean of toil, thick with the refuse of London sewers, all distilled into a lapping ribbon of desperation and sorrow. The gentleman turned and acknowledged his presence with a curt nod as he veered down an alley. Reed pursued, hopeful for more than a doorway fuck: being invited back to a fellow's rooms meant a proper wash and maybe a meal afterwards. As he turned the corner, the gentleman was waiting for him beside his waiting carriage, a highly polished black affair that, to the boy, screamed menace and money.

Why do the two always go together? He thought and wavered.

The man held his calling card up in the air. Reed instinctively reached for it, for any opportunity really, but the man held it higher aloft. The dim light of the street lamp showed him to be only a few years older than Reed, though sallow cheeks and unfocused eyes implied vices the paperboy had yet to employ.

"First things first. You're that lad who used to hawk papers, calling out the headlines near Euston Station?"

"Yes sir!" He was thrilled that his mark knew him, might have been nursing a long-held infatuation.

"Good, good, your timbre is excellent."

"My mother was an actress," he lied. "Long gone from the pox, I'm 'fraid," he added, instantly regretting the premature attempt to gain sympathy.

The man pointed a white, gloved finger at the soiled crotch of Reed's threadbare trousers.

"And no French gout? I don't like my sausage spoiled."

"No sir, clean as a whistle!"

"Hmmmm, I bet you've had your whistle cleaned quite often. Well never mind, I've steady work for a discrete boy. Present this card early in the morning at the address listed and we'll see to it."

Reed stared and the whiteness of the card cradled in his soiled palm. He knew numbers, not letters, and decided to confess as much.

"To be expected, dear lad. Your education begins."

As the gentleman turned toward the waiting carriage he whispered the street address. Reed's thoughts vacillated between his lack of lodgings for the night and the fact that the liquor he had consumed at The Reversal did little to quell his hunger. Also pressing was what, exactly, did his toff mean by *"education"*?

HE FELT BOTH conspicuous and completely ignored on the streets of Arlington, one of the wealthiest, most exclusive neighborhoods in London. Reed was shocked that, after sleeping rough, in the small amount of time it took him to reach the intended address, he had not merely crossed streets but exchanged worlds. Rambling tenements had quickly given way to mansions, sidewalks widened and paving stones righted themselves. The poor and desperate receded and quiet and quick nobs dashed in every direction even though dawn had barely broke.

Reed brushed away nonexistent dust from his filthy overcoat and again straightened the collar. The address he had been given was close to the park, on one of the more private lanes lined with fine coaches and militant doormen. As he approached and was about to produce the card the door opened and a servant jerked his head—a silent signal that Reed should go around back. He did so and the door opened as he mounted the steps, not as if the household awaited his arrival but rather as if such an appearance was routine.

A butler awaited, his coat black and shiny like the midnight carriages rentboys enter never to be seen again. The butler measured him with his eyes and stepped aside to usher him in. Reed was waved down an impossibly long and narrow hall and through a set of doors. The butler motioned for him to undress and wash himself in a steaming tub within the center of the room. He did so gladly, unsure of how long it had been since he had had a bath. As he exited the gentleman from the previous night entered, still in his nightshirt, loose and womanly off his shoulder. He held a steeping cup of tea beneath his nostrils while circling the tub. Reed pretended at shyness, a hand before his enlongated member but low, so ripe bush protruded above extended, chilblained knuckles. The gentleman gave a humored curtsy to this performance so Reed let his hand drop and stood there, a wet anatomical specimen. His toff apparently appreciated candor and closed in for a closer look. The boy tried a steady, seductive gaze, but his observer was interested in something else.

"Right. You'll do just fine. Let's get you dressed and in the study. Pass through the kitchen on your way. I don't want to be distracted by stomach grumbles."

With that he left the room and the butler returned with a night shirt and sack within which he gathered his filthy clothes.

REED CHOKED DOWN a fistful of biscuits and strong tea at a table packed with other household servants who paid him no mind, offered not a word, and again he felt part of an unstated schedule. After he finished his meal, the butler silently shepherded him down another long hallway with more turns than he felt a building should have a right to, and into a vast library. He gasped—so many books, with a brass ladder on wheels to reach the furthest ones. Books like stars, they were so far out of reach. His gentleman stood with pen in hand behind a music stand. The curtains were opened and he looked pale in the sunlight, smaller without the cloak of night, sickly yet still regal.

"And now our labor. We may begin."

Reed gave a practiced leer and started to unbutton his night shirt when the doors flew open and an elderly woman in a dark dress, her hair in a severe bun, entered.

"M'lord." She greeted the master of the house curtly, and began to fuss with a small tray of writing utensils and books.

"Boy, learn your lessons well. You're to do all that Nan asks, and she'll see you're fed, paid, and, if she reports back the appropriate progress, you'll be back for more, I dare say."

With that he exaggeratedly bowed and exited the library. The governess turned and presented Reed with all the instruments with which a small child is taught to comprehend letters. The books on composition were shelved nearby.

She began to march back and forth as she issued instructions, clarifying that she would not repeat herself, swatting the palm of her hand with a small brass whisk from the fireplace for punctuation. Insolence would be rewarded with a knock on his knuckles. He swallowed and stared at the large letters in the book. He recognized their shapes from the papers he had peddled, and concentrated on the amount of promised coin. His determined leer resurfaced; this was a much easier task than buggering that rotund vicar whose thick buttocks made lancing his hole nigh impossible. The sessions were no more taxing than working on the docks or suffering a large, dirty cock in his mouth, one attached to a macer too drunk to cum and too stupid to call it quits. His regular crew of rent boys at The Reversal were none the wiser, as he could not let on he was flush or every hand would be out. The best he could do was let the younger mates crash on the floor of his room with the promise that they pay him later, a debt he had no plans to collect if he could continue to put the squeeze on this lord. He longed to talk about it, however. Often the boys would gather on a favorite rooftop and gossip over a jar of gin as dawn crept across London. They laughed about the odd things that toffs require to get off, though the way some of the lads pulled on their crotches during the round of stories diminished their derision. It was a survival instinct to know just how these scenes ended and Reed was clueless. He was flummoxed on whether he should continue to improve on his own now that he could afford the penny dreadfuls that used to fascinate him, back when he could only stare at the illustrations through a shop window. If he improved too quickly, would the money run out? So far, that hadn't proven to be the case. As his letters had improved, the governess had moved on to elocution lessons. The lord was but a shadowy figure, present only in the mornings, a sleepy ghost floating over the proceedings, bleary-eyed but watchful that his investment was maturing at the right pace.

ONE MORNING THE lord lingered. Reed noticed that none of the writing instruments or school books were present. When the library door opened, instead of the governess, a young man entered the room. By his demeanor and dress, Reed guessed a stable boy.

"Good, good. You there, paperboy, you'll need to do just as I tell you. Pose as for a painter, a painter of words."

With that he took a long pull on his pipe, a queer, thin thing, and held his smoke, bookended between hollowed cheeks. As he exhaled his eyes momentarily closed.

As the stable unlaced his boots, the toff came to life and barked.

"You're in the stable, paperboy! Pretend you've snuck into the master's stable, to steal a nap."

Reed felt a heady mixture of excitement and relief: finally, things made sense. He had long ago mastered his body, and was eager to show the lord what he could do. The lad opposite was a handsome sort and near his age. The smoke wafting through the room was sweeter than tobacco, darker, of midnight deserts and dreams best savored and then forgotten. He breathed deeply and imagined the emerald divan a bale of hay.

"Good, good! Now lad, you're the master, mad that this ragamuffin is trespassing and you know just the punishment he deserves. That's right, loosen your belt and storm the barn!"

He wrote furiously, damp hair matted to his brow, as the young men both took direction as well as improvised. Reed's shirt was above his head, the stable boy between his lifted legs, when a butler interrupted with tea service. The threesome took a break for cucumber sandwiches. The boys ate heartily while the toff kept spooning sugar into his tea until Reed thought that man would prefer a cup of white mud to teeth on. The stable boy looked content in his work, rearranging the plump stiffness in his trousers between bites of his sandwich. Reed was curious about what was being written and tried to peer around the corners of the music stand: the script was beautiful, black, like the lines of a map if maps traced song instead of streets. The story was different than the one being performed, however. Dark, manic deeds raced across the page. He furrowed his brow, trying to gather meaning from the erotic clouds racing up and down the sheets of paper; Reed was more interested in buggering the stable boy, however. The impoverished lad who shared his bed had rolled and stretched against his body all night and Reed had yet to find release. He caught his eye and gave him a signal that the pantomime was over; the other boy looked relieved and stood and undressed. No matter the orders and directions the frustrated lord barked, they grappled with one another as it pleased them.

As HIS LESSONS decreased, Reed was asked back to the mansion by the park to stage a variety of scenes, often but not always with the same youth. One memorable performance concerned the suddenly shy stable boy and a young maid Reed had seen in the kitchen. In the library, she had been transformed into a Queen, bed sheet for a robe, saucer for a crown, ordering the boys to do certain things to her and each other with a surprising relish. The meanings or settings of other scenarios were harder to pin down but Reed took direction and looked to the obviously more experienced stable boy for guidance. There was no end to this sexual circus. He was well paid and leaving the mansion one evening, he nicked a new coat from a neighbor's laundry line—so things were looking up. All of this and the stable boy had a thick staff, and once Reed had figured out how to fit him inside, the boys couldn't keep their hands off each other.

The gentleman only ever stopped writing to pull on his own leaking lobcock or puff the pipe. Some afternoons he would fall asleep on the divan. The naked Reed craved to run his fingers across the spines of the books, and maybe sample the sweetness of his lordship's pipe, but as if on cue, the dark butler always entered, silently directing them to dress, the stable boy back to work, Reed out of the house, palming a half schilling, far less that what the toff would have paid out had he remained awake and writing.

One morning he was ushered into the library alone, no stable boy, no array of items meant to be arranged into a slave ship on the Nile, or, a favorite of late, a vicar accidently locked in an insane asylum overnight. The shades were drawn, the air stale with sickly breath and old smoke. A shallow cough drew him toward the overturned music stand. His gentleman was sitting on the floor, head hung low.

"I'm too dissipated to do so myself."

Reed blinked, unsure.

The gentleman pointed limply toward the divan.

A bound manuscript was placed there, like a paper crown upon a velvet pillow.

"You must deliver it to the printer, Mr. Wright, posthaste. The address is there with the manuscript. I am too ill today. Go. He expects you and will pay you handsomely. Go."

Reed was quizzical but understood the importance and potential finality of the assignment: if the book his toff had been feverishly writing was done, then it was quite possible his visits to the mansion had drawn to an end. The printer was a source of future capital. With the weight of the manuscript in both hands, he slipped out of the room as once again, that prescient butler was there, holding the door.

HE KNEW THE street, he knew the business. Randy sailors would ask where they could buy "Socratic books" and it paid to be well-informed. He turned down an unnamed alley thick with foreign men sleeping in the doorways of opium dens. Upstairs from one such hovel was the print shop renowned for producing political tracts and poorly translated French pornography. He mounted the stairs two at a time and knocked lightly, forgetting that it was a business and not a private house.

"Come in!" A man roared from inside.

Reed sheepishly stepped into the shop. The air was thick with the smell of ink, cigar smoke and perspiration. The printer was a compact, muscular man in a leather apron. His perfectly trimmed ink-black beard and mustache further shaped his already angular face. The thick lenses of his small, wire-framed glasses obscured his eyes.

"Place the manuscript on the floor."

He obeyed and stood there, awaiting further instructions, wondering how much he was to be paid.

"Disrobe. Place your clothes on that chair."

Now used to taking such instructions, Reed complied and as he stepped out of his shabby underwear, just as he had so often in the presence of the stable boy, the memory of whom inspired his emerging erection to bob in the air. Pretending shyness, he bent forward and pulled his shoulders together as if he could fold into himself and conceal his sex. The printer did not appear to notice his act as he moved about the shop.

"Bend down. Down on all fours."

Reed obeyed, the dirty floor was cold, filmy with inky dust.

"Put your arse up, put your nose in the book."

Reed pivoted on his knees and put his face close the bound package of writing. The head of his cock thudded against the floor, leaving a musty ectoplasmic fingerprint of pre-cum in the dust. He felt exposed, like a hungry dog on a narrowing street.

"Untie it and read aloud while I close up shop."

Reed balanced himself on one elbow as he struggled to untie the manuscript and maintain his position on all fours. Cool air caressed his bare ass; his penis lengthened further and again grazed the floor. He shuddered as the words on the page came into focus. The slender, grey salamanders of opium smoke shimmied up through the floorboards. Such words. Delicate script, the wake of a silent ship calmly fording a deep, unexplored ocean of lust. A boot pushed his knees farther apart. He jumped as cool leather met warm flesh.

"I want to hear your voice, I want to see the words."

The first paragraph described incestuous acts between brothers. An erotic shiver launched up his spine as he recalled achieving these very positions with the stable boy. He heard the door lock, the "open" sign turned around. Shades were pulled. The man paced.

"Read on."

The next passage described a youth tenderly washing the elongated penis of a massive, stationary stallion. The printer loomed behind him as he continued to haltingly read. He felt a sensation between his legs and arched his back. A momentary finger—rounded, smooth: gloved?—pressed against his clenched ass and retreated. His cock quivered.

"Use your mouth to turn the page."

The boy tilted his head and pondered. A boot applied slight pressure to the spread of his fingers on the floor so he quickly licked his lips and turned a page with his tongue. Several pages clung together and fell as a whole; he braced himself for unknown punishment. Either the printer didn't notice or didn't care. He again read aloud.

This new passage concerned a naked boy on all fours on the floor of a bookshop, reading aloud.

Reed shuddered as Mr. Wright circled him. Silver wisps of opium curled up from the shadowy den below. As he read, the printer withdrew a quill from its stand, moistened it on his tongue, and inserted it in his supplicant's rear.

As Reed read those very words aloud gloved fingers pressed the writing utensil further in. He stammered but knew that where there was a glove, there was boot, so with a whisper he continued the story of the boy's ecstasy and as described on the page, a pinion wound its way inside him.

"He expects you and will pay you handsomely." Yet his gentleman said he had planned on going himself but fell ill...

Like every Limehouse paperboy, he'd buggered and been buggered. Before the stable boy's ample staff there were back alley assignations for a sixpence, flophouse floors for warmth. This was different. As he read and as the quill traveled farther in, he felt its original feather form return and multiply into the lush wing of a golden griffin. He wanted to lie completely still and focus on this new and painful pleasure but the hand now on his neck steered him to read and the words poured out and his cock ached and an effusive, molten heat dibbled forth, quickly caught by an extended finger and fed back to him.

His tongue, no longer dry, turned the page.

Here was a sonnet about a sonnet written in blood and Reed did not follow the meaning of the poem, though his whole body shivered as the printer's circling pace around him quickened.

The quill was still inside him and he arched his back further, as if he could ignite the griffin's pinion into full wings when really, the hand of a practiced falconer was required.

That gloved hand returned, hovering near his testicles. He tensed. Once an overweight gentleman in a top hat had offered him ten shillings to get in the back of his hansom cab and Reed eagerly complied, loosening his trousers as the driver shut the door. The older man, inebriated, his beard wooly with spilt snuff, pulled Reed's pants down and clutched his sac with such brutality that the youth cried and kicked his way out of the lurching cab, naked from the waist down, which set the whores of Charring Cross laughing.

The grip on his neck tightened. Face against the page, he could see the imperfections of the ink as lines began to stretch and yearn, like branches reaching for the sun. The letters pulsed and opened as if hungry flowers. Still he read. A stack of books in the corner shimmered as if about to dissemble, paper into sand, the printed words angry mad ants that would ravage the room.

Reading aloud a passage wherein a mad Queen tortured two servant boys, he tripped over the word "cunt" and with a guttural laugh the printer entered him roughly, pushing forward, heavy and brutish in his rhythm. Cheek on the floor, pages scattered and still he read aloud. Fading purple smoke from below filled his nostrils. One leg bent, the other outstretched, he clutched the nearest sheet of paper and read, words punctuated by the grunting man riding him hard. Eyes tearing, the letters went in and out of focus as his penis thickened. Pages fluttered across the room, out of reach, the printer grunting above. So he read the titles off the spines of the books on the shelves. He gasped and gulped and in between his recitations, he listened for the flap of griffin wings.

Mr. Wright lifted him roughly off the floor and turned him over and straddled his naked body, now coated in sweat. He held Reed's head by his damp hair with one hand while he pulled on his own cock with the other. The boy parted his lips just as the printer unfurled in his mouth and Reed's semen shot out and onto the floor, hitting loose pages of manuscript. The printer's glasses fell and anger crossed his face. His eyes were in turn wild and distant. He was blind. He collapsed on top of Reed. His weight crushed the boy's face into the separated pages of the manuscript.

A key worked the door as Reed struggled beneath the bodily press of the printer.

The butler entered and locked the door. Reed panicked and fought to stand up. The butler set a doctor's case down and pulled out a white rag and a clear bottle.

He approached and knelt before the fraught boy.

"Calm down, son, calm down. This won't hurt at all. Apparently, the eyes don't have nerves, as luck would have it."

He dabbed some of the liquid onto the cloth.

"Can't blackmail someone if you can't see the materials 'tis all. You're about to learn a new trade."

Shoe on a scrap of the manuscript, he leaned in. The boy's cheek was slick with his own white splatter, an inverse to the black looping cursive script that told his story. The last one he would ever read.

ALL MY
OCEANS
OF BLOOD
AND INK

Matthew Bright

1: Theatre Royal, Dublin, 1867

TELL ME: WHAT purpose does the carnal drive of a man serve?

I ask this with no guile. What use is something powerful enough to lead a man astray from his normal life, all for a brief explosion of pleasure? For all of the significance we pay to restraint with our words, it takes the merest moment for us to be denuded of all pretence and find ourselves gripped by something altogether more physical. It's for this reason that in half the streets in the south of the city can be found harlots who, for a few pennies, can be taken in an alleyway for the cheapest fumble. Perhaps, spent and shuffling home to their wives, the men who frequent these women promise themselves that the carnal drive will never again get the better of them, but even they know this to be a lie—all it will take will be the right stretch of skin, or the right glimpse of a stocking, the threat of exposed bosom in hot weather, and then they are once again priapic, ready to debase themselves anew.

For myself, I have always regarded this with some degree of bafflement. Why have I never felt this visceral reaction to a woman the way my fellows have? And yet—here I find myself, the blood singing in every art of my body, breathless with desire.

For him.

Him: an actor on the stage. A young lover ensnared in comic misapprehension. I cannot be the only one captivated by his performance tonight; the adoring expression upon the faces of many of the audience members enforce this, and I find myself madly, irrationally jealous—jealous of anyone upon whom his gaze is bestowed.

I am invisible from the stage; there is no way my face could be picked out by him as he looks across his audience, and this single, hitherto-unremarkable fact awakens a bizarre anger in me, a catastrophic sense of unfairness that by ill fate of my seat I can be so overlooked.

The audience stand to applaud him vigorously at his curtain call. I try and raise my voice louder than the throng so he will notice me. When the curtain has fallen for the final time, I seat myself as the others around me begin to dress and leave. I was sent here to write a review, and as I was wont to do I had brought paper and a pen with me with which to make notes from which to martial my thoughts later on, but all I had written throughout the performance was his name, in neat block capitals.

I closed the notepad, tucked it away in my coat, and joined the stream of people leaving.

Outside, I broke away from the crowd. A thought—a plan, even, one might be so bold as to call it—suggesting itself to me. The stage door of the Theatre Royal is discreet, practically unknown by most theatregoers, and therefore rarely attended by eager audience members hoping to apprehend the stars on their exit, but I knew where the side street could be found. When I arrived, I was the only one present, and I found myself obscurely pleased; I felt that the presence of others would have somehow diluted my adoration, made it somehow less special, commonplace. I lurked by the door, feeling conspicuous and ill at ease. I fiddled with my paper, thinking to add something while I waited, but could think of nothing, and returned it to my pocket still bearing only the two words I had written earlier: HENRY IRVING.

Which was when I noticed that the stage door stood ajar.

Well—I ask you: what would someone such as yourself have done? Or someone such as myself, who prides himself on his journalistic spirit, his will to discover? What should I have done?

Perhaps I should have waited outside, but I did not.

I shall not bore you with the description of the theatre's backstage; they are as unremarkable as all the many other theatres I have seen since then. All you need to know is that I found myself at the dressing room door of the man upon whom I had spent the night fixated. You need not know the length of time it took me to summon the courage to knock, or the nauseous elation that churned my stomach bitterly when he answered. All that needs to be known here is that by hook or crook, I had found myself alone in Henry Irving's dressing room.

"Hello," he said, a prosaic greeting that still—to my ears at least—sounded like poetry springing from his lips. "And you are...?"

I stepped forward, removing my hat, stretching out a hand awkwardly. "Mr. Irving, my apologies for the intrusion. I—well, the stage door was open, and I took the opportunity. I hope you don't mind, but I was so moved by your performance that I felt I must visit you and express how—"

He swivelled and regarded my hand with a stony look of suspicion. "Yes, all that as may be, young man, but perhaps we could start with a name?"

I dropped my hand. "Stoker. Abraham Stoker. I'm with the *Evening Mail,* I was sent here to review the show. I—"

"Ah, of course. ," said Henry. "I gather you enjoyed the show, then?"

"Remarkable. I have seen a number of version of *The Rivals*, and this was really one of the finest performances I've had the pleasure of seeing."

"That's more than kind of you." Henry withdrew to his dressing table. He was an imposingly tall man, even more so away from the stage and in the stuffy confines of a dressing room, and he had to stoop considerably to look into the mirror clearly. "I assume the *Mail* has sent you to ask some questions for the edition?"

"Actually..." I winced. "No, they haven't. I confess I simply was so entranced by your performance that I wanted to come and tell you in person. I felt—" He straightened, and turned towards me, and I swallowed. "I felt compelled."

"Did you now?" He stepped towards me, holding up a cloth in my direction. "Perhaps you could also be compelled to assist me with something? My makeup—it's rather a devil to remove, and I have quite a time of it when I try myself. Would you be so kind?"

He drew close to me, closing his eyes and inclining his head up into the light, pressing the cloth into my hands. Our bodies were practically touching; until that day I would never have considered such a proximity to another of my own gender be so full of sexual intimations, and yet here and now I found myself shivering. "Gentle pressure," he said, "and it'll be right off."

I trace the cloth across his face, removing with it the light film of greasepaint beneath. His skin paled beneath my ministrations, and I realised that the makeup had added a rosy tiny to his skin that was otherwise absent—though do not let my description conjure an image of pallor or coldness, for as pale as he was, his skin was warm, even without touching it.

I drew first nearer, and then bolder, and, dispensing with the cloth, I removed the last traces of makeup from the crease of his eye with the pad of my thumb, allowing my fingertip to skim down over his sharp cheekbone. Up close, I could see that, despite the composed image he projected on stage, his face was drawn from exertion, his hair damp with sweat. I moved my fingers up to a lock that had fallen to his forehead and stuck there, pushed it back to join the rest of it's slicked-back brothers.

"Was my performance really that good?" Henry said without opening his eyes. I felt his breath against my face as he spoke.

"It was the finest I've ever seen." My eyes fixed upon his lips, and the thought appeared in my mind: my god, I want to kiss him.

"You can," he said. "I'd welcome it."

And so I did.

At first he didn't respond, allowing me only to move my lips against his, to press my tongue into the gap between and attempt to invade his mouth, but then he relinquished and gave me access, his own tongue returning my movement. His hands were at first on my shoulders, holding me still as we kissed, and then they were gone; I felt the absence keenly only to open my eyes and see that he was divesting himself of his clothing. His long, nimble fingers plucked apart the thick buttons of the military costume he had been wearing, and he stripped away the coat, revealing his naked torso beneath. The lack of an undershirt below the coat seemed obscene; between my legs, my body reacted to the obscenity.

His body was as marvellous as I had anticipated from a distance, compact as steel and whipcord; the muscular force that lean, lithe body contained was extraordinary. He backed away from me, lowering himself until he was seated on the edge of his dressing table, hastily pushing its contents away. He spread his legs, then lifted his arms wide and above his head, until he resembled the

Vitruvian man. In the oil lamps set upon the table, his sweat-slicked body gleamed, the evidence of a hard night's labours laid out before me.

"Was it really the finest performance you've ever seen?"

I leaned in to kiss him, but he tilted his mouth away. "Riveting," I said, into his cheek. "Incomparable." I kissed his chest, opened my lips against the skin and tasted him. "Transcendent." I began to explore the length of his torso, gripping him by the waist and pulling him to me, baptising his skin with my own saliva, possessed by a desire to lick his body clean, to demonstrate my adoration for him with my mouth. I descended to the tantalising edge of his breaches, kissing their perimeter; his hands tangled in my hair, gripped tight. "Breathtaking," I murmured into his taut belly, and rose. Once again he avoided my mouth, and instead guided me to his armpits, where I buried my face. The hair was sparse, sharp, and I found he tasted different, as if he was another man entirely. The thought thrilled me: after all, shouldn't an actor taste like a multitude of men? Didn't that make sense—all those myriad roles he had played, written in sweat upon his body?

He pushed me away, and began to fumble with his trousers. I pushed his hands away, unfastened him, and pulled down the remains of his clothing, undergarments and all. The tight costume stuck halfway down his calves. Impatient, I ducked beneath them, emerging in the triangle of space between his legs. His sex stood, short but thick, arising from a briar of coarse dark hair, his testicles heavy-hanging below. "Ennervating," I told him, and provided them the attention I had accorded the rest of his body, causing him to moan so loudly I feared we would draw unwanted attention, and so I pulled back, returning to my baptism of his skin, tracing my way across his inner thighs, the length of his legs, drawing back the tight clothing inch by inch until they finally separated from his body, leaving him—at last—fully naked. "You bared your soul," I told him, raising his feet to my faith. I ran my tongue over their length, between his toes. I was reminded of the biblical stories of the woman who washed Jesus' feet with her tears, but as I bent to my task I told myself that there could be no greater act of worship than my own at that very moment.

I was wrong; I felt his hands upon my head, pushing me back as he repositioned himself on the dressing table, pushed back against the mirror so that there appeared to be two of him now, the him-before-me and the him-in-the-mirror. He pulled back his legs, exposing himself further to me, and clasped me to him, guiding my face between his buttocks, my tongue into the bitter, coppery-tasting tangle of hair around his hole. Above me, I could feel frantic movement as he worked his sex.

"The best performance you've ever seen?" he panted. His fingers were tight in my hair, so tight now that it hurt, and I struggled to breathe. I managed what sound of assent I could, and he groaned. "Astonishing," I tried to say, into him, and I felt him tighten around my tongue, his thighs press close—and then he released me. I was freed in enough time to watch his speed spill from his cock, and I bent to consume it.

He reclined, him and his mirror image back to back on the dressing table, spent. His eyes were closed, and he didn't move for long enough that I began to feel awkward upon my knees and, despite my own unaddressed arousal, I stood, rearranging my clothing.

"I should go, Mr. Irving. It's been a pleasure. And—it—it really was a fine performance."

He neither spoke nor moved, and so I retreated to the door. It was only as I was about to close it quietly behind me that he spoke. "Thank you. Perhaps we'll see each other again, Mr. Stoker?"

"Perhaps," I said, and closed the door.

And so I ask again: what purpose does the carnal drive of a man serve? Can that explosion of pleasure, however brief, be enough? For now I'm here, in my small room, with my paper and my pen, and I am writing. Below a name in block capitals, I have created with words an encounter capable of both provoking and disappointment me in equal measure. Perhaps it's even a performance to equal Mr. Irving's—though this will only ever be for my own private audience, and yours, perhaps.

But with the stage door firmly closed, and the alley chilly and empty, it's all I have.

2: The Grand Hotel, Whitby, 1895

When I was a child, I could not walk. The reasons for this have never been clearly established, though my father engaged and dismissed a series of doctors who posited multiple theories of increasing unlikeliness, but until the age of seven my ability to walk was at best an unsteady hobble and at worst complete paralysis.

Somewhere in my eighth year this changed. I couldn't say what the catalyst for this was, but I made up for my own youthful malaise by throwing myself headlong into every sporting activity my education and leisure could provide. It would appear the enforced confinement of my childhood years was long forgotten, both to myself and to my family.

And yet, as you may way well know yourself, some things never quite leave us, not fully.

As I child I would dream. It was a recurring dream, not quite a nightmare, but never pleasant. I had taken to sleeping lying on my front. It displeased my mother greatly, who thought me in danger of choking in my sleep, but even when she would gently turn me over in my sleep, by morning I would have rolled back. In my dream, I would awake in the dark, face down on the bed, unable to move. The room would be lit by the sallow moonlight slipping through the narrow window, casting vague, elongated shadows across the floor. And then, I would sense a presence; that neck-tingling, primal feeling that there is something in the nothing behind you.

But I cannot turn to look. I can do nothing but lie there, feeling my own breath tighten in my throat. Until, eventually, something moves. What I have taken for the shadow of a chair separates, reveals a figure who has been sitting in it. He is an extraordinarily tall, narrow man who strides purposefully across the room, and stoops over my bed.

I feel a cold whisper against the back of my neck, and then I awake.

This particular dream lasted long into my adolescence and then, as my life became busier, as I married, moved to London, became ensnared in the business of showbusiness, it vanished as if it had never been there. Until tonight, when, for the first time in decades, I dreamed once again of the narrow man in my bedroom and I awoke in a cold sweat to find my room in the Grand Hotel as empty as it had been before my slumber.

Unable to return to sleep, I crossed to the writing desk by the window. I opened the curtains and gazed out across the harbour. Whitby was blue in the moonlight, it's jumble of gambrel roofs and pitched houses half-lost in a thick brume that had rolled in off the sea and hung over the water. Here and there lights in the windows marked the streets that lay within in, but the bridge that connected East Cliff to West Cliff was invisible. Directly opposite me, I could pick out the narrow band of the hundred and ninety-nine steps that snaked up to the Abbey rising up out of it, its base lost to sight.

It was a night like this, I thought, in which the narrow man in my dreams could so easily be real. Even now he might be stalking through the streets, the sea mist curling around him as he came towards me, for who knew what purpose.

I fixed upon the image, and rummaged through the papers on the desk—letters, endless letters, half-written, half-read, all in my own hand, some never to be sent—until I found a blank sheet. I smoothed it out, and neatly lettered a title at the top: THE DEAD UN-DEAD.

Several hours later, I had filled forty sheets of paper, my handwriting growing increasingly illegible. I had conjured images I had not known were contained in my head: a castle in a foreign land, daemonic temptresses, storm-swept seas, and a seductive, implacable man who, in my story, was even now setting foot on the cobbles of Whitby.

I returned to the window. Most of the lights had gone out now; the town was dark. But I could see him moving, engulfed by the mist but visible in the eddies and swirls that disturbed it. He was coming up through the gap in the cliff, along the road towards the Great Hotel, visible now, a shadow who raised its face towards my window, and—

You will have surely guessed whose face it was.

Even the most casual observer of our engagements over the decades could have described by devotion to him without the faintest of trouble. I would have willingly sacrificed any treasure in my life for him, and so I found myself, with a particular failing I could recognise as if standing far enough away to observe but powerless to alter, unable to raise even the slightest criticism of him. Did I care if my name appeared at the bottom of every program—*Acting Manager: Bram Stoker*—as if I was an insignificant part of the circus that kept him on the stage? Not a whit; this was my job. Did I care that my careful cultivation of contacts and favours won him accolades and riches, and yet I was left to fend for myself when my own finances suffered? Not a jot; it was my pleasure. Did I care if I wrote fifty letters a day to stoke the fires of his career, and yet he had ceased to sign his letters to me as 'with love'?

No, I did not. And yet here was my narrow man, with the face of my beloved, written large across the scattered pages, in my own indelible hand.

Finding my heart beating faster, the same cold sweat arising as if I had just woken once again from my nightmare, I retreated from the window. My nightshirt felt tight, constricting, and I fumbled it off, leaving me naked and shivering in the chill from the window. I seized my fountain pen and the remaining blank pages from the desk and threw myself onto the bed. I pressed my face into the pillow, held it tight until stars woke behind my eyelids and I couldn't breathe. I raised myself on my elbows, pulled the paper towards me, and wrote:

He is here. In the room.

He is behind me. I know it though I cannot turn to look.

Henry is here.

And I felt his touch on my neck. Fingertips between my shoulder blades, at first gentle, and the insistent, applying pressure until I could no longer stay fixed on my elbows and I fell forward. His lips kissed my spine, descending, and then his hands gripped my thighs. He spread me, pulled back to view my supplicatory position.

He spat—his own version of my baptism of his body, I suppose, the issue of his mouth greasing the way. And then his weight was on top me. He pressed sharp against me, seeking entry. I rose to facilitate, and he slid inside me. The pain was sharp, consuming my entire body, and I cried out, threw my head back against him. In my clenched fist, the fountain pen spilled ink into my palm; he plucked it from my grasp and flung it away. He stayed within me, unmoving but for his lips and his teeth nibbling against my neck. When I let my head fall, he began to move over me, slow and insistent.

At length his thrusts became harder, his whole body supine against my back. He whispered in my ear, though I shall not repeat those words; despite my candour I cannot bear to impart those sentiments to another for fear it would diminish them. He raised me, pulled me to my knees, freeing me from the bed, thrusting his last until he spent inside me. I had expected to feel his issue, but instead felt only the sensation of his body collapsing exhausted onto mine. Nevertheless, the knowledge of his seed within me was provocation enough—with a few strokes of my own hand I had matched him. I shuddered, emitting moans loud enough to shock even myself, ejaculating a thick, syrupy gout of black ink across the bed.

The blue blossomed on the white cotton, soaking into the fabric, and they began to curl and shiver beneath it. Henry let a tired hand fall against my chest and his touch released the last of me; I cried out again, shooting a final spray of ink across the papers that had long-since fallen from the table. The words I had spent my evening setting down vanished into my black splatter. The papers whipped up as if a strong wind had them in its breath. The floorboards joined them in concert, shuddering and straining, wildebeest restrained only by the nails that held them in place. My fountain pen bounced and leaped across the floor. First dust then masonry rained down upon our union as I collapsed facedown upon the vibrant mess we had made.

Beneath us, the floor cracked, and we descended in a tumult of stone and mortar until we were submerged in liquid.

We arose, coughing, clinging to each other in a sea foaming red and blue around us, an ocean of ink and blood. In the gloaming of a fresh dawn, Henry kicked against the tide, kissing me passionately on my lips and neck. The Grand Hotel's foundations clung futilely to the cliffs, the rest of it's walls long gone, broken apart by our lovemaking. Henry's arms were tight around me, pulling me below the surface of the sea, and we sank, lips pressed together, sharing the air in our lungs. To either side of us plunged the remnants of a town—the shattered buttresses of the Abbey sinking past us to one side, the other the whalebone arch, bones detaching and turning slowly away from each other into the dark below. We sank past fishing boats and carts, beachhuts and lobsterpots, until we reached the ocean floor, and amidst an unfolding cloud of filth we kissed until there was no more air in our lungs and we had no choice but to kick back towards the surface.

We rose towards a new day's light, and as we left the enveloping dark of the deep behind us, Henry's face screwed tight with terror. He opened his mouth to scream, the last bubbles of lifegiving air escaping in a stream. I clung to his thin body, but I could do nothing to prevent what followed; as the rays of sunlight reached him through the water, his body disintegrated, flowed through my fingers as insubstantial as the sediment at the bottom of an inkwell, and was swept away.

I arose, gasping, to the surface of a briny, salty green sea watched over by the slowly-awakening, fully-intact town of Whitby. The sun rose, and I choked at length, crying bitter tears as I swam painfully back to the shore.

3: Lyceum Theatre, London, 1897

Tell me: what purpose does the carnal drive of a man serve?

What use is something powerful enough to lead a man to blindly give a loyalty that goes unpaid—a loyalty paid in time, in words, in love, and yet so bitterly unrewarded. How trivial it seems, when one puts one's mind to it, that a man—that I—can allow the urge to touch and to taste another's body to rule so many other more substantial concerns. Consider the bleak moment after one has spent, in which the other's body seems like nothing but a collection of parts reeking of the aftermath—that moment, that so quickly fades, perhaps in that moment is wisdom.

A single word was all that he gave me, at the conclusion. Years of work, and all he gave me was one word, and so here I found myself, in my office, gripped by an unutterable rage. Perhaps I should convince myself that a lifetime of friendship does not necessarily presume that he should love my work without calculation; I could tell myself that his objective opinion is a boon. And yet, I do not believe it to be that, for I am convinced of the quality of my play.

All the horrors I have imagined for the past years, laid out on the page. But I can admit to you, perhaps, that this is not really what wounds me. A simple dismissal perhaps I could stomach, were it not for *this* play, for *this* part. How could he fail to notice for who this was written?

Perhaps then I could convince myself that it was the performances that had let it down. The actors had done their best with the barely-bound-together script I had assembled for them, and Jones was passable, but the role was written for Henry—the part of the narrow man that inhabited my dreams, written for the narrow man that inhabited my waking hours. Henry could have given it the life it deserved, but no—I was left merely to grapple with his single word of judgement.

There was a knock at the door, which I ignored. I was in no mood for conversation. Momentarily, the door opened anyhow, which meant it could only be one person.

"Henry, I warn you, I'm foul company."

I did not turn to look at him, but could hear movement behind me. The sound matched a familiar movement; he had sat himself on the edge of my desk—the rustle of papers, scrape of an inkwell as he moved it aside—the same as he always did.

"I presume you would like an apology." There was an odd cadence to his voice, an air of performance, as if he was reading the line from an unfamiliar script.

"I expect nothing of the sort," I said. "You have made your pronouncement, and that will be that. *The Undead* is no doubt now quite dead."

"Perhaps." A pause. He would be fiddling with something on the desk, no doubt. He usually did—a pen, perhaps. "Did you hold hope that it would work, truly?"

I turned to him. My fists were clenched, fingernails digging into my palms. I had never felt like this in his presence before; I was so accustomed to control, to the sensation of containing the deep wellspring of feeling that I held for him, that it was at once exhilarating and terrifying to feel so close to letting all of that go. "I'd really rather be alone."

"The thing that it was missing," he said, as if he had not heard me, "was a clear focus. Your Dracula—he is meant to be both monster and seducer, and yet I could not see in what way he was either."

He looked old, I realised; it is so rare that we study someone's face in detail, and we so often simply store the imagined version of what they look like. Nothing some greasepaint and well-placed stage lights wouldn't fix, of course, but not quite the visage I had envisioned as I wrote. But then, age comes to us all.

"That as may be. I wish to be alone, Henry. To consider, and to write."

"To write?" A small ghosted across his lips, then he stifled it. "More of *The Undead?*"

"No. My letter of resignation."

He stood up, limbs unfolding like a crane. "Your resignation?"

"Yes."

"But...why?"

I took a long, steadying breath. "Henry—I see no gain in discussing that with you now."

"Bram—your play aside, I would never want you to—"

"Henry."

He looked baffled—an expression I had never seen on his face, except in a play, and then it had looked quite different. He was always so assured, always the person in control of the room, even when it was me that had made everything in that room happen. "Bram, surely we can't fall out over such a small thing as a play?"

"*A* play, perhaps not, but *my* play—yes."

"The Lyceum won't survive without you."

This was flattery, but possibly true. I looked around the office, noted the cracked plaster, the gloomy, unwashed windowpanes, the peeling playbills. But of course, he didn't really mean the theatre. "Perhaps the Lyceum's time is up," I said, "just like yours."

One learns, in a friendship of a lifetime, how to break somebody.

"Bram..." He stepped close to me. "Bram...I...do you need me to apologise?" His pleading must have been an unfamiliar role.

"No. I do not."

"Then—then what will make amends?"

He kissed me. It was unexpected, and after so many imagined kisses—a multitude of kisses in every form and setting once could conjure—it was at once disappointing and electric. I opened my mouth against his, tasted cigars, then pulled back.

"Henry..."

"I've always known." He kissed me again, There was fervour—he was thrusting his tongue into my mouth, pulled at my clothing. A button flew off, skittered into a corner, and his hands fell on my body, fingernails scraping against the soft flesh. He gripped me by the waist and spun me around, pressing me against the wall, his mouth on the back of my ear. The breath was catching in my throat; I felt like I was caught in the beginnings of an earthquake.

But then I remembered the single word, and suddenly his fingers felt awkward his mouth clumsy and wet; what I had mistaken for fervour was merely inexpert enthusiasm. I turned and pushed him away. "Is that it?" I cried. "Is that what I've been waiting for? That pathetic attempt?" I shook my head.

He reached for his own clothing, stripping himself with little to no ceremony until he stood before me naked. His body was still steel, still as I had imagined from all those stolen glances over the years—age had come to us all, but to him it had hardened him.

I armed myself with his own words. "Dreadful!"

He began to cry.

I waited until they had stopped, and he had turned away from me as he wiped his eyes out of my gaze.

"Bend over," I said.

He didn't move, shoulders still hunched and then he spread his hands and prostrated himself over the desk. His chest was flattened against the discarded leaves of my play, sprung free of their makeshift binding. I imagined their ink imprinting onto his skin, the handwritten notes, stage directions written across his ribs, dialogue spiralling around his navel. I was hard.

I removed my own trousers and positioned myself behind him. This should have been an opportunity for observation; too long I'd relied on imagination, had fantasised about the texture, the shape, the taste of every part of the body displayed before me. In my mind, I had debased myself upon every inch of him, but now I felt no desire to attend to any part of him save one.

When I entered him he did not make a sound. I thrust to the base, pressed myself against him, heavy on top of him. My hands found his wrists, held them against the desk as I fucked. He kept his head pressed against the desk, his forehead rested against the hastily prepared poster for tonight's reading.

It was a curious feeling to be inside him, unlike any I'd experienced before. The prevailing feeling was heat, a heat that surrounded my cock so fully that every part of my body was already tensing to spend with him, to fill his hellfire innards with my own seed. I released his hands, and straightened myself, spread his buttocks to witness my penetration of him. The sight of my cock, stretching him as I entered, was vivid and pornographic in a way that none of my fantasies had ever been— they had been so lavish, so decadent, even when the walls had been coming down around us. This was entirely different: it was carnality, and rage—and blood.

Beneath me he tore. The seam ran from my cock up towards his neck, splitting as if all the threads had suddenly given way, spraying a precise crimson line up my torso from navel to chin. He peeled away, revealing the viscera beneath, the shocking white of his spine dividing his bloody insides into two beating, pulsing halves. Around my cock the muscle was giving way, and I found myself stumbling forward, wrongfooted, falling into the disintegrating mass of him. My hands that had a moment ago grasped tightly to him now caught in his skin, as if I was dressing in the dark, and it sloughed away from the rest of his body as my fingernails tore through.

I pitched forward, my face pressed suddenly and intimately into him, the ridges of his vertebrae splitting my lip. My mouth filled with the taste of copper;

his blood and mine. I opened my mouth to cry out and instead found myself choking as his veins divulged their contents onto my tongue.

His skin slid from his body, and I with it, facedown. I dared not crane my neck to see what remained of him standing, this meat and bone assemblage still twitching on what remained of its legs, bent over the desk. Bloodied sheets of paper dislodged by our fucking floated down, sticking where they fell. I coughed—Henry's blood, gouts of it from my lungs—and sank against the floor. Except it wasn't the boards I was resting against, it was the shapeless sack of skin that had fallen away from Henry. My forehead was against what had been the back of his neck, where the split had ended. I nuzzled against it like a new-born lamb against its mother, found myself bleating needfully, until—as if it had been made for me—the lip of the skin slipped over my head. The slick, jellied inside settled over me; I felt his eyelashes settle against mine, the ragged edge of his lips meet mine, the tangle of frayed nerves that dangled behind behind his nipples like an uprooted weed settled over mine and set them alight.

I crawled to my feet, pulling on this new suit, straightened myself: tall, narrow.

There was a rarely used mirror tucked away behind a cabinet. I dragged it out, dusted it down, and regarded my new self. I licked my—his—lips. "Astonishing," I said, trying it out. "Incomparable."

It felt so alien to see Henry stare back at me with such an open attention in his gaze. It made my skin prickle beneath his. "Breathtaking!" I mouthed at my reflection.

I stooped and plucked several of the pages of the play—those that were still readable—from the floor. "'Listen to them—the children of the night! What music they make!'" I could see it now, Henry as Dracula; commanding, the role he was born to play, the role I had made for him. I tried another: "'I have crossed oceans of time to find you.'"

Yes!—this: this what I had dreamed of.

The papers fell. I found new words to fit into Henry's mouth. "He is meant to be both monster and seducer, and yet I could not see in what way he was either."

I took a breath, and turned to him, sat so benignly on the edge of my desk. My fingernails had cut bloody tracks into the inside of palms. The pain felt fresh and vital, but when I looked into the face of the man to whom I had devoted so many of my thoughts—waking and dreaming—for the better part of my lifetime, I saw my own exhaustion reflected back at me. We were both too old for this; the time for us both to be fresh-faced and adored had past.

"Yes," I said, wearily. I bent to gather together the unbound leaves of my play scattered across the floor, and think to myself that this is the last time I will bow to Henry. "I imagine you would not."

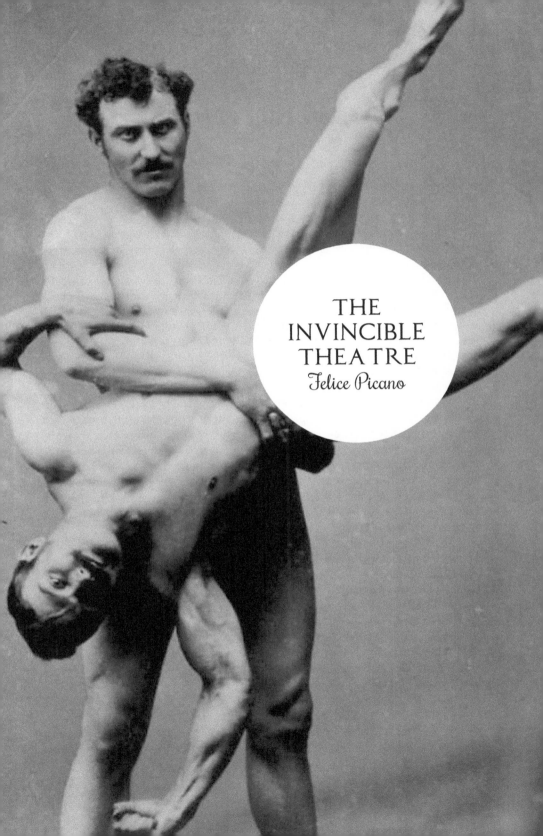

THE
INVINCIBLE
THEATRE
Felice Picano

A THEATRICAL TROUPE suddenly arrived unannounced in Covent Garden late one very breezy afternoon when all of us were going starkers chasing after our bonnets, hats, cash boxes and stray stalks of airborne gladiolus.

The actors clangorously trundled into the square within two large, overblown, colorful, horse drawn caravans, and immediately camped at the far northeastern corner, where infrequent "entertainment" customarily set up stage.

The latter had, during my time there so far, been constituted of: a wagon full of cheerless, fly-blown marionettes in so-called dramatizations of old legends that even young Zoe Newholl disdained as puerile. I also recall an ancient Punch and Judy Show, from somewhere in Essex, last costumed and painted up in the time of King George Second. Most recently, we'd been "treated" to a family dance company from Scotland purporting to be "Hebrides-bred and authentikal," of which the less said about it the better for any future intercourse with our northern neighbour.

"Monsieur Guillaume Darrot and The Invincible Theatre," read the man-sized placards of the new troupe, stood on either side of the little stage that was quickly erected between ends of two high-sided caravans parked six yards apart in the corner. Hand bills distributed by myself, as a hired lad, named the individuals of the company, which besides M. Darrot, included Mademoiselle Suzette Darrot; Mademoiselle Antoinette Genre; M. De Sang Pur—doubtless the large, bearded, bald headed fellow I had noted moving large objects about so much;– and a "Grande-Madame de St. Clement-En-Hors-de-Combat," whom we were assured would play roles deemed "Domestic, Deistic and Outlandish."

I laughed as hard as the other flower vendors, fruiterers and marrow-sellers, reading aloud for them this piece of Frenchified gallimaufry. Even so, two nights later I joined an audience of several score, requiting my Ha'pence for the troupe's first performance: "The Most Despicable and Horrible Tragedy of the Tyrone Family of ____ County, Ireland — after a tale written by that estimable Mr. Joseph Bodin de Sheridan Le Fanu." And, like the other three score in the audience, I was terrified, frightened, and moved. Moved so much, in fact, that four days later and after having seen every one of their performances, I resigned The Covent Garden, flower-selling, and the Hellenically-inclined Newholl family forever, and I joined the Invincible Theatre troupe.

M. DARROT TURNED out to be an individual no more exotic than a Mr. William Darrow, or Billy-Boy Dee, as his sire, another member of the troupe, one Jonathan Darrow, (.i. e. Mr. Pure Blood, or De Sang-Pur,) called him. For all his age and for all of his considerable airs, Darrow the Elder, was no more well-born than your humble servant, My Lord, and hailed from some inconsequential townlet in Surrey.

And the purity of his blood, if it ever existed, must do daily battle with prodigious amounts of gin and whiskey to discover which liquid would prevail.

Still, the old reprobate was docile and had been for many long moons an actor with other troupes, including what remained of The Kings Men during the realm of the last Regent, and so he had memorized his acting parts, or at any rate had gotten several resonantly long speeches by heart.

It was those speeches that Darrow the Younger had pilfered, and around them that he had since begun to scribble his own plays, far more popular adaptations of our then contemporary literature as found in various three volume novels and periodicals, along of course with those foreign dramas he happened upon and then "lifted" wholesale. Add to those, two or three expurgations of Mr. Shakespeare filled with blood, thunder, ghosts, and revenge, and there you have the troupe's entire repertoire.

You may then easily guess from these explications that the great female dramaturge of the company, Madame Suzanne Darrot, was in fact Susie Darrow nee Semple, wife to Billy-Boy; also that Mademoiselle Antoinette Genre was in truth her niece by blood, a Miss Amy Green. As for the fifth member of the company, it would be many months before I uncovered that remarkable personage's complete identity and rather odd verity.

Meanwhile during their short engagement at the Covent Garden's out of doors corner, I had progressed with The Invincibles from being a mere set-up helper, to a placard boy, and on to becoming a constant "stage-handy lad," assisting Billy in setting up the changes of scenery. These commonly consisted of two parts: a painted background or as they called it "rear scrim," and a variety of deal or other lightweight wood (and thus quite mobile) furniture upon which the actors would perch and lean for verisimilitude, though few might actually hold the full weight of the somewhat rotund Darrow Elder for longish periods of time. I also "drew the curtains" to open and close the show as well as to register the so called Entr'actes.

An immediate fascination with their art attracted me into the circle of The Invincible Theatre. Growing knowledge and increasing appreciation of their craft and all it comprised, indeed required, drew me even more tightly into their tiny realm. Thence, a kind of juvenile passion with those two lovely, and one bizarre, women, enmeshed me ever more approximate.

Remember that I was at this time in that mid-age between boy and man that my former employer, Theogones, so abhorred. But I must admit that finally it was my total fixation upon Billy Darrow that at last folded me into the troupe's most intimate circle — for while I had before idolised members of the female sex, for the first time in my life, I found a male worthy of my uttermost infatuation.

Was he handsome then, this leading actor, you will ask, My Lord? Of course he was; he was a leading man of an acting troupe, after all. But then again, feature by feature, he was not especially remarkable. He had learned through stage make-up to over-benefit the advantages of his better facial features: his fine glittering black eyes he emphasised by further application of dark paint to his eyebrows and by thickening to ebony his eye lashes. His nose I knew for a fact at close sight to be slightly bent to the left. No matter, he painted a straight line down to its tip despite the bone, and shaded it from either side, and it appeared ferrule-straight. He re-limned and then daubed into the new outline his upper lip so it might be as voluptuous as its mate. He oh so softly rouged his cheekbones so they shone not quite so high, to make himself more cherubic for younger roles. Even so, later on, when a play-described "brilliant beau" was required for a walk-on role, Billy was the first to toss my own self, clad in gilt velvet with silver frogging, onto that never-very-steady movable stage in lieu of himself for the audience to ooh and aah over. True his figure was slim, and long, but almost, he believed, simian, with his somewhat apelike long arms and large hands. His posture was never quite Royal, unless it must be for a role. No, he was ever an indifferent "King", preferring always that his Elder or even the mysterious and multi-named fifth member take over those majestic roles when they were of a short duration.

As compensation, Billy was, however, most lithe, most flexible, and most assuredly athletic. He could juggle, he could somersault, he could leap high enough to make audiences gasp, and he would then just barely alight, one shaky foot atop a single shivering beam, his entire body vibrating as though he would topple over, and yet hold his ground steady — to everyone's amazed relief. In short, he could, with no trouble at all, incur every viewer's eye by a score of differing means and hold it—just as long as he wished. If his voice was nothing especial, a fair tenor; still he could sing several airs of Mr. Handel and Herr Mozart with perfect tone and pitch and he would leave a tear in your eye and a throb in your breast. But for the grand dramatic speeches, he must drag in that old sot, his sire, whose resounding baritone was a natal gift. So, as the lad Billy Boy had watched his Pater to learn, so watched I him every moment onstage, whether in rehearsal or "on show," to educate myself into what turned out to be an only middling grasp of the actor's craft.

And if Billy Darrow was admirable, he was even more so when he had someone to admire him. By this tenth year of The Invincible Theatre's existence, that meant no one other than my self. His wife was by then quite inured; his father was, as always, uninterested; and who knew what the fifth member thought, as we only heard uttered speech onstage; even Billy's niece by marriage, his last conquest before me, was looking about for someone other to engage her esteem.

It was she, Miss Amy, who, three months into my employment with the troupe, made the discovery that despite all my larking about London town, among some of its most unsavoury haunts and disreputable gutters, that for sensual experience, I was still "pure as the driven snow."

We had left London some week past and only just set up stage in the large, second common green of Sheffield town, and I had just returned from depositing our placards about those shop fronts that would countenance our adverts in their windows, when she faced me down. Her arms akimbo, her chestnut hair all flying about, her cheeks reddened from proximity to the boiling hot water: in short, quite notably "natural" for once and if I must say so, quite lovely too. The scene was the outdoor fire where she and her aunt were laundering the troupe's clothing in preparation for the week to come. By this time I had come into a second set of shirt and trowsers, and so had given in my originals for cleansing.

"What's this then?" she asked pointing to a stain no more remarkable to my eye than any other, except perhaps its location, slightly above the Y of my trowser legs. As I looked, she looked me in the eye and said, "Jizz, is what. Look Ess, how he does stain himself at night. "

I was unaware of staining myself at night or any other time and said so, unawares they were japing with me, until Mrs. Darrow asked "Have you then no dreams of at all, a lad your age, of ladies fair?" Upon which I blushed to recall one such dream about her self.

She laughed, but quickly enough the two of them calculated, and then asked, "Haven't you ever? . . . With a lass or lady?" And what was I to say. I turned and fled, murmuring some work that must be attended to immediately.

That night, my idol roused himself from his conjugal bed within caravan number one and came to where I had cobbled together my own more makeshift sleeping quarters on the street beneath caravan number two.

"Come, my love," for that was how Billy spoke to all of us, my love, my darling, my sweetheart: "Come up to bed with Susie and me."

I was to say the truth amazed, for the cobblestones were especially iron-hard with ice that night with autumn coming on, despite my many efforts to disguise them with slats and cloths; any softer lie-down would be preferable.

No sooner had we crept into the caravan and I was at the edge of the bed, viewing by faint candlelight Mrs. Darrow herself, all pink skinned, wrapped in warm covers atop softer pillows, then from behind, I felt his hands upon me. Before I knew what he was about, he'd had stripped off my trowsers and shirt and pushed me atop her. From there, she took over, and any questions I may have uttered were stilled by first her and then him. Soon were we all three as Nature made us, and almost as quickly was I between her large soft breasts, my self being fondled and kissed, manipulated and managed from in front and in back by one and the other simultaneously, until I had found a wet harbor below and pushed to it. I found a rhythm and soon began to gasp. What heaven! Twice more did I consort with the distaff, while the husband consorted with the lady from behind, and alternately encouraged me with many caresses and lewd remonstrations. Through it all, I encountered and experienced so many differing sensations and emotions, that when it was all over, and the three of us were at last spent to our utmost, I lay between them both, and murmured my double adoration, before I collapsed into utter debilitation.

Once having tasted such delights, how then was I to be denied? I was not.

From then on, for months on end, I bedded with my master and my mistress. True it was that the lady tired of our frolics earlier some nights than the fellow did, and would fall asleep, leaving Darrow to divert me. Increasingly as I appeared, I would in vain seek her, and be told she was sharing Amy's bed that night. Or more simply, "Getting her much needed sleep, for she worked hard today, two shows and three parts, and she knows she'll get little enough sleep with you about." Said sternly, just before Billy kissed my lips and rifled my undergarments with his monkey-quick hands.

In vain did I attempt to draw Miss Amy into our nocturnal diversions. "Leave her be, the poor thing," Susie would exclaim. "Haven't she enough of men folk during the day!" This latter not so much directed at myself, who outside of the bed at Caravan One remained as shy and diffident as before; nor did it refer to our leader, much as I would come upon him all unawares staring at the lass when she knew not he was about, and he surely appeared to have more than theatrical ambitions upon his mind.

No, but it did allude to Mme. Genre's slow but certain new appearance, her growth, both physical and dramatic, lending her far greater stature and her experience, providing greater repute, so that when his wife complained of too much labor, our Billy Boy simply transferred the roles to his niece. Amy took them on with a loud enough grumble and a demand for "more meat and less gristle," but despite these noises, in truth she took on the new parts joyfully and acquitted herself very well indeed.

So well that she acquired admirers, by the by. Indeed, by the time we had arrived as far as Nottingham Shire, Mme. Genre could rely upon several gentleman's carriages to be parked just outside the circle that comprised our audience; the owners seated upon fold-out seat-contraptions prepared by their valets or drivers, near enough to the stage where they might admire Amy from closer quarters — an advantage Darrow charged a half shilling for, per head. I would not have been amazed to have closed down in one town and set up for travel to another and seen our little tripartite retinue followed by another entire and quite longer cortege of Amy's guest-admirers.

"They used to follow me so," Susie whimpered very early one morning, when we had shared a bed together again, all three, she , I and Billy. The back curtains of the van formed a little vee out which I could see the pre-dawn constellation Cassiopeia clearly against the cobalt night. Her husband soothed her, holding her tight about as she sobbed on, "Even more admirers than she. Even higher born. Do you remember, Billy?" He did remember, loyal mate that he was and he said so, and they reminisced about Lord This and Baron That until she was mollified a bit, at which she caught sight of me and declared, "Does it never go down? I ask you, truly. Never? Ah, well, at least one handsome lad admires me," and turned to cover me with her soft form, and so I was forced to somewhat awaken, while Darrow added his own domestic admiration from behind her.

I mentioned triple vans because we had gained a third, somewhat smaller and older than the others and thus in a more parlous state, yet withal useful, because that's where Darrow the Elder, and the silent and apart from us but for the stage Fifth Troupe Member now slept and kept their costumes and other belongings, Susie having moved many of hers to be with Amy. So I now had a home up off the cobblestones and while not my own bed, at least the first real example of such an object since I was an infant.

Partly this was ascribable to our increased "box-office" as the nightly monetary receipts were euphemistically spoken of, there being a box, if no office. Amy's increase of new followers certainly were partly responsible for that boon, but so it turned out was I. For I soon became a performer in The Invincible Troupe myself, and if I may be immodest, a not terribly unimportant addition to the company: especially to the lasses and women-folk, for by now I too had grown, almost as tall as Darrow, and had sprung soft down upon my lip and cheek and chin, which Susie and even Billy did fawn upon.

The manner of it coming to pass was thus: I have written of how I had slowly accustomed myself to the boards—and boards indeed they were, eight of them of the same thickness and width, that I myself put up and took down along with Billy Darrow. I had gone onstage first in the various non-speaking roles that Darrow's repertoire called forth. In one act was I a silent Royal personage before whom a duel would be fought, or in another a judge, with but one word to utter –"guilty" or "released." For these I naturally enough took upon myself the coloring that stage powders and paints could provide, and I appeared stern or elderly or authoritative as the role called for. No sooner was my one word said or my four gestures made, then I was off the stage and returned to my duties as stage-handy lad moving about this or that scrim or prop— short for furnished property, i.e. part of the objects needed for the play. On occasion, as I've also written, I was a great beau, or fop, costumed with extraordinary style and panache but with little enough "lines" to say or "action" to do.

Even in the most stalwart of troupes, actors "go down"—get ill, or depressed, or vanish two days on end larking with some townsperson, or refuse to leave their caravan from "a case of the sulks."

Our fifth ordinarily silent troupe member was the first to become ill, with a catarrh that interfered mightily with her ability to speak sans a cough. She did lovely work of hiding it or stitching it into the scenes she played, just as though it belonged there. The first two nights, at least, she did. The third night proved impossible for her to get out of bed or leave caravan three for her feverish state, and thus was I was cast in her place.

The play was The Bard's *Tragedy of Romeo and Juliet* and the most unlikely part I was to take over for her was a small female role, that of Lady Montague, Romeo's mother: with but a handful of lines. The largest role that night however I must slip into, in her stead, was that of Mercutio, playing to Billy as my best friend. I had learned by heart the two speeches already: one fantastical and the other pathetic. Later on, I was to play gruff Friar Laurence, and what lines I was unsure of would be whispered to me by someone or other in the company, offstage at the time.

In the first role of the young smart, I japed much with Billy who played Romeo, and who in turn flirted back at me, giving a new significance to these young men's close friendship in the play. This impelled one Oxonian within the audience to laugh out loud, "Why! Look! They are as *Greek* as ever were *Italian lads*! And I'll wager as prompt at each other with their *cods* as with their *daggers!*" a comment that earned much merriment.

Later on, as the Friar, my beard did itch badly as did my monk's cowl, and I was eager to be rid of those, but the applause was delightful, and when Mercutio was called for, I vanished and reappeared sans beard and blanket but wearing the other's doublet and feathered hat, and bowed to even greater kudos.

Later that night, as we sat in the local public house gobbling down our late and by no means undercooked dinner, t'was Susie who said of me, "He's bit. Why look. As surely as though it were a gadfly upon his neck, he's bit by the streaming limed-lamps he's fired up himself and by the yokels' hand claps–stage-bit, the great dolt!"

I coloured deeply for it was not entirely untrue. Darrow Elder — who seldom spoke once his tankard was in hand — deigned to utter to me: "A capital 'Queen Mab,' lad." Then pondering. he added, "A somewhat less creditable death speech." Which drove us to hilarity, for he could not give ought, not even words, but he must take something back, all the time.

After that night I remained on stage with The Invincible Theater troupe, earning my own sobriquet, Monsieur Addison Aries, a name conjured by the Darrows, husband and wife, out of my own given name and an old Astrological Almanack one of the company had snitched somewhere in Northern Wales and which they followed closely: for they were a superstitious lot, all of them, our mysterious Fifth (now Sixth) actor included. None of the women stepped onstage without first spitting behind herself and twirling her index finger in a curlicue while uttering below her breath, "Pigs foot!" Though none could tell from whence it all derived.

The elder Darrow would not call a single playwright by exact name, but rather referred to one as "The Immortal Bard," another as "The French Rapscallion" for Moliere-whose Scapin we travestied rather absurdly. Novelists that we adapted likewise underwent a sea-change, from Dickens to "Frick'em," for example, and when once I had come upon and was reading a single volume novel about the Antipodes titled *Harry Heathcote of Glangoil*, the old thing took a look at the author's name and said, "Anthony Scollop is it? I read once a book by him—concerning a Mrs. Prudie!" To which I smiled and made myself scarce, for Darrow Elder being friendly was more frightening by far than him being his usual drunken self.

And so, My Lord, I passed my 13th, 14th and 15th birthdays as Mercutio and Tybalt, as Friar Laurence and Lady Montague, as Lord Marchmell and the Duke of

Tickles, as Raggs the Sheep-herd and Stiggs the Scrivener, as Charles Surface, and Young Dornton, as Captain Absolute (to Billy's seductive Catesby) and Sir Derleth Tyrone the Younger, as Doctor I. M. A. Dandy and Mlle. Camille du Sprech, as Young Fool and Old Liar, as Unknown Bandit, and First Soldier, once even as Lord Beverley, and twice as Lord Mayor of London; but in short, as a repertoire-actor. For Billy Darrow was no fool and knew that whatever extra I earned from him on the boards I soon brought in trebled in farthings, quickly gaining for that new Invincible Troupe actor, M. Aries his own little "claque" or group of youths, for so one's followers are named.

I was furthermore useful in so many other ways to his company: as stage worker, as tender lover to his wife, who thus minded less her usurpation in the company by her niece, and thus didn't make the expected trouble; and not least of all useful as Billy's own personal Antinuous, for I was rich with spunk, and he was determined to mine it out of me one way or t'other.

I have mentioned before the mysterious fifth (and after I joined them) *sixth* member of the Invincible Travelling Theatre. But have always done mysteriously and for good reason: mysteriousness seemed to hover about this troupe member from morn 'til night and despite the greatest illumination thrown from a beneath a fire-lighted stage lime-light.

I have said this actor played both male and female. No surprise when so did myself at different times, as did Amy Green. I have also said this actor possessed a voice of surpassing range. Singing from a higher soprano than Suzie Darrow down to bass notes that our senior-most fellow, old Jonathan Darrow, might–and regularly did in his speeches — encompass. Recall that they boarded together in one wagon; yet utterly apart; and it did not signify that anyone knew the better nor associated the more with this Theatrickal Enigma.

More than once did I ask Billy Darrow who this *Personne de Grand-Chance* might be, in truth.

"Leave it be, Addison, my love, for no good can come of your needing to know."

"But surely that person is not of the Darrow kith and kin?"

"That is so."

"Then how came this person to your troupe?"

"By slow degrees. By a downfall from a greater estate," Billy said.

We were pulling up stakes for the tented enclosure against poor weather that some folks paid a shilling for extra, at this time, so I well recall our conversation. "But surely, a smart lad like your self has already discovered that for himself."

"You mean because of this person's great adaptability?"

"That too. But mostly because who else among us can hold an audience so completely rapt?"

"Why yourself," answered I, ever loyal, "With your tumbles and leaps and tricks."

"Aye that foolishness–and only betimes!"

"And your sire, too, with his tragic speeches."

"All five of them — when he chooses to be sober."

"And Miss Green, when she wears her bodice low upon her bust and flirts."

"And yourself for all that, when you are dressed in gold and well peruked and flirt with the ladies in the second row," he answered. "But surely you've noted how different our Great Person to be?"

I had and yet could not put it into speech, and so I held my own.

"Do not be bothersome to any one in the troupe, Addison, or I shall have to whip you too, among the many fleshly duties I already manage."

So was I warned.

By this time we had begun a new play, Mr. Shakespeare's *The Twelfth Night*, much expurgated, naturally enough given our audiences and their general understanding, chopped back to no more than two hours, albeit full of wit and flirtation.

None more so than between the maid Viola, dressed as a man to court the noble Olivia for Duke Orsinio, and Olivia herself. Who then mistakes Viola's stranded brother, Sebastian, for her as "Cesario" and forces him to wed her.

We had rehearsed this, myself as Sebastian for the Invincibles, but most of all playing opposite Suzie, with whom I had been second husband for nigh three or more years by now (although only a boy of fifteen years by then) with whom I felt most congenial.

All the more of a surprise then, when Amy, "Mlle. Genre," came down with a rotten tooth and could not play the opening. An even a greater surprise to myself that Suzie Darrow would then play Viola, a role she knew well, and that our fifth person then "took over" the role of Lady Olivia; evidently having been several roles in the play in previous years—or decades—I knew not which.

This I discovered only as I made the announcement of the parts and the cast, that is to say, before the curtain, and upon "opening day," in a rather large market square at the town of Croydon.

I then ran "back-stage" where I was fitted into my first costume and went 'on stage" in my first role as retinue to old Jonathan's (with a young- painted face) Orsinio. Billy played Toby Belch and Antonio and other clownish roles.

Our mysterious sixth actor as Olivia flirted believably and also gave the part emotion, and even evoked tears in the cheeks of the females of the audience with her sad plight: more than one of them had loved a youth and not been loved in return. Suzie as Viola/Cesario, played charmingly and affectingly too.

So we arrived at Act Four, Scene 1, before Olivia's house, where I as Sebastian have arrived and now seek to rid myself of Billy's clown. He returned in a minute as Sir Toby and we had at each other with soft-sticks, stopped by Lady Olivia's importuning words.

She has only just noticed Sebastian and thinks him Cesario. Billy had "cut" that act's second scene and so here we are at scene 3, and all of a sudden, Lady Olivia begins making love to Sebastian. He, being a healthy youth, responds to her beauty and advancements. Passionately and loving, we troth our pledge and Sebastian is dragged off to a parson to be married. I well knew how to play this part, ardently and adoringly.

Astonish me then when our mysterious sixth player drops all the reserve that had surrounded her with mystery; she grasps my hand tightly, clasps me about the body tightly, whispers -stage whispers—insinuating and lovingly, and then kisses me so deeply I thought I might lose my wits. Baffled I looked then—- as fitted Sebastian in the play—but in reality too. For one who had never before as much as regarded me, now seemed to have adored me from afar, and only just then allowed me to understand that fact. Rustlings among the front seats showed that they too had intuited or somehow understood the real passion exerted betwixt us two. From the back-most standees came low whistles and even a growl or too, marking me as a "lucky dog."

Nor was I physically released during the short scene behind the curtains, but held ever more closely, with much hand fumbling about my person, so that I must stick out like some fool jackanapes, did I not put my clothes in order in time for the final scene in which Viola and Sebastian are re-united and the Duke and she become as one, while Sebastian and Olivia again passionately and loving retroth our pledge and all exeunt, leaving Billy all alone on stage to sing "When I was a tiny little boy, with a hey-ho, the wind and the rain."

Behind the curtains once again, I turned to our mysterious sixth player and said, "Tonight. At ten o'clock. Be certain old Darrow is dead drunk." She responded with a hand upon my manhood.

And so, as the clapping endured — and we two were especially applauded— was that stage that has been my life, your Lordship–and I do not at all mean that little makeshift stage that was the Invincibles Theatre — set for its next quite dramatic act and transformational scene.

How inflamed I was after that provincial premiere of Billy's expurgated *Twelfth Night* you may easily imagine. Seldom have I been quite so heated.

The hours I must wait dragged by like Eternity itself and it was all I could do to not drink myself Ale-blind, as we four, Suzie, Billy, Jonathan and myself, celebrated our quite substantial "take" from our performance in a local pub, named–and this is one of those coincidences that makes my life so piquant — The Fallow Deer. Naturally Billy was looking forward to future performances as we were already the talk of the town, especially as several townsfolk did stop by our table and asked for a repeat the following night. More cheer followed that, you may be assured.

At last we all wandered away to our wagons, Jonathan drunk, Billy and Suzie cordially tipsy, and myself in a quiet frenzy of anticipation, albeit acting as though I too were inebriated.

So they pushed me into sick Amy's wagon, where she slept snoring away and none too clean smelling neither, while they celebrated with a rare husband and wife cohabitation.

As the 'vans were placed together in one side corner of a minor lane of the main square, I could, by peeping out of the curtains sometimes even see what took place in the other two. Thus, at ten o clock sharp–by the local steeple bells—I was on the flagstones outside the smaller van, as washed and close to undress as I dared be, making my whistle-signal to the *Grande Personne* her self.

Naturally, the interior was dim-lit, a mere candle-end set upon a carton of costumes that served as a bed stand. Through the wooden partition, I could easily hear the stentorian gasps and wheezing, snores, and assorted harrumphs of old Jonathan in his sleep.

And there lay my Love, all soft and white skinned amid her furled bedclothes. Her hair lay in shining ringlets upon her noble neck, and tumbled a bit upon one ivory shoulder. I might easily make out the softly ridged concavity of her back, guarded as it was by her two pillowy softnesses. She turned an unpainted face toward me and with one finger, soubrette style, to her lips bade me be very quiet.

She lay like that as I removed my shirt and trowsers—I'd come barefoot—as though musing, and she seemed most pleased, as she reached for my extremity—which greeted her so avidly.

Soon enough I was atop her and fondling. Unlike Suzie or even Amy, she was slender rather than voluptuous, smooth-skinned, free of that padding wherein I might lose myself after passion. Her breasts were small and almost firm but were as much her weakness as any other female once I had them well in hand. Soon enough was I hand-guided to her lower regions and there she equalled Suzie well enough.

As on stage, her kisses were intoxicating and I will even use the oft repeated term breath-taking. At times, I believed I might never recover my breath unless I detached myself from those avid lips. I did so less and less as she guided me within herself, and from atop and behind her I began my manly ministrations.

Believe me, My Lord, when I report I never had encountered before and seldom since, such passion from a partner in love making. Most ladies merely *receive* a gentleman, some with greater motion than others, few with such enthusiasm and few with her (I thought of the words at the time) athleticism and un-stanched hunger.

Quickly enough, despite my efforts, did we rise and fall toward that bliss that is common to all. Much as I resisted, much as I had been taught by Suzie and Billy Darrow to resist, all teaching went for naught in that bed. Nor were either of us satisfied even then, but we must start up again for a second time, and while that lasted longer and we rose to new feats of intertwining, never mind conclusion, did even that suffice— but we must try a third time.

If I seem somewhat muddled in the telling now, My Lord, you may well imagine how utterly fuddled with longing and lust was I at the time. And so I shall attempt to write it as I recall, precisely and in order.

Firstly, we had risen off the mattresses, such as they were, and now were standing up, my mistress holding onto the curbed upper inner bars of the caravan for support, myself holding onto her chiefly and every once or twice in a while, also grasping an overhead strut.

As I was riding my way into my final *voyage de amour*, one hand cupping her small breast slid downward; to it I joined my second hand and just as the great heat was upon me, it slipped further down and encountered–how can I write it? — manhood as large and stiff as my own! Yes, right there, inches above a distinctive womanhood.

I gasped quite loudly. At the same time, I felt myself drawn in ever more deeply, and closely. She spent. I spent. And all the while I had one hand on her manhood and another upon her womanhood.

In that same instant the partition shook and splintered and Jonathan Darrow himself, wide awake and bulging red with drink thundered, "Must you? Must you? Must you yet again?"

His complaint was stopped by the vision that even a vat of ale and a decanter full of Scots Whiskey could not undo: the vision that is, of ourselves, standing before him in *flagrante* and possessing not two but instead three sets of genitals!

"What then...." He stammered. "What demons be ye?!" he added, doubtless quoting lines from some play we knew not. And fell over the partition and onto the bed alongside us.

My companion pulled free of me and leapt to the bit of floor where clothing was tossed all about until some semblance of costume was put on. I stood there I fear in great astonishment, and clad as I was the minute I was born. Old Jonathan rose in his fusty bedclothes and lurched toward me. I fought him down and rushed out the 'van following my partner who, now dressed, had alighted and stood in a defending posture, looking like a very Achilles in those prints by Mr. Flaxman.

Roused by the great noise, Bill and Suzie and even Amy had looked out of their curtains, just as Jonathan tumbled out of the 'van after me and lunged toward me, only to be stopped by a perfectly aimed and quite powerful full-fisted blow to the nose by —not I—but *my lady transformed into man*.

He howled in pain and soon, those in the pub's inn chambers nearby had thrust up their window sashes and the scene was there for all to see.

My hermaphrodite pushed past me once more into the 'van and thrust my clothing at me where it fell upon the cobbles, and in a minute he/she had run to the front exit, and leapt onto one of the old Bays kept there un-shafted and roused it with a kick. Minutes later we witnessed our Sixth Actor riding upon it, bareback as any American Indian or Amazon warrioress, off across the square of Croydon and rapidly into the frosty night.

By this time the entire plaza and surrounding streets was lighted up, as I pulled on my trowsers. Folks were shouting and calling jibes at us, and throwing down objects upon our heads.

"Damn your hot blood!" Billy Darrow shouted at me, and rushed out at me. "Didn't I tell you *not to*?"

Luckily he stumbled in his ill-timed charge at me.

In short time I was up and inside, past Suzie and gathering my belongings and hidden pay.

By the time I was upon the ground again, it was in time to hear Billy railing,

"You've ruined everything. Everything! Everything!"

Still not fully clad, I pushed on my shoes as best as I could, and then I blew Suzie a kiss, and I too sped off, on foot, in the direction of the most surprizing lover of my life. . . . although toward where exactly, and what I expected to find, I could not say.

EXTRACT:
MY
SECRET LIFE
Anonymous

After Walter's first brush with homosexual sex, under the auspices of a bisexual threesome, he finds himself obsessed with his male partner, at once ashamed and overwhelming curious to repeat the experience alone. And ultimately, as one will not be shocked to learn, curiosity wins...

THE EVENING CAME, and how strange! I felt part of my old nervousness. — He put on his silks and boots, which Sarah kept. — At the sight of his white flesh, and roly poly pendant, mine stood upright. We stripped. I pressed his belly against mine, grasping him round his buttocks (he was smooth as a woman), and his prick rose proudly at once. I handled his prick, pleased with the soft feel of the loose skin. — "Fetch me, or I'll frig myself, I shall spend a pail full" — I wetted both our pricks and bellies with soap and water, then putting him on his back on the bed, mounted him. Our pegos were pressed between our bellies, and grasping each other's rumps, and shoving our pricks about as well as we could, the heat and friction drew both our spunks, and we lay quiet till our tools shrunk down over our balls, forming a heap of testicles and pricks.

Then came a dislike to him and disgust with myself that I often had felt recently. But it vanished directly, I felt lewed again and when I felt his cock. It was stiff soon. As he finished washing it he turned round, and I saw it thick and swollen. Just then Sarah rushed in and prayed me to go. "Do, oh do pray, or there will be a great row — for God's sake go." She was much agitated, I had never seen her so before. "You must — you shall go, — or I shall be half ruined." Yielding I went as quickly as I could, and he did after me, I heard.

Next night I saw her out, and could get no explanation about her agitation; but she told me I could not go to the house for a week or ten days.

What gave me about that time such hot fits of lust it is not easy to say, but I was in full rut. At times a fellow's prick stands much more than at others, some-times it is idleness, sometimes stimulating food, some-times strength. For some days before I saw him again my prick stood constantly, I was again alone in town, and why I did not ease it by fucking don't recollect — Sarah I could not see any where, and I did nothing but think how I would frig him, and tail her, when we met. When at length we met, he told me he had not spent since I'd made him. Laughing, Sarah said, "The beg-gar wanted to have me, but I wouldn't let him." Perhaps a lie — I touched his cock which sprang up stiffly at once. He stripped, and his red tipped, white stemmed sperm spouter would have fascinated any woman — I undressed, my cock stiff as his, and libidinous frolics began.

"Have you buggered him" — Sarah's question came suddenly into my mind as I handled his throbbing prick, his rigid piercer. "Fetch me, frig me, then you fuck Sarah and let me fuck her after — go on — I'll frig myself — I must spend" — said he, and began frigging.

I stopped him. I put him in various attitudes and looked at his naked rigidity — feeling it, kissing it, glorying in my power — with my own prick upright. Both were wanting the pleasure sorely, yet I dallied and my brain whirled with strange desire, fear, dislike, yet with intention. Then I placed him bending over the bed — his bum towards me, his head towards the looking glass — I stood back to look. There were his white buttocks and large womanly white thighs, his legs in silk, his feet in feminine boots. — Not one could have imagined him a man, so round, smooth, white, and womanly was his entire backside and form. It was only looking further off that I missed the pouting hairy lips, and saw a big round stone bag which shewed the male. His prick was invisible, stiff against his belly.

I closed on him, put my hand round and gave his prick a frig — his bum was against my belly. — "Fetch me — oho — make haste, I'm bursting" — looking down I saw his bumhole and the desire whirled thro my brain like lightning. Without pausing or thinking, I felt his prick from under his balls, and whilst he al-most shivered with desire — "Oh! make haste, fetch me" — I put both hands round him, feeling his balls with one, his prick with the other; and my own stiff prick I pressed under his ballocks, saying, "Let me put my prick up your bum."

"That I won't," said he disengaging himself and turning round, "that I won't."

Furiously I said, "Let me — I'll give you ten pounds." "Oh no." "I will give you all I have" — and going to my trowsers I took out my purse, and turned into my hands all the gold I had — it was, I think, more than ten pounds.

"Oh no, I can't, it will hurt," said he, eying the money. "It won't." "It will. When I was apprenticed, a boy told me a man did it to him, and it hurt him awful."

I don't know what I replied — but believe I repeated that it would not hurt, that it was well known that people did it, and as I talked I handled his prick with one hand, with the other holding the gold.

"It will hurt — I'm frightened, but will you give me ten pounds really?"

I swore it, talked about that of which I knew nothing — that I had heard it was pleasure to the man whose arsehole was plugged — that once done they liked nothing so much afterwards. His prick, which had dwindled under fear, again stiffened as I frigged, he ceased talking and breathed hard, saying, "I'm coming." — I stopped at once.

"Let me." "I don't think you can, it seems impossible — if you hurt me will you pull it out?" "Yes yes, I will."

He turned to the bed again and kneeled, but he was too high — I pulled him off — then it was too low. Again on the bed and I pulled his bum to the level of my prick, I locked the door, I trembled, we whispered. I slabbered my prick and his hole with spittle. His prick was still stiff. There was the small round hole — the balls beneath — the white thighs. — I closed on him half mad, holding him round one thigh. I pointed my prick — my brain whirled — I wished not to do what I was doing, but some ungovernable impulse drove me on. Sarah's words rang in my ears. I heard them as if then spoken. My rod with one or two lunges buried it-self up him, and passing both hands round his belly I held him to me, grasping both his prick and balls tightly. He gave a loud moan. "Ohoo I shall faint," he cried. "Ho, pull it out."

It's in — don't move or I won't pay you, or some-thing of that sort — I said, holding myself tight up to him. "Ohooo, leave go, you're hurting my balls so" — I suppose I was handling them roughly — but his bum kept close to my belly.

I recollect nothing more distinctly. A fierce, bloody minded baudiness possessed me, a determination to do it — to ascertain if it was a pleasure — I would have wrung his prick off sooner than have withdrawn for him, and yet a disgust at myself. Drawing once slightly back, I saw my prick half out of his tube, then forcing it back, it spent up him. I shouted out loudly and baudily (Sarah told me), but I was unconscious of that. She was in her sitting room.

I came to myself — how long afterwards I cannot say. — All seemed a dream, but I was bending over him — pulling his backside still towards me. — My prick still stiff and up him. "Does it hurt now." "Not so much."

His prick was quite large but not stiff. A strong grip with my hand stiffened it, I frigged hard, the spunk was ready and boiling, for he had been up to spending point half a dozen times. My prick, still encased, was beginning to stiffen more. — He cried — "I am coming, I am coming" — his bum jogged and trembled — his arsehole tightened — my prick slipped out — and he sank on the bed spending over the counterpane — I stood frigging him still.

He spent a perfect pool of sperm on the bed. The maddening thought of what I had done made me wish to do it again. I forgot all my sensations — I have no idea of them now — I knew I had spent, that's all. "Let me do it again." "That I won't for any money," said he turning round.

Then I frigged myself and frigged him at the same time furiously. Fast as hands could move did mine glide up and down the pricks. Pushing him down with his arse on the sperm on the counterpane, I finished him as he lay, and I spent over his prick, balls, and bally. In ten minutes our double spend was over.

Immediately I had an inaffable disgust at him and myself — a terrible fear — a loathing — I could scarcely be in the room with him — could have kicked him. He said, "You've made me bleed." At that I nearly vomited — "I must make haste," said I looking at my watch, "I forgot it was so late. — I must go." All my desire was to get away as quickly as possible. I left after paying him, and making him swear, and swearing myself, that no living person should know of the act.

Yet a few days after I wrote the narrative of this blind, mad, erotic act; an act utterly unpremeditated, and the perpetration of which as I now think of it seems most extraordinary. One in which I had no pleasure — have no recollection of physical pleasure — and which only dwells in my mind with disgust, tho it is against my philosophy even to think I had done wrong.

ABOUT
THE
AUTHORS

соб фот Д.Быстрова

HENRY ALLEY is Professor Emeritus of Literature in the Honors College at the University of Oregon. He has four novels, *Through Glass* (Iris Press, 1979), *The Lattice* (Ariadne Press, 1986), *Umbrella of Glass* (Breitenbush Books, 1988), and *Precincts of Light* (Inkwater Press, 2010). His story collection, *The Dahlia Field* (Chelsea Station Editions) appeared in Spring 2017. For nearly fifty years, literary journals have published his stories. Most recently, one was chosen for *Best Gay Stories 2017*, and he, along with his husband, Austin Gray, was awarded a Mill House residency by Writing by Writers.

NICK CAMPBELL lives in South London, is a bookseller by day, and has written for Lethe Press, Obverse Books and Titan.

TOM CARDAMONE is the author of the Lambda Literary Award-winning speculative novella *Green Thumb* and the erotic fantasy novels *The Lurid Sea* and *The Werewolves of Central Park* as well as the novella *Pacific Rimming*. So far he has cobbled together two short story collections, *Night Sweats: Tales of Homosexual Wonder and Woe* and *Pumpkin Teeth*, which was a finalist for the Lambda Literary Award and a Black Quill Award. Additionally, he has edited *The Lost Library: Gay Fiction Rediscovered* and the anthology *Lavender Menace: Tales of Queer Villainy!*, which was nominated for the Over The Rainbow List by the LGBT Round Table of the American Library Association. His short stories have appeared in numerous anthologies and magazines, some of which have been collected on his website www.pumpkinteeth.net.

DALE CHASE has written gay men's erotica for twenty years with over 200 stories published in magazines, anthologies, and collections, including translation into Italian and German. Her third novel *The Great Man* was published by Lethe Press in 2017. Chase lives near San Francisco.

VERONA HUMMINGBIRD was born and raised in Oregon. Though she no longer calls it home, her years in the Pacific Northwest instilled in her a love of the outdoors, an appreciation for natural beauty, and a keen sense of wonder. Passion, temptation, and communication are cornerstones of her marriage as well as her stories. She is thankful every day for her husband, family, and friends.

RHIDIAN BRENIG JONES lives in Wales with his husband, Michael, and French bulldogs, Coco and Cosette. He leads an adult literacy programme and writes before work, when the three best things in his life are still asleep.

MATTHIAS KLEIN keeps the body of nir childhood cat in the freezer in the hope of one day performing mad science on him. Nir partner insists on keeping the other dead things ne collects in the garage. Find nem probably not being morbid enough on twitter @daystromreject.

KOLO is but one aspect of a Hilo boy who grew up poor and found love in a foreign land. Now, he dedicates much time and love to writing romances set in Hawaii's past, present, and future—and perhaps even alternate Hawaii's. Kolo recognizes that Hawaiians have always been a mischievous bunch that celebrates sexuality in its many permutations and is proud to be such a Hawaiian.

As a nomadic entertainer and musician, KATIE LEWIS is fortunate to encounter a plethora of exciting people, places and events that inspire her writing. She hopes to be a regular staple in your naughty literature collection.

DALE CAMERON LOWRY lives in the Upper Midwest with a partner and three cats, one of whom enjoys eating dish towels. It's up to you to guess whether the fabric eater is one of the cats or the partner. Dale is the author of the short story collection Falling Hard: Stories of Men in Love and editor of Myths, Moons, and Mayhem, a collection of gay paranormal erotica from Sexy Little Pages.

JEFF MANN grew up in Covington, Virginia, and Hinton, West Virginia, receiving degrees in English and forestry from West Virginia University. His publications include two collections of personal essays, Edge: Travels of an Appalachian Leather Bear and Binding the God: Ursine Essays from the Mountain South; six novels, Fog: A Novel of Desire and Reprisal, which won the Pauline Réage Novel Award, Purgatory: A Novel of the Civil War, which won a Rainbow Award, Cub, Country, Insatiable, and Salvation: A Novel of the Civil War, which won both a Lambda Literary Award and the Pauline Réage Novel Award; and three volumes of short fiction, Desire and Devour: Stories of Blood and Sweat, Consent: Bondage Tales, and A History of Barbed Wire, which won a Lambda Literary Award. In 2013, he was inducted into the Saints and Sinners Literary Festival Hall of Fame. He teaches creative writing at Virginia Tech in Blacksburg, Virginia.

Like Sharon Stone and the zipper, MIKE MCCLELLAND originally hails from Meadville, Pennsylvania. He has lived on five different continents but now resides in Georgia with his husband, son, and a menagerie of rescue dogs. His first book, Gay Zoo Day, was released in September 2017 by Beautiful Dreamer Press, and his work has appeared in several anthologies and in publications such as the Boston Review, Queen Mob's Tea House, Permafrost, Heavy Feather Review, and others. Keep up with him at magicmikewrites.com.

CHARLES PAYSEUR is an avid reader, writer, and reviewer of all things speculative. His fiction and poetry have appeared at Strange Horizons, Lightspeed Magazine, Dreamspinner, and many more. He runs Quick Sip Reviews and can be found drunkenly reviewing Goosebumps on his Patreon. You can find him gushing about short fiction (and occasionally his cats) on Twitter as @ClowderofTwo.

FELICE PICANO is the author of more than thirty books of poetry, fiction, memoirs, nonfiction, and plays. His work has been translated into many languages and several of his titles have been national and international bestsellers. He is considered a founder of modern gay literature along with the other members of the Violet Quill. Picano also began and operated the SeaHorse Press and Gay Presses of New York for fifteen years. His first novel was a finalist for the PEN/Hemingway Award. Since then he's been nominated for and/or won dozens of literary awards. Picano teaches at Antioch College, Los Angeles.

CLAUDIA QUINT is writes fantasy, romance, and erotica, exploring fairy tales and myth. Her work has been published in *Timeless Tales* magazine, non-fiction in *Bright Wall, Dark Room,* and a Robin Hood novella *Arrows Fletched With Peacock Feathers* from Less Than Three Press. She is currently at work on a fantasy novel, *Diary of a Centaur.* In her other lives by other names, she is a graphic designer, a voice actor, and an astrologer. Keep up with her at claudiaquint.wordpress.com

ROB ROSEN (www.therobrosen.com), award-winning author of the novels *Sparkle: The Queerest Book You'll Ever Love, Divas Las Vegas, Hot Lava, Southern Fried, Queerwolf, Vamp, Queens of the Apocalypse, Creature Comfort, Fate, Midlife Crisis,* and *And God Belched,* and editor of the anthologies *Lust in Time, Men of the Manor, Best Gay Erotica 2015, Best Gay Erotica of the Year, Volume 1* and *2* and *3,* has had short stories featured in more than 200 anthologies.

ABOUT THE EDITOR

MATTHEW BRIGHT is a writer, editor and designer who's never quite sure what order those titles should go. His fiction has appeared most recently in Tor.com, *Nightmare's Queer Destroy Horror, Steampunk Universe, Clockwork Iris, Harlot* and *Glittership*. He's the editor of *The Myriad Carnival: Queer and Weird Tales from Under the Big Top, Threesome: Him, Him and Me* (which landed on *Publishers Weekly's* Most Anticipated Titles of Spring 2017), and *Clockwork Cairo: Steampunk Tales of Egypt*. By day he works as a book designer to pay the bills and keep his dog in the life to which she has become accustomed.

A NOTE ON THE IMAGES:

All the images used in this book are genuine period photographs (though the images accompanying 'The Blacksmith's Son' and 'Teleny' have have their backgrounds mildly altered for design purposes.) In addition, the image for 'The Blacksmith's Son' actually dates from nearer the 1920s, but we took some artistic license because, well, have you *seen* him? If you'd like to explore more about them and their histories, I highly recommend the following blogs who do wonderful work in curating these:

flowers-in-his-hair.tumblr.com
antique-erotic.tumblr.com
victoriangentlemeninlove.tumblr.com

Lightning Source UK Ltd.
Milton Keynes UK
UKHW010635221122
412637UK00001B/33